Emmanuel Guibert

# ARIOL

## The Teeth of the Rabbit

PAPERCUTZ™
New York

# ARIOL Graphic Novels available from PAPERCUTZ™

ARIOL graphic novels are also available digitally wherever e-books are sold.

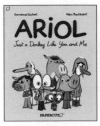

Graphic Novel #1
"Just a Donkey Like
You and Me"

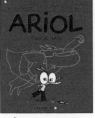

Graphic Novel #2
"Thunder Horse"

Graphic Novel #3
"Happy as a Pig..."

Graphic Novel #4
"A Beautiful Cow"

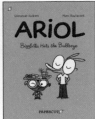

Graphic Novel #5
"Bizzbilla Hits the
Bullseye"

Coming Soon

Graphic Novel #6
"A Nasty Cat"

Graphic Novel #7
"Top Dog"

Graphic Novel #8
"The Three Donkeys"

Graphic Novel #9
"The Teeth of the
Rabbit"

Graphic Novel #10
"The Little Rats
of the Opera"

Boxed Set of Graphic
Novels #1-3

Boxed Set of Graphic
Novels #4-6

"Where's Petula?"
Graphic Novel

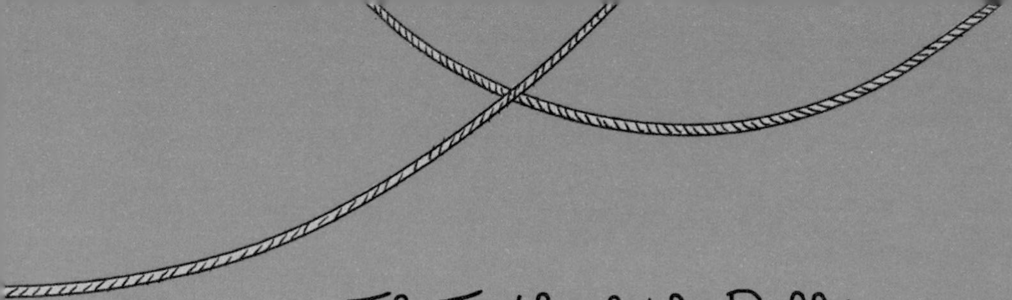

# The Teeth of the Rabbit



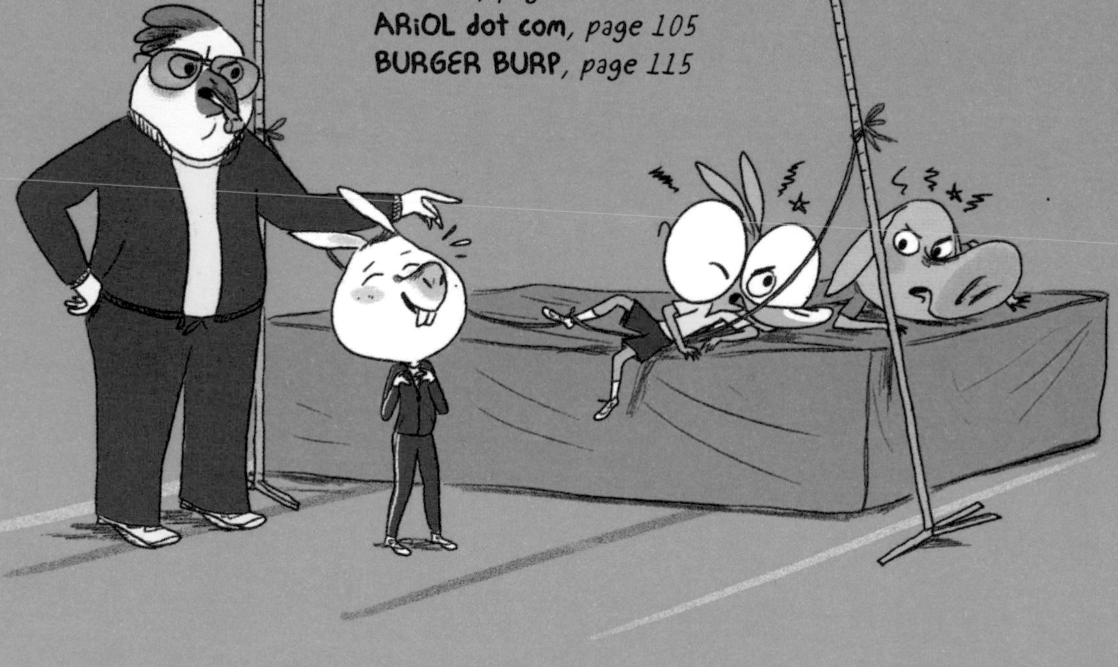

To Mr. Le Goff.
— Emmanuel Guibert

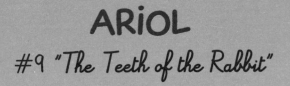

# ARIOL
## #9 "The Teeth of the Rabbit"

Emmanuel Guibert — Writer
Marc Boutavant — Artist
Rémi Chaurand — Colorist
Joe Johnson — Translation
Bryan Senka — Lettering
Dawn Guzzo — Production
Rachel Pinnelas — Production Coordinator
Jeff Whitman — Assistant Managing Editor
Jim Salicrup
Editor-in-Chief

Volume 9: Les dents du lapin © Bayard Editions, 2014

ISBN: 978-1-62991-602-6


Printed in China
Manufactured by Regent Publishing Services, Hong Kong,
Printed November 2016 in Shenzhen, Guangdong, China


Papercutz books may be purchased for business or promotional use.
For information on bulk purchases please contact Macmillan Corporate and Premium Sales Department at
(800) 221-7945 x5442.


Distributed by Macmillan

First Papercutz Printing

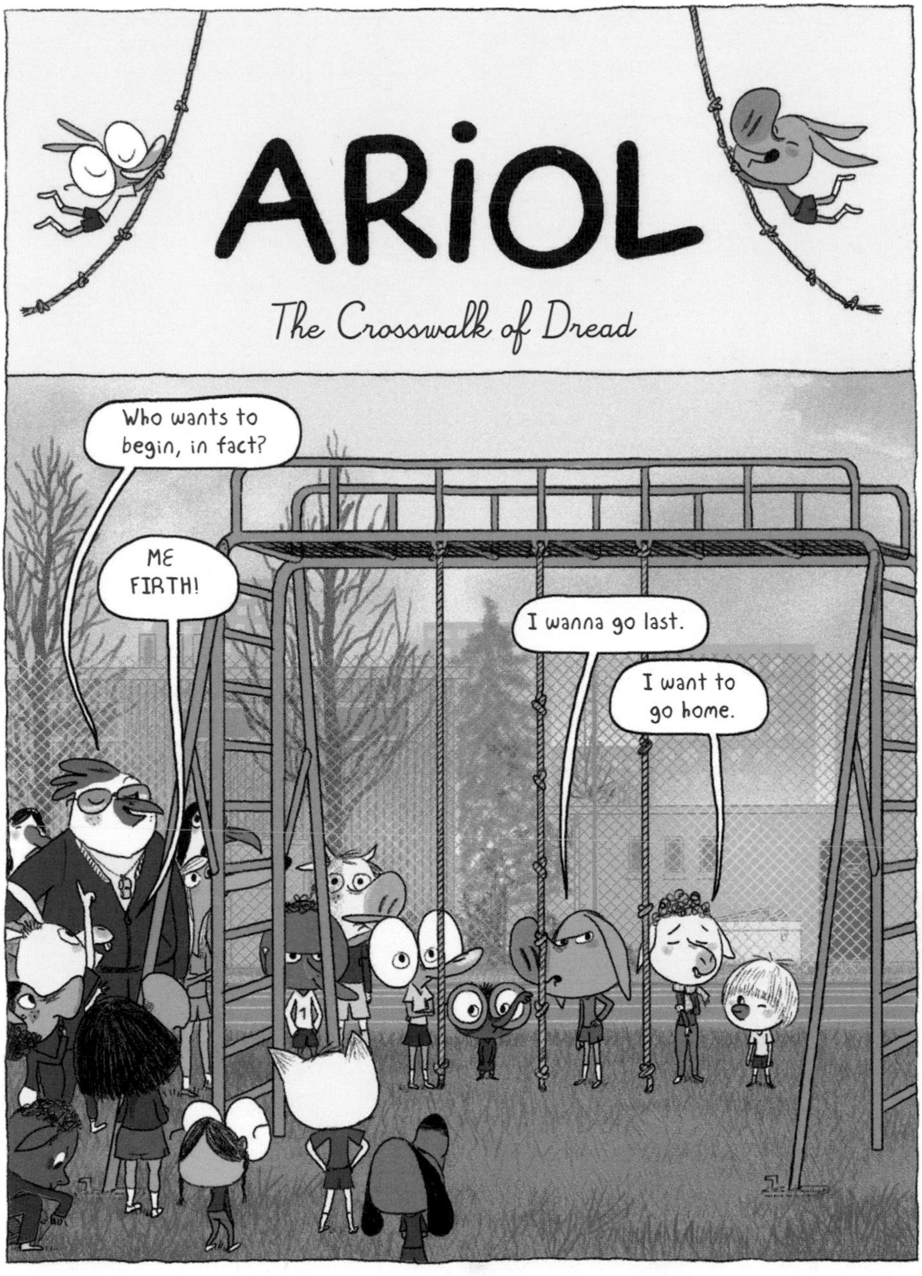
ARiOL
The Crosswalk of Dread
Who wants to begin, in fact?
ME FIRTH!
I wanna go last.
I want to go home.

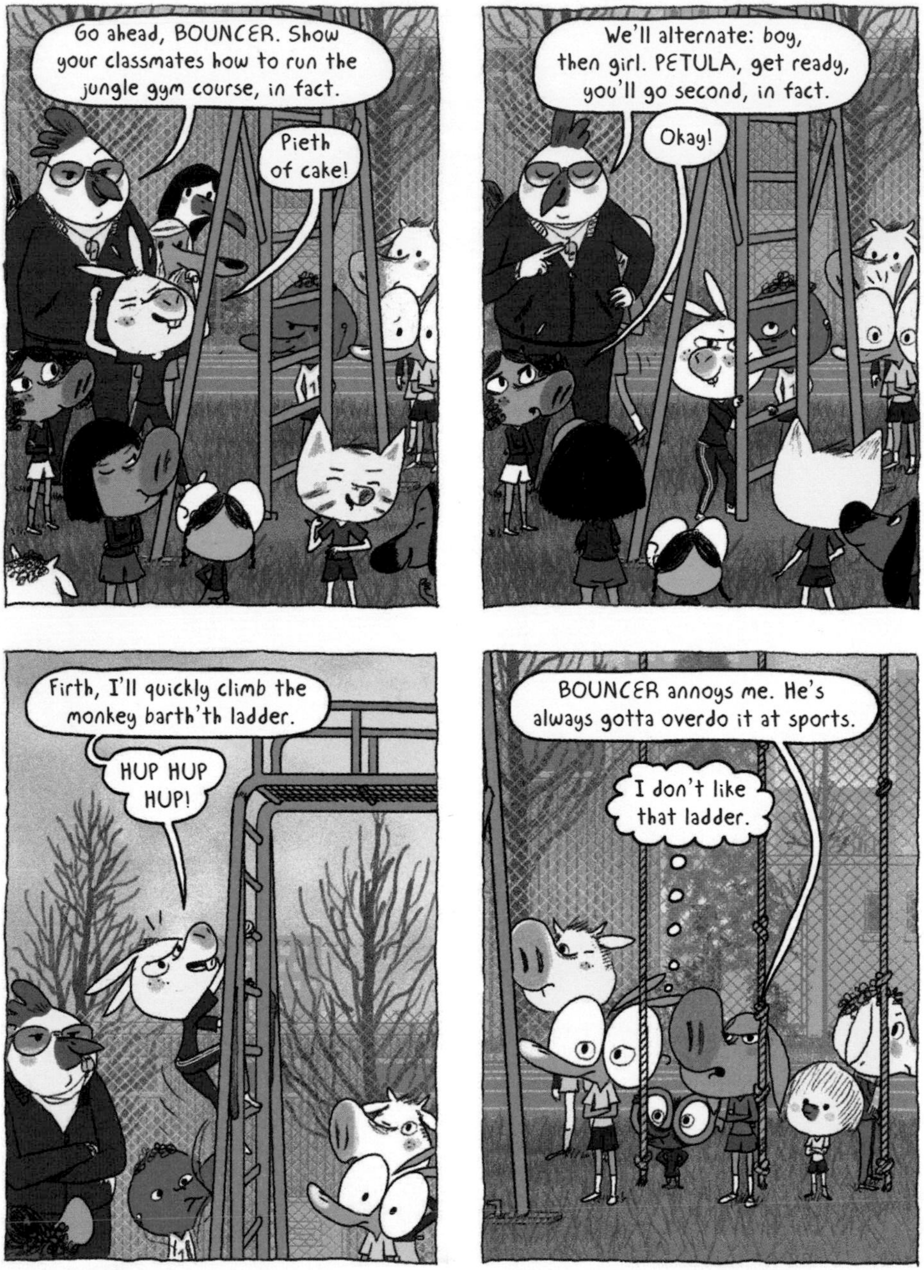
Go ahead, BOUNCER. Show your classmates how to run the jungle gym course, in fact.
Pieth of cake!
We'll alternate: boy, then girl. PETULA, get ready, you'll go second, in fact.
Okay!
Firth, I'll quickly climb the monkey barth'th ladder.
HUP HUP HUP!
BOUNCER annoys me. He's always gotta overdo it at sports.
I don't like that ladder.

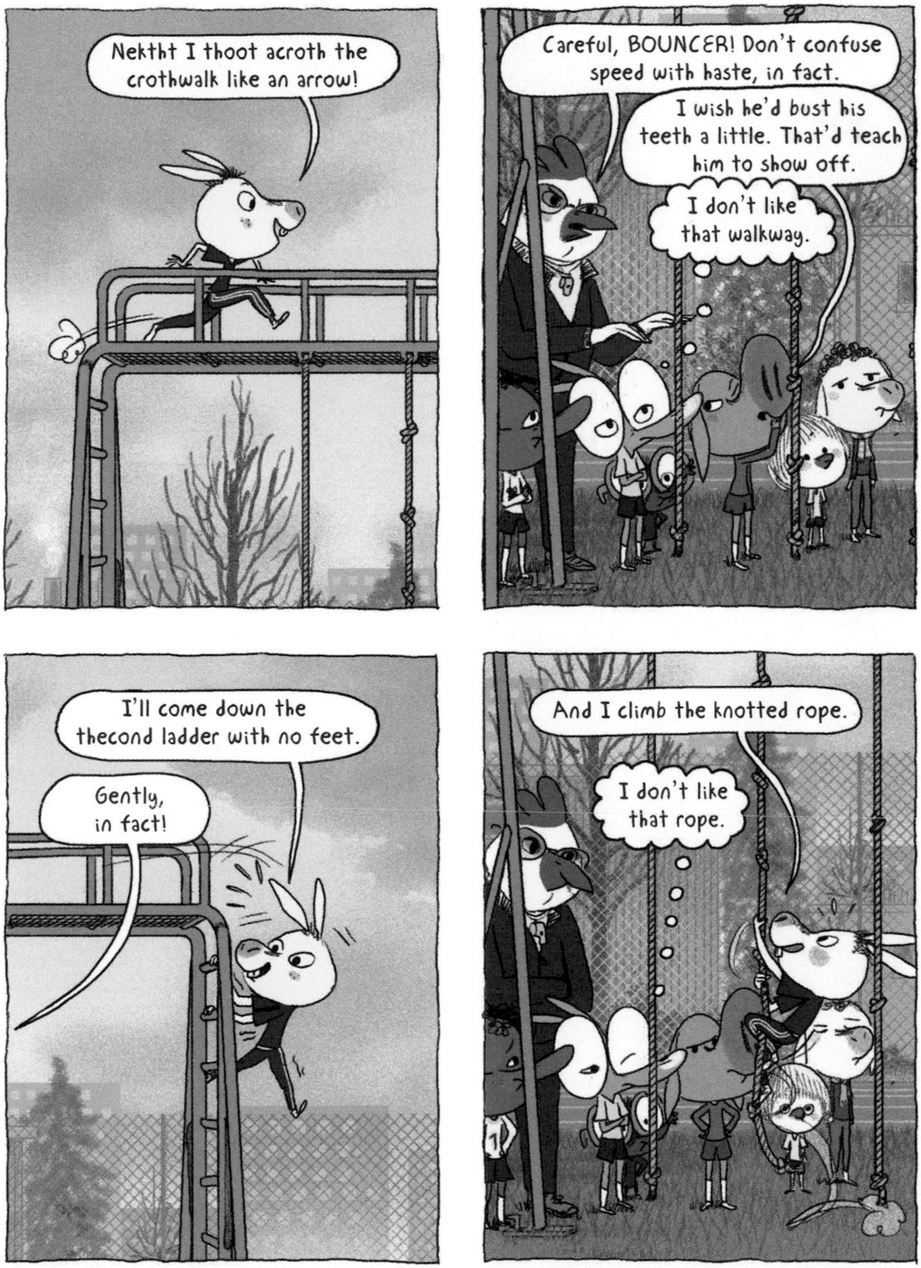
Nektht I thoot acroth the crothwalk like an arrow!
Careful, BOUNCER! Don't confuse speed with haste, in fact.
I wish he'd bust his teeth a little. That'd teach him to show off.
I don't like that walkway.
I'll come down the thecond ladder with no feet.
Gently, in fact!
And I climb the knotted rope.
I don't like that rope.

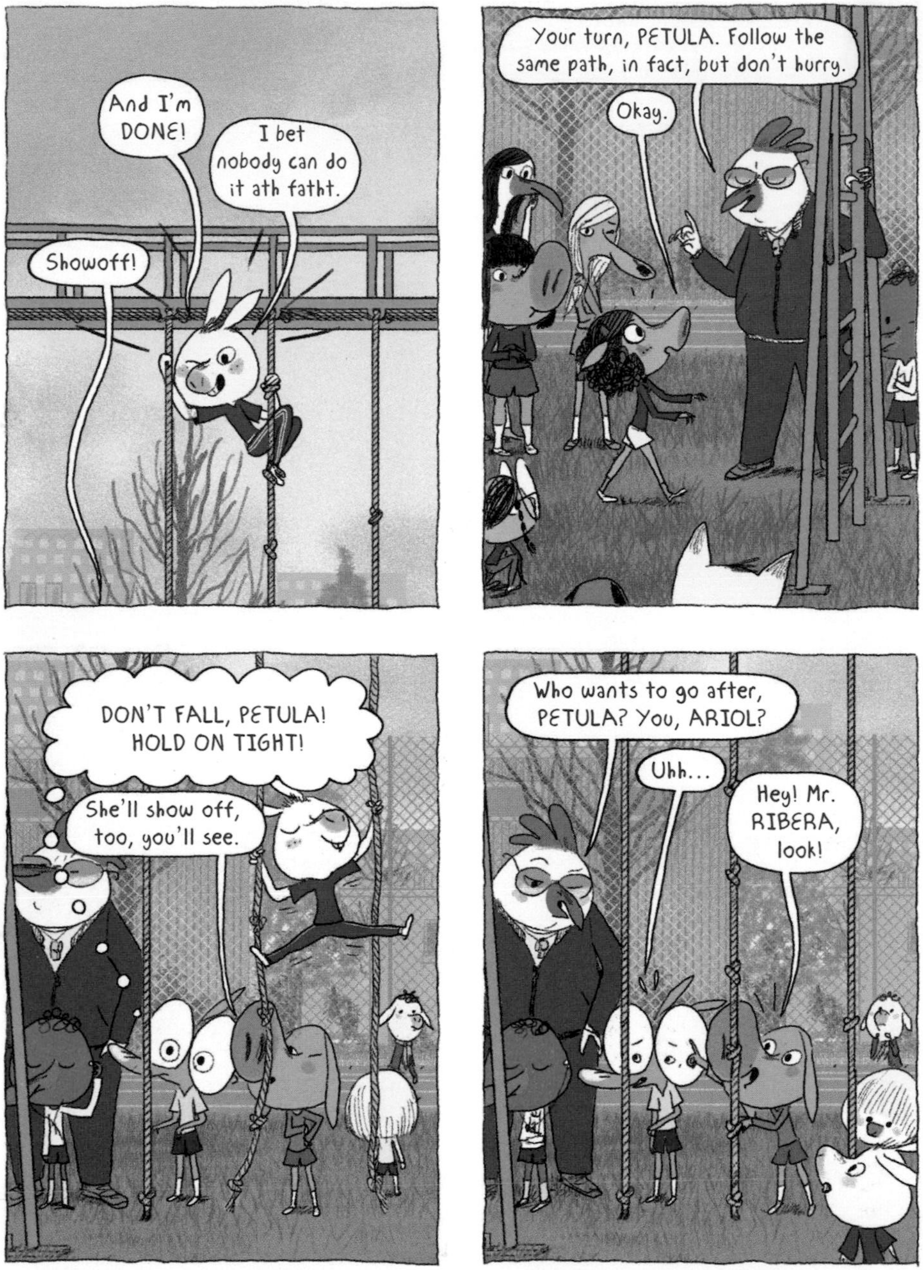
And I'm DONE!
I bet nobody can do it ath fatht.
Showoff!
Your turn, PETULA. Follow the same path, in fact, but don't hurry.
Okay.
DON'T FALL, PETULA! HOLD ON TIGHT!
She'll show off, too, you'll see.
Who wants to go after, PETULA? You, ARIOL?
Uhh...
Hey! Mr. RIBERA, look!

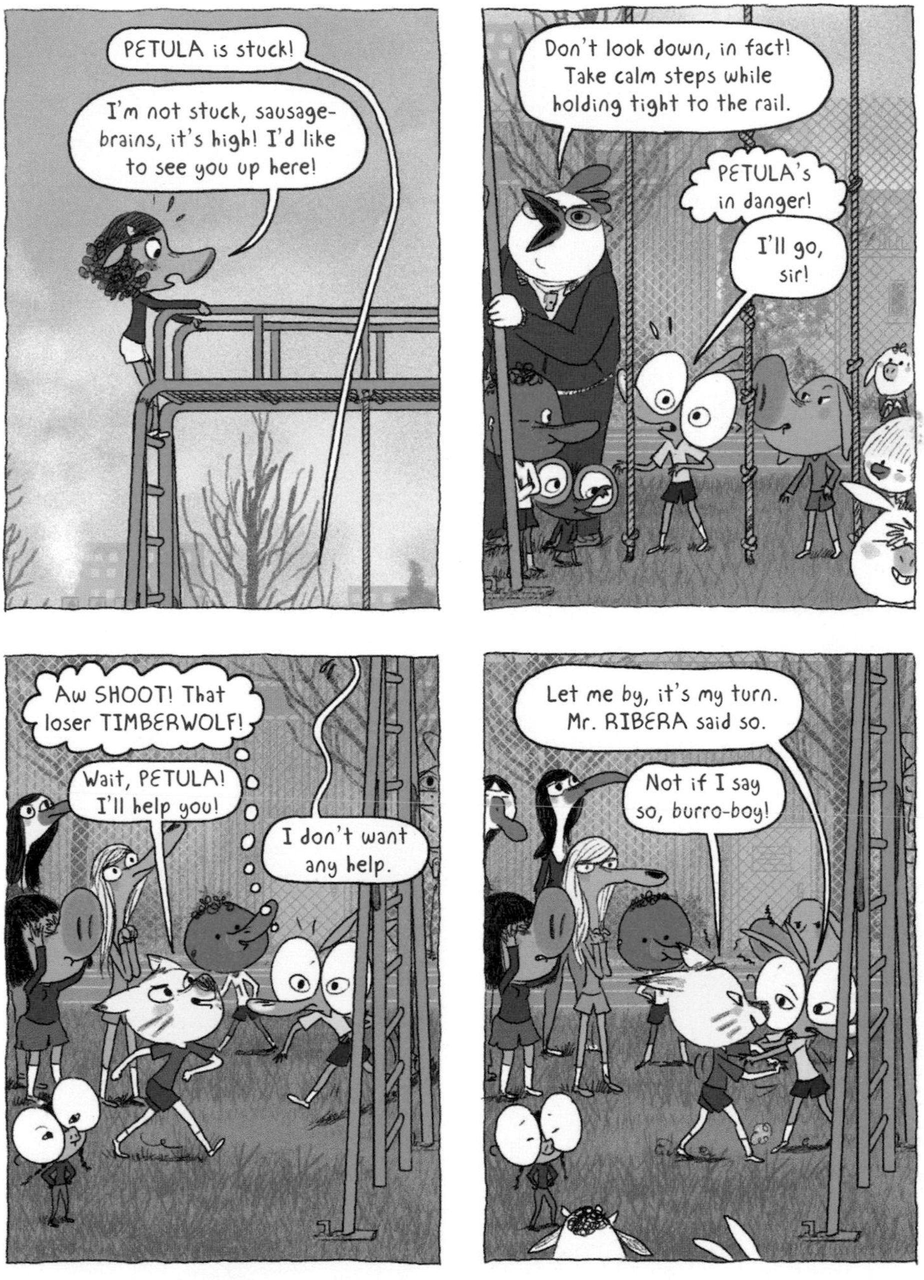
PETULA is stuck!
I'm not stuck, sausage-brains, it's high! I'd like to see you up here!
Don't look down, in fact! Take calm steps while holding tight to the rail.
PETULA's in danger!
I'll go, sir!
Aw SHOOT! That loser TIMBERWOLF!
Wait, PETULA! I'll help you!
I don't want any help.
Let me by, it's my turn. Mr. RIBERA said so.
Not if I say so, burro-boy!

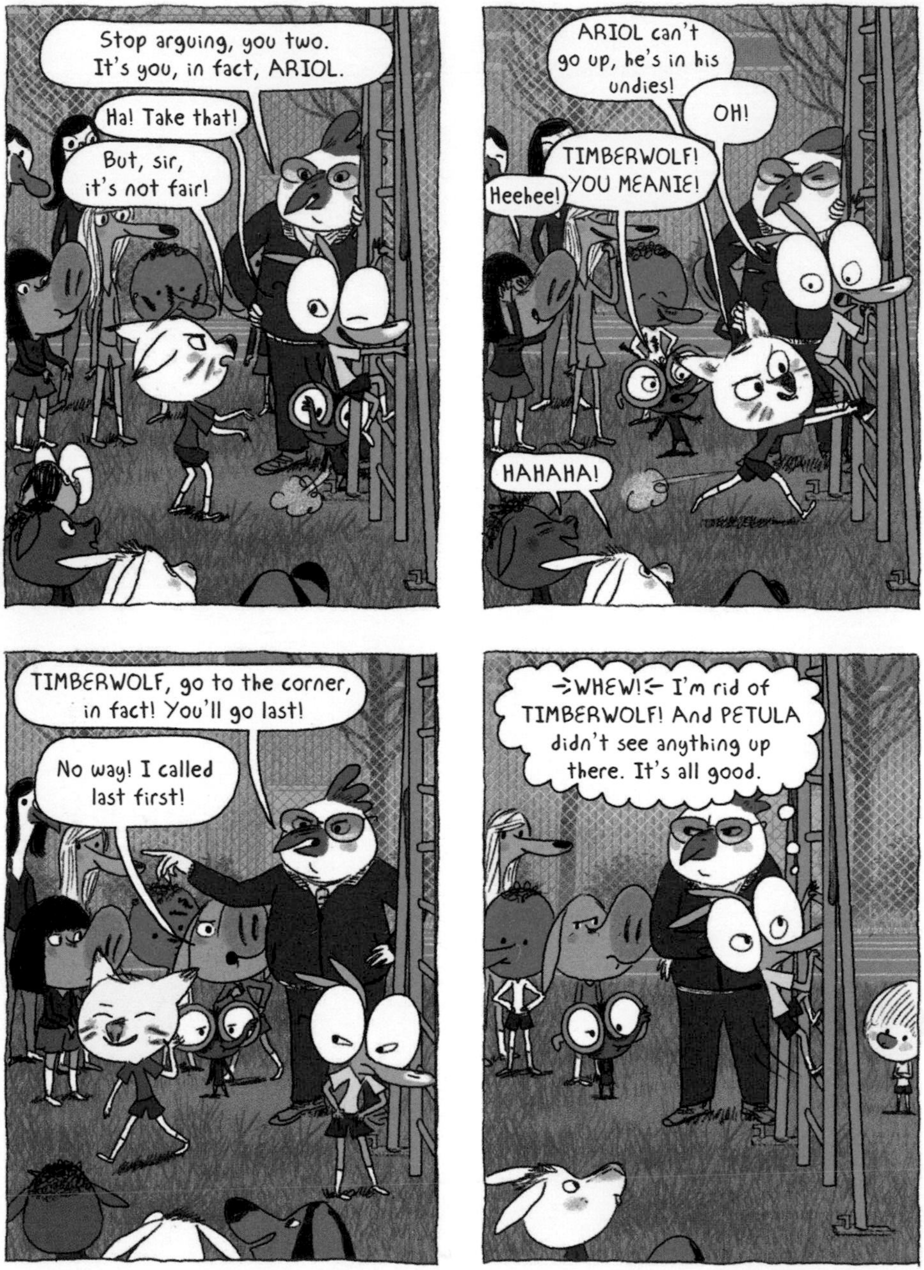
Stop arguing, you two. It's you, in fact, ARIOL.
Ha! Take that!
But, sir, it's not fair!
ARIOL can't go up, he's in his undies!
OH!
TIMBERWOLF! YOU MEANIE!
Heehee!
HAHAHA!
TIMBERWOLF, go to the corner, in fact! You'll go last!
No way! I called last first!
WHEW! I'm rid of TIMBERWOLF! And PETULA didn't see anything up there. It's all good.

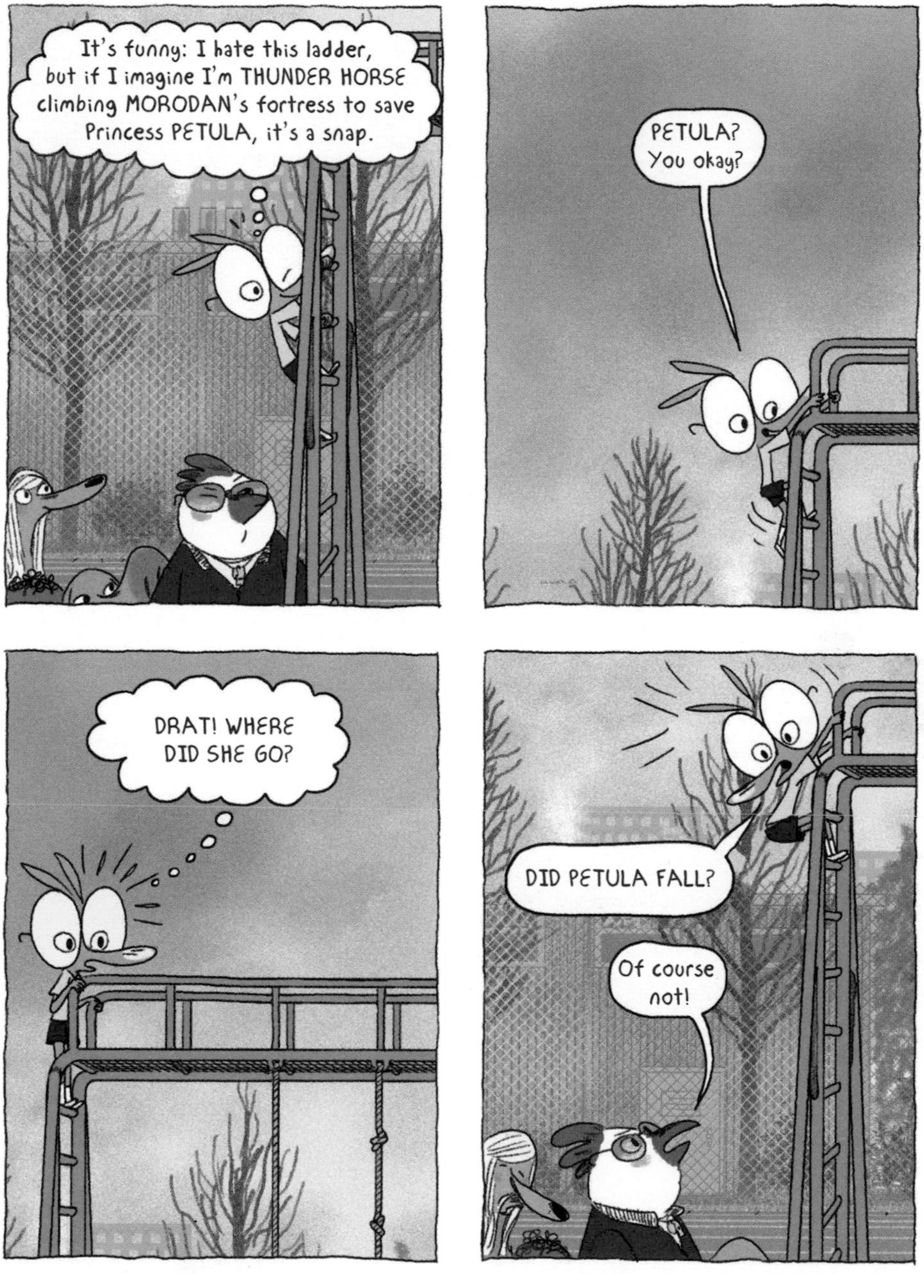
It's funny: I hate this ladder, but if I imagine I'm THUNDER HORSE climbing MORODAN's fortress to save Princess PETULA, it's a snap.
PETULA? You okay?
DRAT! WHERE DID SHE GO?
DID PETULA FALL?
Of course not!

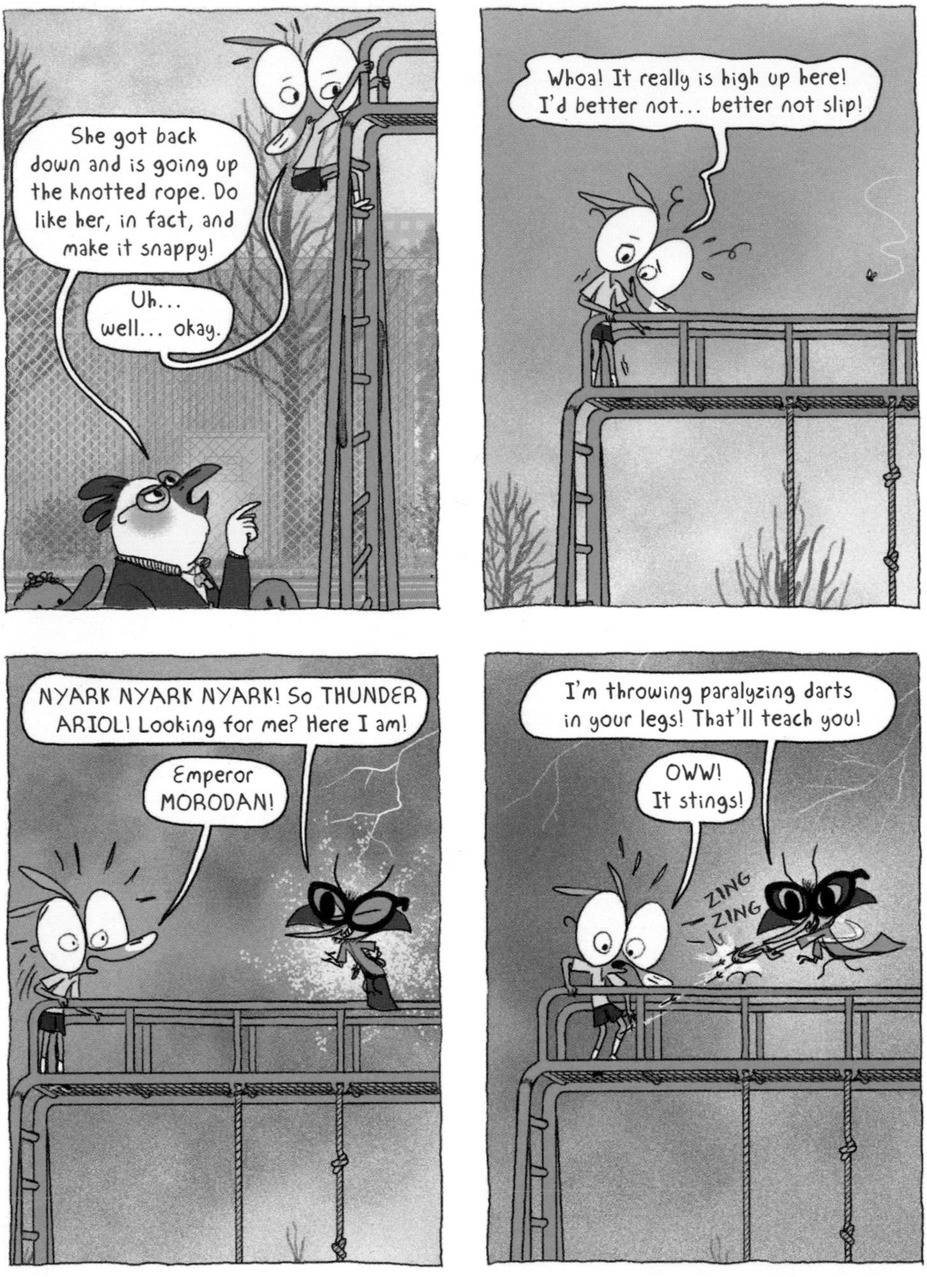
She got back down and is going up the knotted rope. Do like her, in fact, and make it snappy!
Uh... well... okay.
Whoa! It really is high up here! I'd better not... better not slip!
NYARK NYARK NYARK! So THUNDER ARIOL! Looking for me? Here I am!
Emperor MORODAN!
I'm throwing paralyzing darts in your legs! That'll teach you!
OWW! It stings!
ZING
ZING

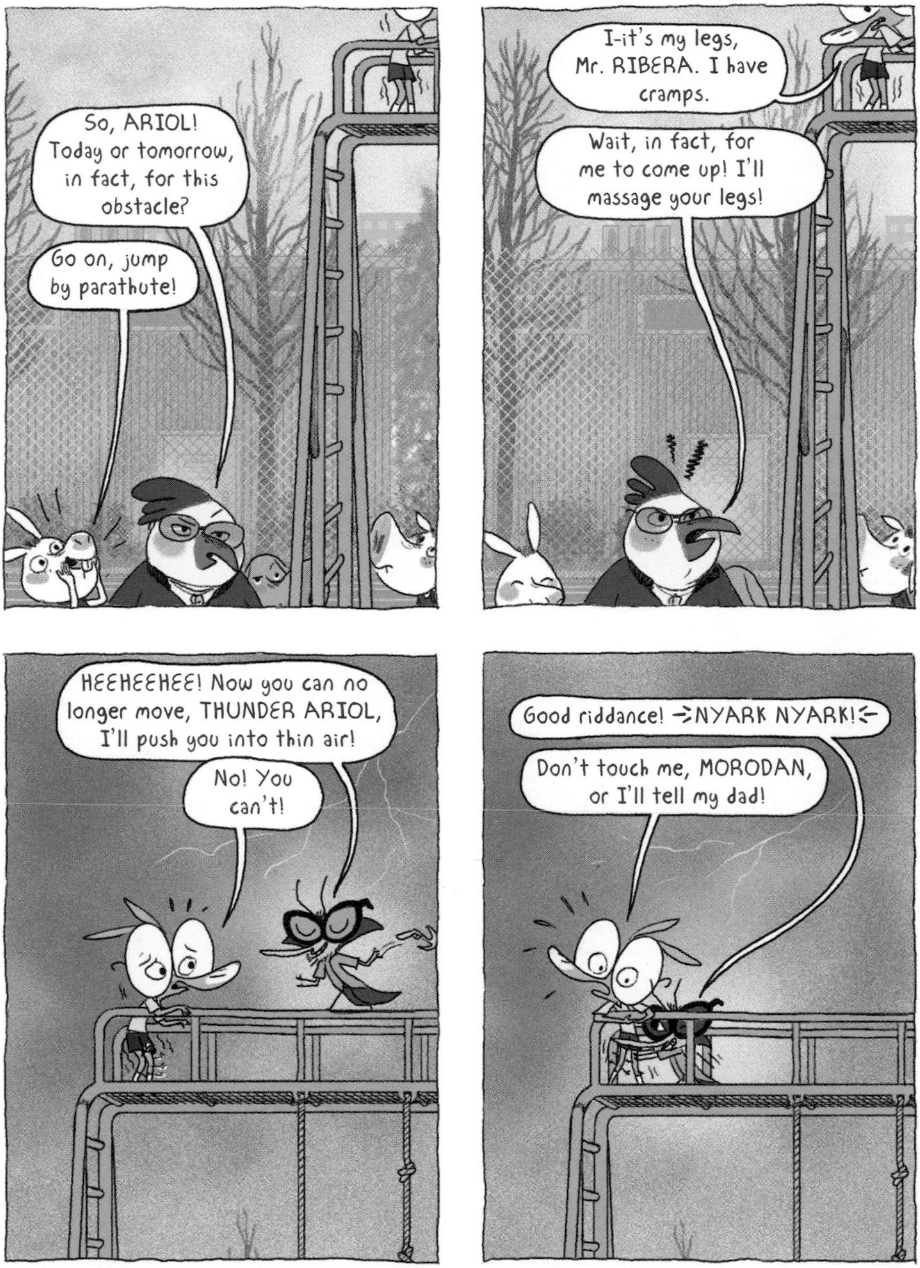
So, ARIOL! Today or tomorrow, in fact, for this obstacle?
Go on, jump by parathute!
I-it's my legs, Mr. RIBERA. I have cramps.
Wait, in fact, for me to come up! I'll massage your legs!
HEEHEEHEE! Now you can no longer move, THUNDER ARIOL, I'll push you into thin air!
No! You can't!
Good riddance! NYARK NYARK!
Don't touch me, MORODAN, or I'll tell my dad!

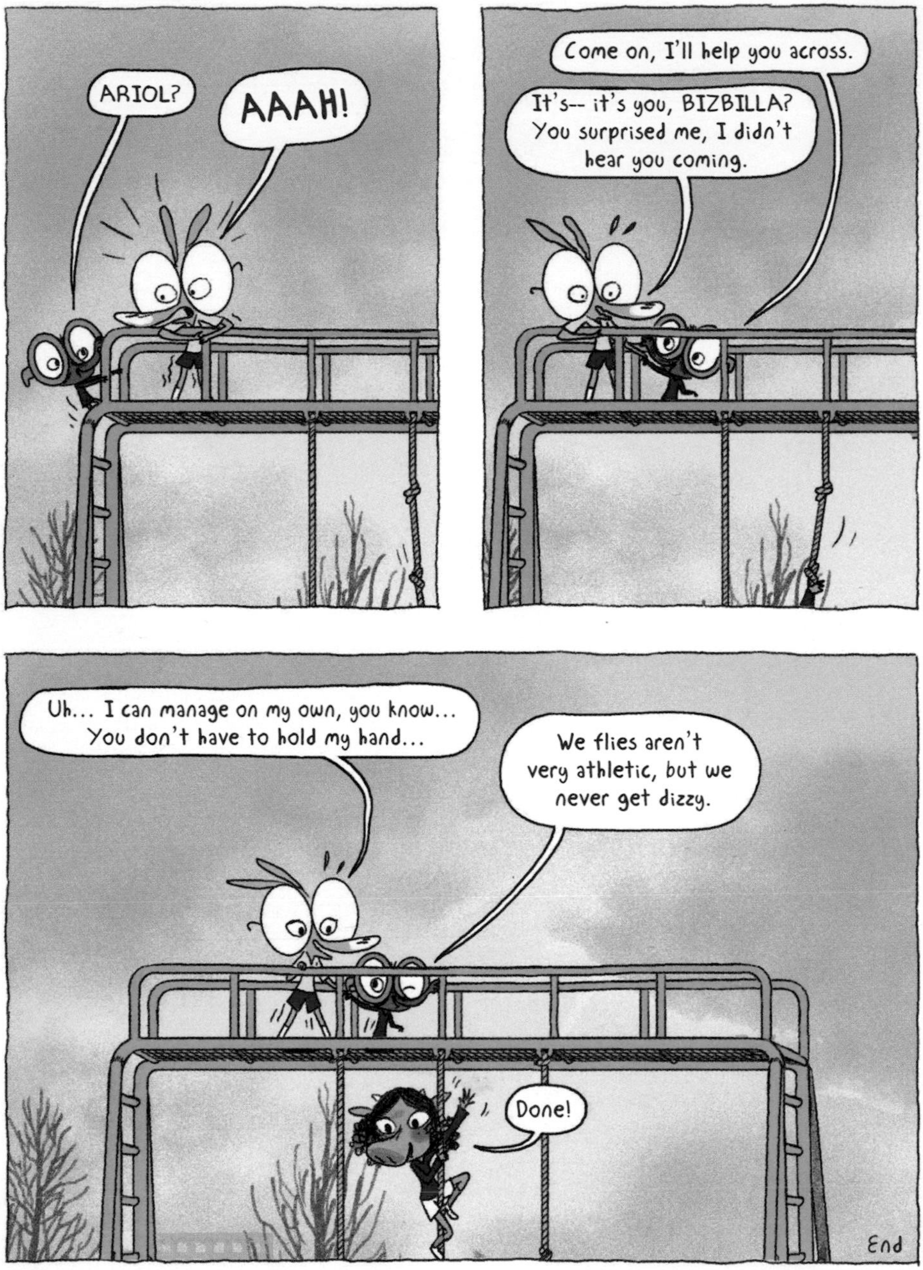
ARIOL?
AAAH!
Come on, I'll help you across.
It's-- it's you, BIZBILLA? You surprised me, I didn't hear you coming.
Uh... I can manage on my own, you know... You don't have to hold my hand...
We flies aren't very athletic, but we never get dizzy.
Done!
End

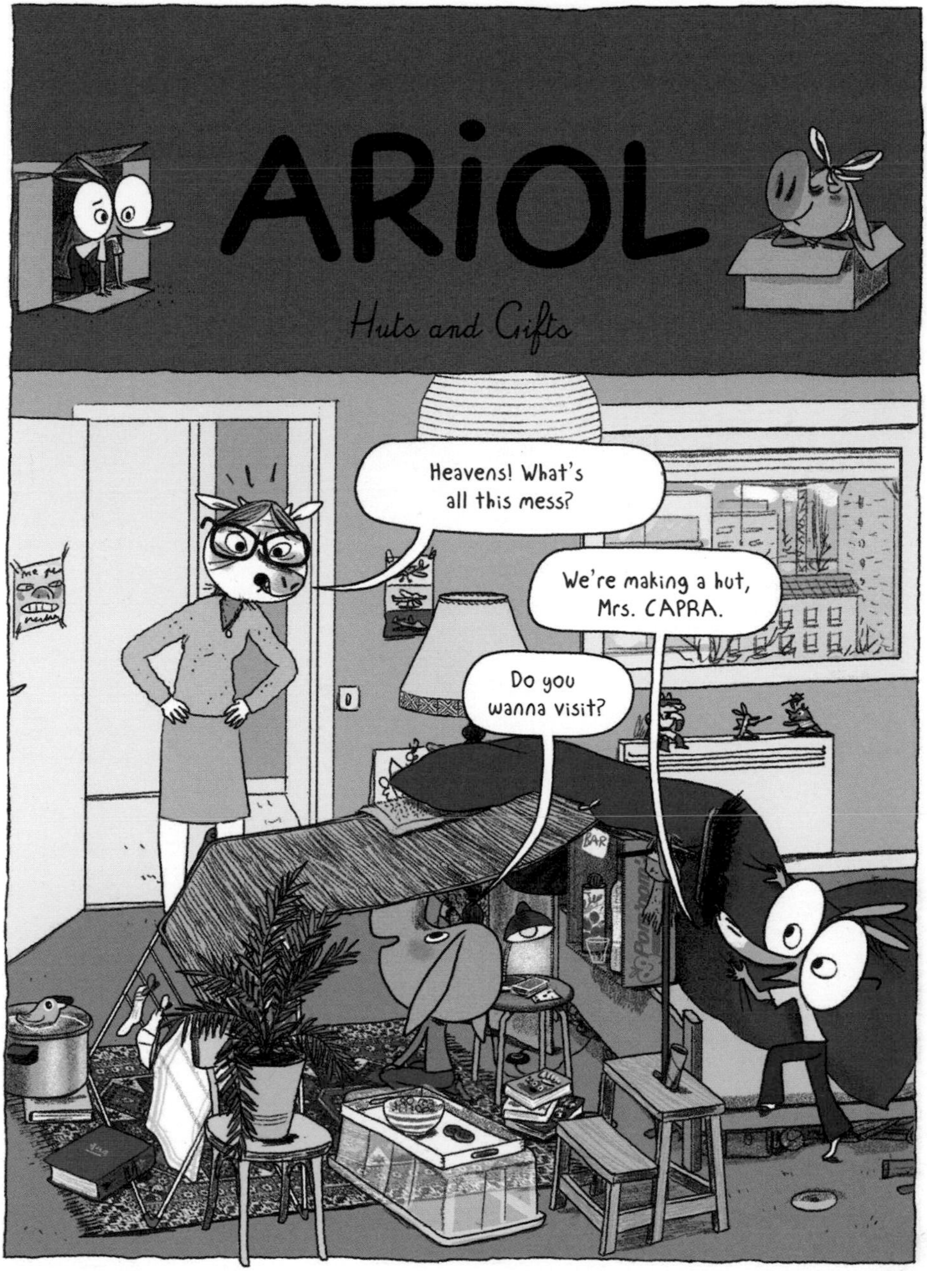
ARiOL
Huts and Gifts
Heavens! What's all this mess?
We're making a hut, Mrs. CAPRA.
Do you wanna visit?

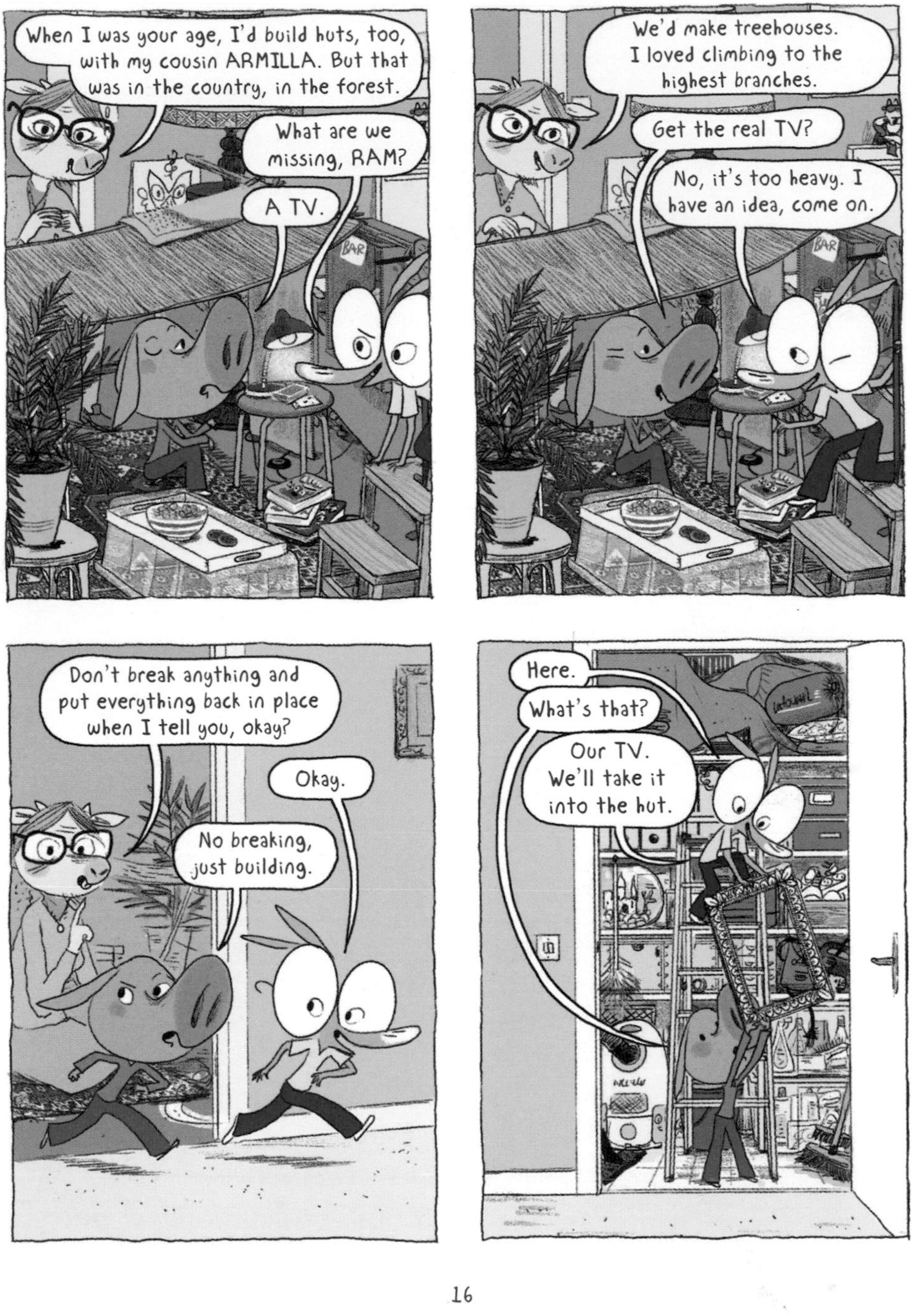
When I was your age, I'd build huts, too, with my cousin ARMILLA. But that was in the country, in the forest.
What are we missing, RAM?
A TV.
We'd make treehouses. I loved climbing to the highest branches.
Get the real TV?
No, it's too heavy. I have an idea, come on.
Don't break anything and put everything back in place when I tell you, okay?
Okay.
No breaking, just building.
Here.
What's that?
Our TV. We'll take it into the hut.

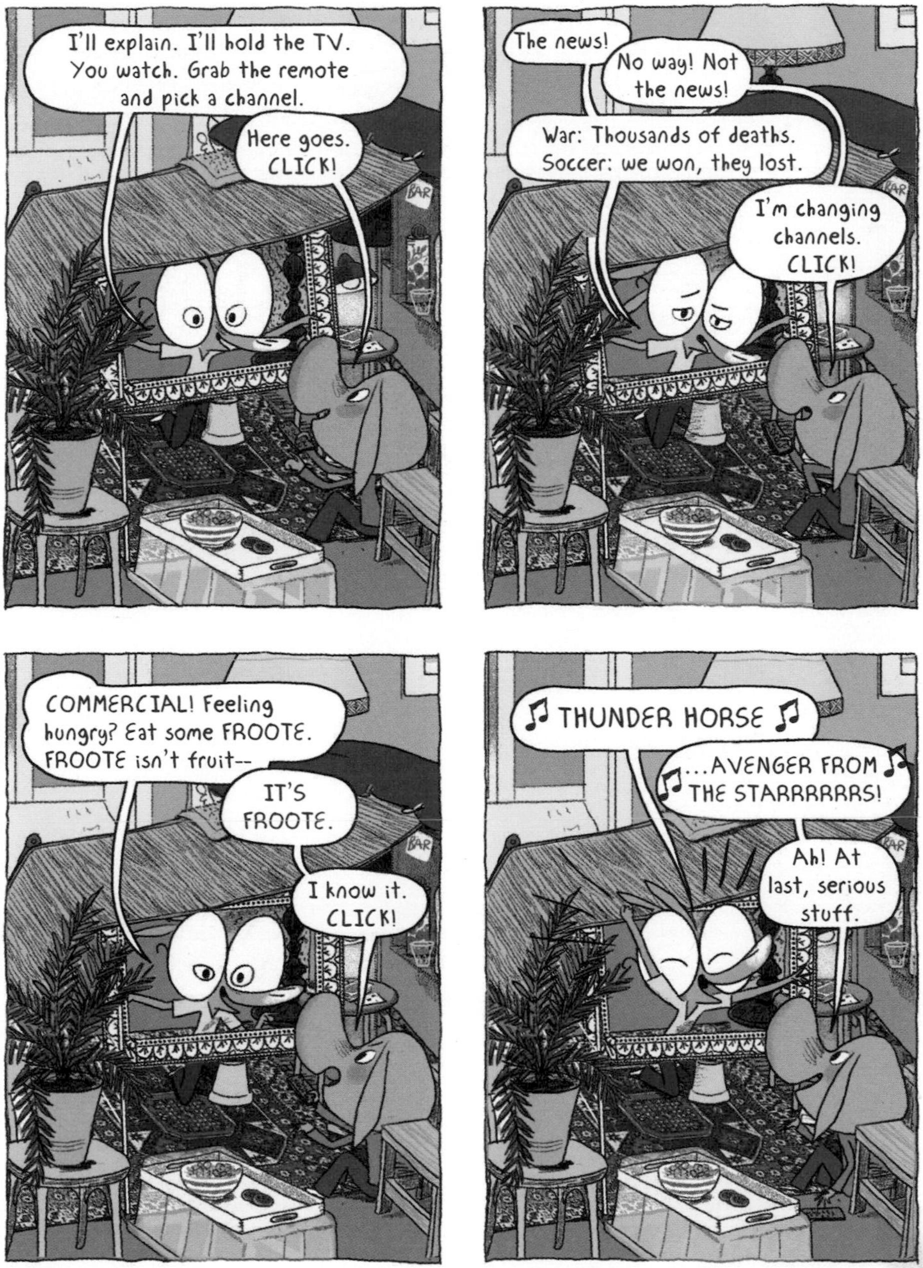
I'll explain. I'll hold the TV. You watch. Grab the remote and pick a channel.
Here goes. CLICK!
The news!
No way! Not the news!
War: Thousands of deaths. Soccer: we won, they lost.
I'm changing channels. CLICK!
COMMERCIAL! Feeling hungry? Eat some FROOTE. FROOTE isn't fruit--
IT'S FROOTE.
I know it. CLICK!
♫ THUNDER HORSE ♫
♫ ...AVENGER FROM ♫ THE STARRRRRRS!
Ah! At last, serious stuff.

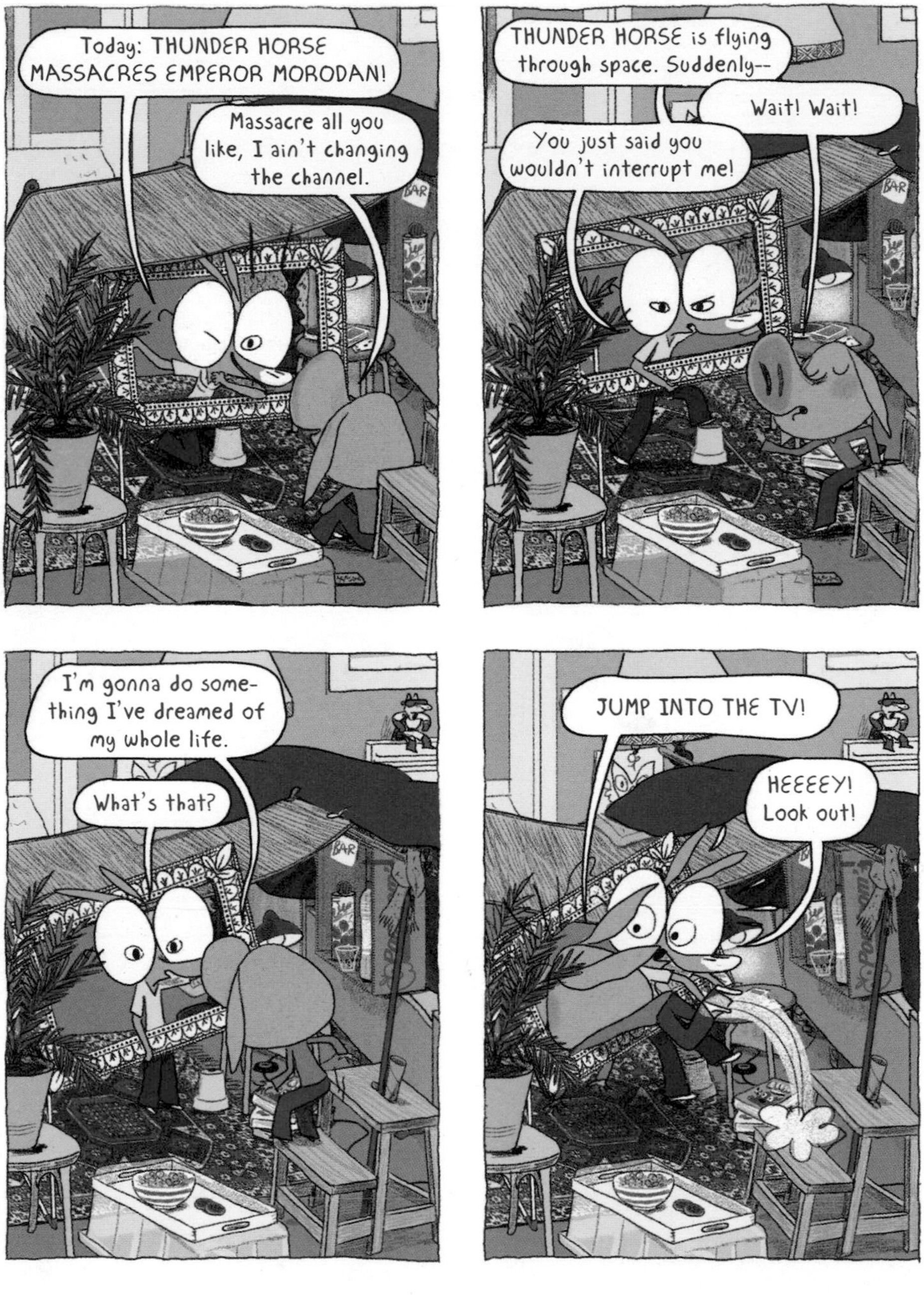
Today: THUNDER HORSE MASSACRES EMPEROR MORODAN!
Massacre all you like, I ain't changing the channel.
THUNDER HORSE is flying through space. Suddenly--
Wait! Wait!
You just said you wouldn't interrupt me!
I'm gonna do some-thing I've dreamed of my whole life.
What's that?
JUMP INTO THE TV!
HEEEEY! Look out!

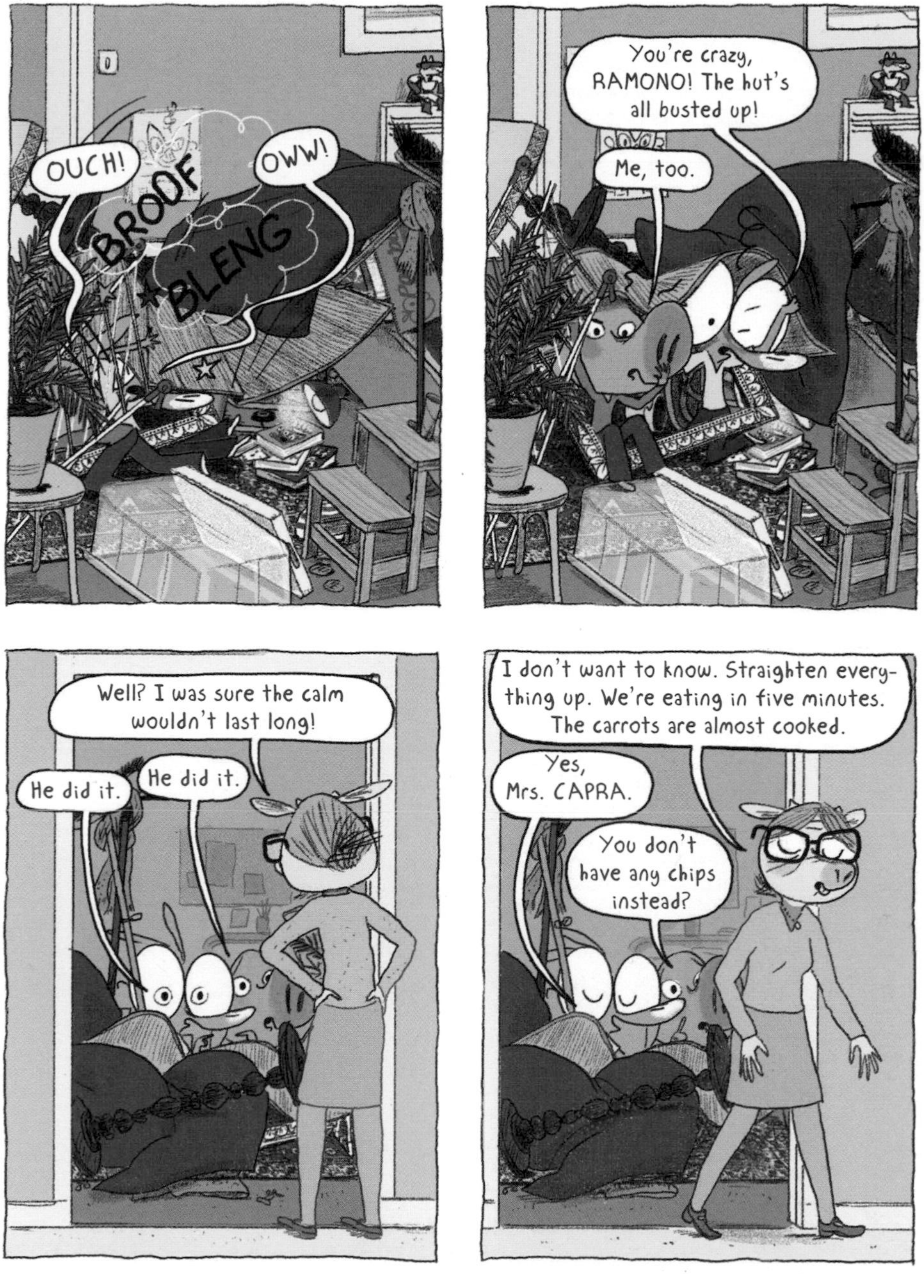
OUCH!
BROOF
OWW!
BLENG
You're crazy, RAMONO! The hut's all busted up!
Me, too.
Well? I was sure the calm wouldn't last long!
He did it.
He did it.
I don't want to know. Straighten everything up. We're eating in five minutes. The carrots are almost cooked.
Yes, Mrs. CAPRA.
You don't have any chips instead?

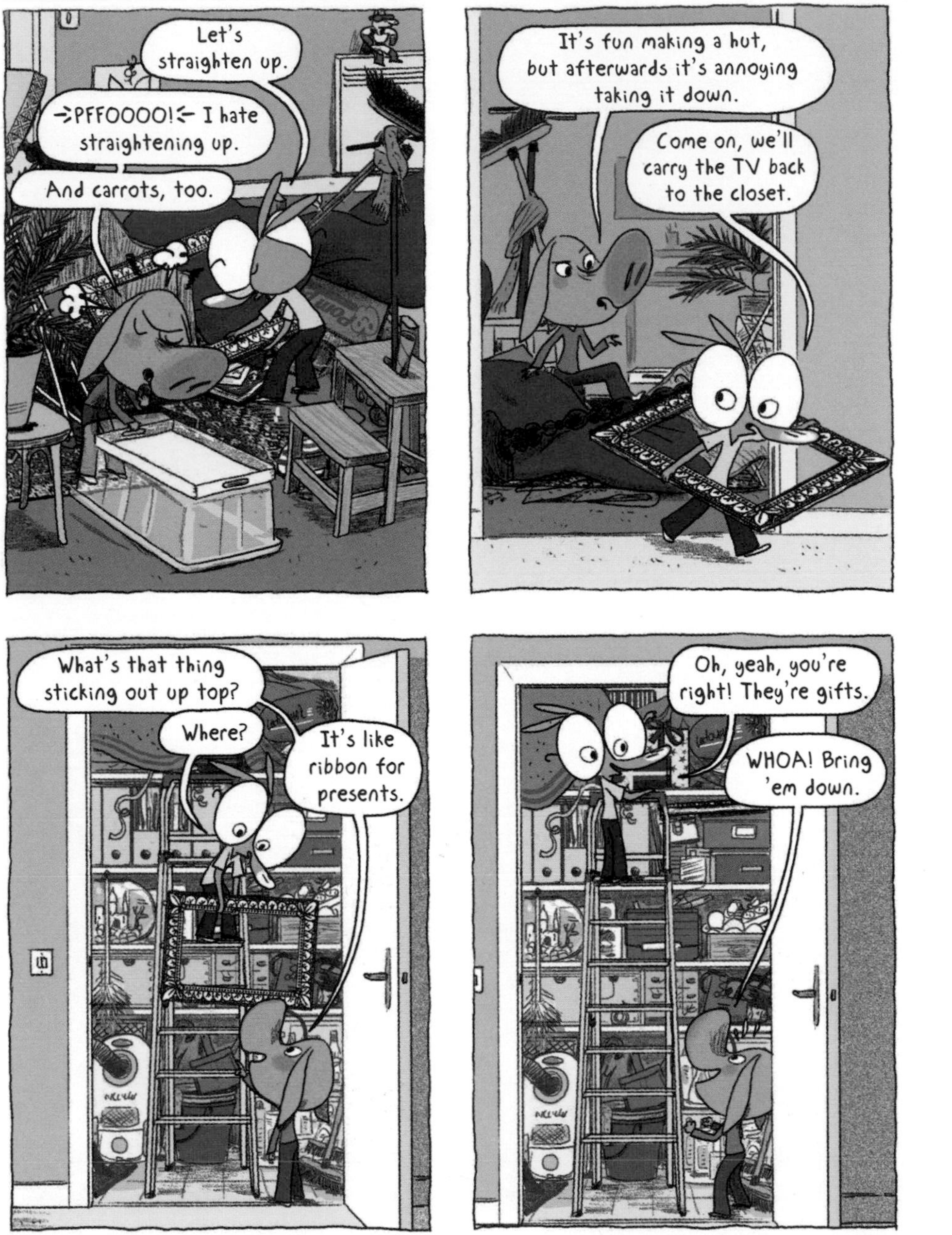
Let's straighten up.
⇢PFFOOOO!⇠ I hate straightening up.
And carrots, too.
It's fun making a hut, but afterwards it's annoying taking it down.
Come on, we'll carry the TV back to the closet.
What's that thing sticking out up top?
Where?
It's like ribbon for presents.
Oh, yeah, you're right! They're gifts.
WHOA! Bring 'em down.

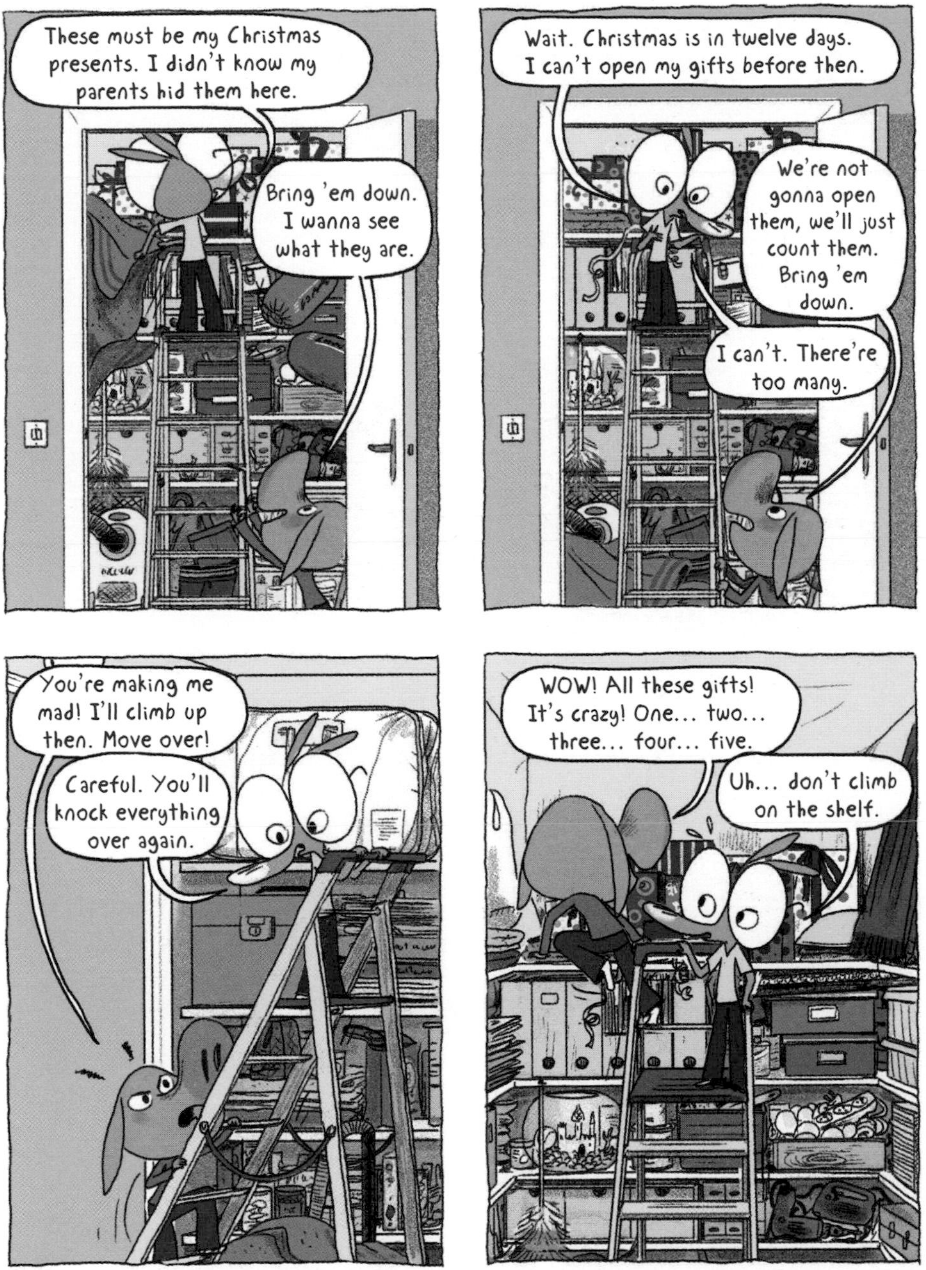

These must be my Christmas presents. I didn't know my parents hid them here.
Bring 'em down. I wanna see what they are.
Wait. Christmas is in twelve days. I can't open my gifts before then.
We're not gonna open them, we'll just count them. Bring 'em down.
I can't. There're too many.
You're making me mad! I'll climb up then. Move over!
Careful. You'll knock everything over again.
WOW! All these gifts! It's crazy! One... two... three... four... five.
Uh... don't climb on the shelf.

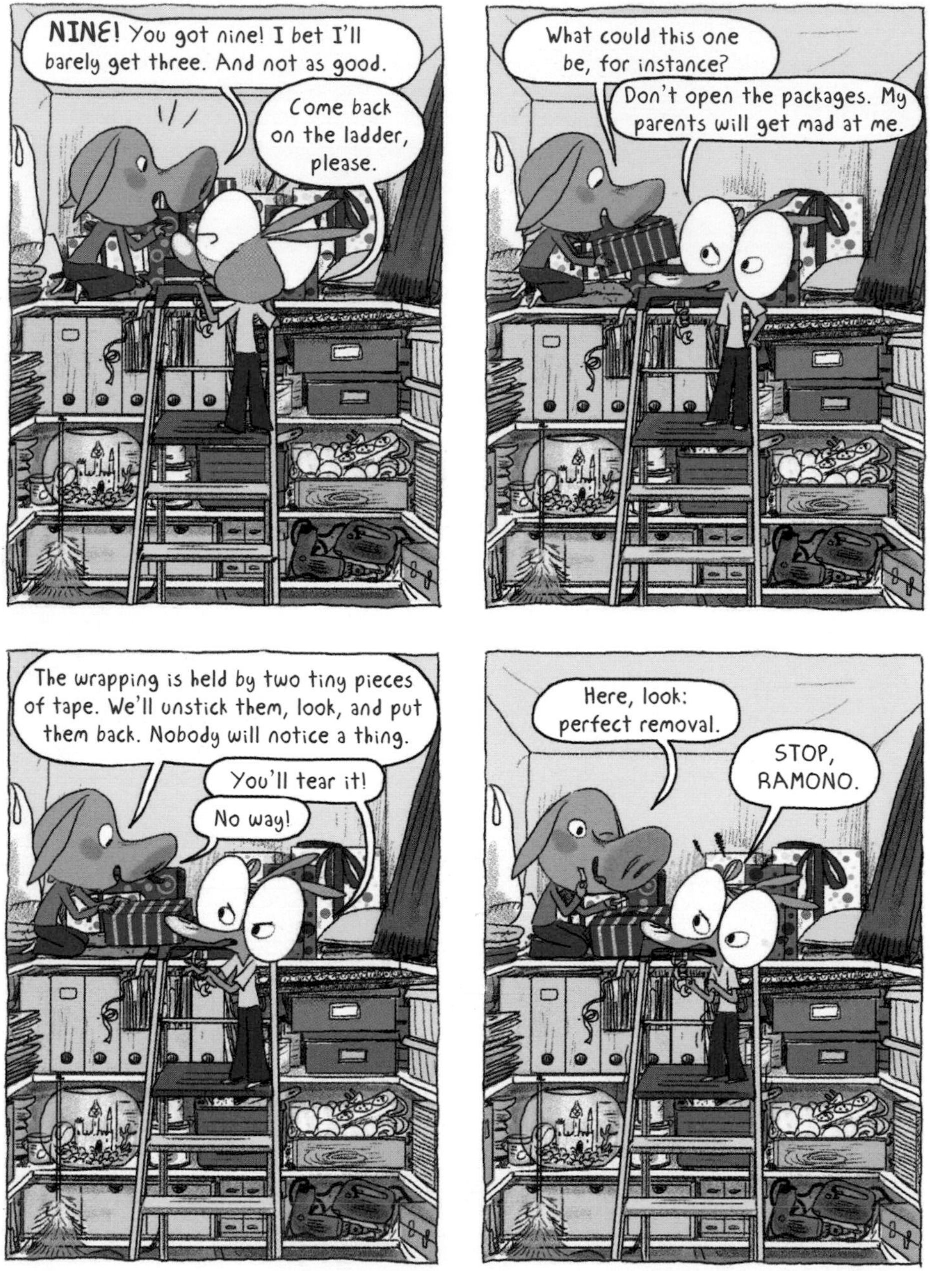
NINE! You got nine! I bet I'll barely get three. And not as good.
Come back on the ladder, please.
What could this one be, for instance?
Don't open the packages. My parents will get mad at me.
The wrapping is held by two tiny pieces of tape. We'll unstick them, look, and put them back. Nobody will notice a thing.
You'll tear it!
No way!
Here, look: perfect removal.
STOP, RAMONO.

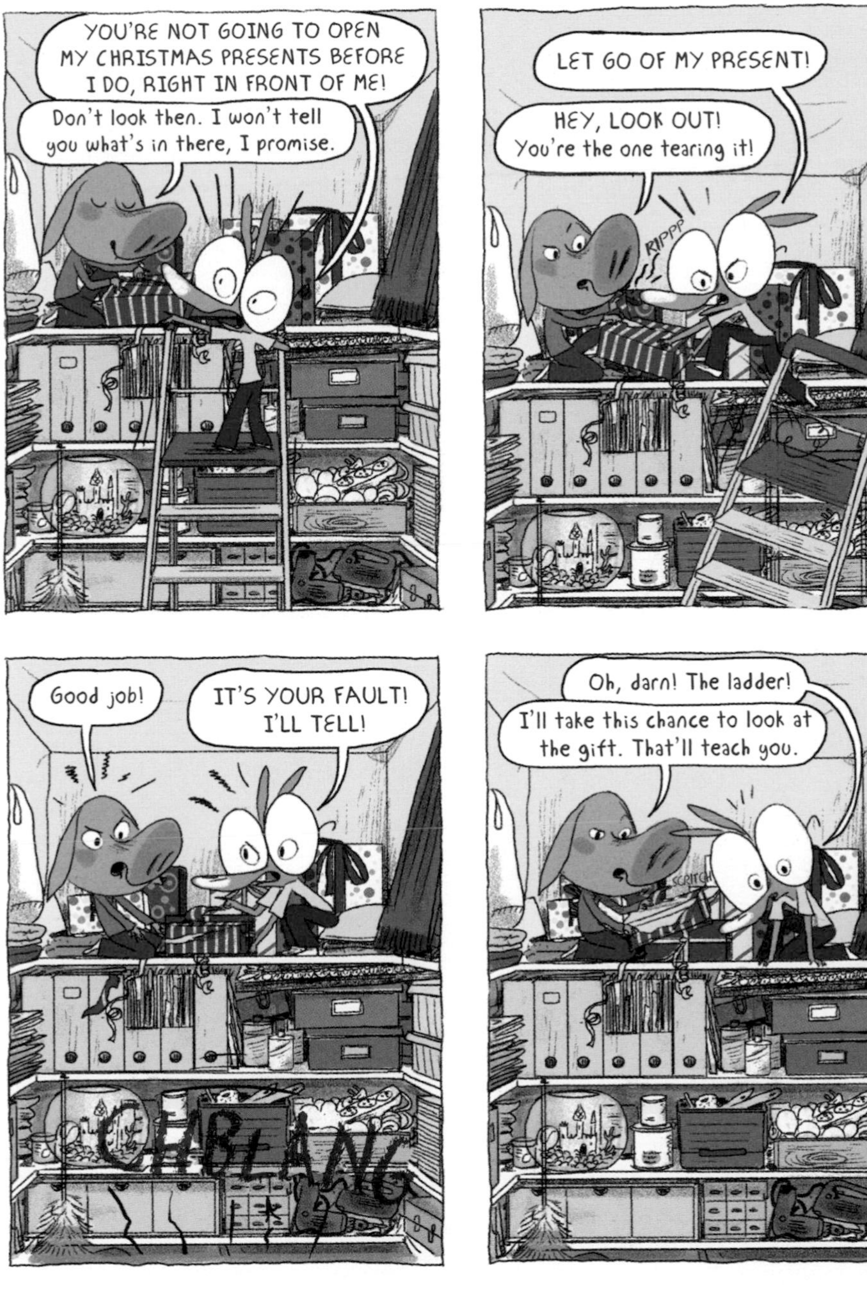

YOU'RE NOT GOING TO OPEN MY CHRISTMAS PRESENTS BEFORE I DO, RIGHT IN FRONT OF ME!
Don't look then. I won't tell you what's in there, I promise.
LET GO OF MY PRESENT!
HEY, LOOK OUT! You're the one tearing it!
RIPPP
Good job!
IT'S YOUR FAULT! I'LL TELL!
CHBLANG
Oh, darn! The ladder!
I'll take this chance to look at the gift. That'll teach you.
SCRITCH

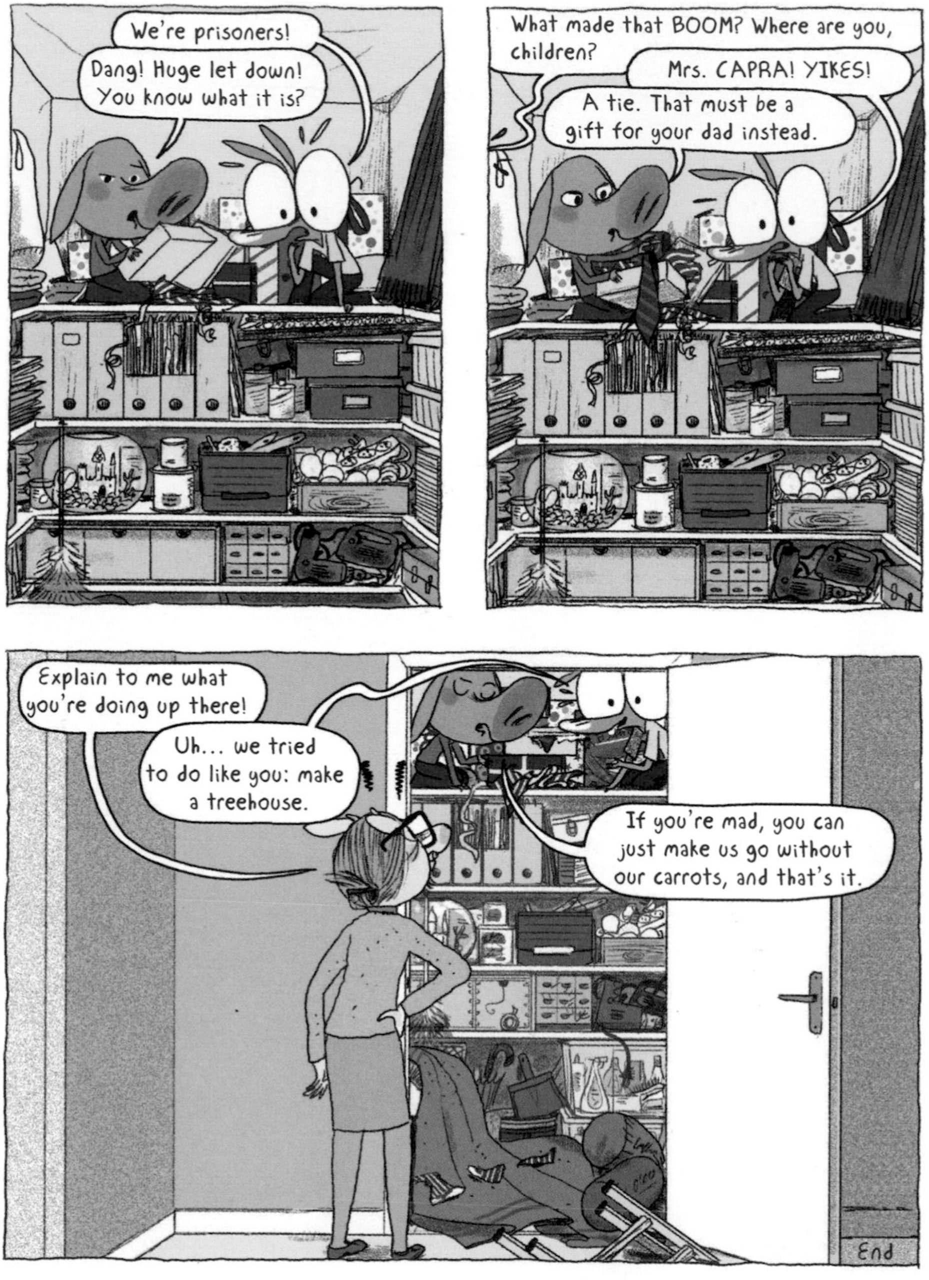

We're prisoners!
Dang! Huge let down! You know what it is?
What made that BOOM? Where are you, children?
Mrs. CAPRA! YIKES!
A tie. That must be a gift for your dad instead.
Explain to me what you're doing up there!
Uh... we tried to do like you: make a treehouse.
If you're mad, you can just make us go without our carrots, and that's it.
End

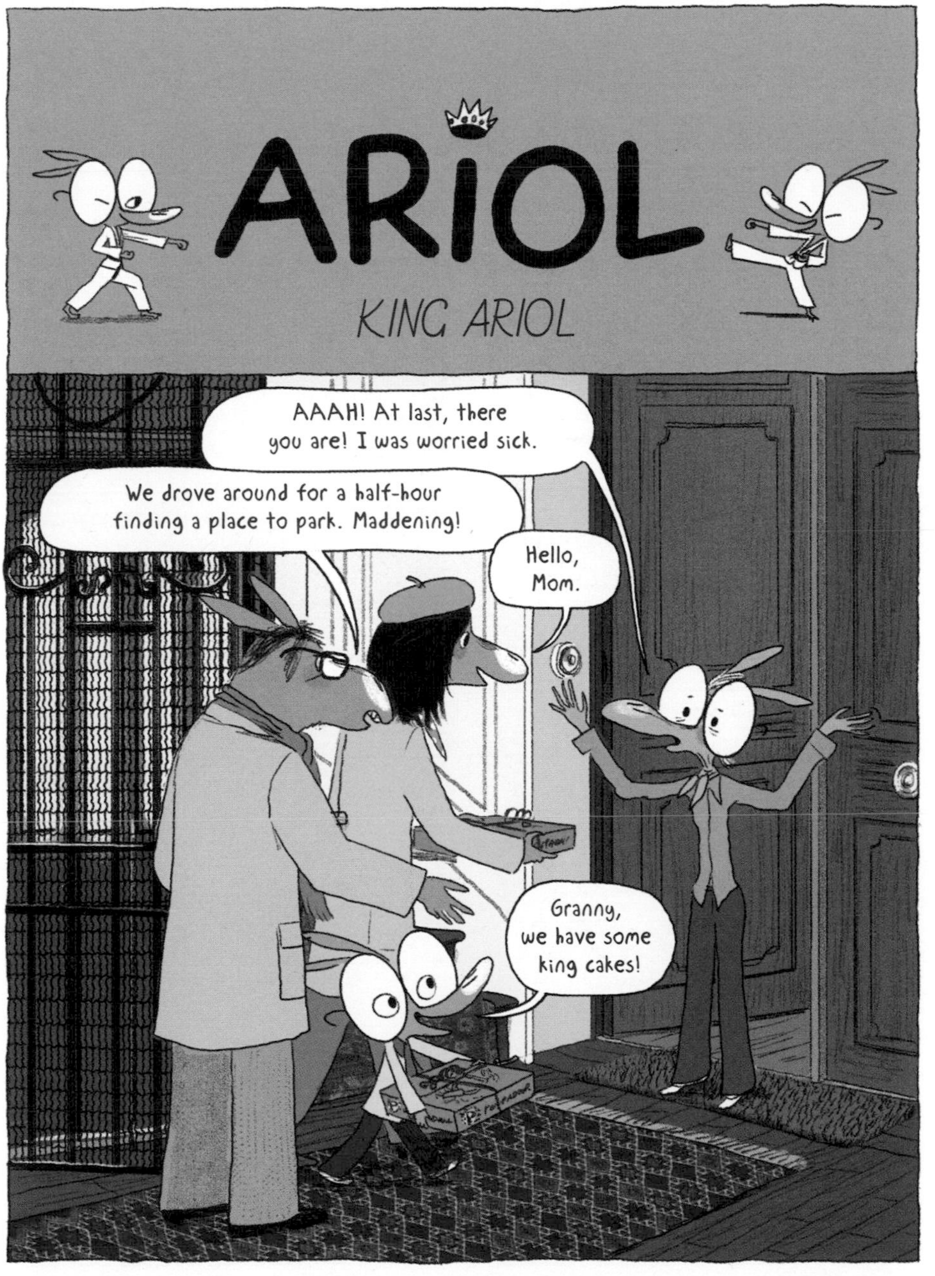
ARIOL
KING ARIOL
AAAH! At last, there you are! I was worried sick.
We drove around for a half-hour finding a place to park. Maddening!
Hello, Mom.
Granny, we have some king cakes!

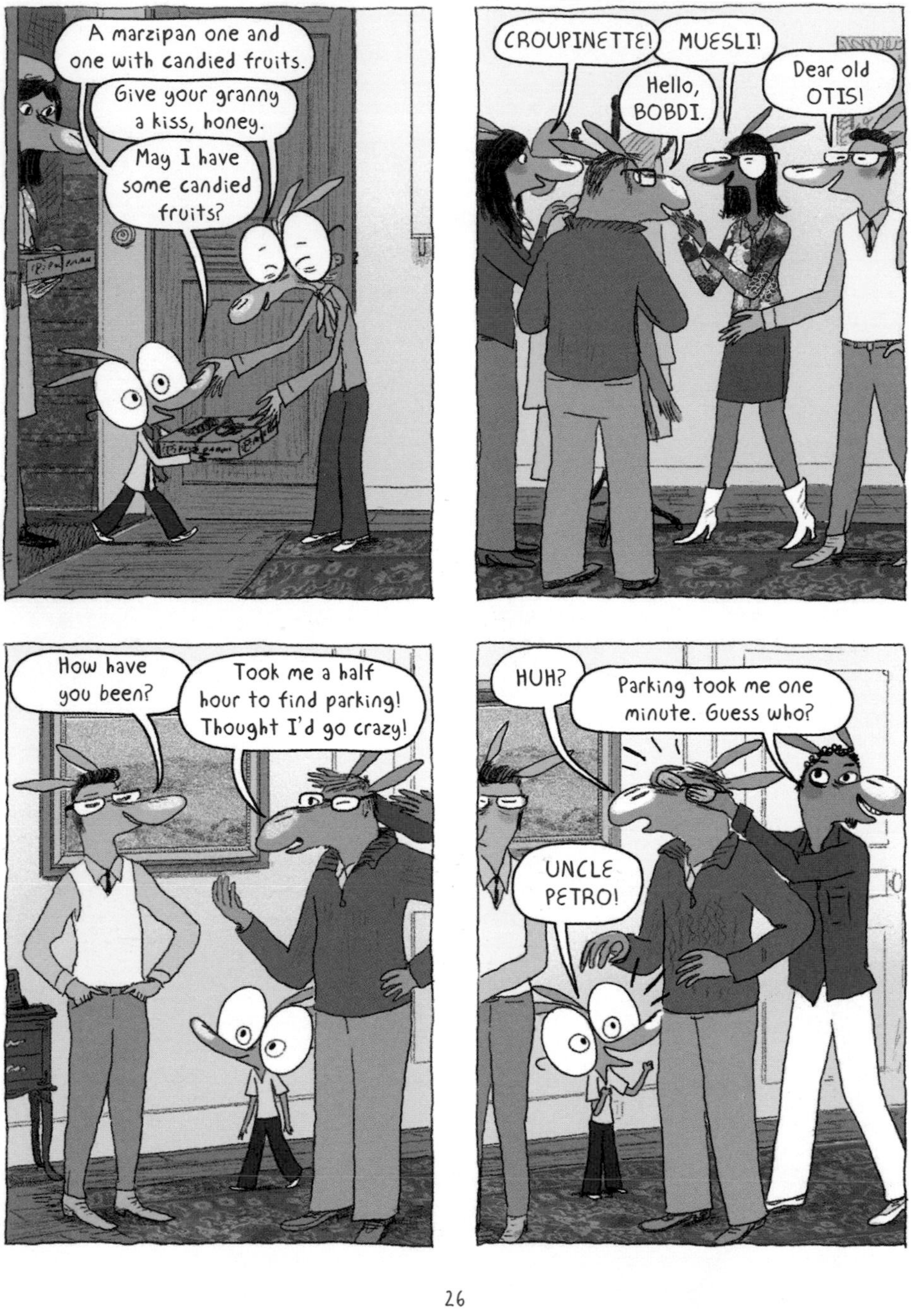
A marzipan one and one with candied fruits.
Give your granny a kiss, honey.
May I have some candied fruits?
CROUPINETTE!
MUESLI!
Hello, BOBDI.
Dear old OTIS!
How have you been?
Took me a half hour to find parking! Thought I'd go crazy!
HUH?
Parking took me one minute. Guess who?
UNCLE PETRO!

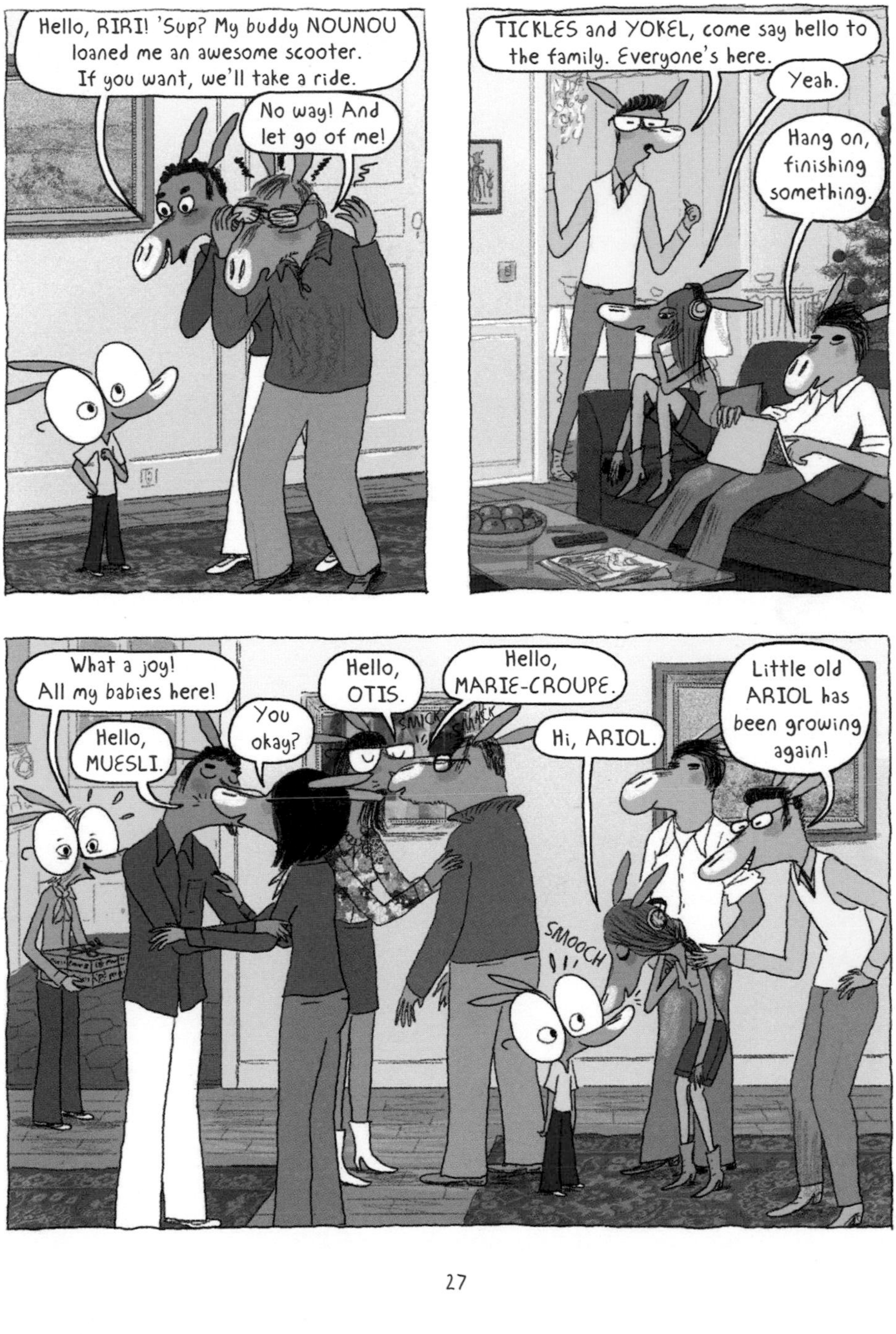
Hello, RIRI! 'Sup? My buddy NOUNOU loaned me an awesome scooter. If you want, we'll take a ride.
No way! And let go of me!
TICKLES and YOKEL, come say hello to the family. Everyone's here.
Yeah.
Hang on, finishing something.
What a joy! All my babies here!
Hello, MUESLI.
You okay?
Hello, OTIS.
SMACK
SMACK
Hello, MARIE-CROUPE.
Hi, ARIOL.
Little old ARIOL has been growing again!
SMOOCH

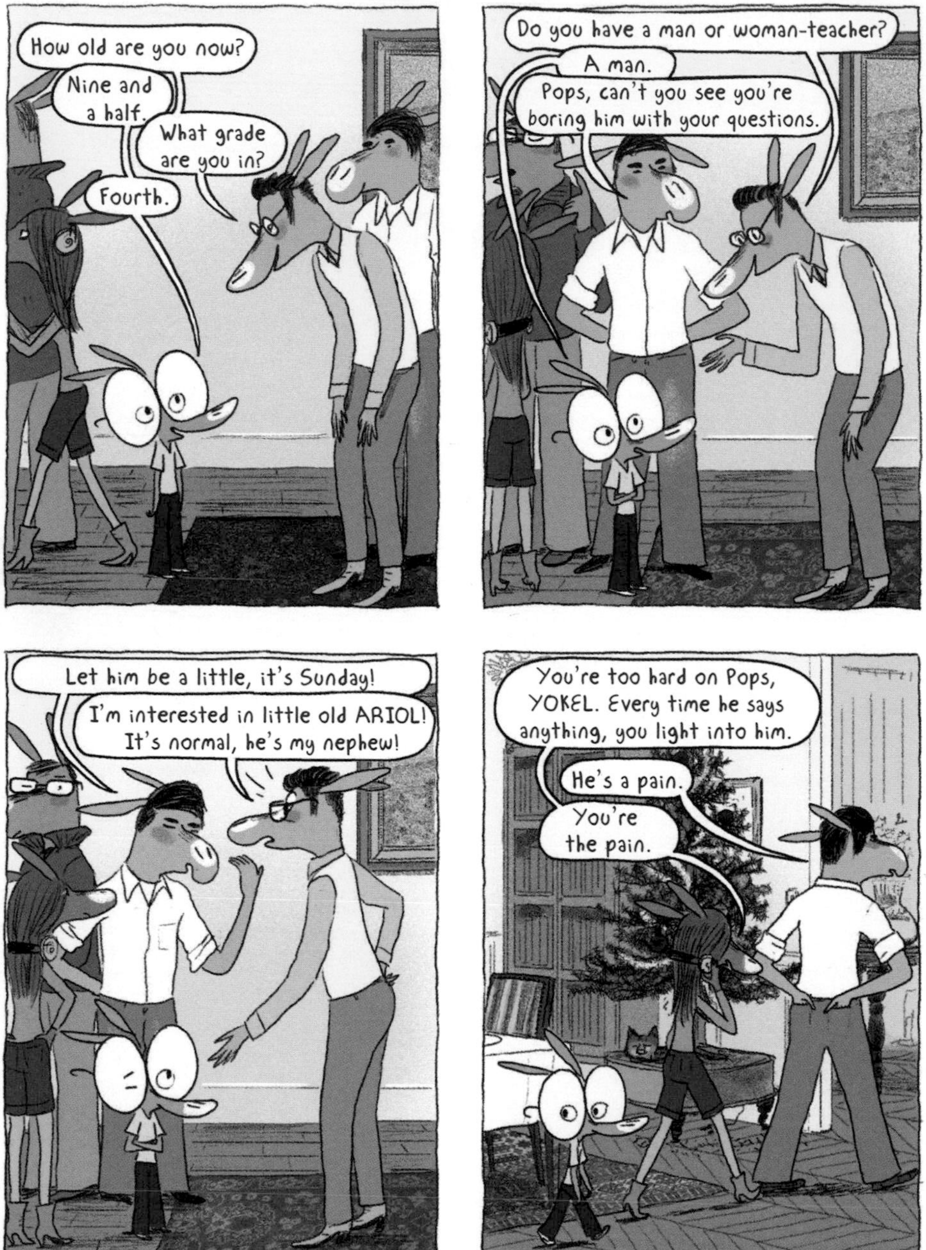
How old are you now?
Nine and a half.
What grade are you in?
Fourth.
Do you have a man or woman-teacher?
A man.
Pops, can't you see you're boring him with your questions.
Let him be a little, it's Sunday!
I'm interested in little old ARIOL! It's normal, he's my nephew!
You're too hard on Pops, YOKEL. Every time he says anything, you light into him.
He's a pain.
You're the pain.

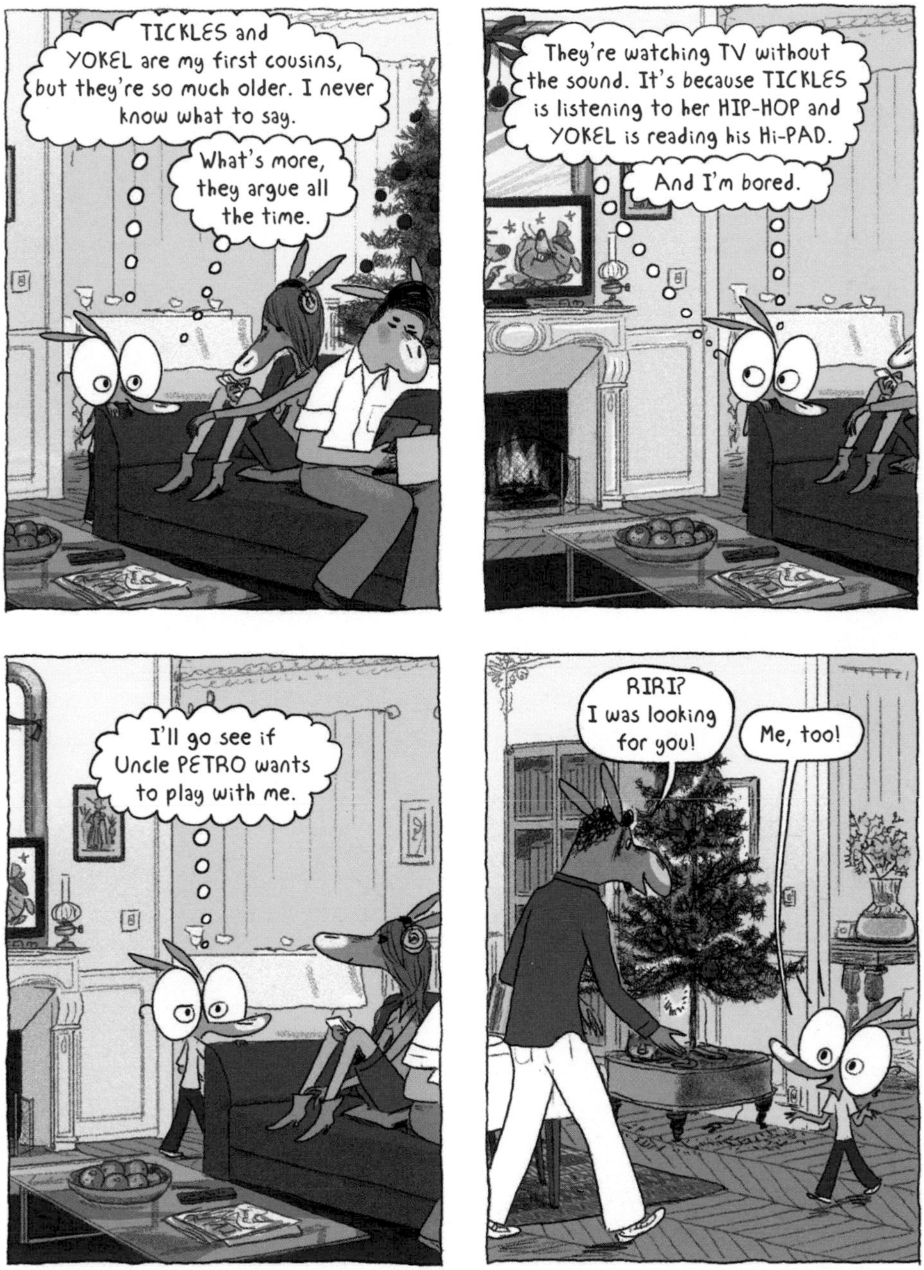
TICKLES and YOKEL are my first cousins, but they're so much older. I never know what to say.
What's more, they argue all the time.
They're watching TV without the sound. It's because TICKLES is listening to her HIP-HOP and YOKEL is reading his Hi-PAD.
And I'm bored.
I'll go see if Uncle PETRO wants to play with me.
RIRI? I was looking for you!
Me, too!

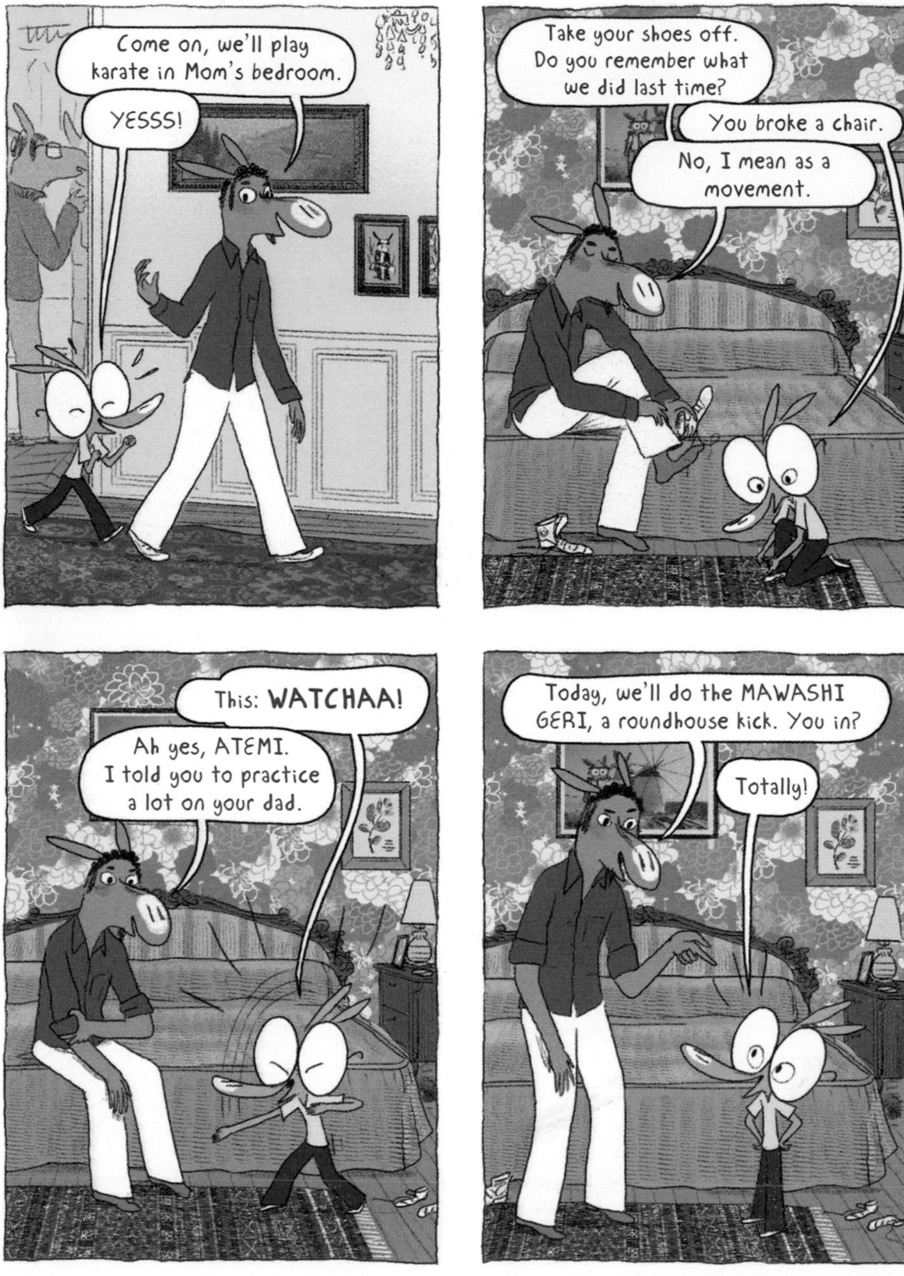
Come on, we'll play karate in Mom's bedroom.
YESSS!
Take your shoes off. Do you remember what we did last time?
You broke a chair.
No, I mean as a movement.
This: WATCHAA!
Ah yes, ATEMI. I told you to practice a lot on your dad.
Today, we'll do the MAWASHI GERI, a roundhouse kick. You in?
Totally!

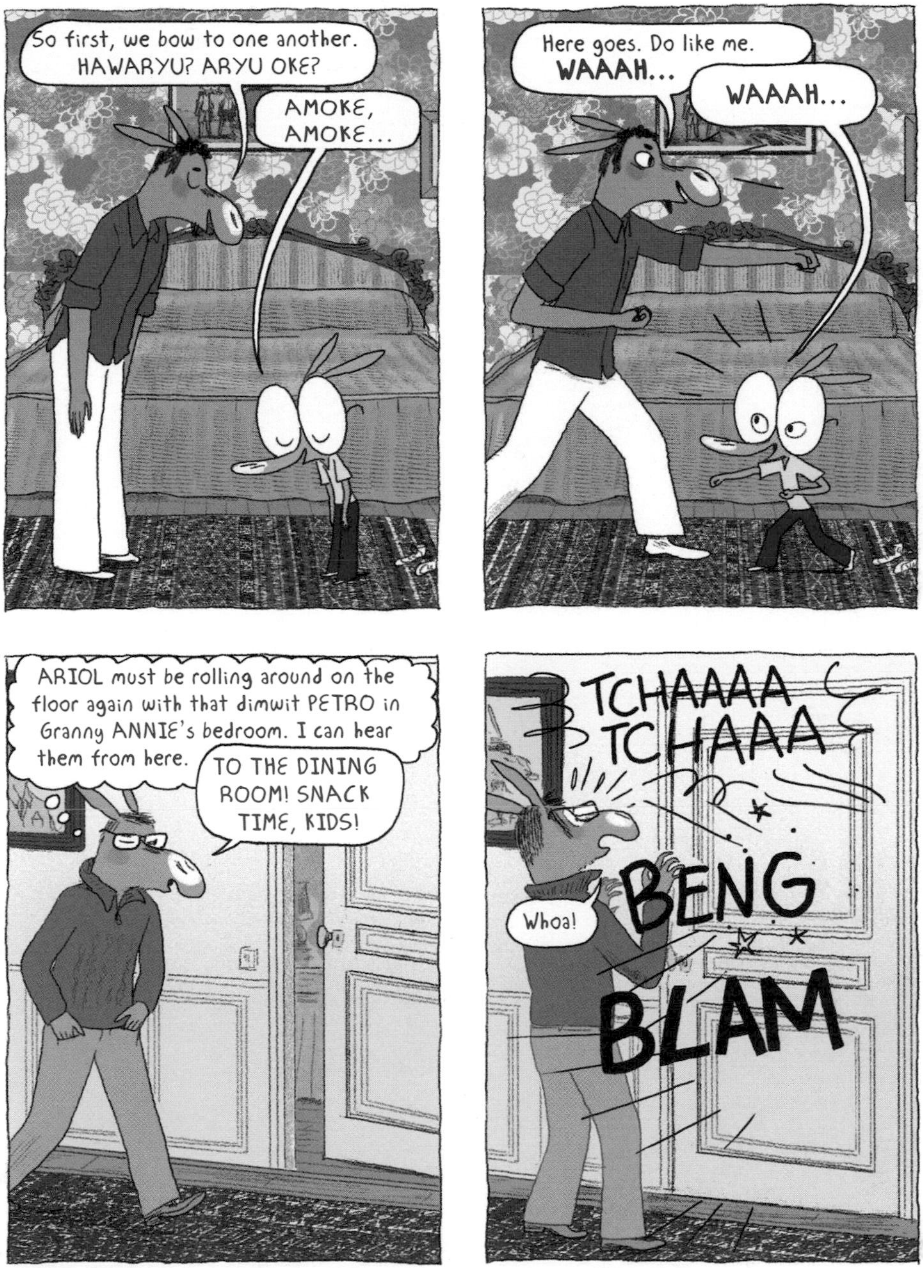
So first, we bow to one another. HAWARYU? ARYU OKE?
AMOKE, AMOKE...
Here goes. Do like me. WAAAH...
WAAAH...
ARIOL must be rolling around on the floor again with that dimwit PETRO in Granny ANNIE's bedroom. I can hear them from here.
TO THE DINING ROOM! SNACK TIME, KIDS!
TCHAAAA TCHAAA
BENG
Whoa!
BLAM

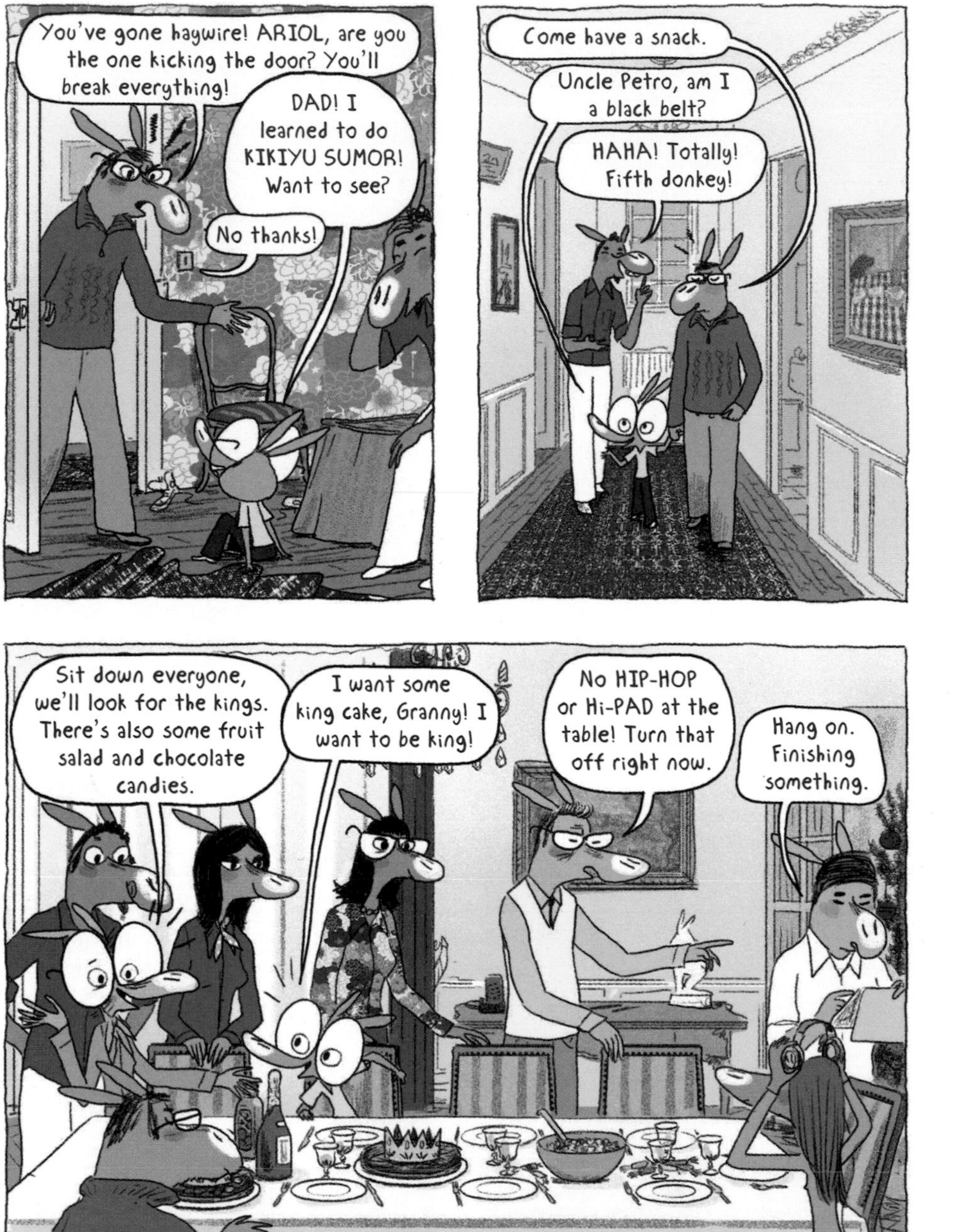
You've gone haywire! ARIOL, are you the one kicking the door? You'll break everything!
DAD! I learned to do KIKIYU SUMOR! Want to see?
No thanks!
Come have a snack.
Uncle Petro, am I a black belt?
HAHA! Totally! Fifth donkey!
Sit down everyone, we'll look for the kings. There's also some fruit salad and chocolate candies.
I want some king cake, Granny! I want to be king!
No HIP-HOP or Hi-PAD at the table! Turn that off right now.
Hang on. Finishing something.

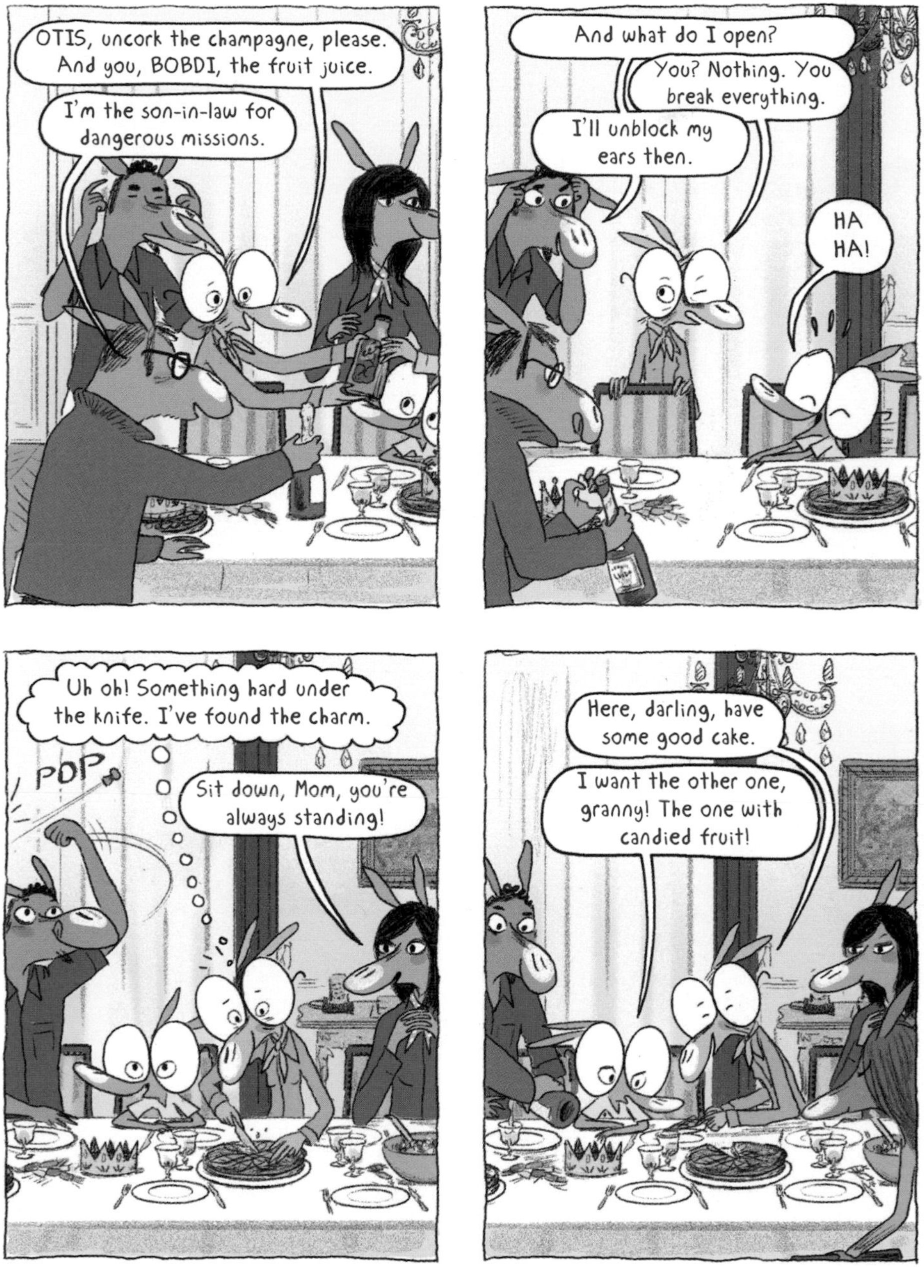
OTIS, uncork the champagne, please. And you, BOBDI, the fruit juice.
I'm the son-in-law for dangerous missions.
And what do I open?
You? Nothing. You break everything.
I'll unblock my ears then.
HA HA!
Uh oh! Something hard under the knife. I've found the charm.
POP
Sit down, Mom, you're always standing!
Here, darling, have some good cake.
I want the other one, granny! The one with candied fruit!

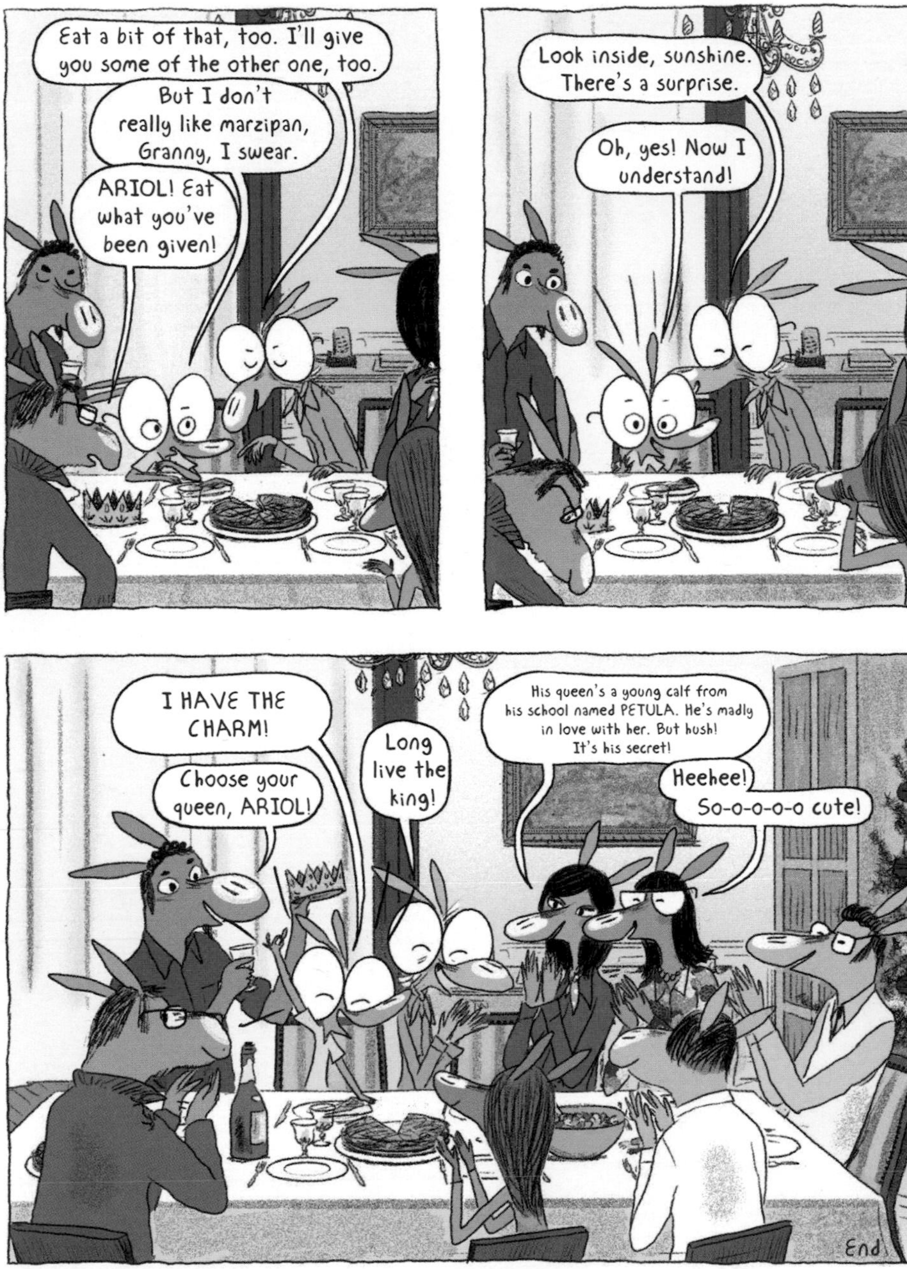
Eat a bit of that, too. I'll give you some of the other one, too.
But I don't really like marzipan, Granny, I swear.
ARIOL! Eat what you've been given!
Look inside, sunshine. There's a surprise.
Oh, yes! Now I understand!
I HAVE THE CHARM!
Choose your queen, ARIOL!
Long live the king!
His queen's a young calf from his school named PETULA. He's madly in love with her. But hush! It's his secret!
Heehee!
So-o-o-o-o cute!
End

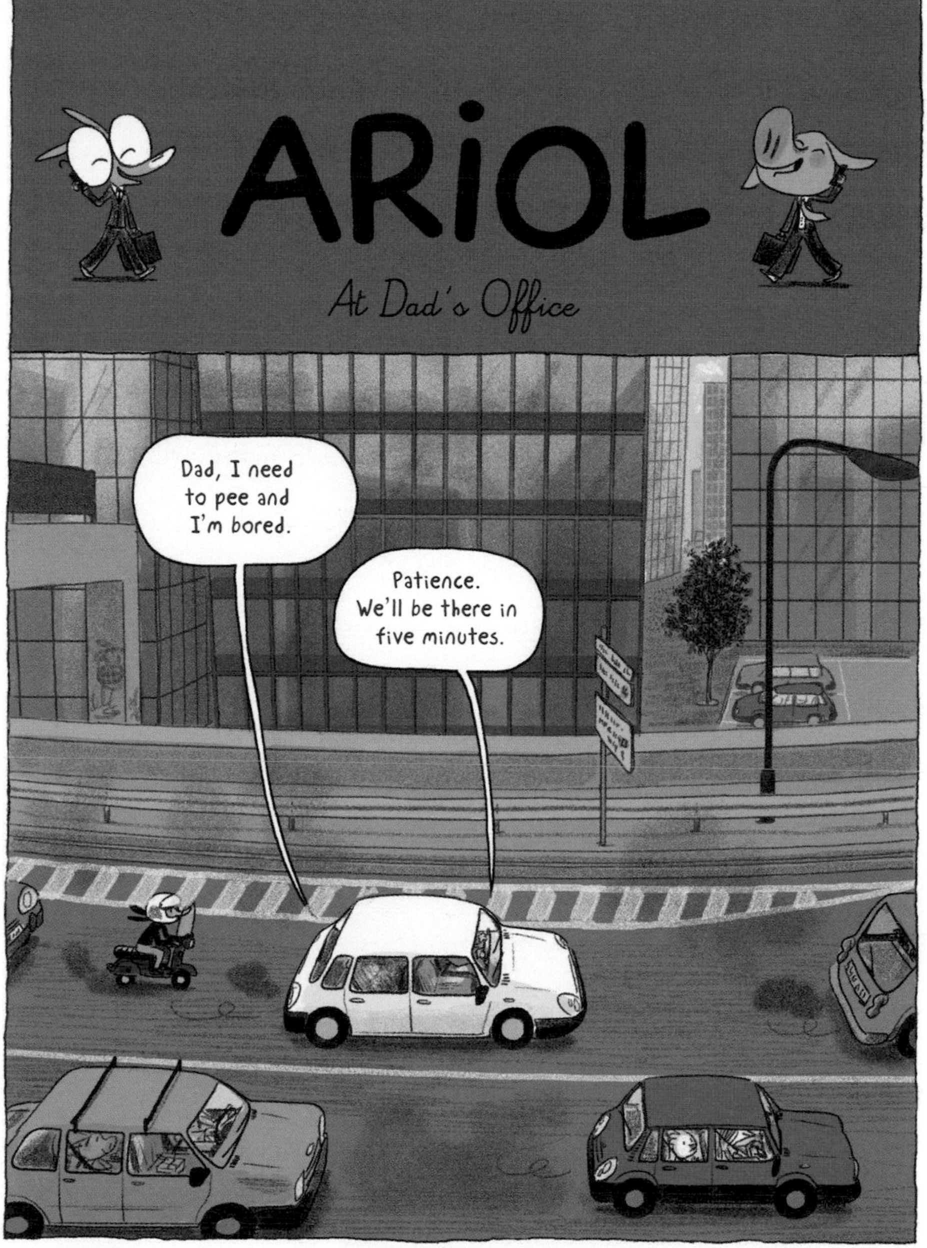
ARiOL
At Dad's Office
Dad, I need to pee and I'm bored.
Patience. We'll be there in five minutes.

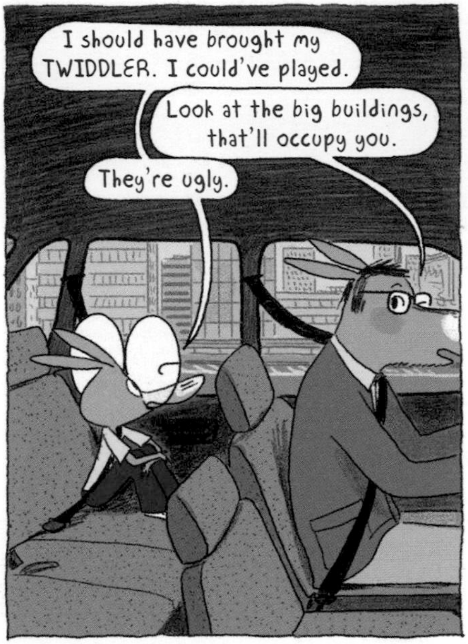
I should have brought my TWIDDLER. I could've played.
Look at the big buildings, that'll occupy you.
They're ugly.

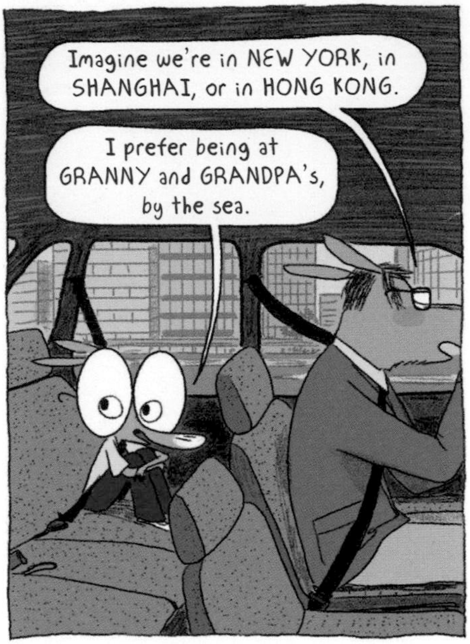
Imagine we're in NEW YORK, in SHANGHAI, or in HONG KONG.
I prefer being at GRANNY and GRANDPA's, by the sea.

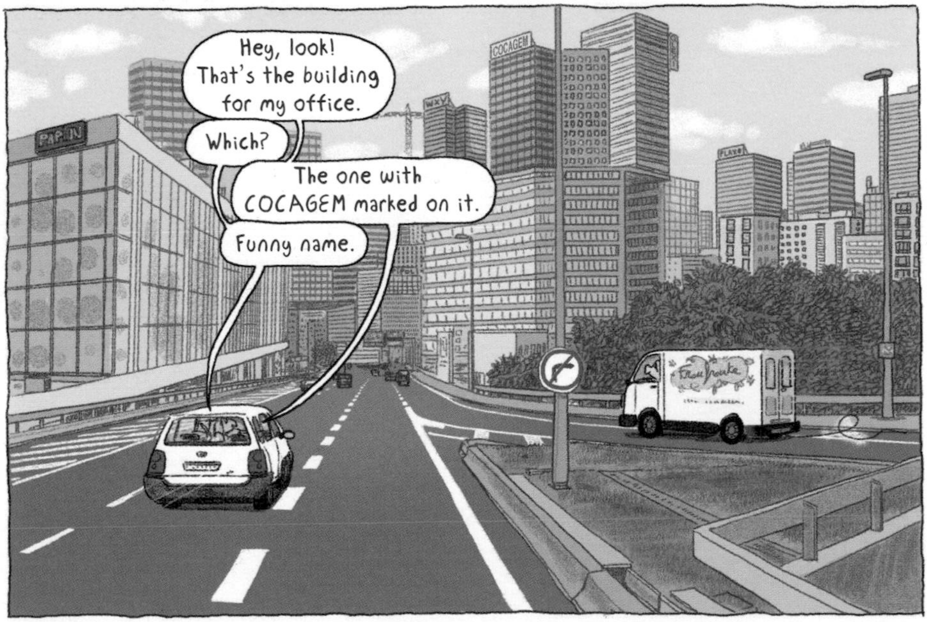
Hey, look! That's the building for my office.
Which?
The one with COCAGEM marked on it.
Funny name.
COCAGEM

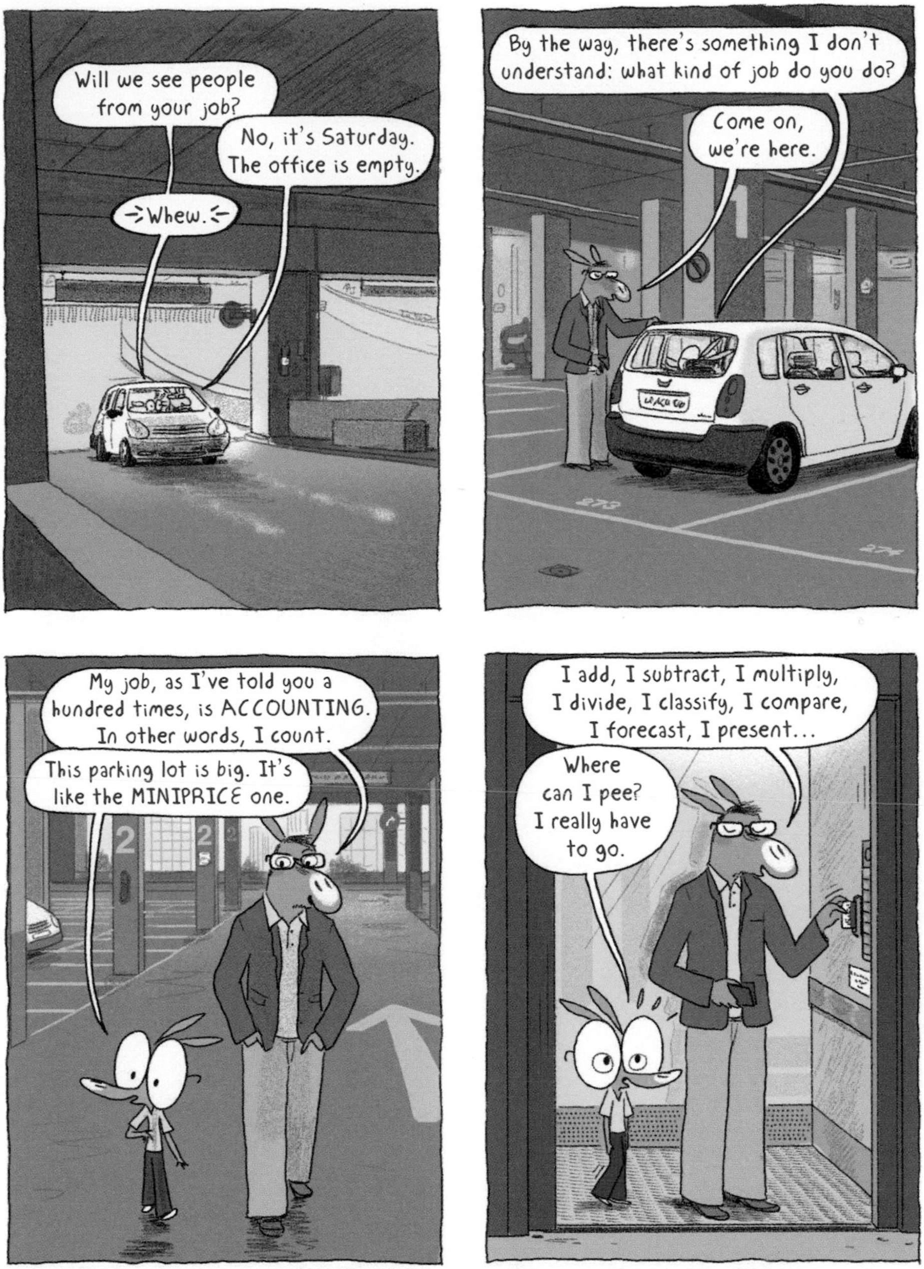
Will we see people from your job?
No, it's Saturday. The office is empty.
Whew.
By the way, there's something I don't understand: what kind of job do you do?
Come on, we're here.
My job, as I've told you a hundred times, is ACCOUNTING. In other words, I count.
This parking lot is big. It's like the MINIPRICE one.
I add, I subtract, I multiply, I divide, I classify, I compare, I forecast, I present...
Where can I pee? I really have to go.

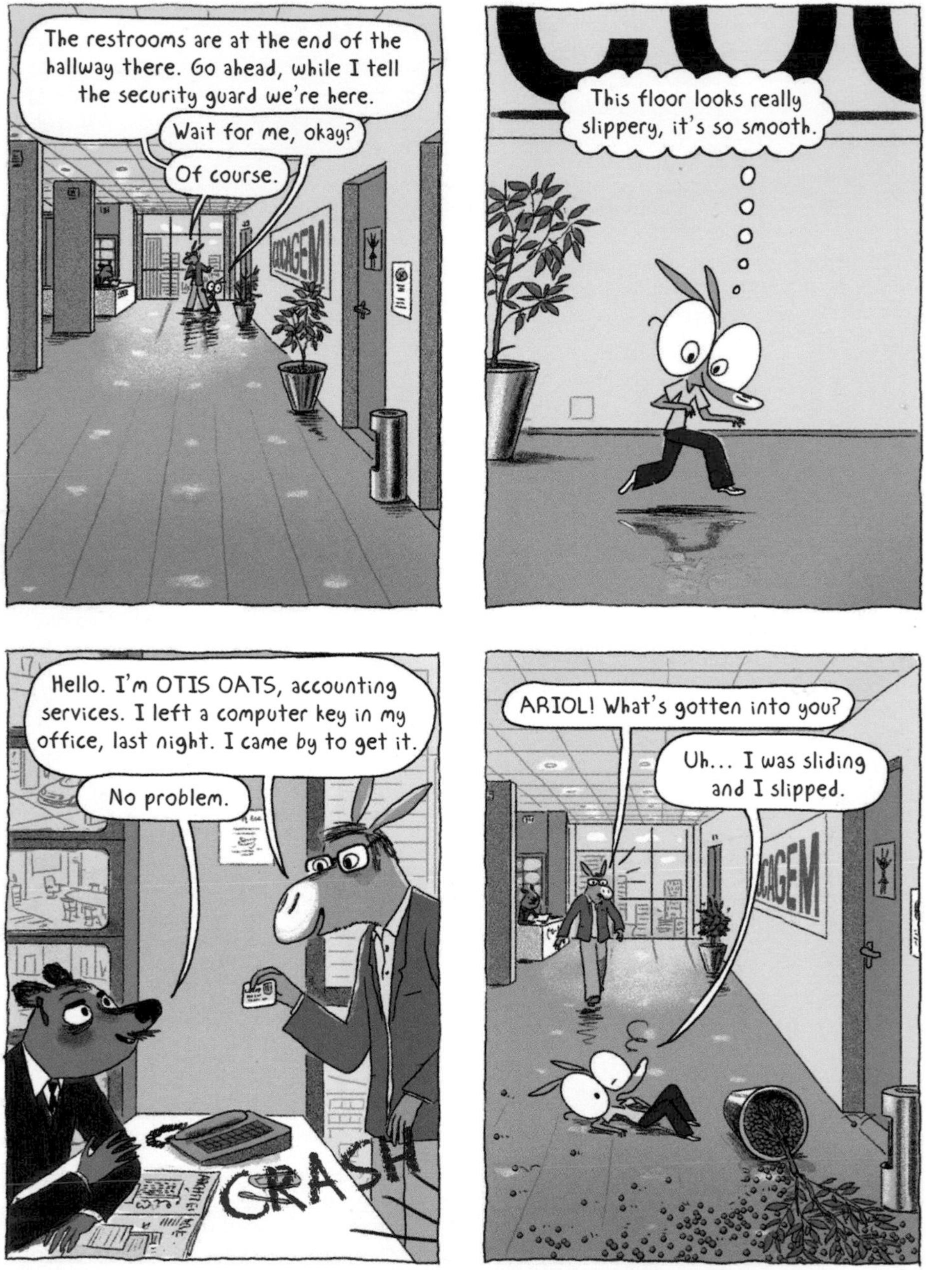
The restrooms are at the end of the hallway there. Go ahead, while I tell the security guard we're here.
Wait for me, okay?
Of course.
This floor looks really slippery, it's so smooth.
Hello. I'm OTIS OATS, accounting services. I left a computer key in my office, last night. I came by to get it.
No problem.
CRASH
ARIOL! What's gotten into you?
Uh... I was sliding and I slipped.

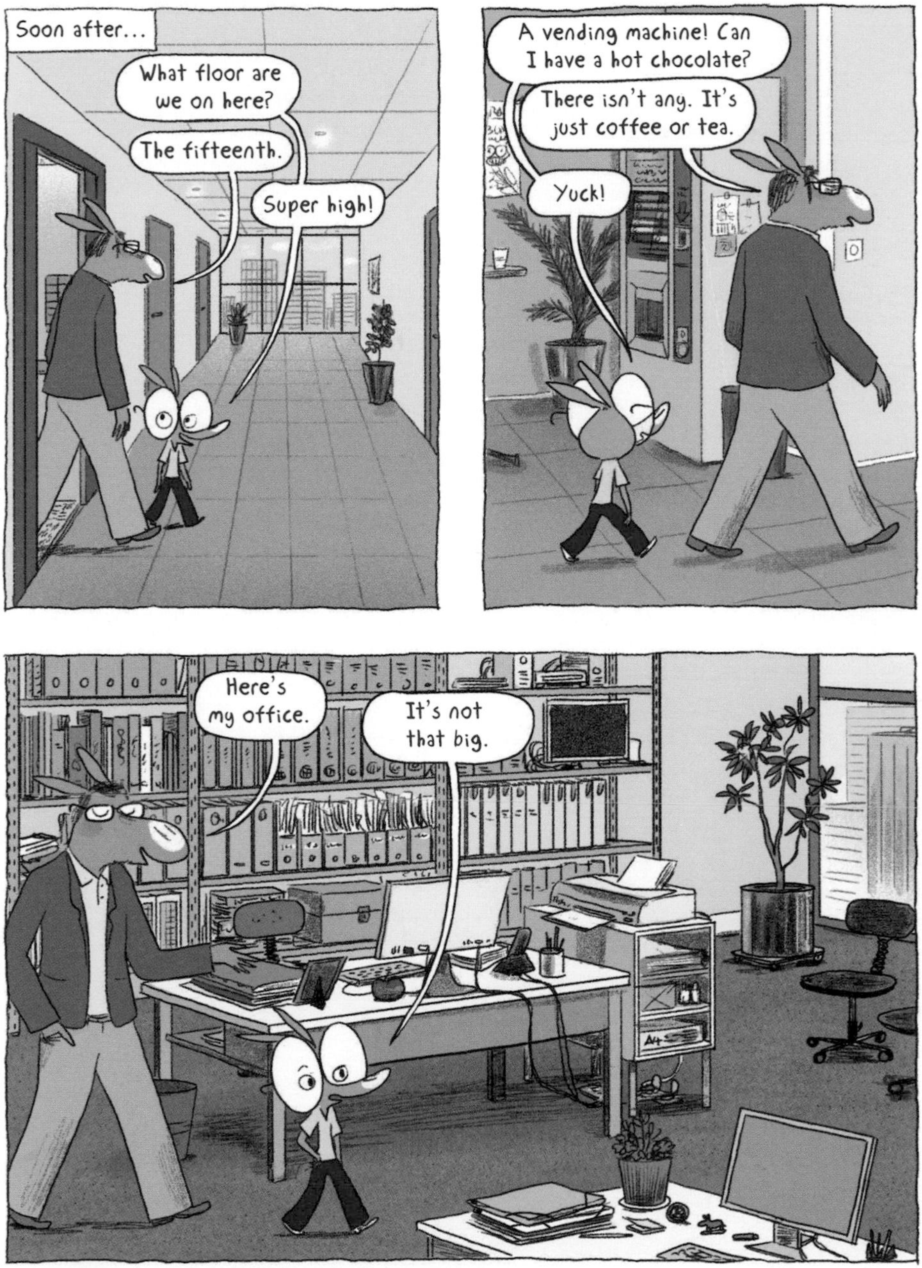
Soon after...
What floor are we on here?
The fifteenth.
Super high!
A vending machine! Can I have a hot chocolate?
There isn't any. It's just coffee or tea.
Yuck!
Here's my office.
It's not that big.

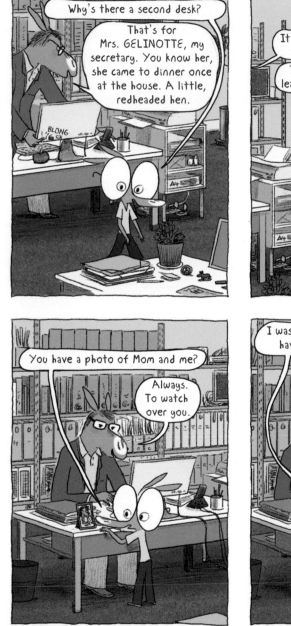

Why's there a second desk?

That's for Mrs. GELINOTTE, my secretary. You know her, she came to dinner once at the house. A little, redheaded hen.

BLONG

The view's blocked by those big buildings.

It's pretty at night. It's all lit up.

Yes, but you leave at night.

You have a photo of Mom and me?

Always. To watch over you.

I was little, and Mom didn't have the same hairstyle.

I'm checking something on my computer. I'll be five minutes. Sit down and wait patiently.

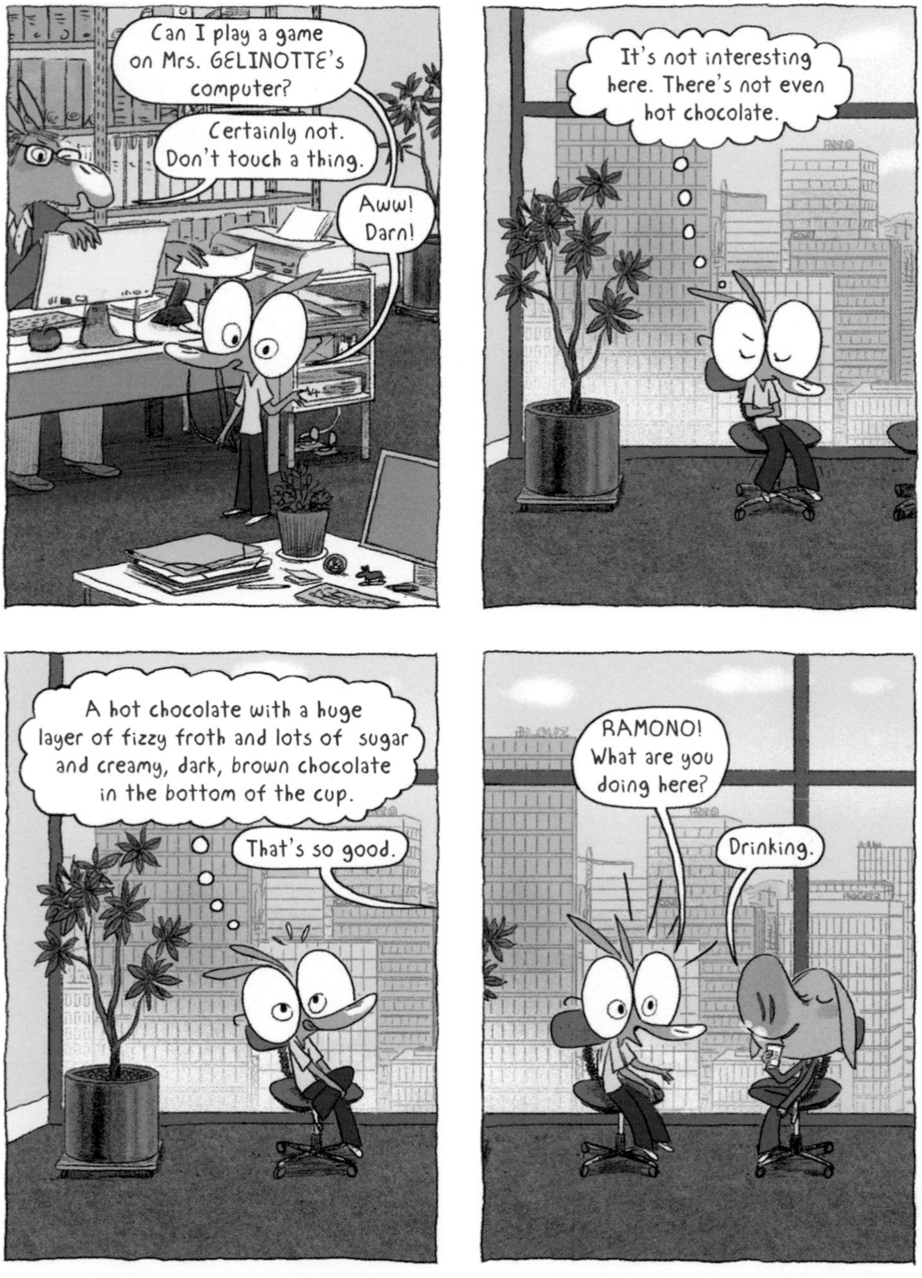

Can I play a game on Mrs. GELINOTTE's computer?
Certainly not. Don't touch a thing.
Aww! Darn!
It's not interesting here. There's not even hot chocolate.
A hot chocolate with a huge layer of fizzy froth and lots of sugar and creamy, dark, brown chocolate in the bottom of the cup.
That's so good.
RAMONO! What are you doing here?
Drinking.

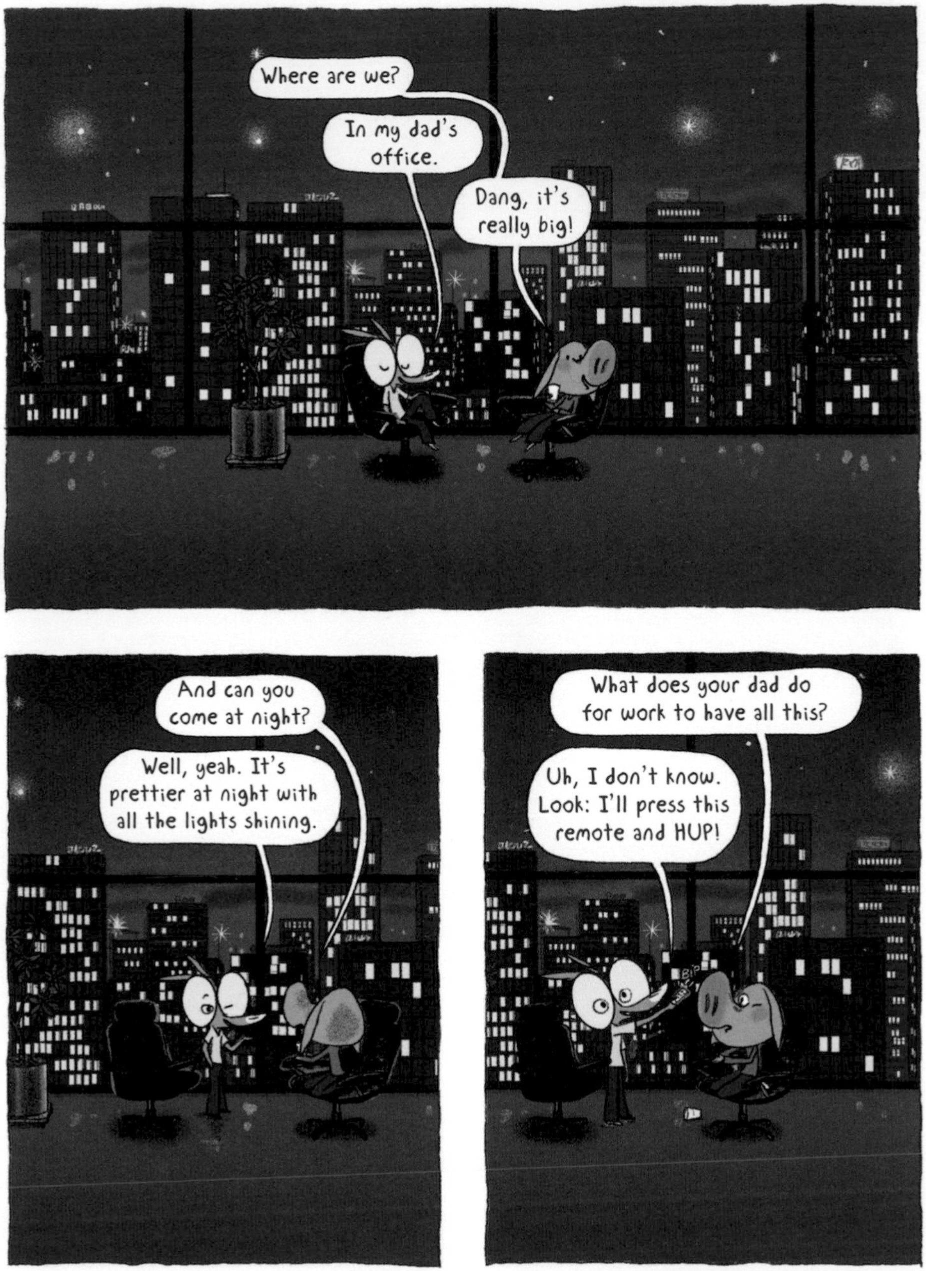
Where are we?
In my dad's office.
Dang, it's really big!
And can you come at night?
Well, yeah. It's prettier at night with all the lights shining.
What does your dad do for work to have all this?
Uh, I don't know. Look: I'll press this remote and HUP!
BIP

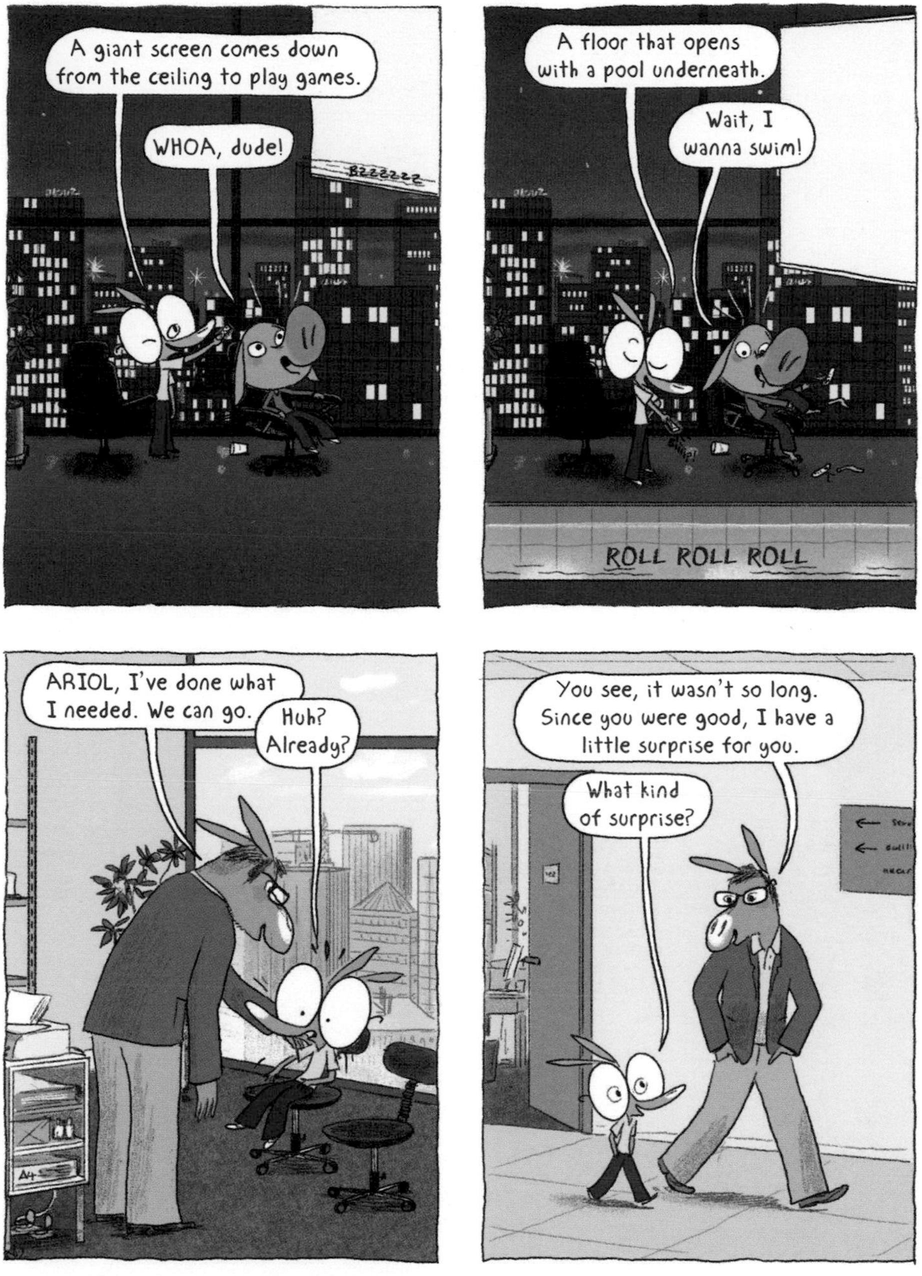
A giant screen comes down from the ceiling to play games.
WHOA, dude!
BZZZZZZ
A floor that opens with a pool underneath.
Wait, I wanna swim!
ROLL ROLL ROLL
ARIOL, I've done what I needed. We can go.
Huh? Already?
You see, it wasn't so long. Since you were good, I have a little surprise for you.
What kind of surprise?

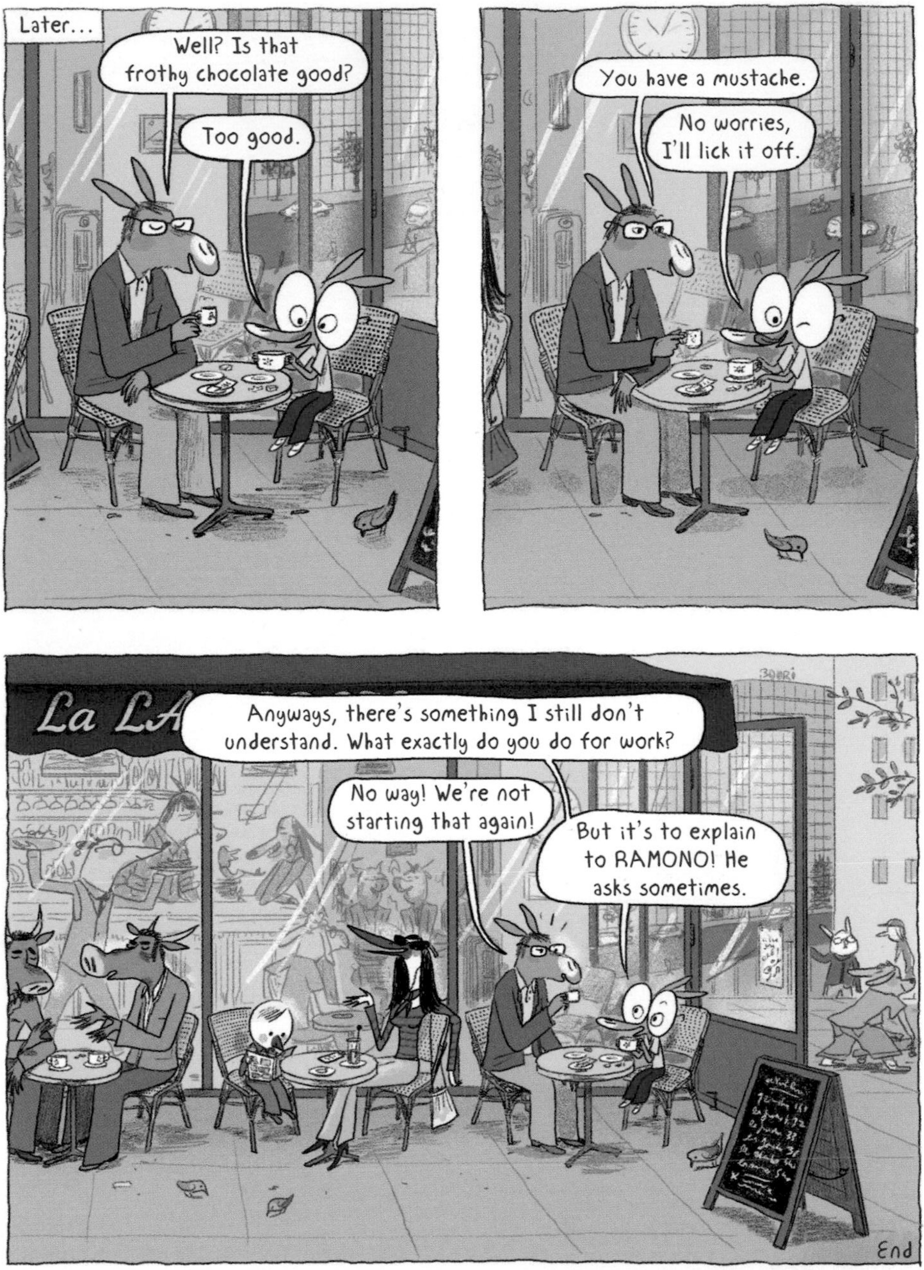
Later...
Well? Is that frothy chocolate good?
Too good.
You have a mustache.
No worries, I'll lick it off.
La LA
Anyways, there's something I still don't understand. What exactly do you do for work?
No way! We're not starting that again!
But it's to explain to RAMONO! He asks sometimes.
End

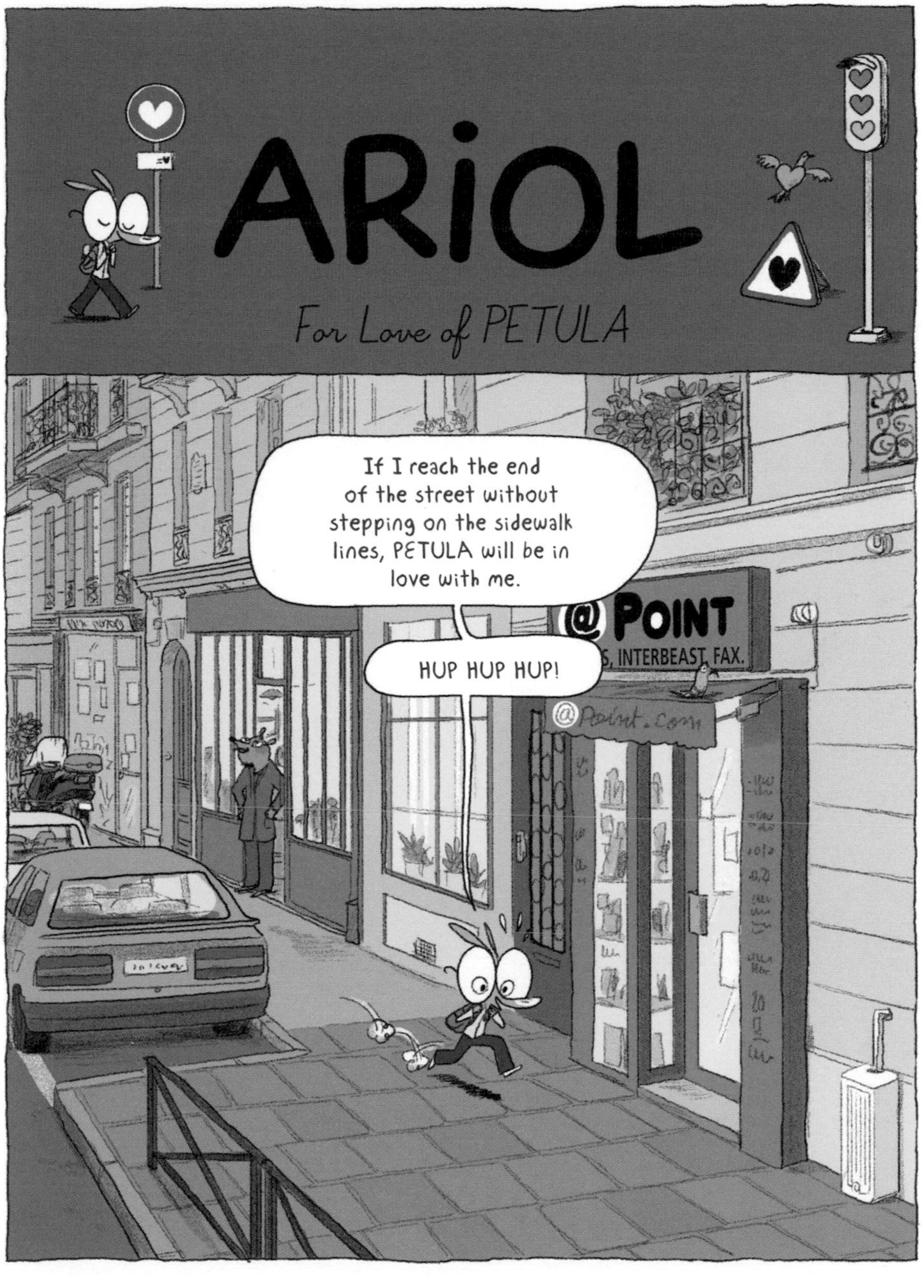

ARiOL
For Love of PETULA
If I reach the end of the street without stepping on the sidewalk lines, PETULA will be in love with me.
@POINT
S, INTERBEAST, FAX.
HUP HUP HUP!
@Point.com

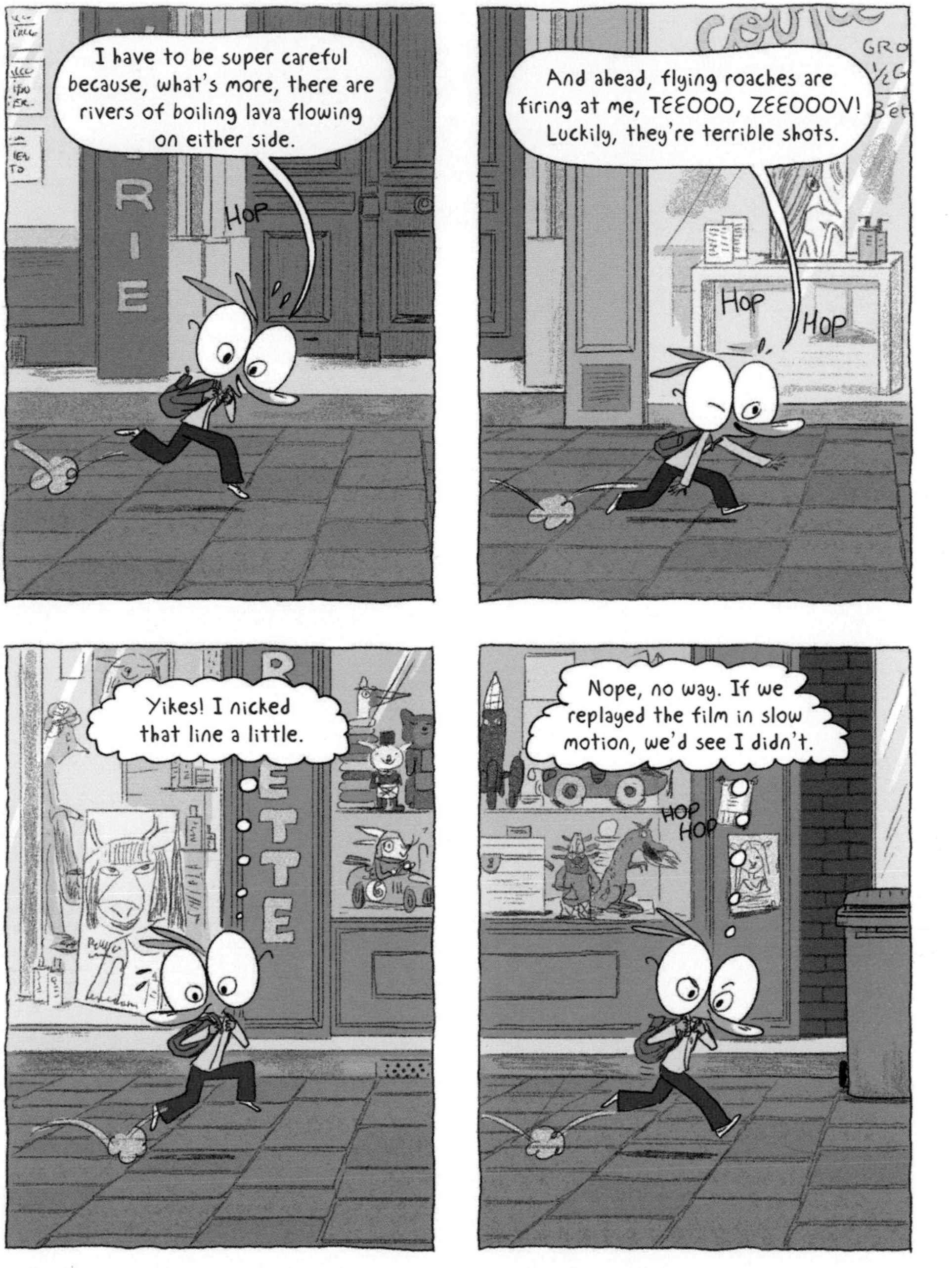
I have to be super careful because, what's more, there are rivers of boiling lava flowing on either side.
HOP
And ahead, flying roaches are firing at me, TEEOOO, ZEEOOOV! Luckily, they're terrible shots.
HOP
HOP
Yikes! I nicked that line a little.
Nope, no way. If we replayed the film in slow motion, we'd see I didn't.
HOP
HOP

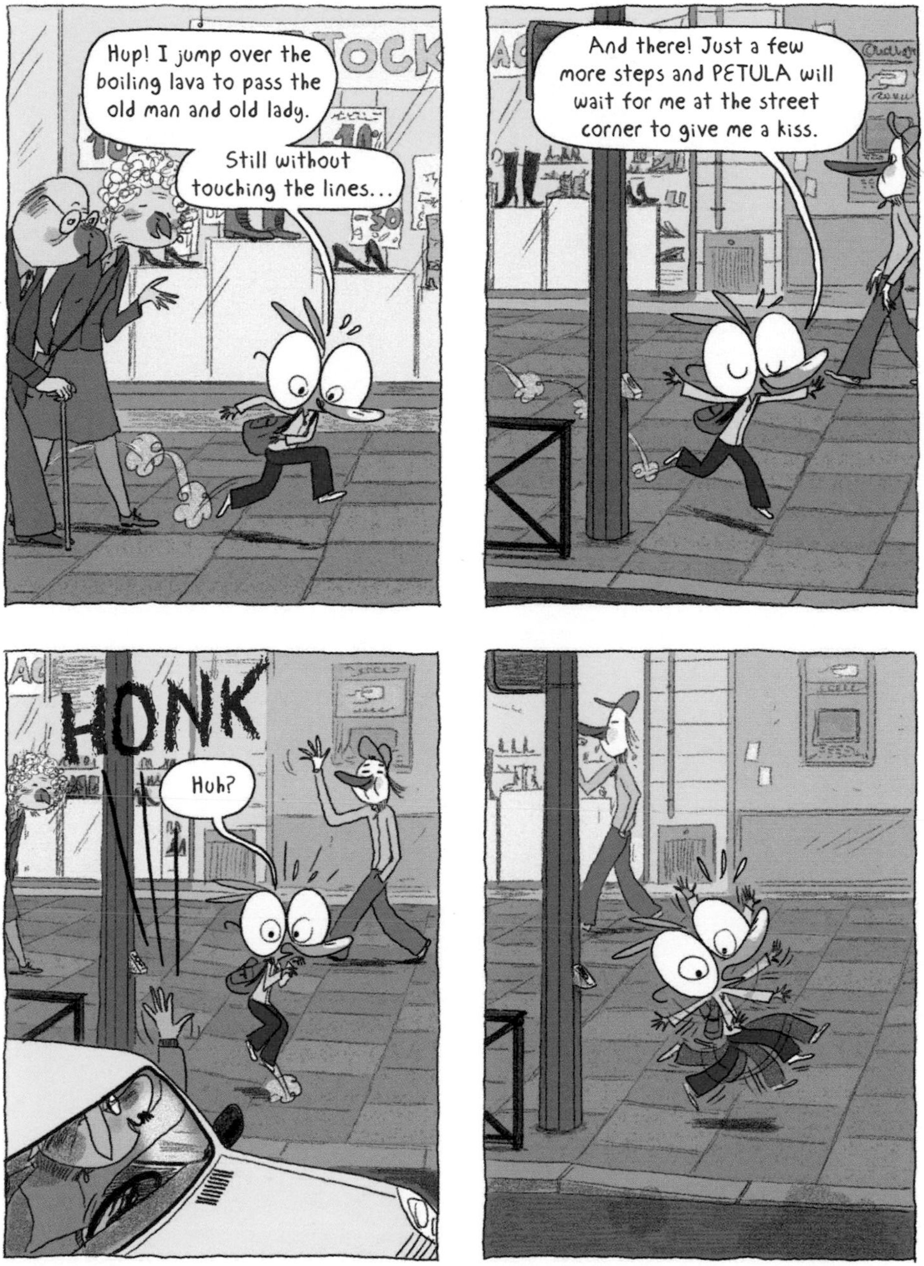
Hup! I jump over the boiling lava to pass the old man and old lady.
Still without touching the lines...
And there! Just a few more steps and PETULA will wait for me at the street corner to give me a kiss.
HONK
Huh?

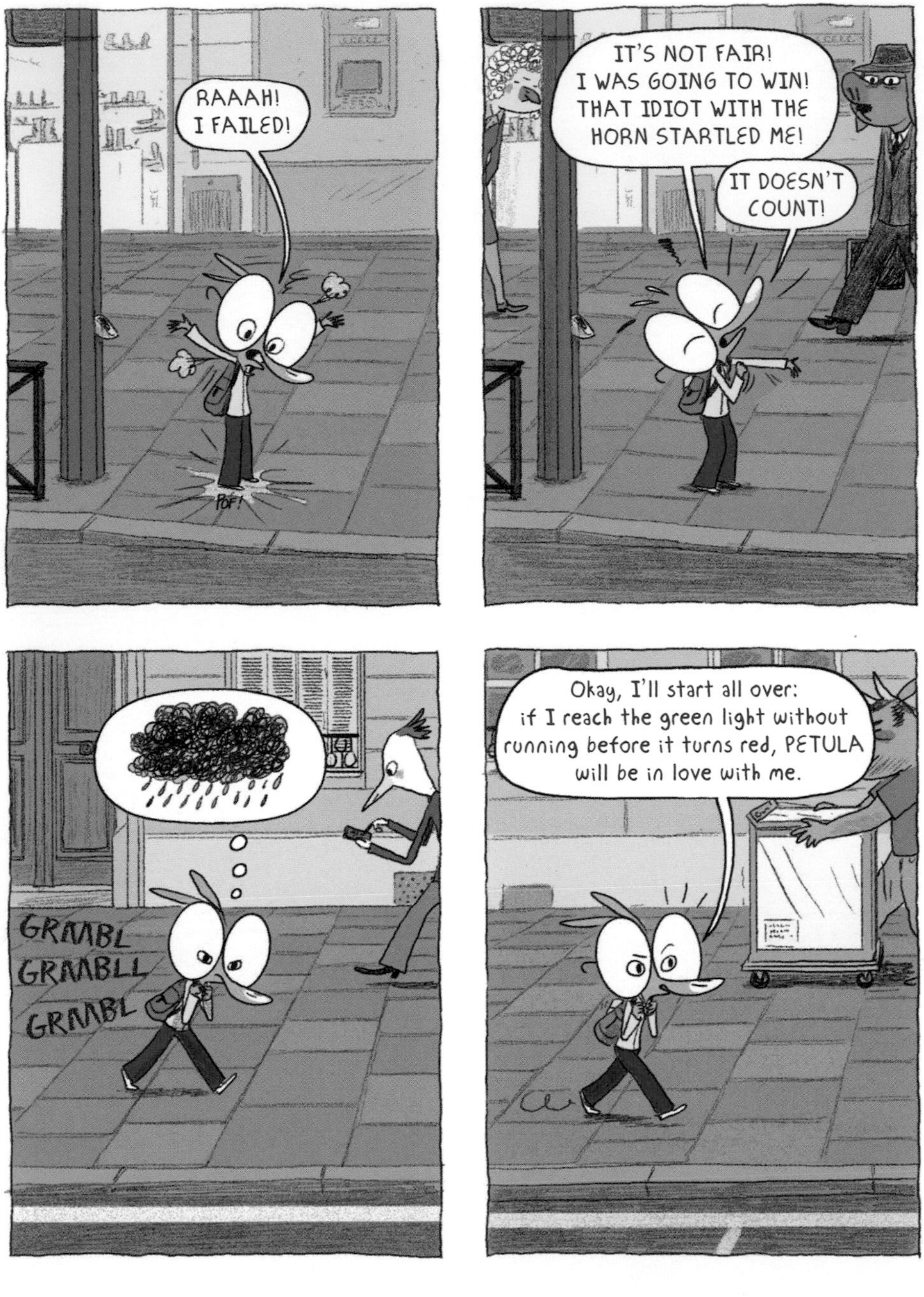
RAAAH! I FAILED!
POF!
IT'S NOT FAIR! I WAS GOING TO WIN! THAT IDIOT WITH THE HORN STARTLED ME!
IT DOESN'T COUNT!
GRMBL
GRMBLL
GRMBL
Okay, I'll start all over: if I reach the green light without running before it turns red, PETULA will be in love with me.

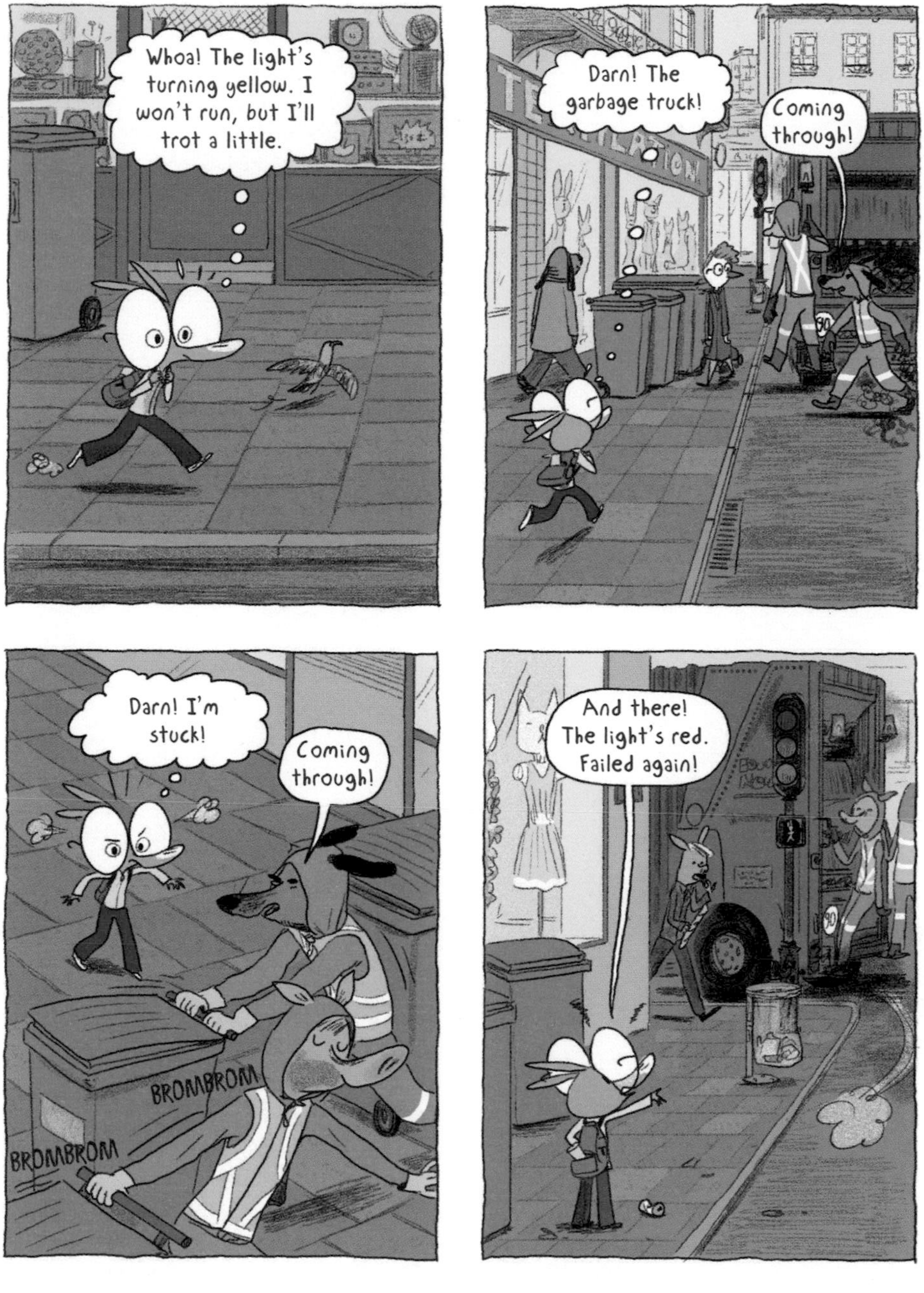
Whoa! The light's turning yellow. I won't run, but I'll trot a little.
Darn! The garbage truck!
Coming through!
Darn! I'm stuck!
Coming through!
BROMBROM
BROMBROM
And there! The light's red. Failed again!

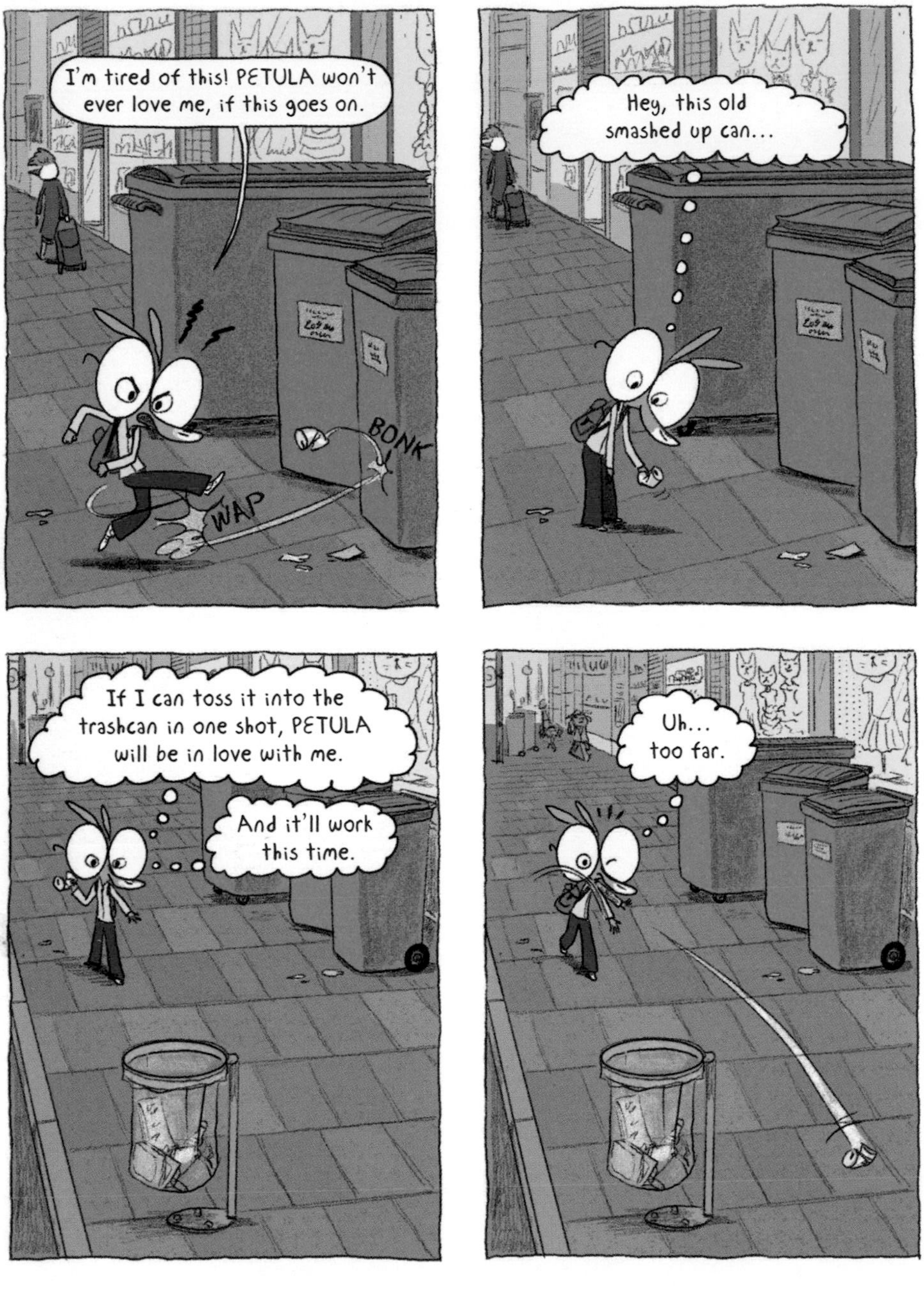
I'm tired of this! PETULA won't ever love me, if this goes on.
BONK
WAP
Hey, this old smashed up can...
If I can toss it into the trashcan in one shot, PETULA will be in love with me.
And it'll work this time.
Uh... too far.

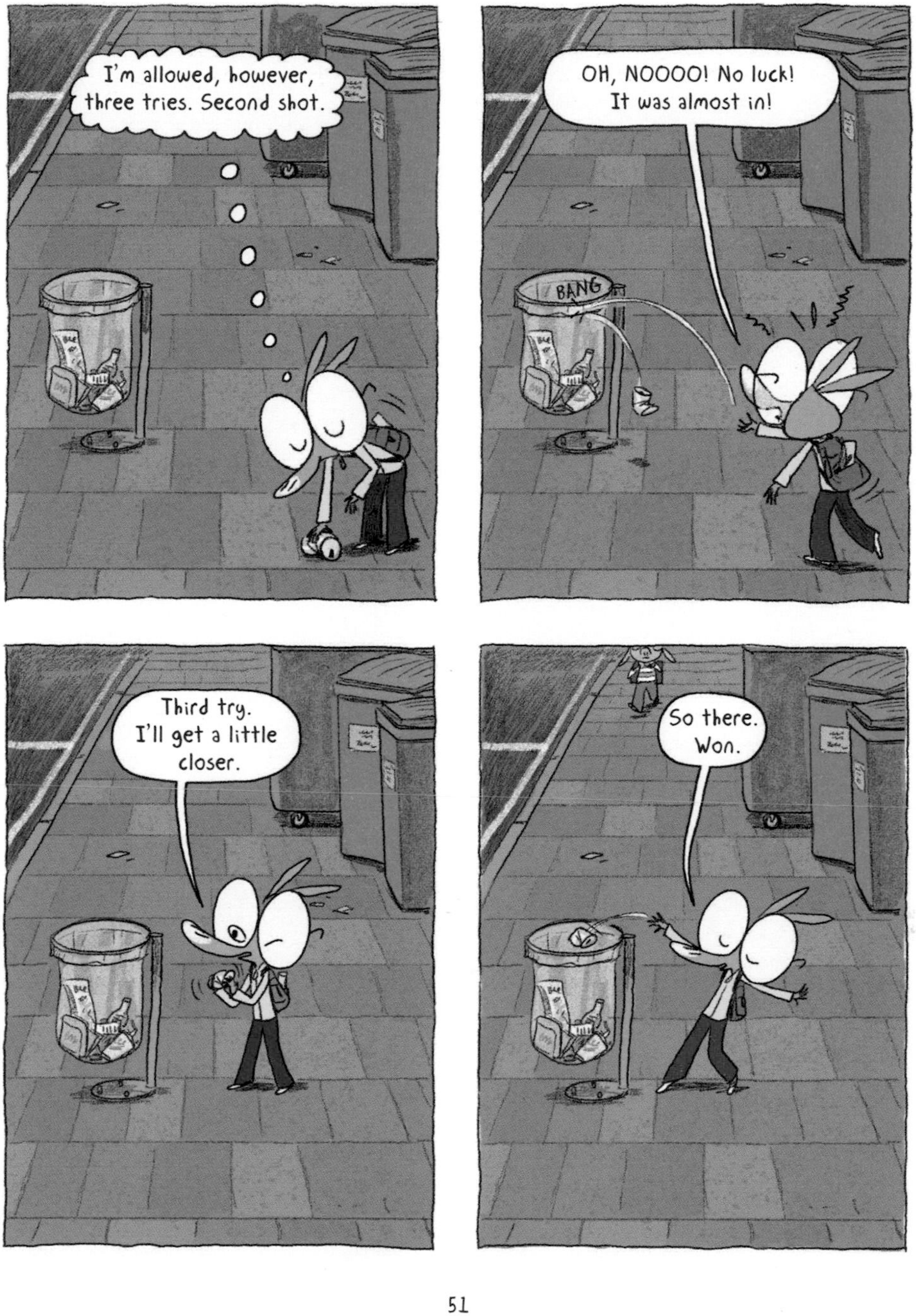
I'm allowed, however, three tries. Second shot.
OH, NOOOO! No luck! It was almost in!
BANG
Third try. I'll get a little closer.
So there. Won.

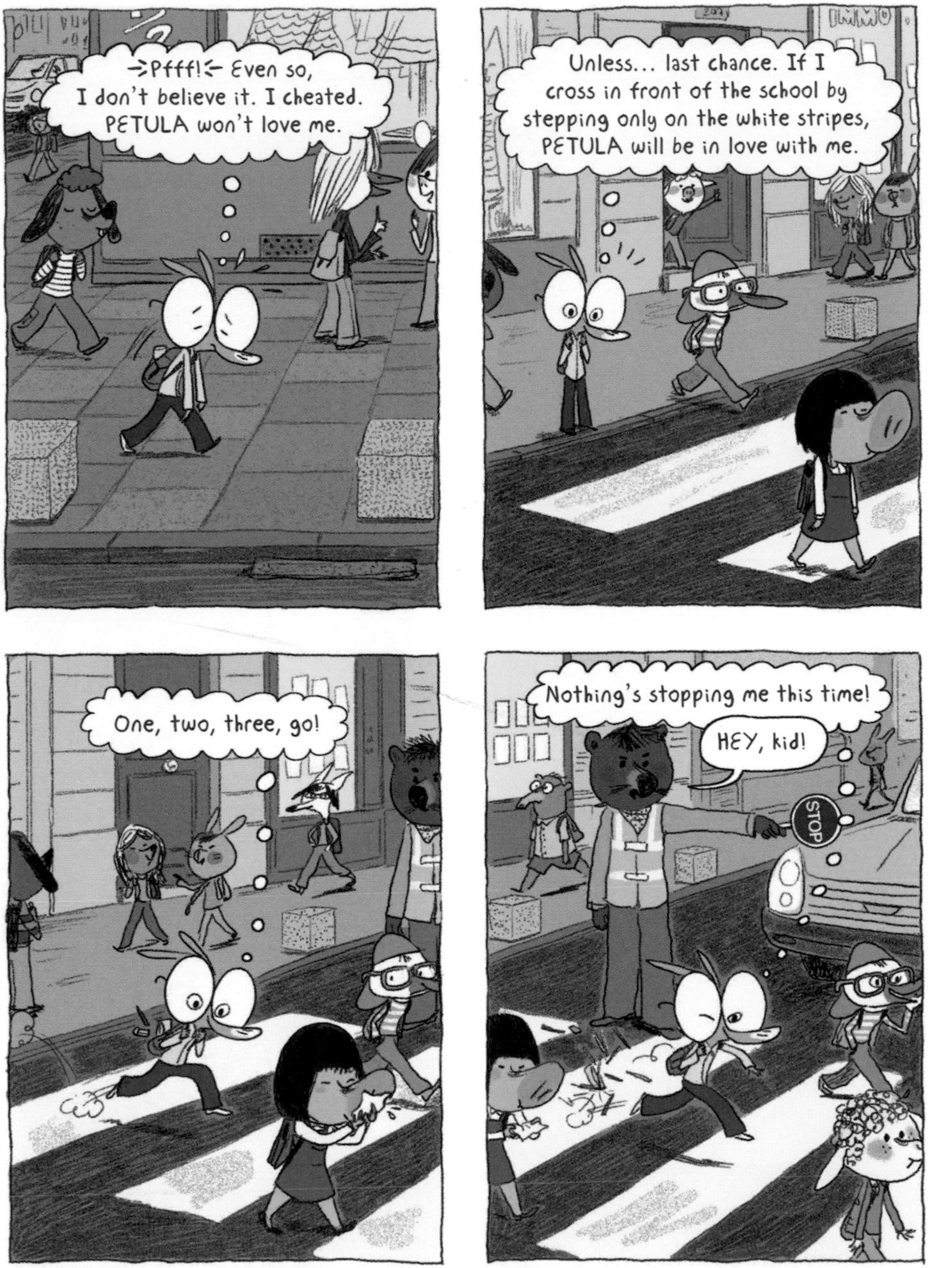
→Pfff!← Even so, I don't believe it. I cheated. PETULA won't love me.
Unless... last chance. If I cross in front of the school by stepping only on the white stripes, PETULA will be in love with me.
One, two, three, go!
Nothing's stopping me this time!
HEY, kid!
STOP

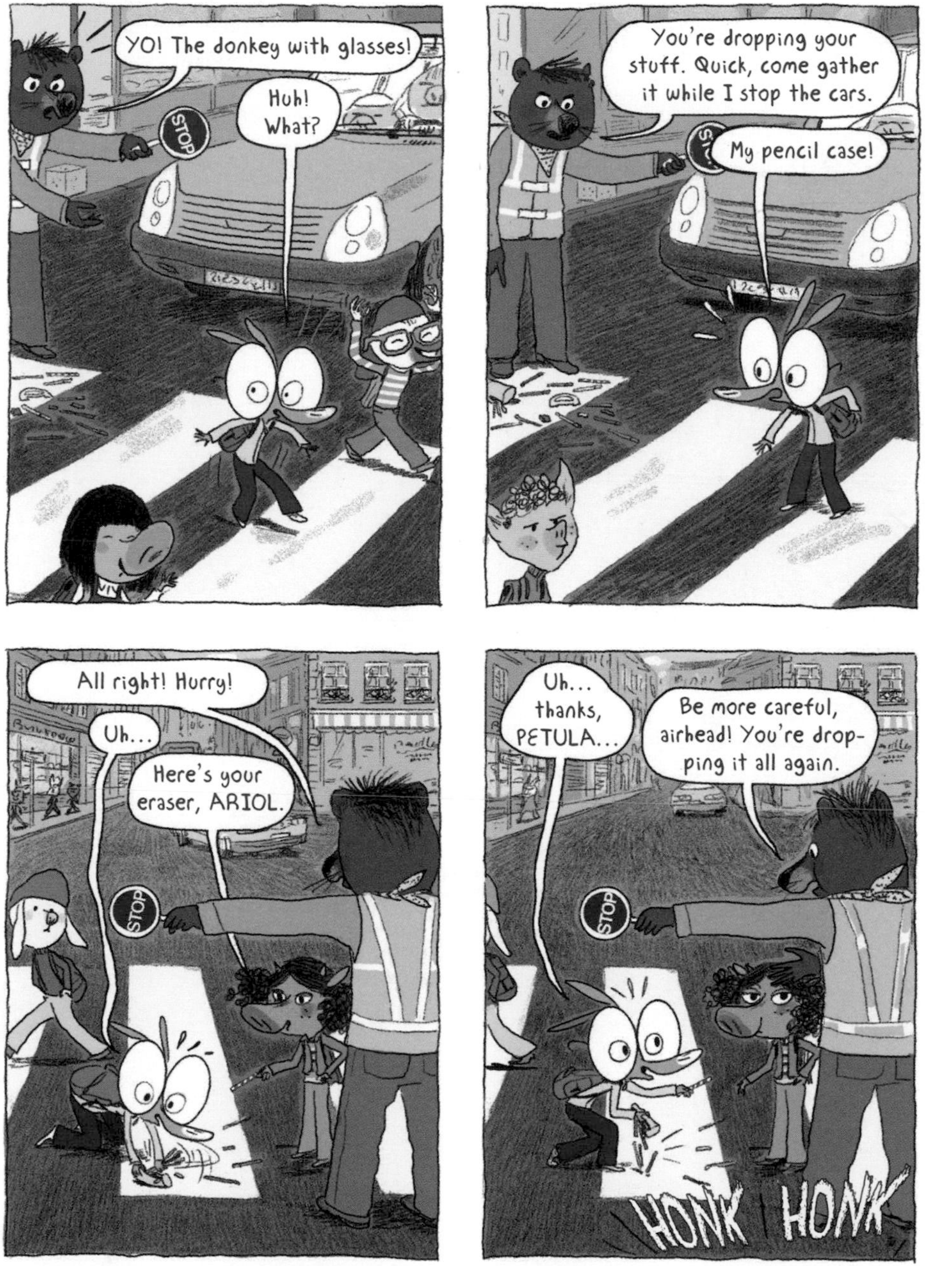
YO! The donkey with glasses!
Huh! What?
You're dropping your stuff. Quick, come gather it while I stop the cars.
My pencil case!
STOP
All right! Hurry!
Uh...
Here's your eraser, ARIOL.
STOP
Uh... thanks, PETULA...
Be more careful, airhead! You're dropping it all again.
STOP
HONK HONK

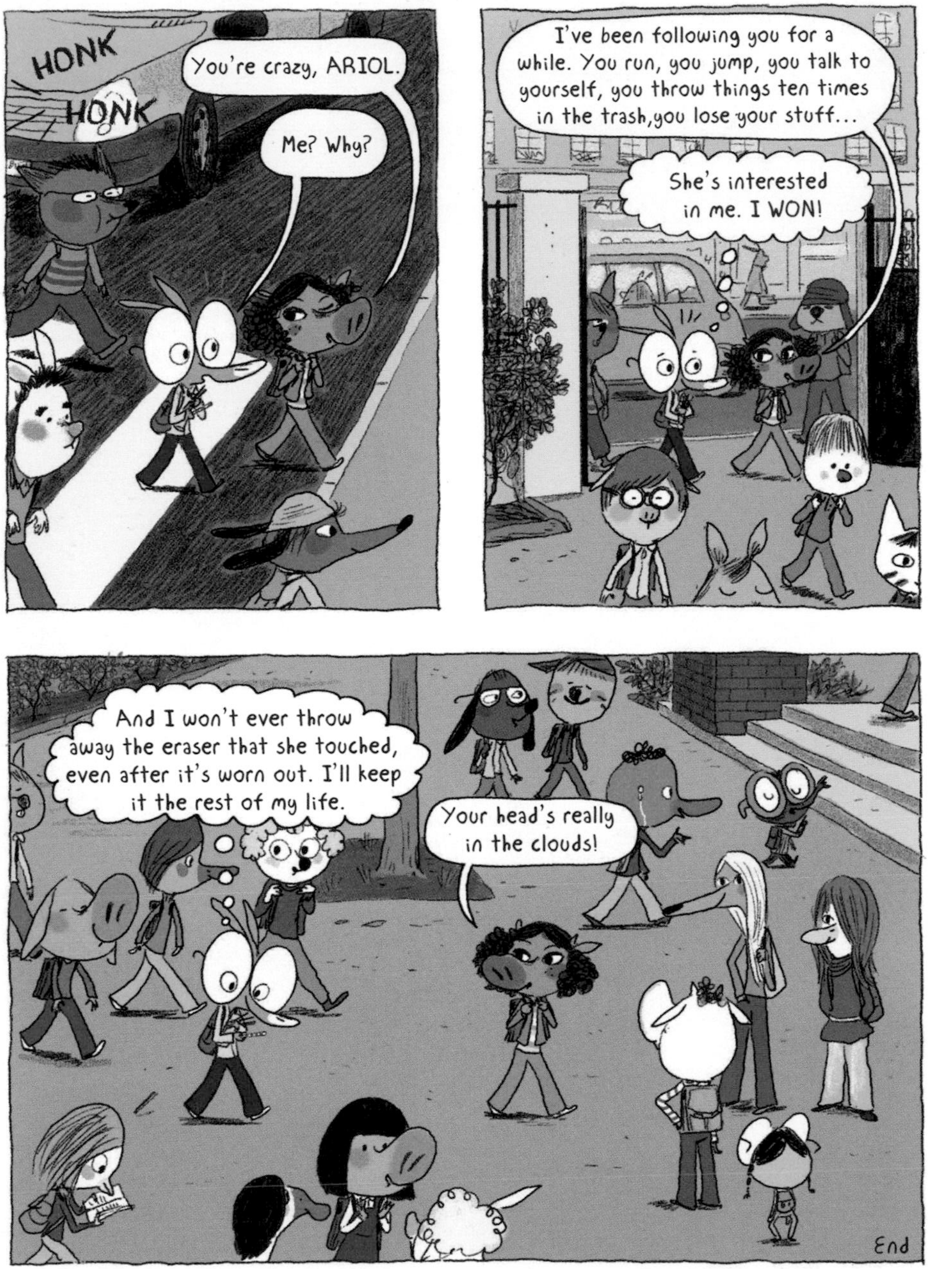
HONK
HONK
You're crazy, ARIOL.
Me? Why?
I've been following you for a while. You run, you jump, you talk to yourself, you throw things ten times in the trash, you lose your stuff...
She's interested in me. I WON!
And I won't ever throw away the eraser that she touched, even after it's worn out. I'll keep it the rest of my life.
Your head's really in the clouds!
End

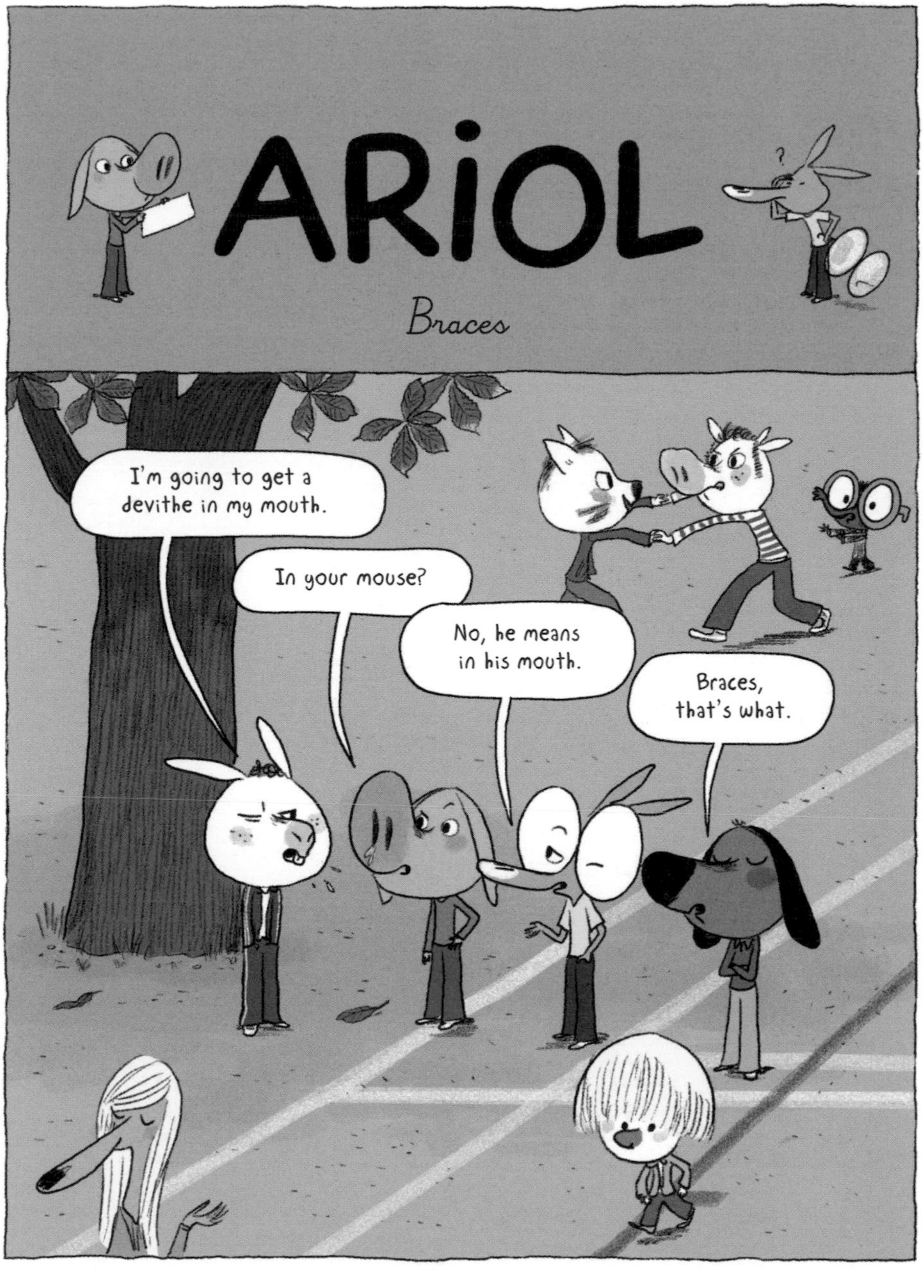
ARiOL
Braces
I'm going to get a devithe in my mouth.
In your mouse?
No, he means in his mouth.
Braces, that's what.

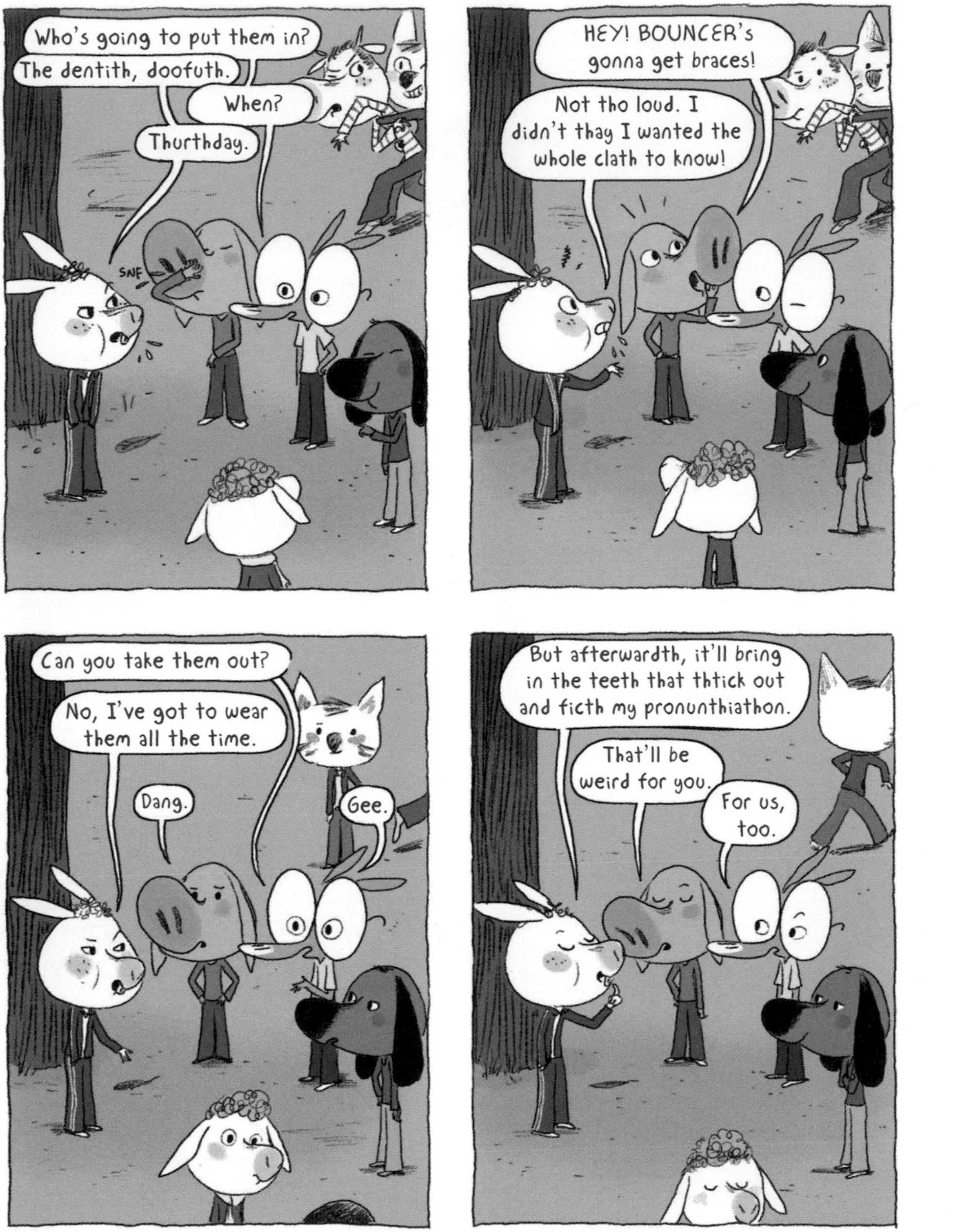
Who's going to put them in?
The dentith, doofuth.
When?
Thurthday.
SNF
HEY! BOUNCER's gonna get braces!
Not tho loud. I didn't thay I wanted the whole clath to know!
Can you take them out?
No, I've got to wear them all the time.
Dang.
Gee.
But afterwardth, it'll bring in the teeth that thtick out and ficth my pronunthiathon.
That'll be weird for you.
For us, too.

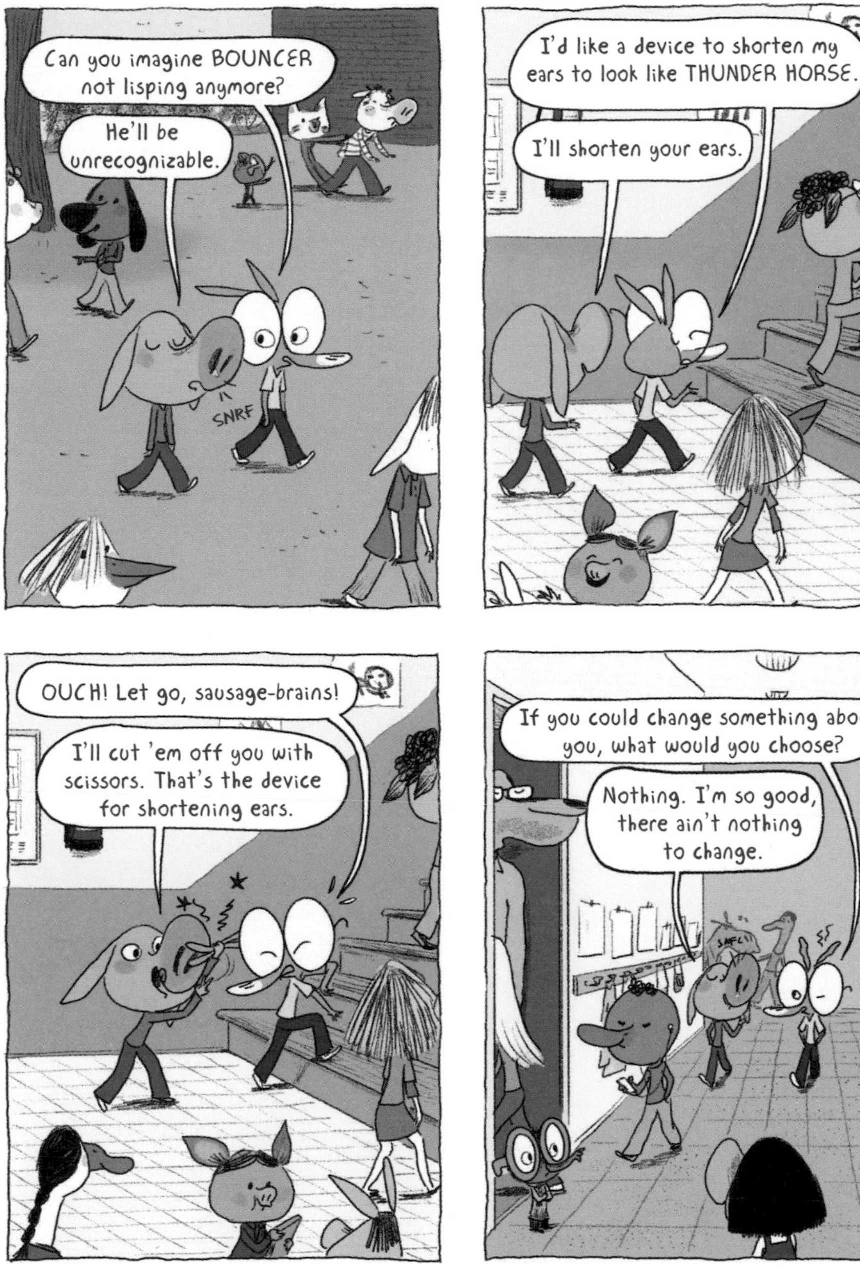
Can you imagine BOUNCER not lisping anymore?
He'll be unrecognizable.
SNRF
I'd like a device to shorten my ears to look like THUNDER HORSE.
I'll shorten your ears.
OUCH! Let go, sausage-brains!
I'll cut 'em off you with scissors. That's the device for shortening ears.
If you could change something about you, what would you choose?
Nothing. I'm so good, there ain't nothing to change.

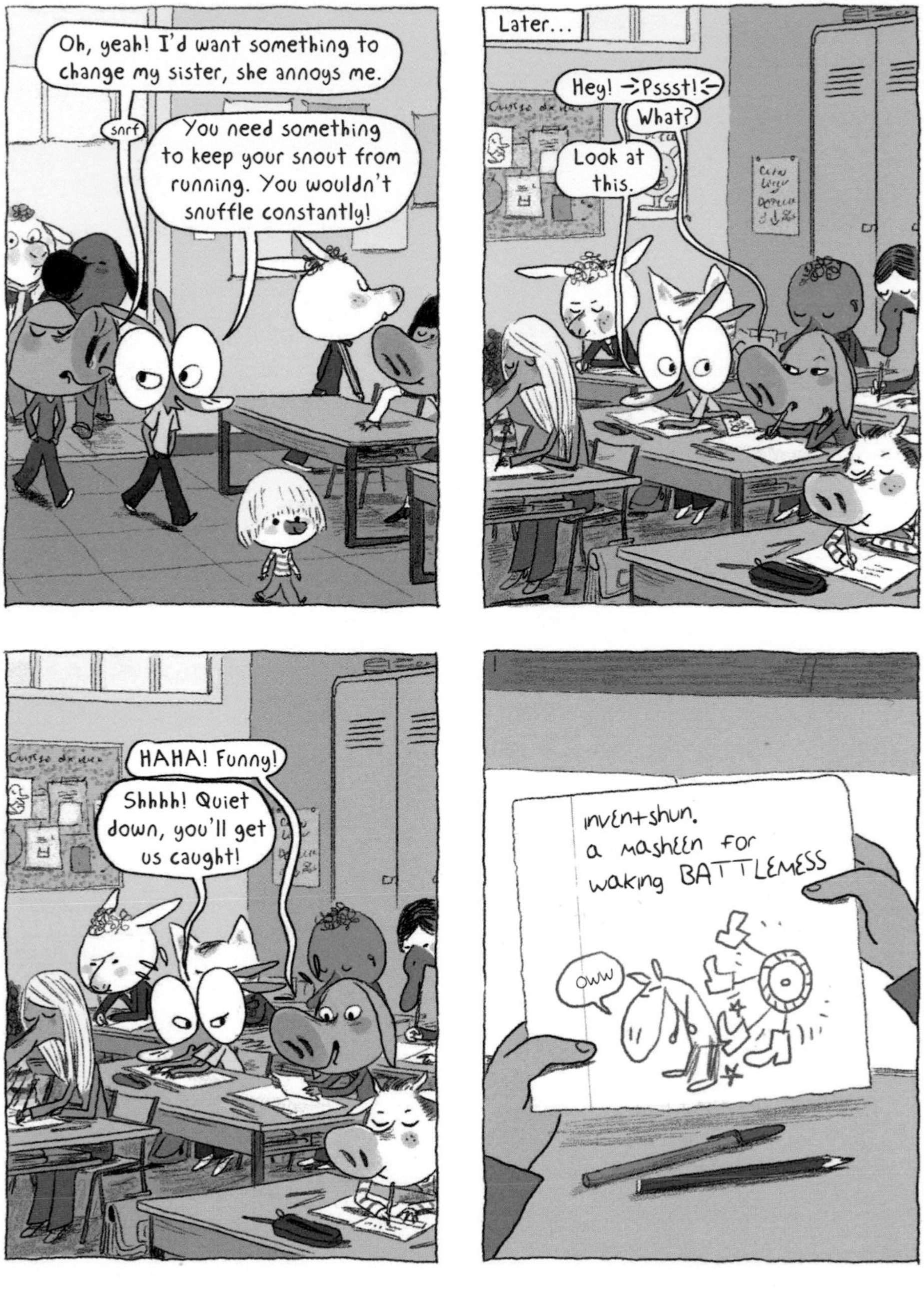
Oh, yeah! I'd want something to change my sister, she annoys me.
snrf
You need something to keep your snout from running. You wouldn't snuffle constantly!
Later...
Hey! Pssst!
What?
Look at this.
HAHA! Funny!
Shhhh! Quiet down, you'll get us caught!
inventshun. a masheen for waking BATTLEMESS
oww

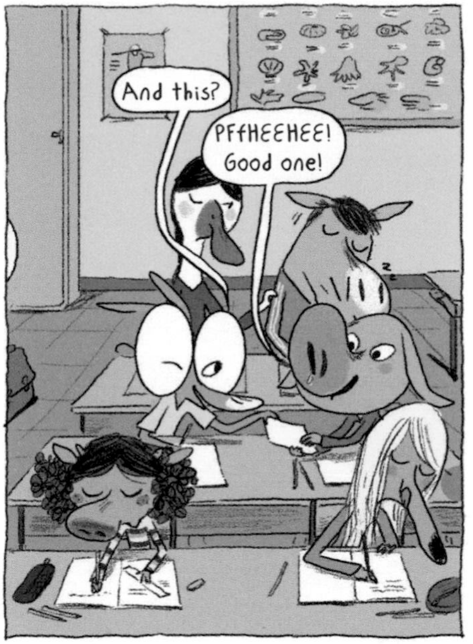
And this?
PFFHEEHEE! Good one!

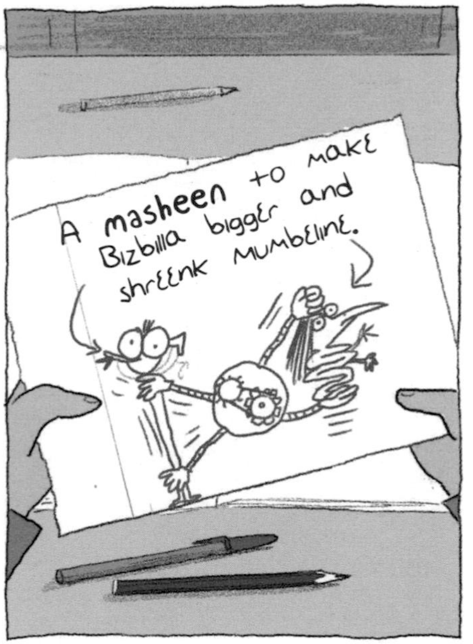
A masheen to make Bizbilla bigger and shreenk Mumbeline.

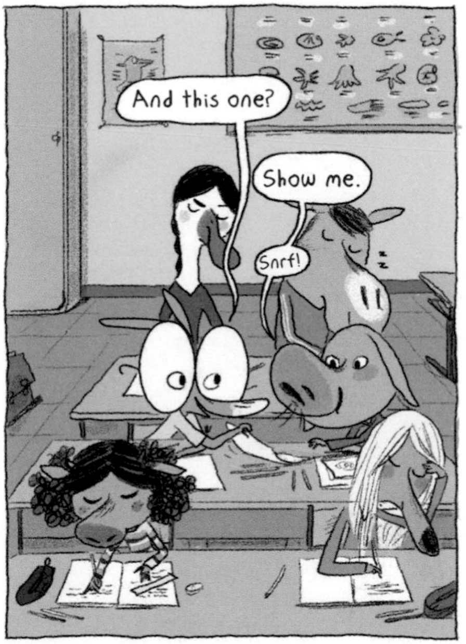
And this one?
Show me.
Snrf!

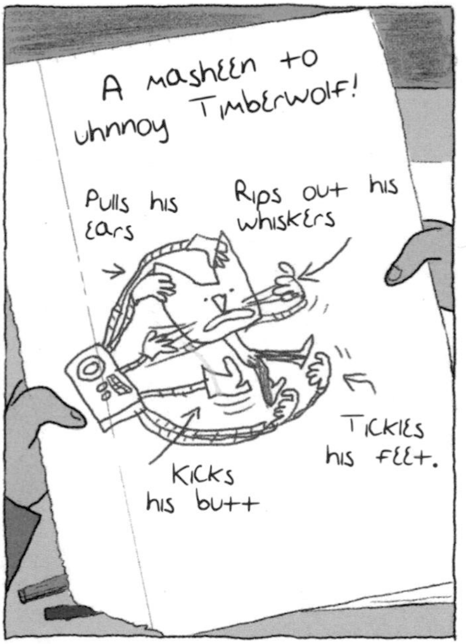
A masheen to uhnnoy Timberwolf!
Pulls his ears
Rips out his whiskers
Tickles his feet.
Kicks his butt

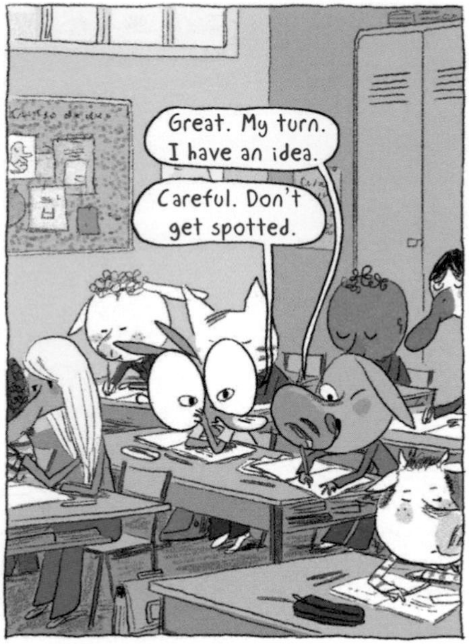
Great. My turn. I have an idea.
Careful. Don't get spotted.

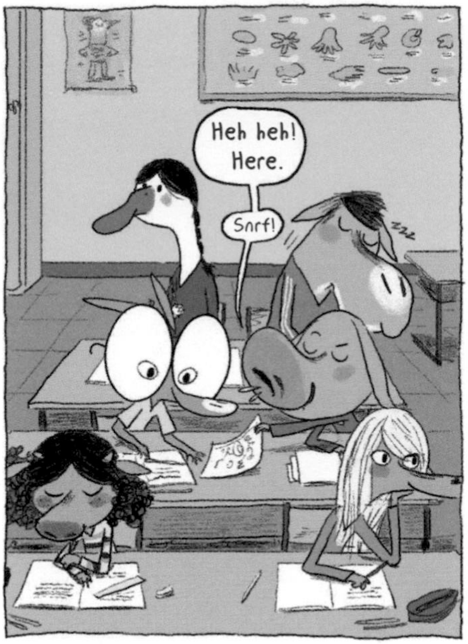
Heh heh! Here.
Snrf!

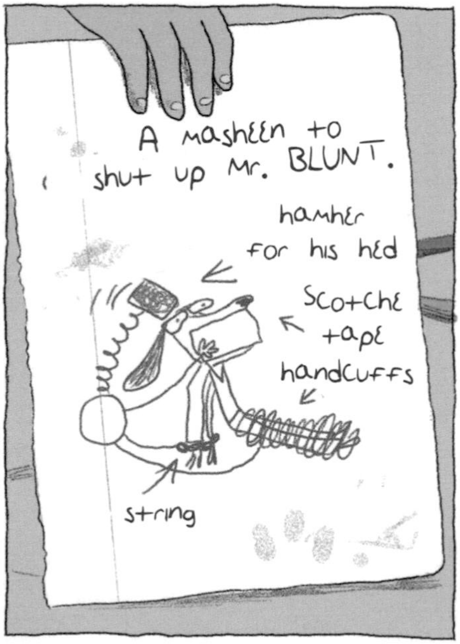
A masheen to shut up Mr. BLUNT.
hamher for his hed
Scotche tape
handcuffs
string

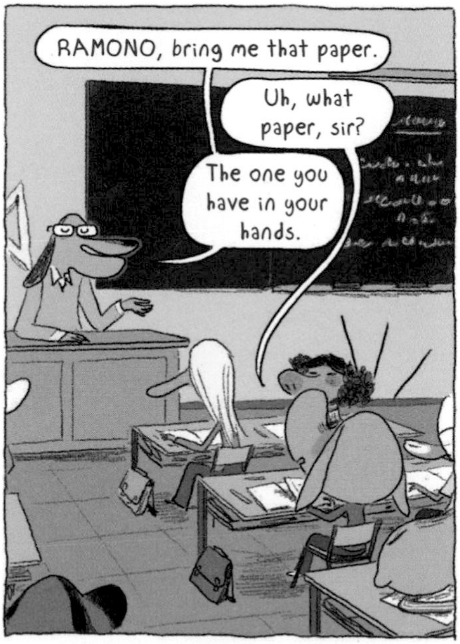
RAMONO, bring me that paper.
Uh, what paper, sir?
The one you have in your hands.

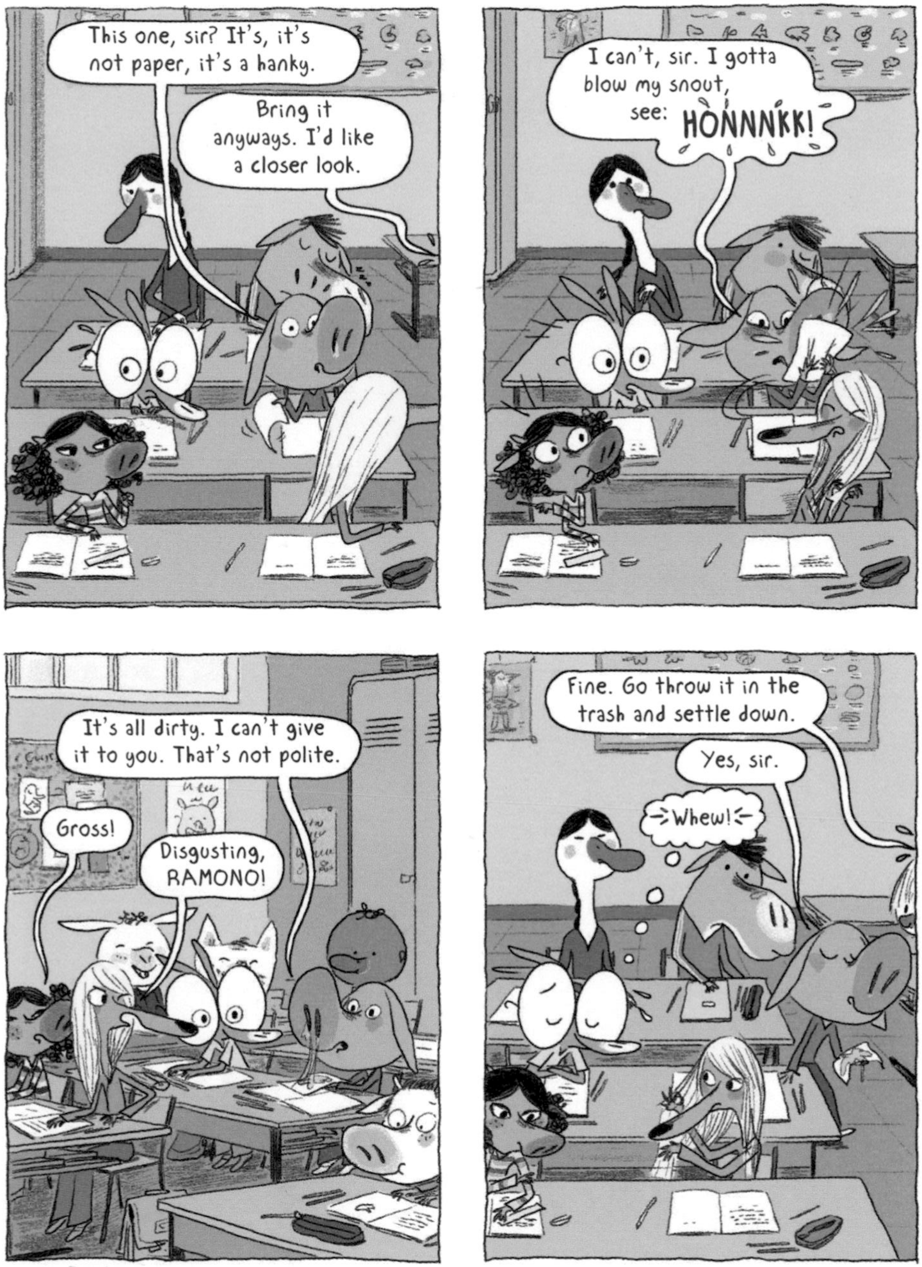
This one, sir? It's, it's not paper, it's a hanky.
Bring it anyways. I'd like a closer look.
I can't, sir. I gotta blow my snout, see: HONNNKK!
It's all dirty. I can't give it to you. That's not polite.
Gross!
Disgusting, RAMONO!
Fine. Go throw it in the trash and settle down.
Yes, sir.
Whew!

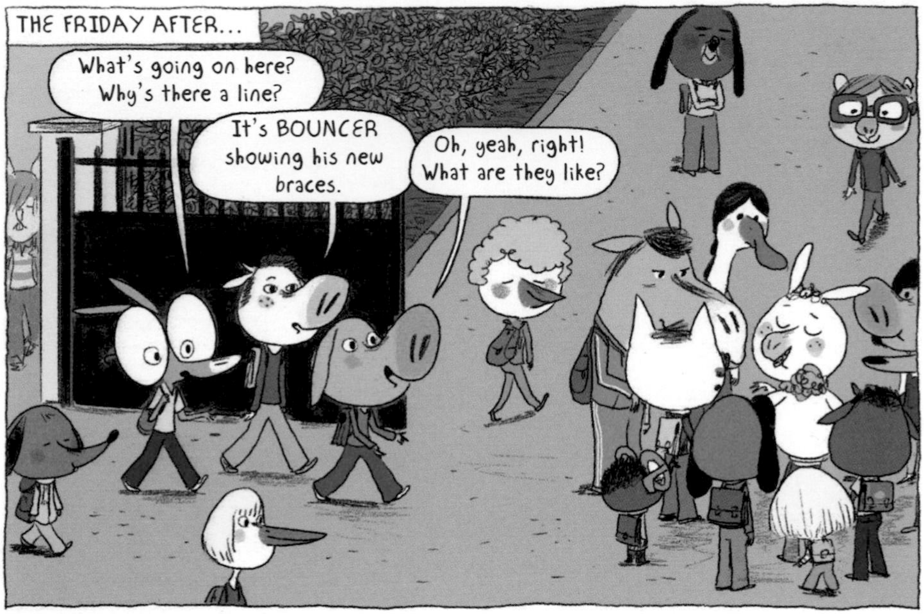
THE FRIDAY AFTER...
What's going on here? Why's there a line?
It's BOUNCER showing his new braces.
Oh, yeah, right! What are they like?

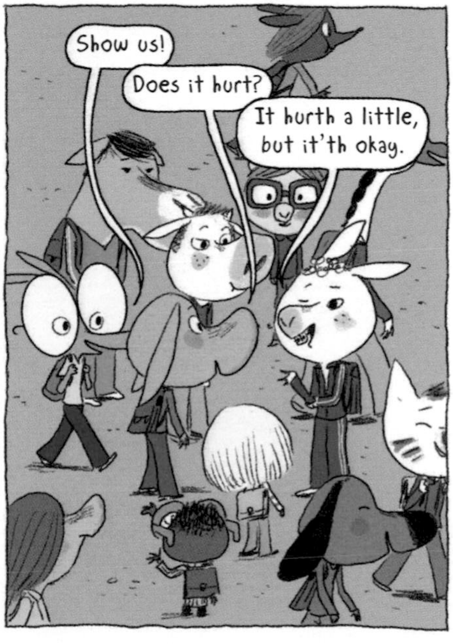
Show us!
Does it hurt?
It hurth a little, but it'th okay.

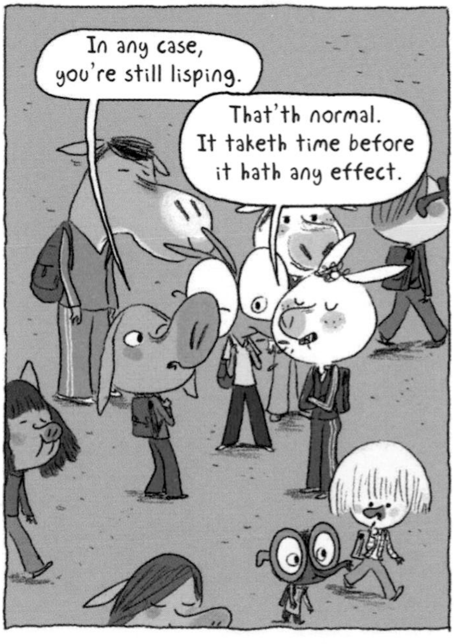
In any case, you're still lisping.
That'th normal. It taketh time before it hath any effect.

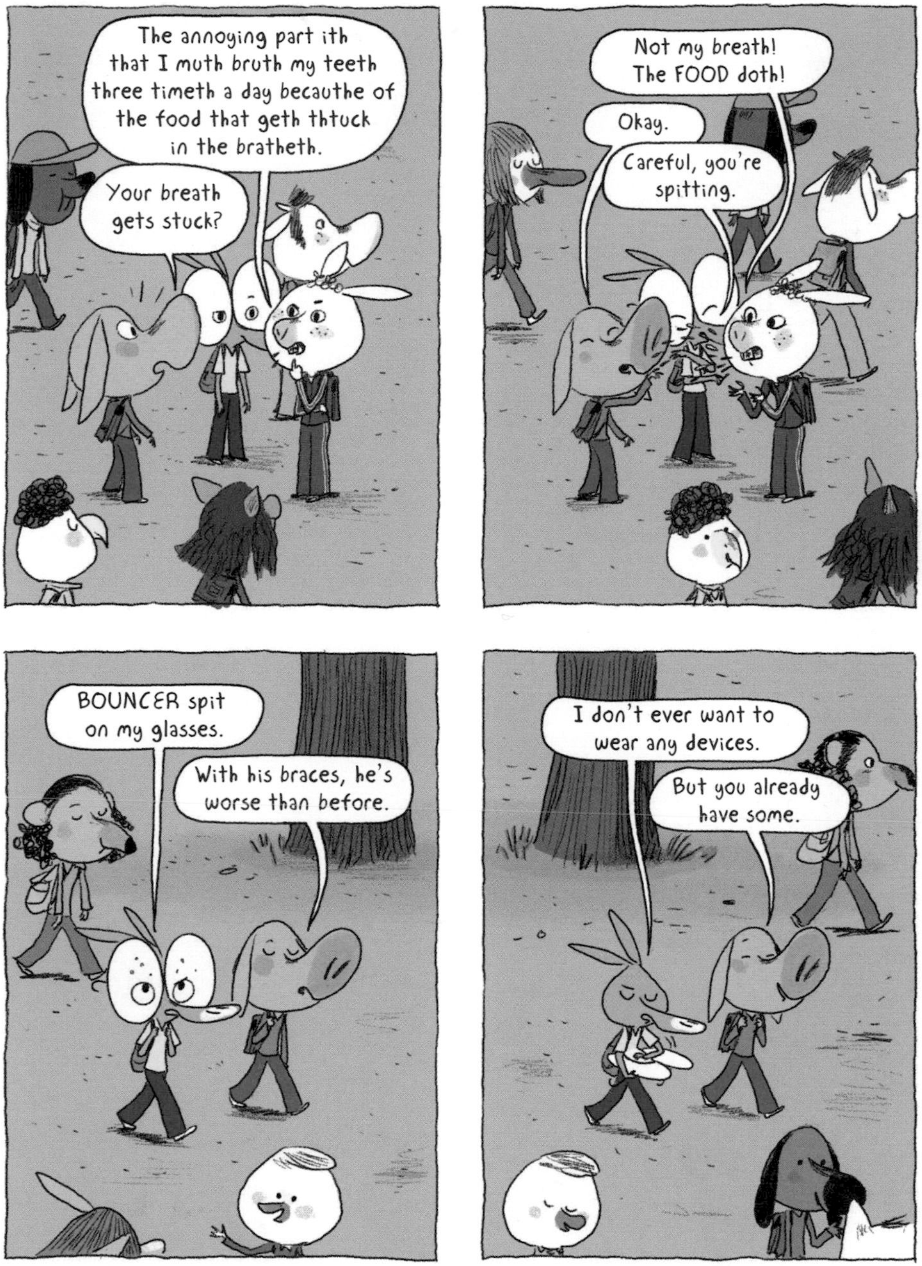
The annoying part ith that I muth bruth my teeth three timeth a day becauthe of the food that geth thtuck in the bratheth.
Your breath gets stuck?
Not my breath! The FOOD doth!
Okay.
Careful, you're spitting.
BOUNCER spit on my glasses.
With his braces, he's worse than before.
I don't ever want to wear any devices.
But you already have some.

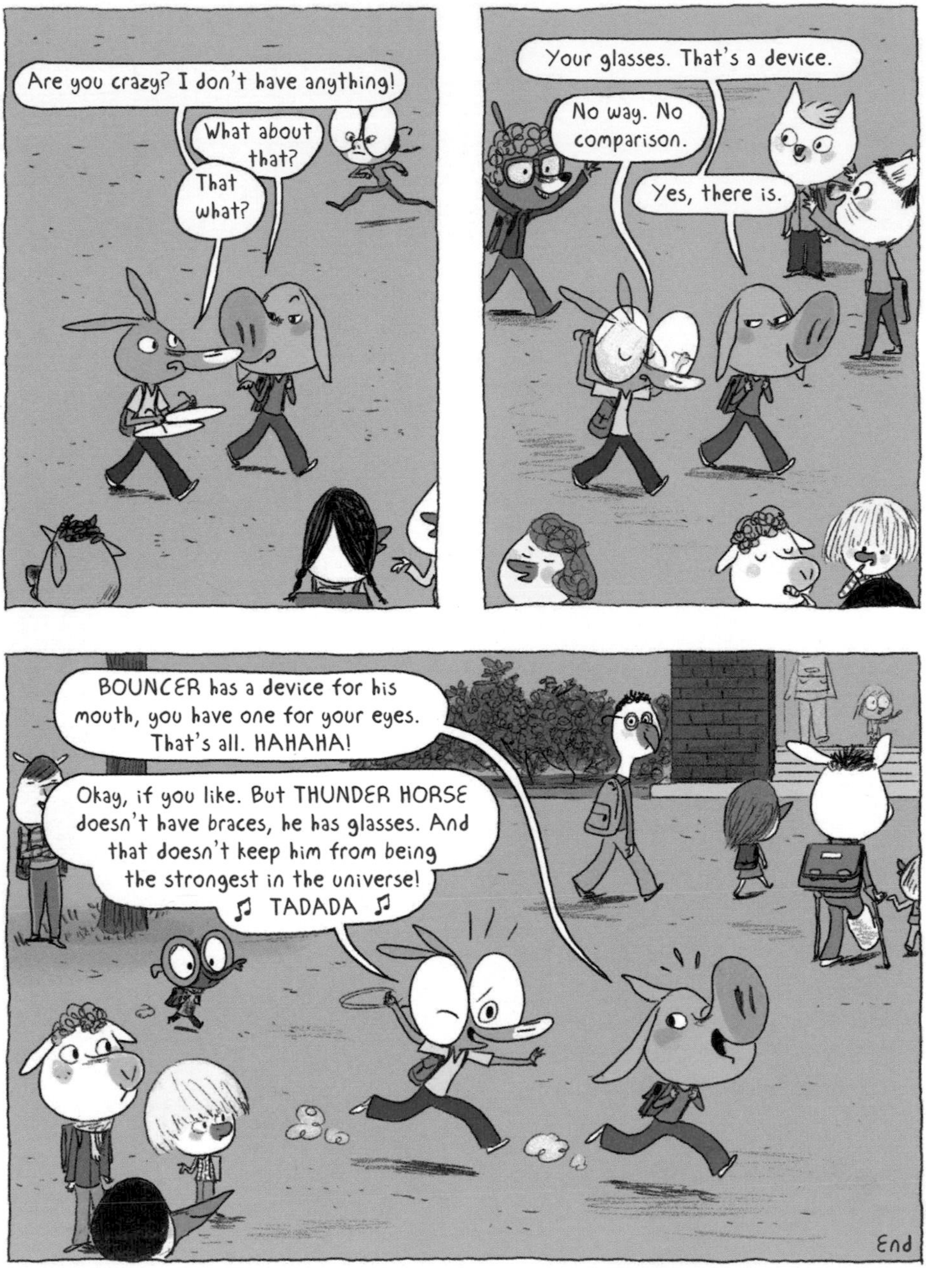
Are you crazy? I don't have anything!
What about that?
That what?
Your glasses. That's a device.
No way. No comparison.
Yes, there is.
BOUNCER has a device for his mouth, you have one for your eyes. That's all. HAHAHA!
Okay, if you like. But THUNDER HORSE doesn't have braces, he has glasses. And that doesn't keep him from being the strongest in the universe! ♫ TADADA ♫
End

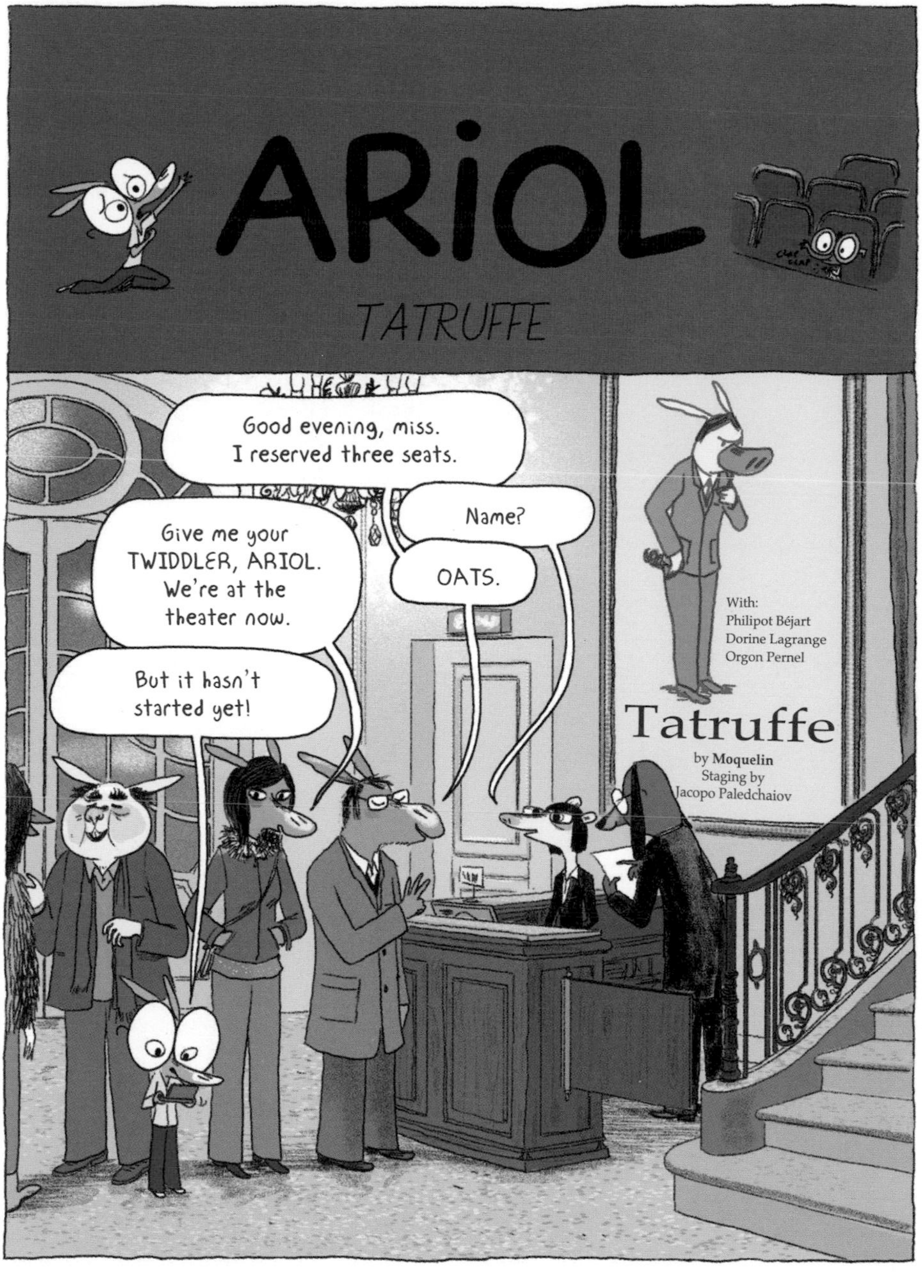
ARiOL
TATRUFFE
Good evening, miss. I reserved three seats.
Name?
Give me your TWIDDLER, ARIOL. We're at the theater now.
OATS.
But it hasn't started yet!
With:
Philipot Béjart
Dorine Lagrange
Orgon Pernel
Tatruffe
by Moquelin
Staging by
Jacopo Paledchaiov

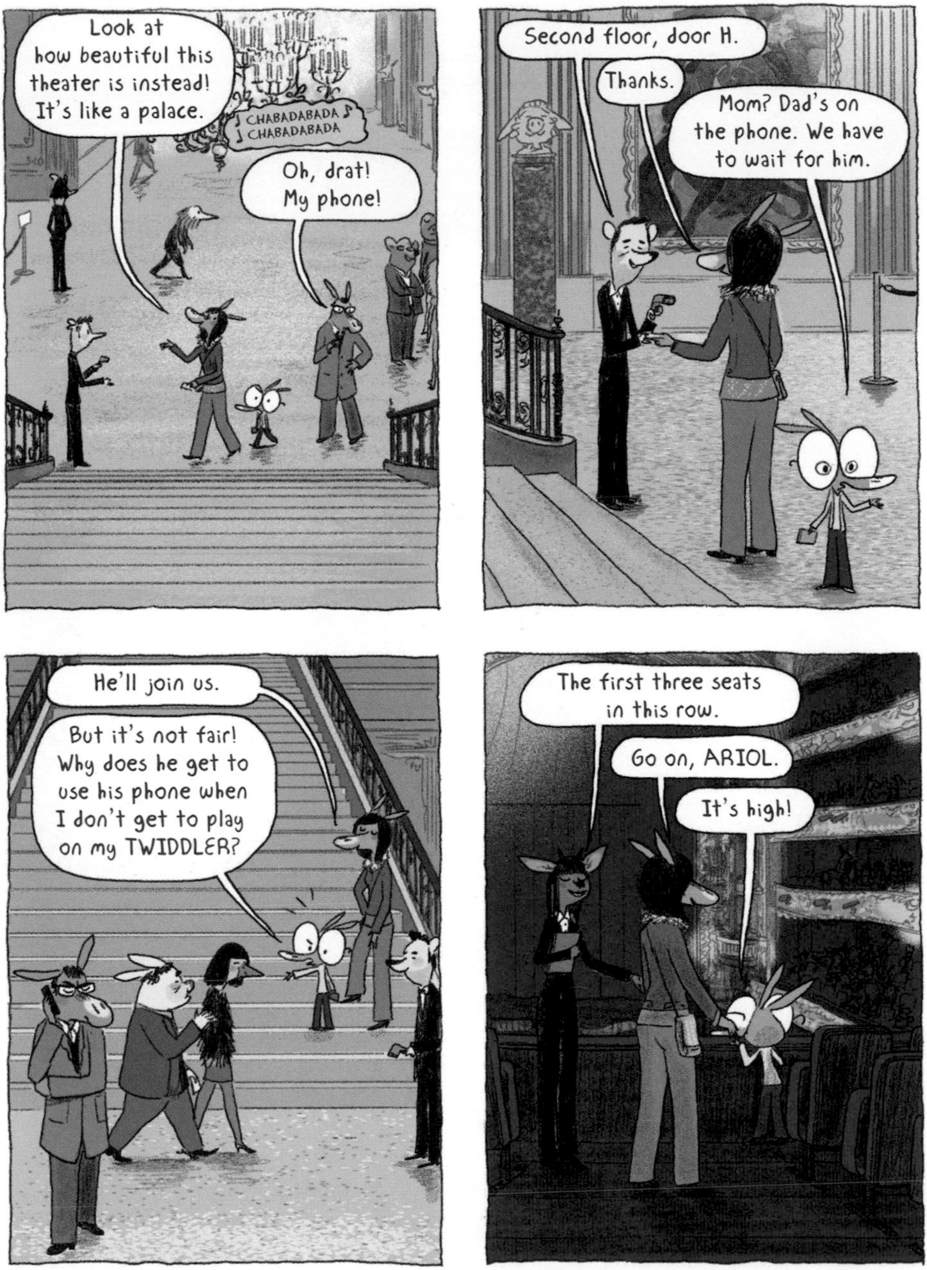
Look at how beautiful this theater is instead! It's like a palace.
CHABADABADA CHABADABADA
Oh, drat! My phone!
Second floor, door H.
Thanks.
Mom? Dad's on the phone. We have to wait for him.
He'll join us.
But it's not fair! Why does he get to use his phone when I don't get to play on my TWIDDLER?
The first three seats in this row.
Go on, ARIOL.
It's high!

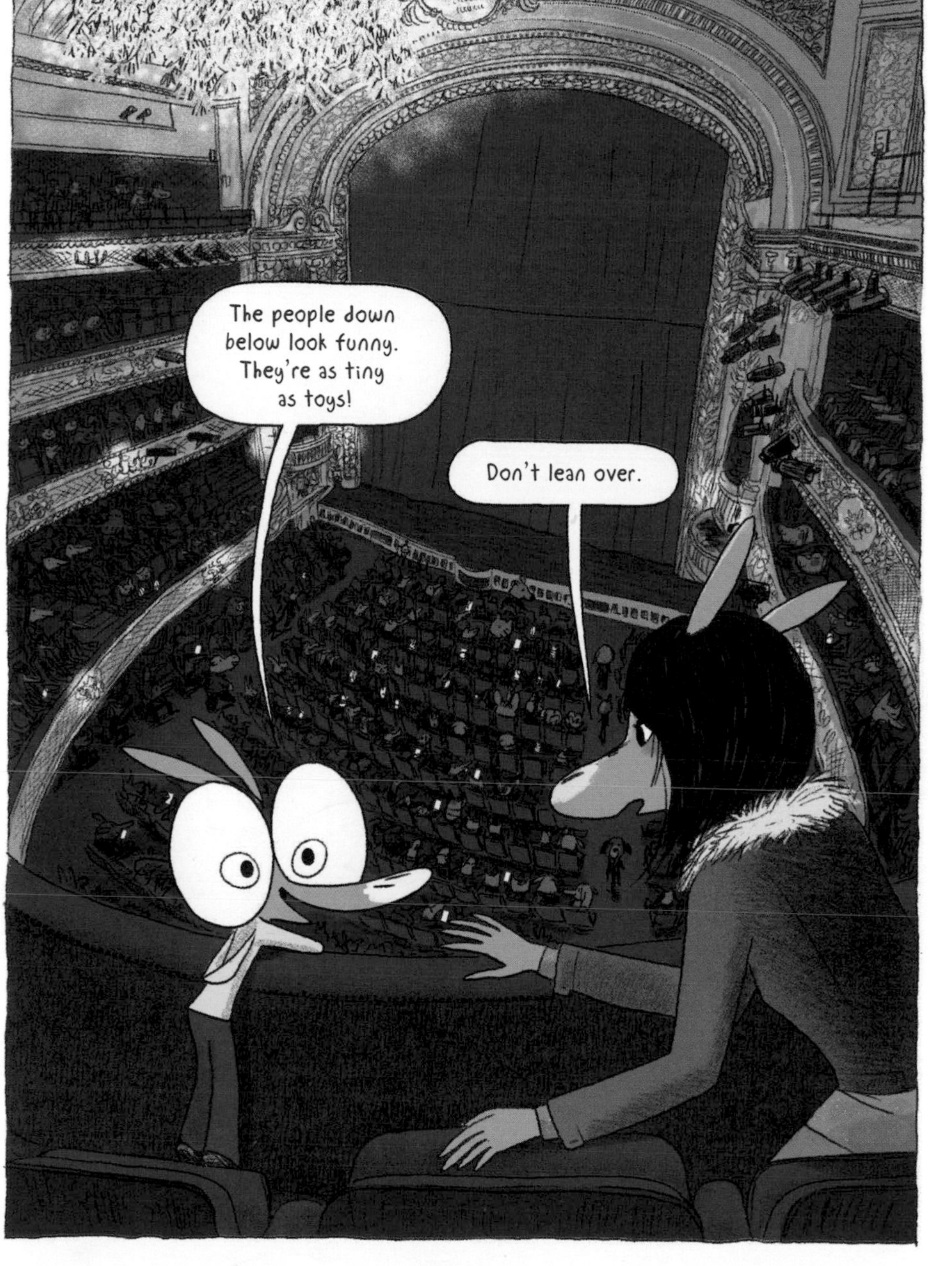
The people down below look funny. They're as tiny as toys!
Don't lean over.

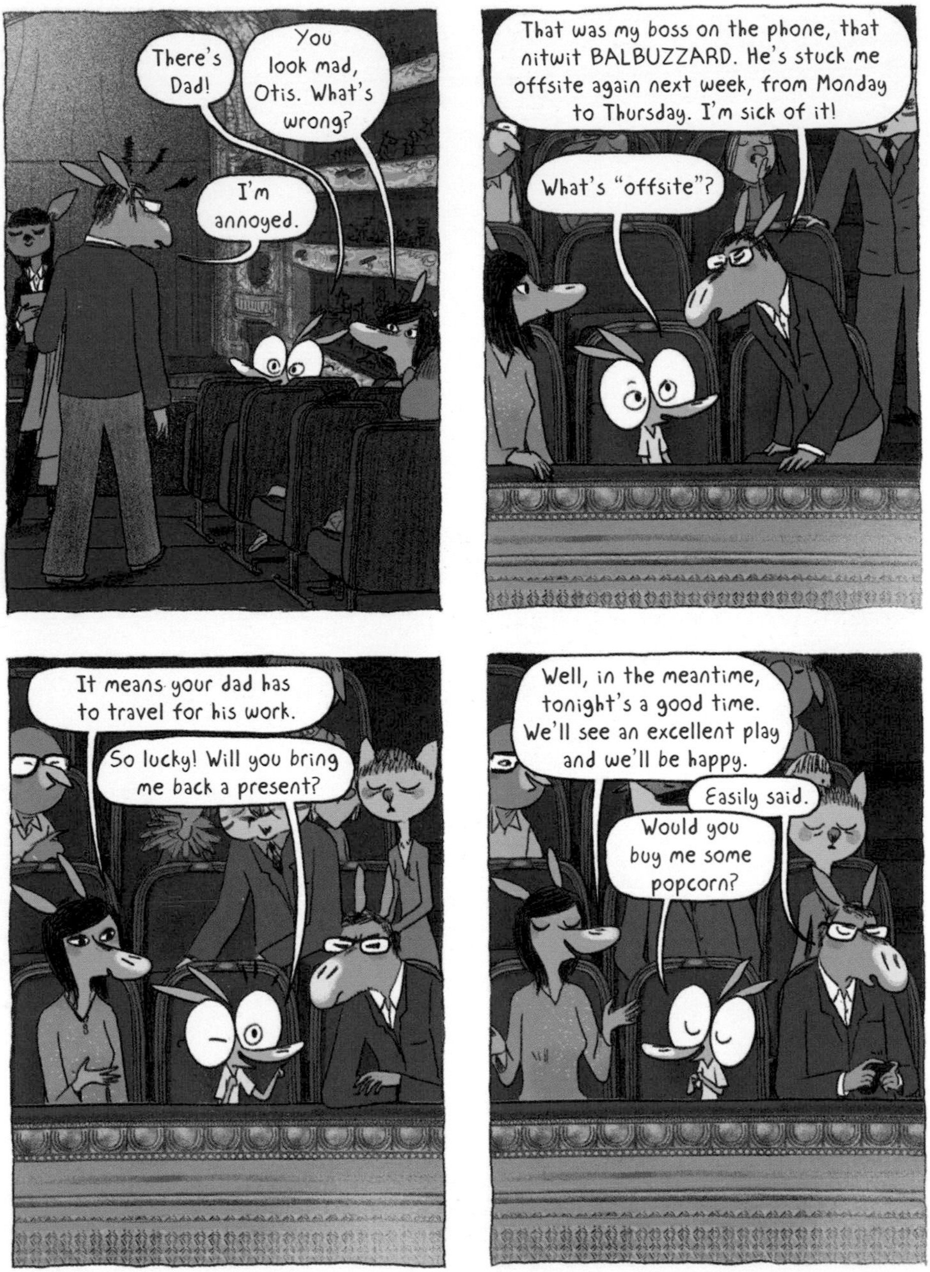
There's Dad!
You look mad, Otis. What's wrong?
I'm annoyed.
That was my boss on the phone, that nitwit BALBUZZARD. He's stuck me offsite again next week, from Monday to Thursday. I'm sick of it!
What's "offsite"?
It means your dad has to travel for his work.
So lucky! Will you bring me back a present?
Well, in the meantime, tonight's a good time. We'll see an excellent play and we'll be happy.
Easily said.
Would you buy me some popcorn?

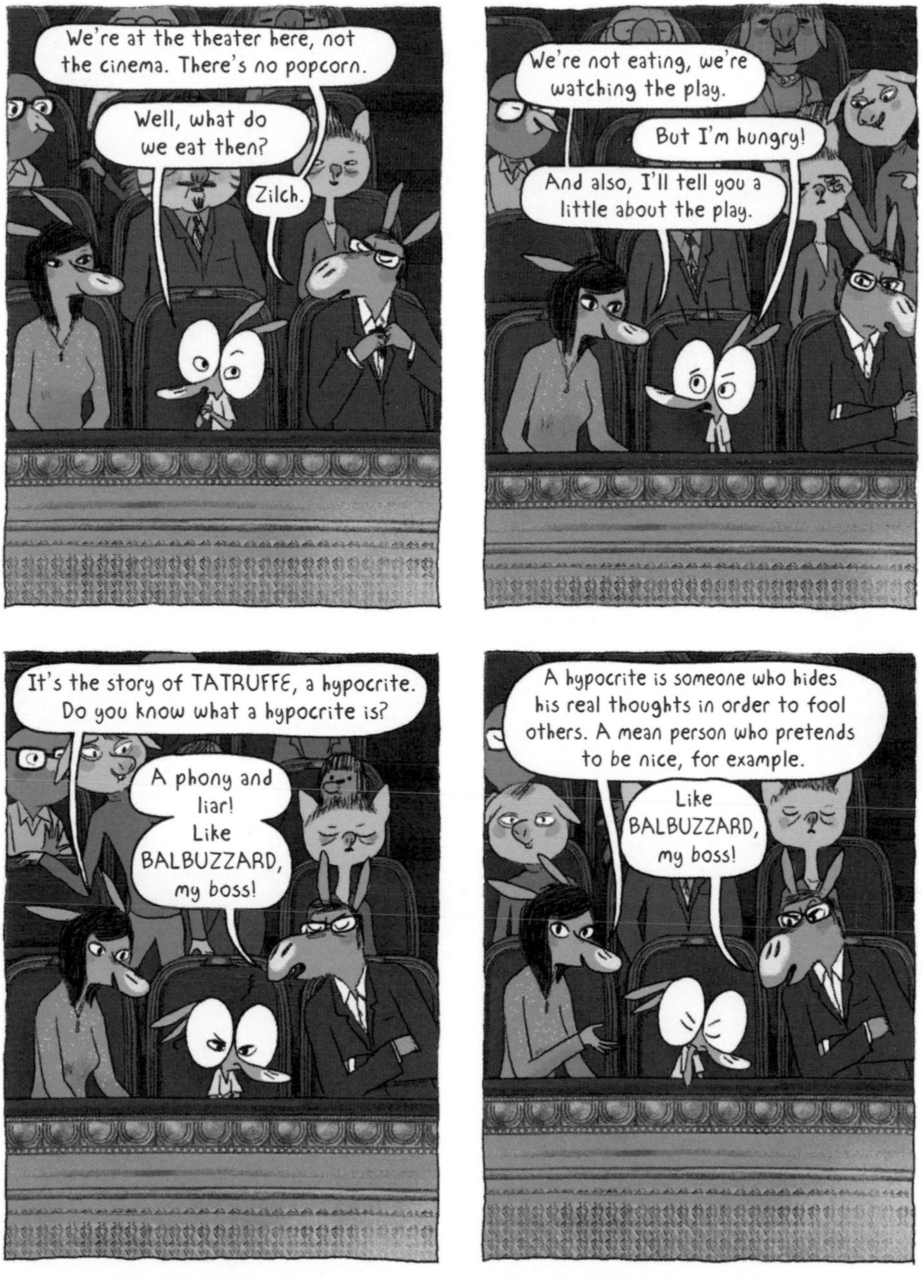
We're at the theater here, not the cinema. There's no popcorn.
Well, what do we eat then?
Zilch.
We're not eating, we're watching the play.
But I'm hungry!
And also, I'll tell you a little about the play.
It's the story of TATRUFFE, a hypocrite. Do you know what a hypocrite is?
A phony and liar! Like BALBUZZARD, my boss!
A hypocrite is someone who hides his real thoughts in order to fool others. A mean person who pretends to be nice, for example.
Like BALBUZZARD, my boss!

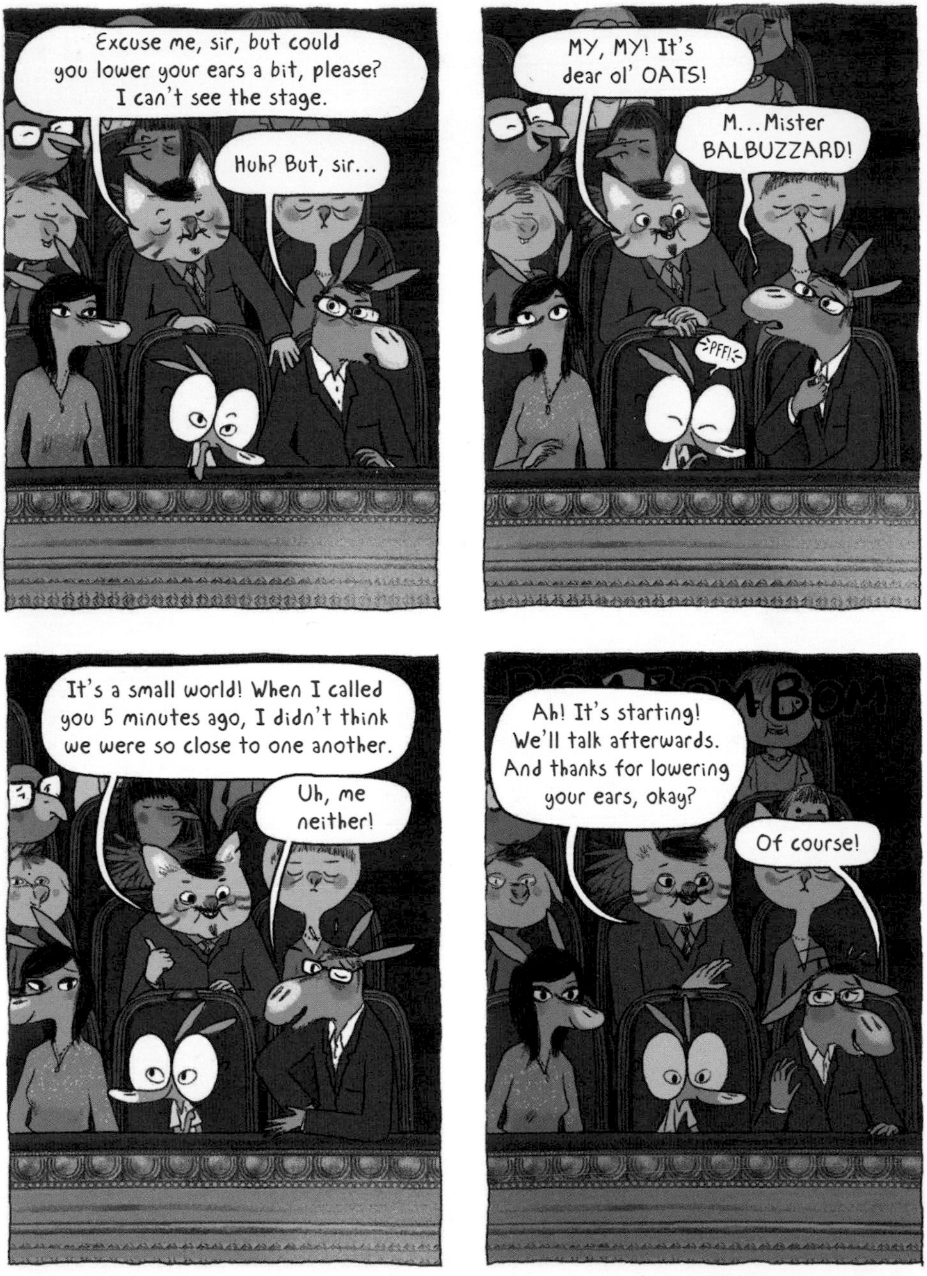
Excuse me, sir, but could you lower your ears a bit, please? I can't see the stage.
Huh? But, sir...
MY, MY! It's dear ol' OATS!
M... Mister BALBUZZARD!
PFF!
It's a small world! When I called you 5 minutes ago, I didn't think we were so close to one another.
Uh, me neither!
Ah! It's starting! We'll talk afterwards. And thanks for lowering your ears, okay?
Of course!

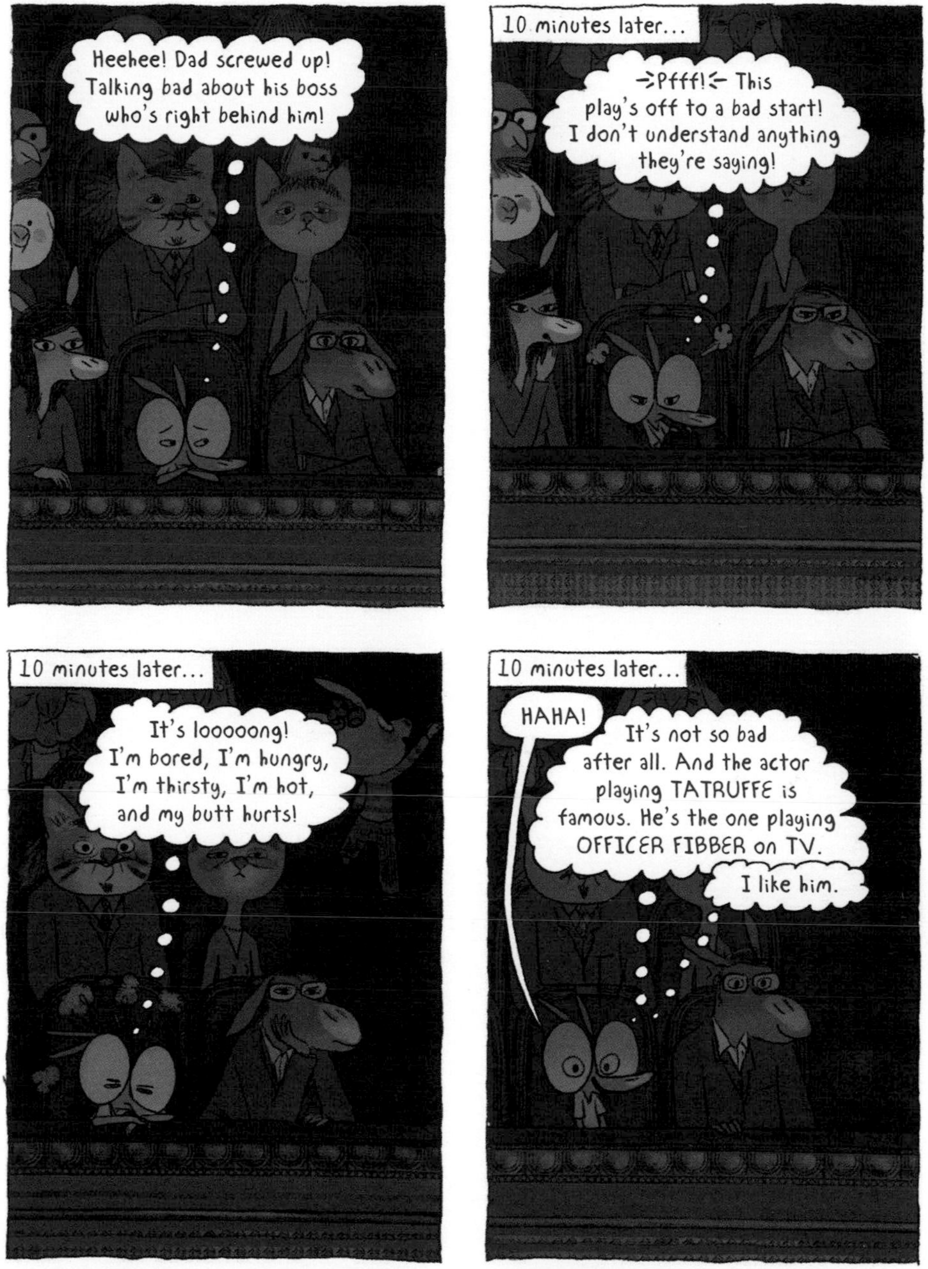
Heehee! Dad screwed up! Talking bad about his boss who's right behind him!
10 minutes later...
Pfff! This play's off to a bad start! I don't understand anything they're saying!
10 minutes later...
It's looooong! I'm bored, I'm hungry, I'm thirsty, I'm hot, and my butt hurts!
10 minutes later...
HAHA!
It's not so bad after all. And the actor playing TATRUFFE is famous. He's the one playing OFFICER FIBBER on TV.
I like him.

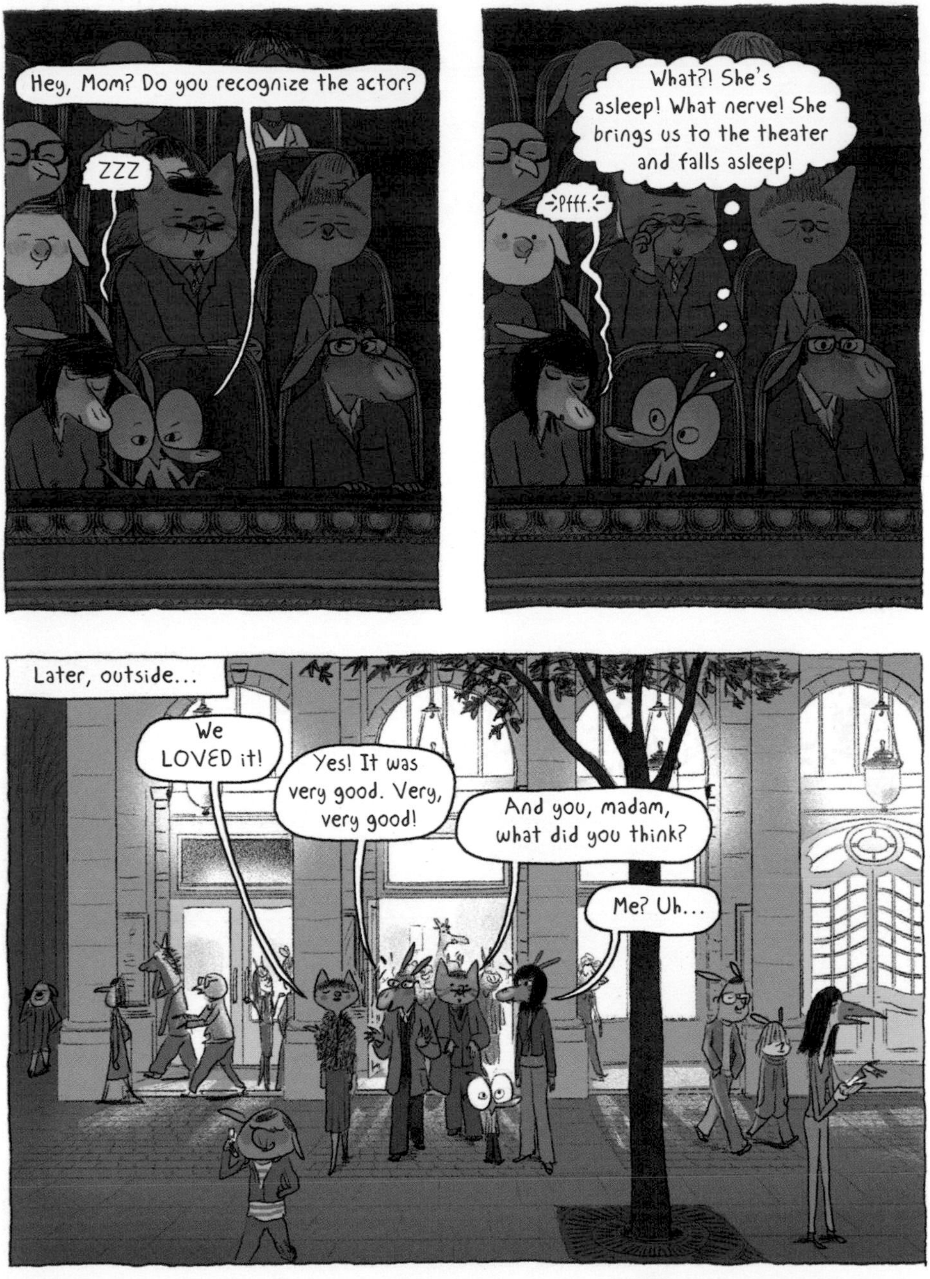
Hey, Mom? Do you recognize the actor?
ZZZ
What?! She's asleep! What nerve! She brings us to the theater and falls asleep!
Pfff.
Later, outside...
We LOVED it!
Yes! It was very good. Very, very good!
And you, madam, what did you think?
Me? Uh...

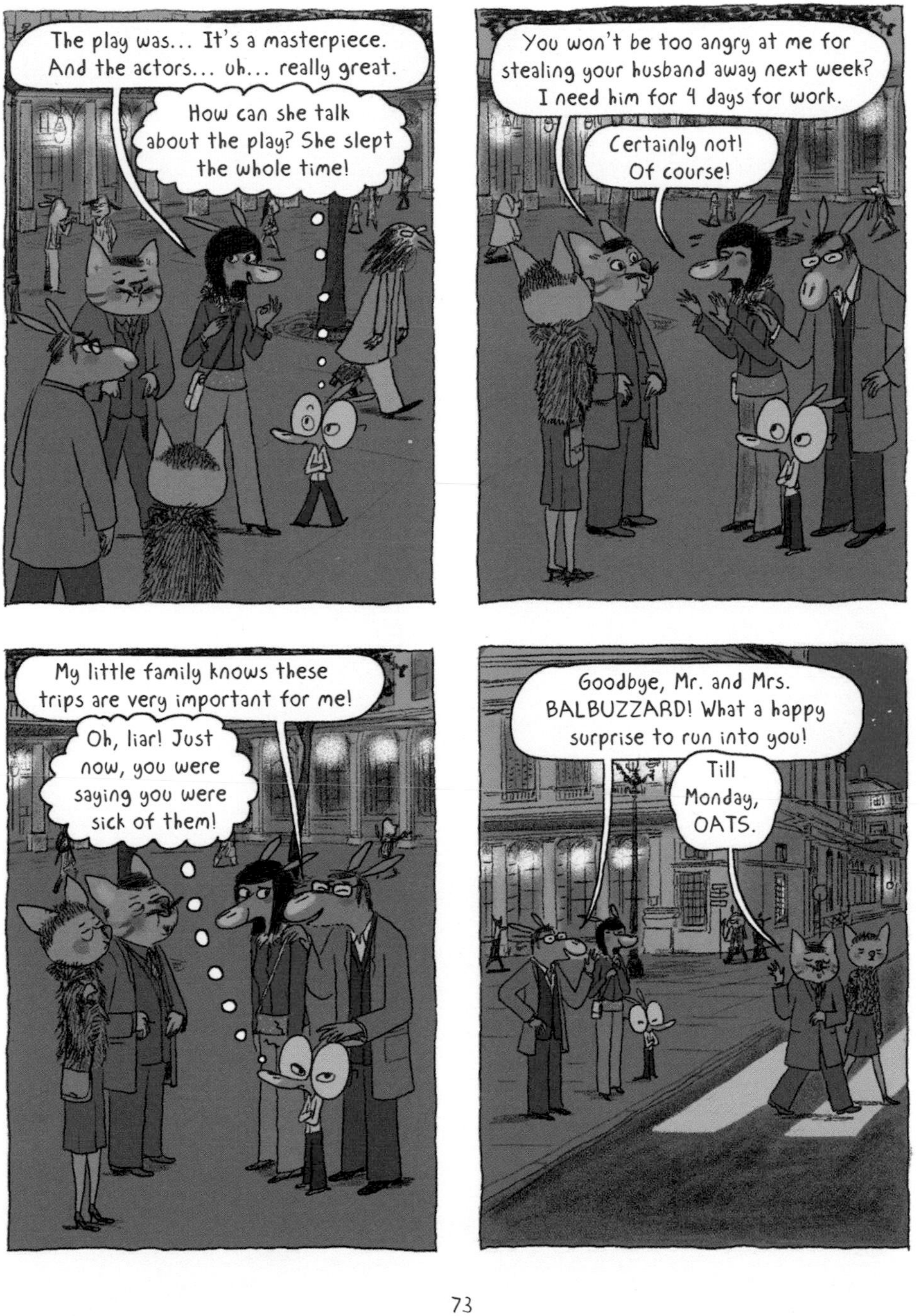

The play was... It's a masterpiece. And the actors... uh... really great.
How can she talk about the play? She slept the whole time!
You won't be too angry at me for stealing your husband away next week? I need him for 4 days for work.
Certainly not! Of course!
My little family knows these trips are very important for me!
Oh, liar! Just now, you were saying you were sick of them!
Goodbye, Mr. and Mrs. BALBUZZARD! What a happy surprise to run into you!
Till Monday, OATS.

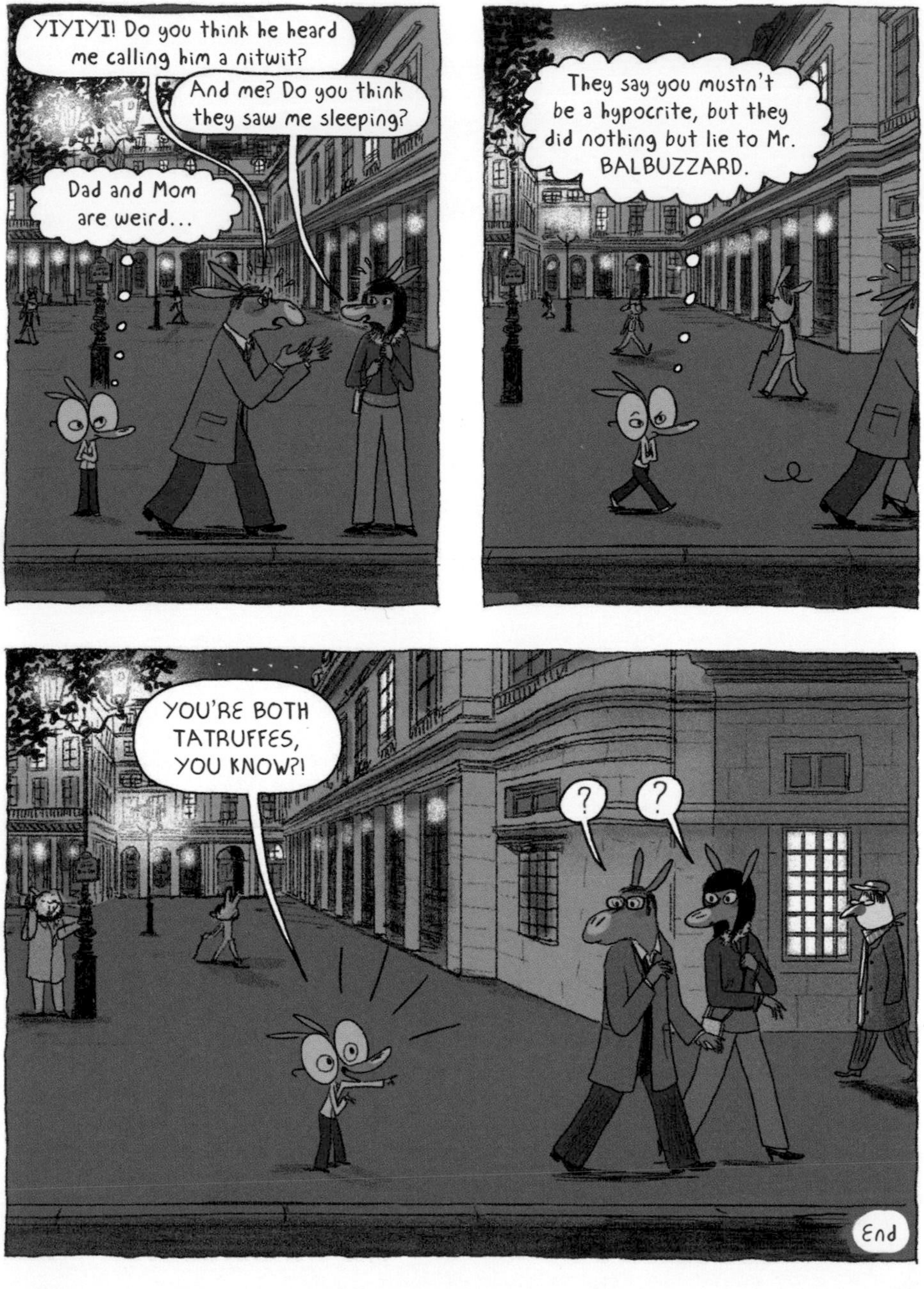
YIYIYI! Do you think he heard me calling him a nitwit?
And me? Do you think they saw me sleeping?
Dad and Mom are weird...
They say you mustn't be a hypocrite, but they did nothing but lie to Mr. BALBUZZARD.
YOU'RE BOTH TATRUFFES, YOU KNOW?!
?
?
End

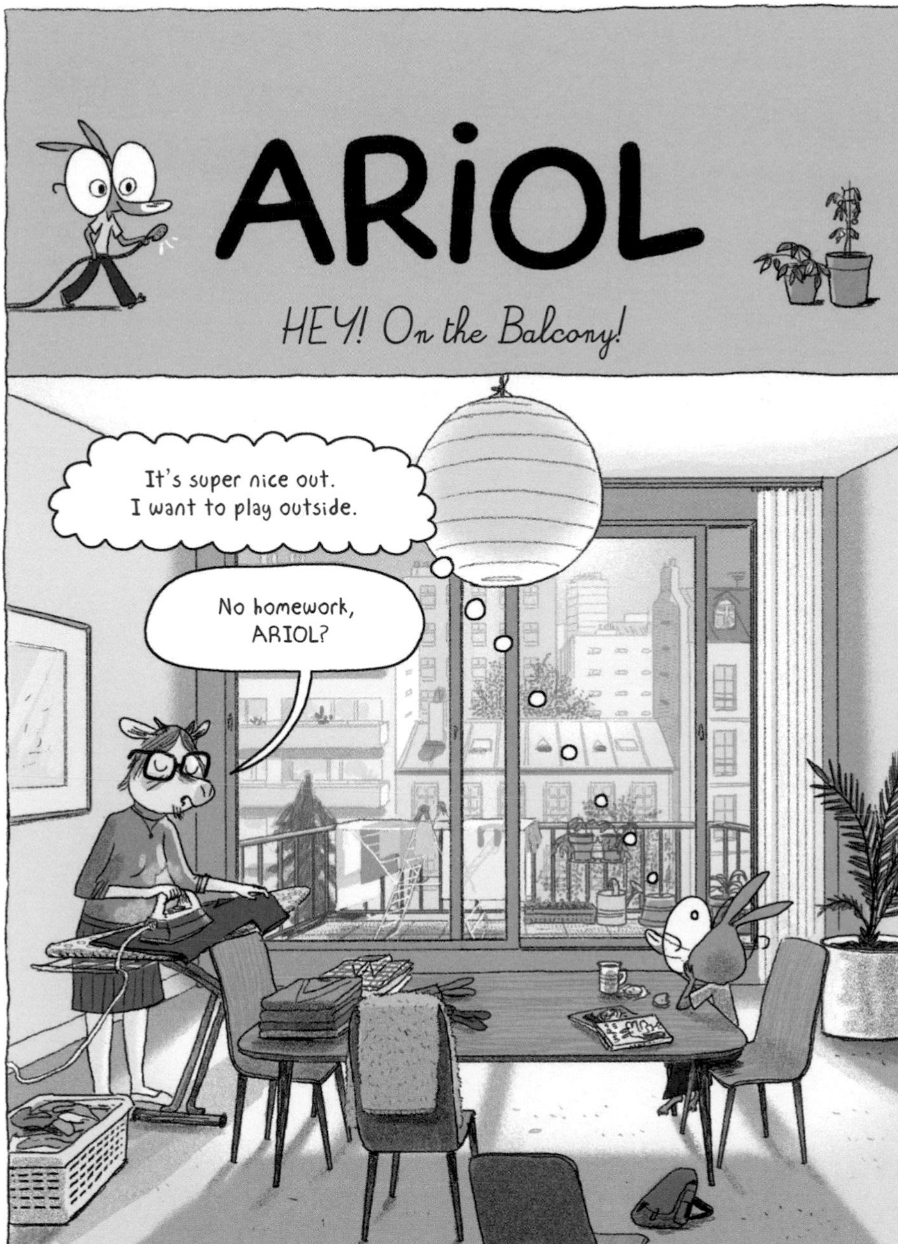
ARiOL
HEY! On the Balcony!
It's super nice out. I want to play outside.
No homework, ARIOL?

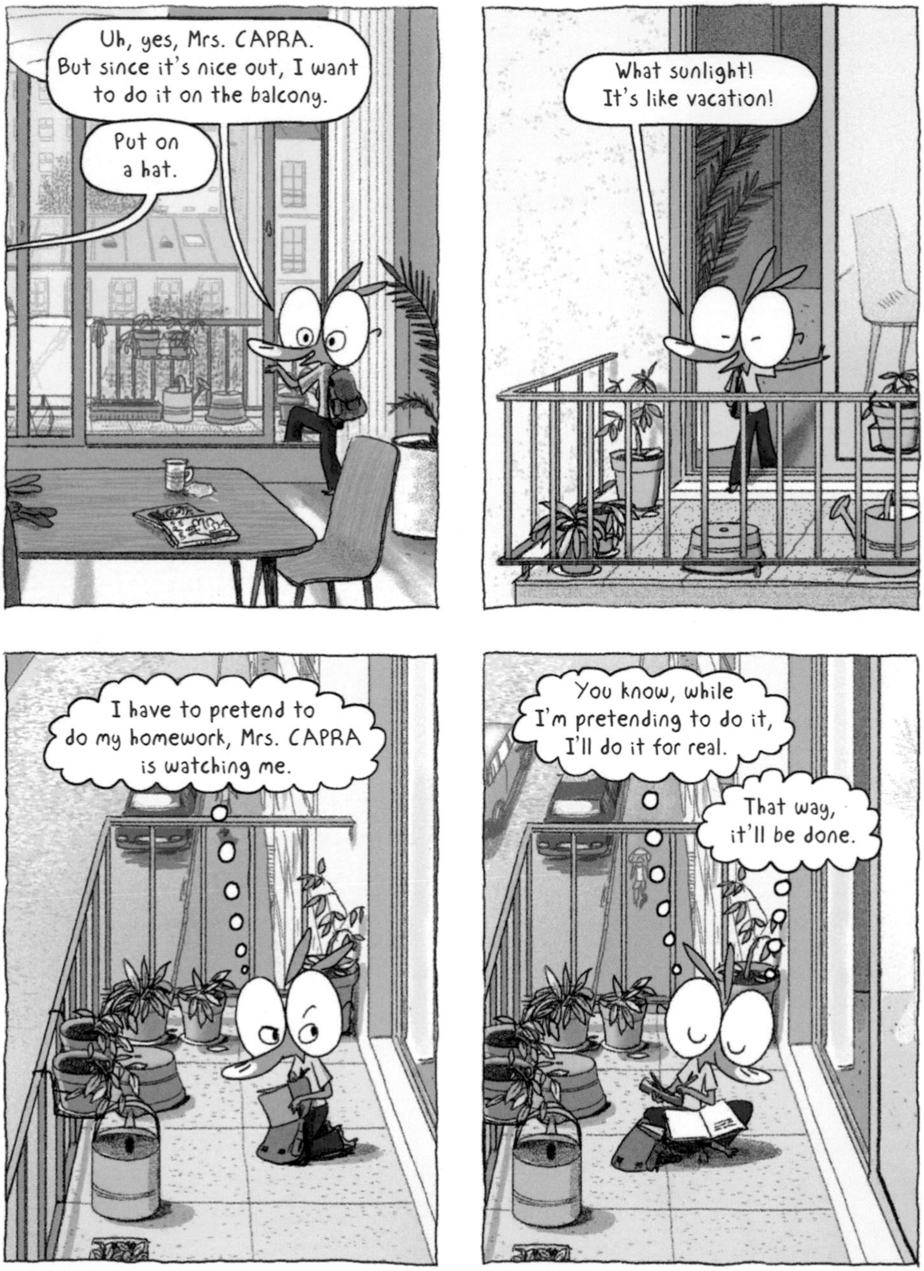
Uh, yes, Mrs. CAPRA. But since it's nice out, I want to do it on the balcony.
Put on a hat.
What sunlight! It's like vacation!
I have to pretend to do my homework, Mrs. CAPRA is watching me.
You know, while I'm pretending to do it, I'll do it for real.
That way, it'll be done.

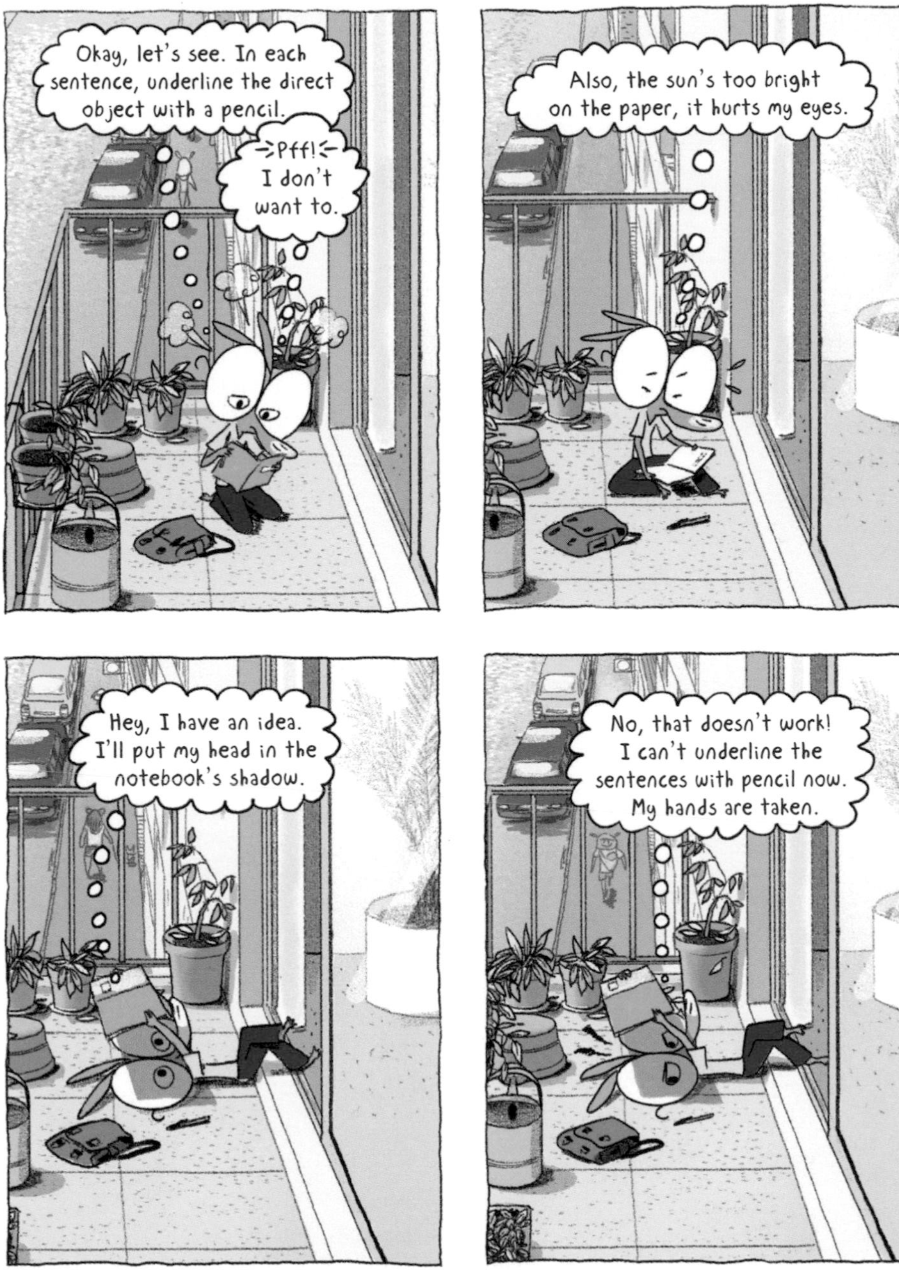

Okay, let's see. In each sentence, underline the direct object with a pencil.
Pff! I don't want to.
Also, the sun's too bright on the paper, it hurts my eyes.
Hey, I have an idea. I'll put my head in the notebook's shadow.
No, that doesn't work! I can't underline the sentences with pencil now. My hands are taken.

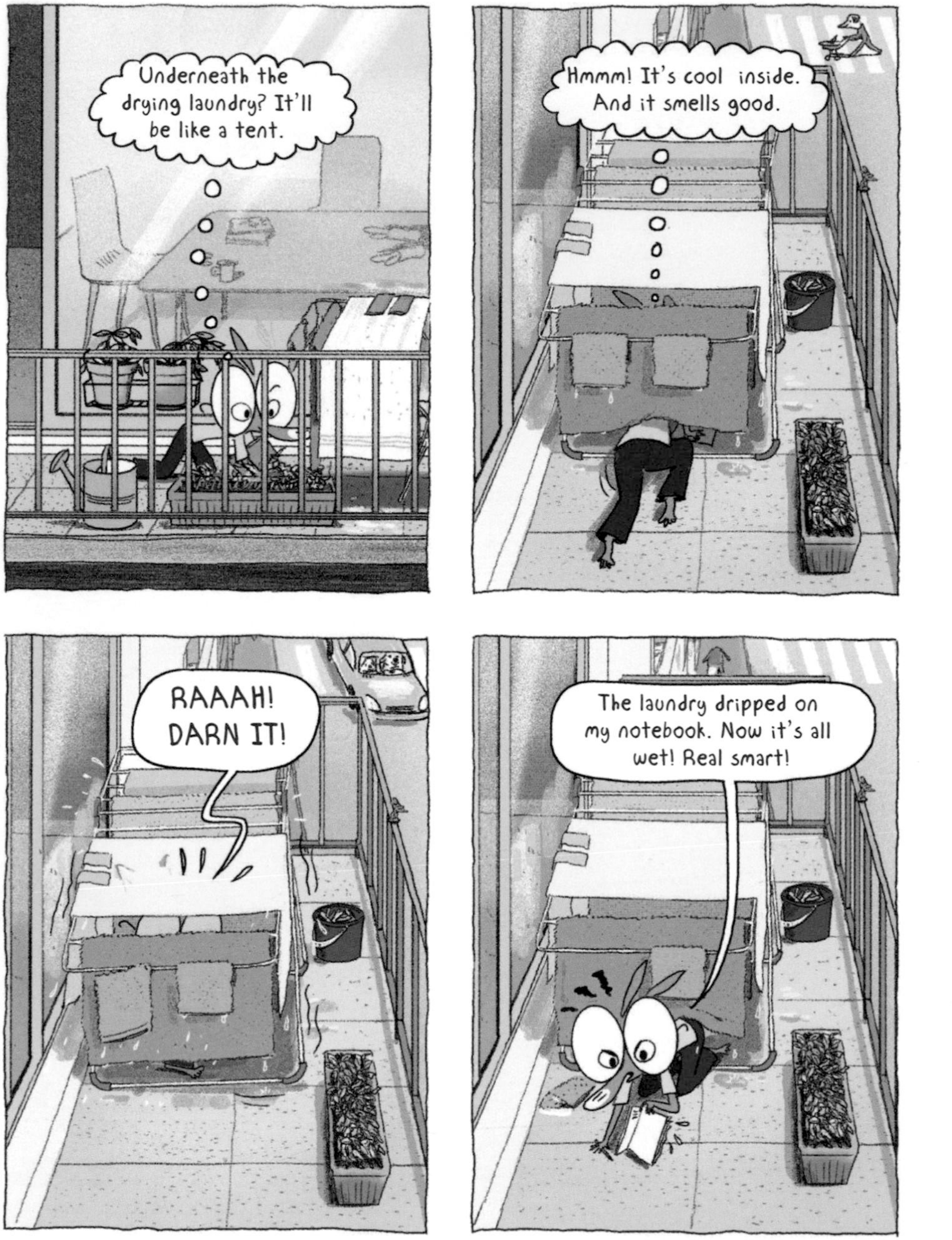
Underneath the drying laundry? It'll be like a tent.
Hmmm! It's cool inside. And it smells good.
RAAAH! DARN IT!
The laundry dripped on my notebook. Now it's all wet! Real smart!

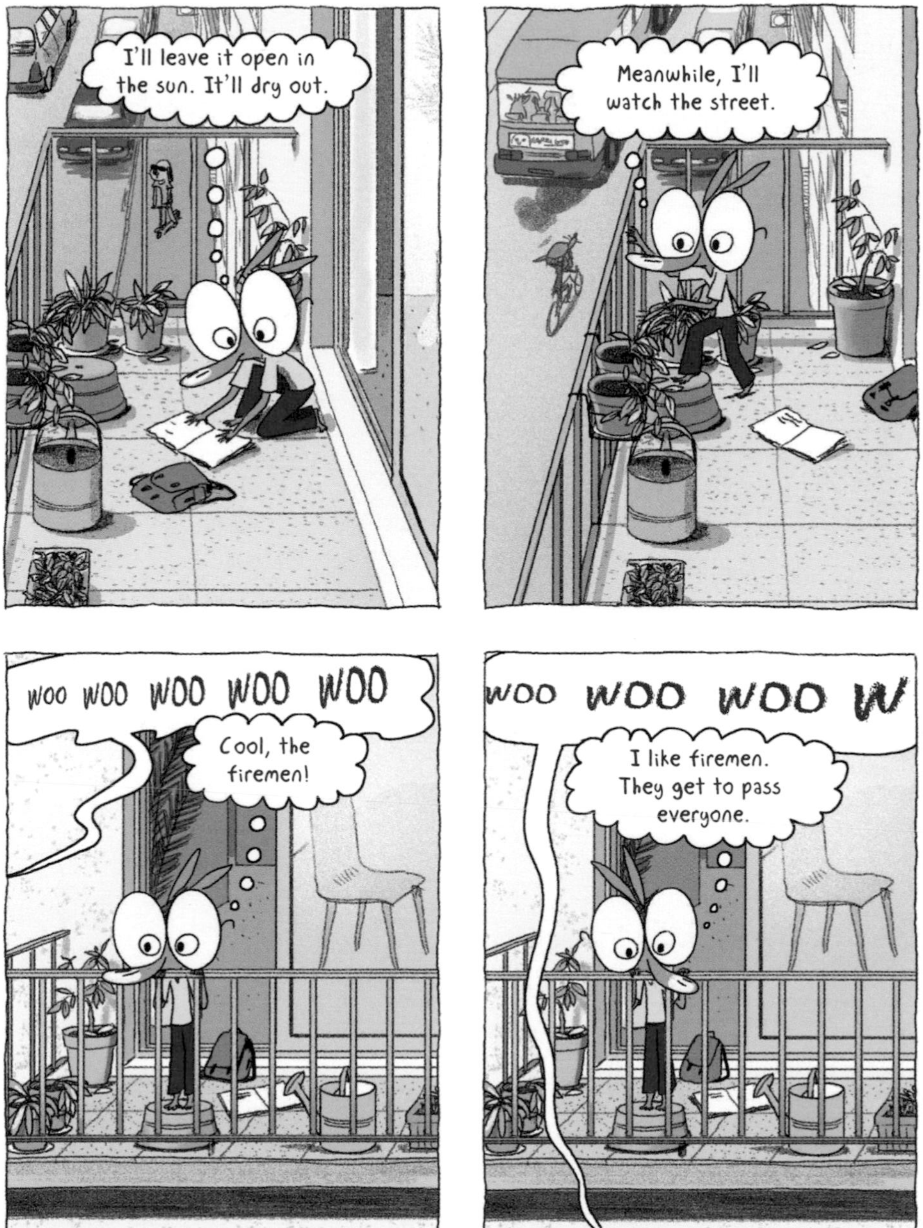
I'll leave it open in the sun. It'll dry out.
Meanwhile, I'll watch the street.
WOO WOO WOO WOO WOO
Cool, the firemen!
WOO WOO WOO W
I like firemen. They get to pass everyone.

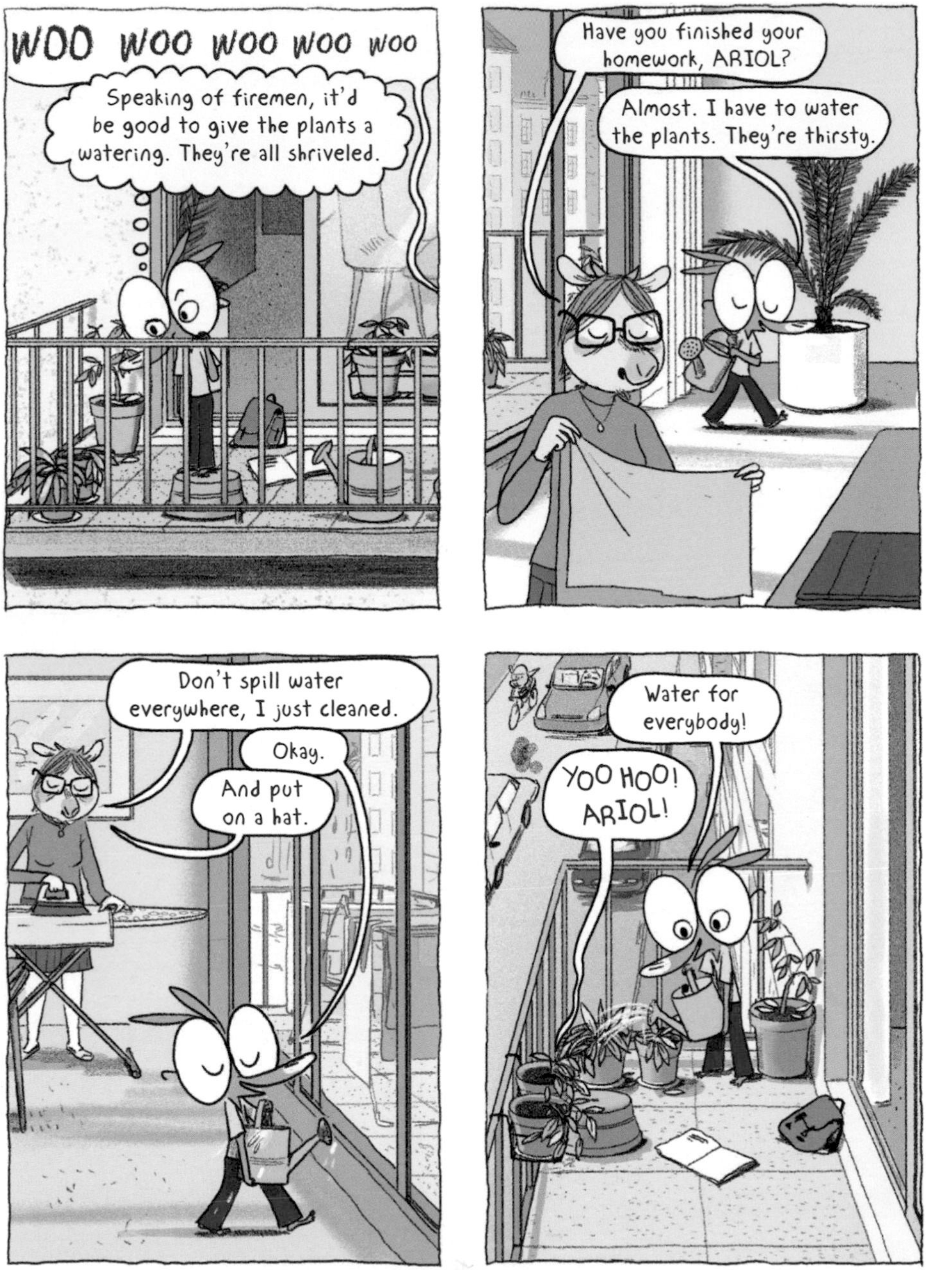
WOO WOO WOO WOO WOO
Speaking of firemen, it'd be good to give the plants a watering. They're all shriveled.
Have you finished your homework, ARIOL?
Almost. I have to water the plants. They're thirsty.
Don't spill water everywhere, I just cleaned.
Okay.
And put on a hat.
Water for everybody!
YOO HOO! ARIOL!

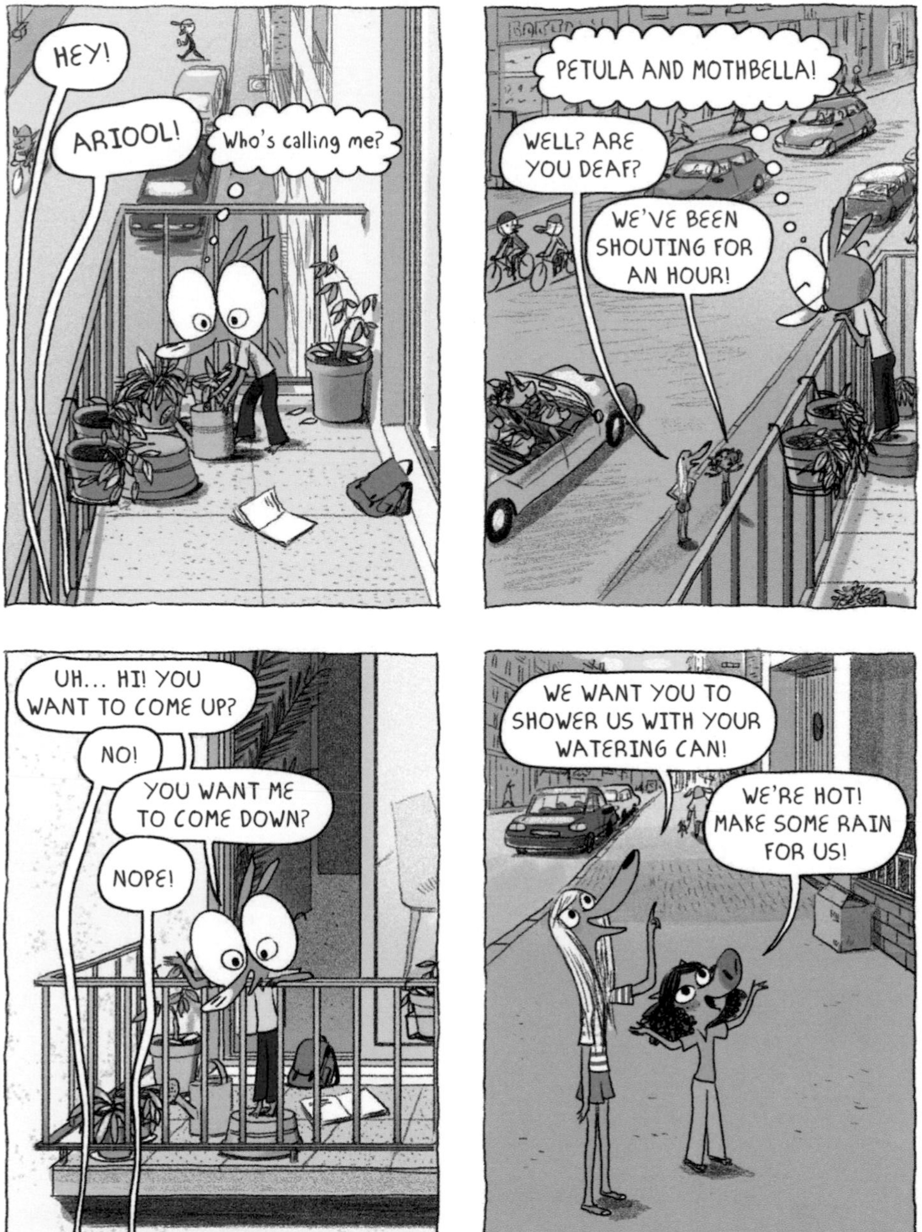
HEY!
ARIOOL!
Who's calling me?
PETULA AND MOTHBELLA!
WELL? ARE YOU DEAF?
WE'VE BEEN SHOUTING FOR AN HOUR!
UH... HI! YOU WANT TO COME UP?
NO!
YOU WANT ME TO COME DOWN?
NOPE!
WE WANT YOU TO SHOWER US WITH YOUR WATERING CAN!
WE'RE HOT! MAKE SOME RAIN FOR US!

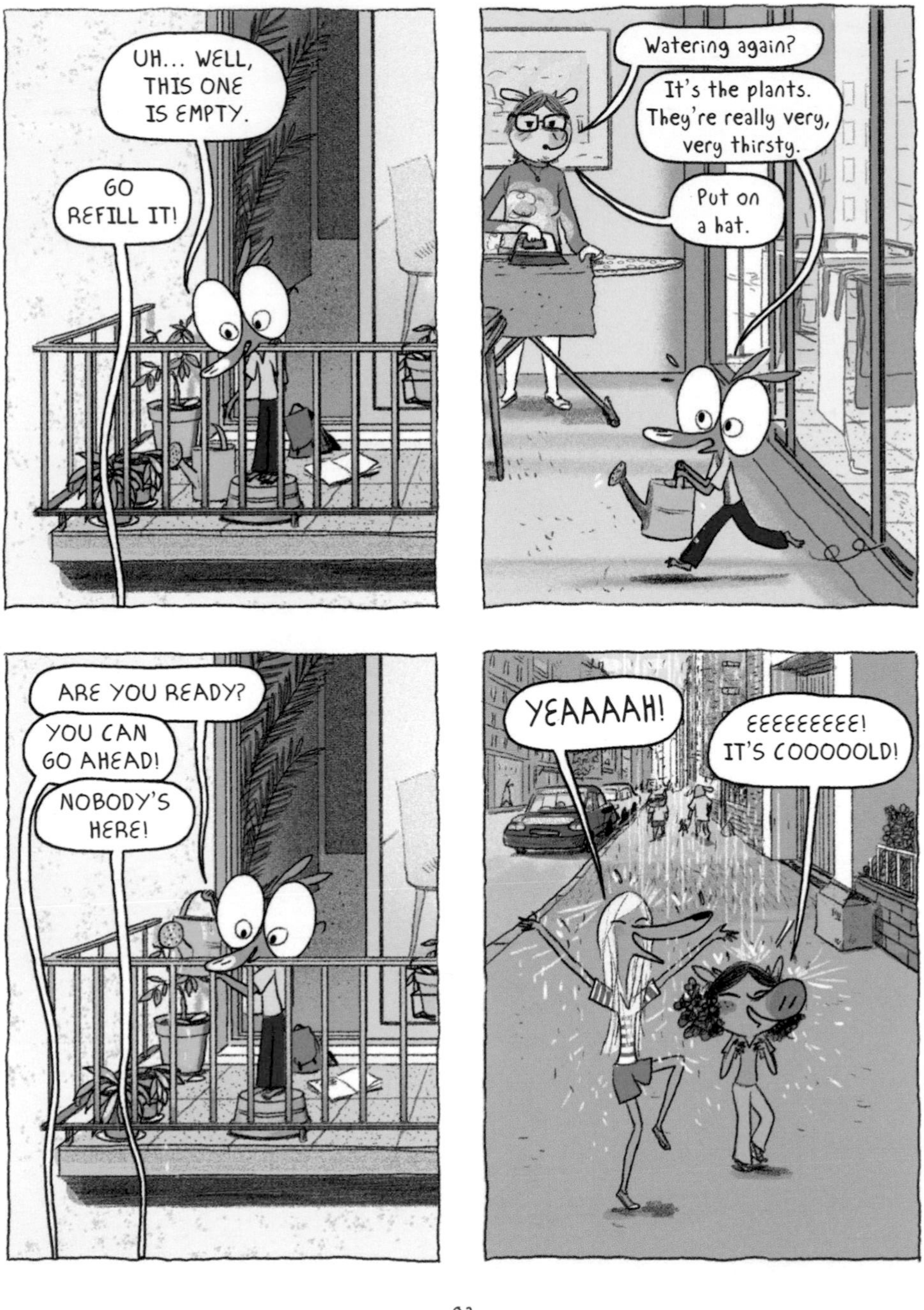
UH... WELL, THIS ONE IS EMPTY.
GO REFILL IT!
Watering again?
It's the plants. They're really very, very thirsty.
Put on a hat.
ARE YOU READY?
YOU CAN GO AHEAD!
NOBODY'S HERE!
YEAAAAH!
EEEEEEEEE! IT'S COOOOOLD!

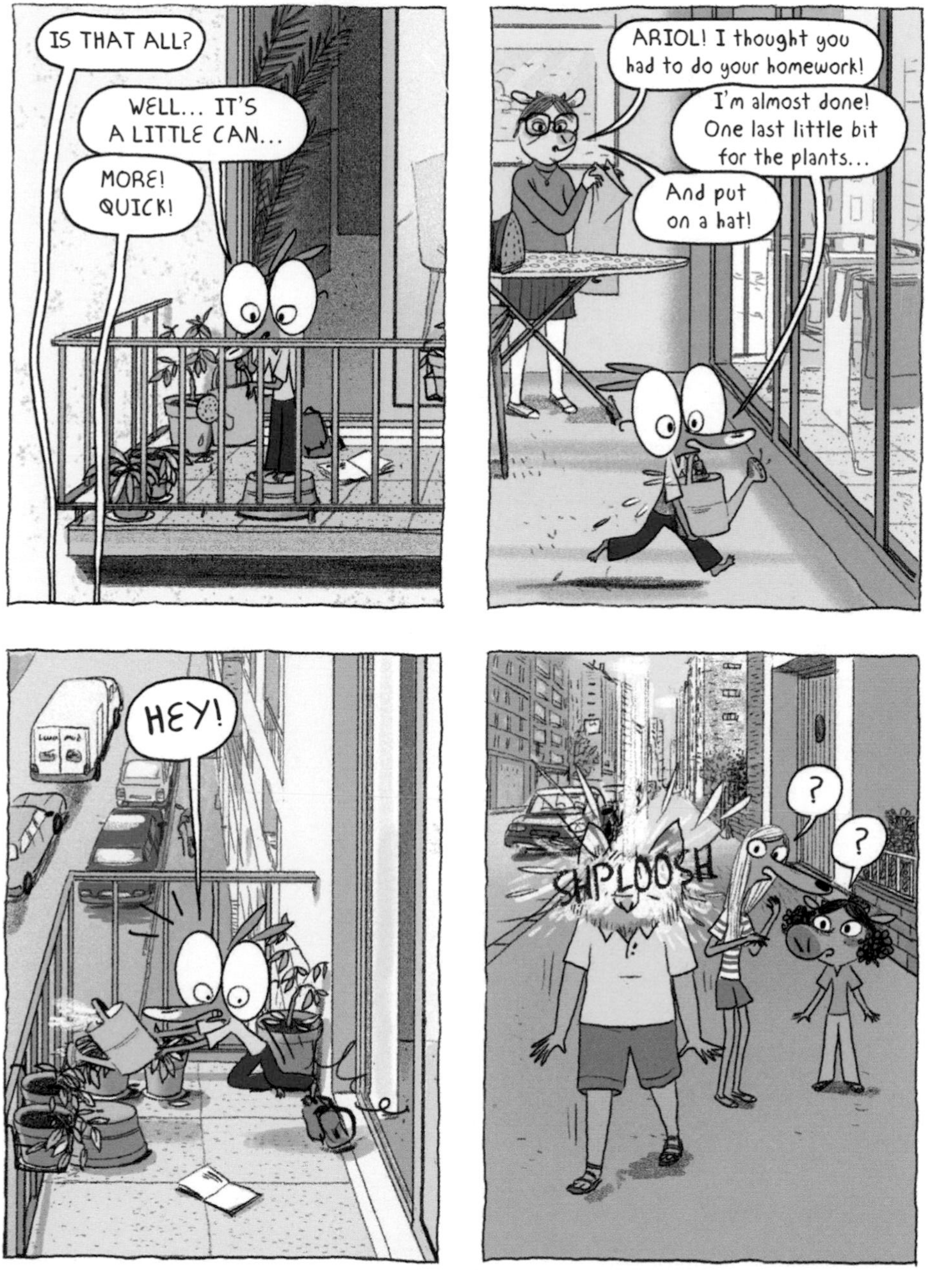
IS THAT ALL?
WELL... IT'S A LITTLE CAN...
MORE! QUICK!
ARIOL! I thought you had to do your homework!
I'm almost done! One last little bit for the plants...
And put on a hat!
HEY!
SHPLOOSH
?
?

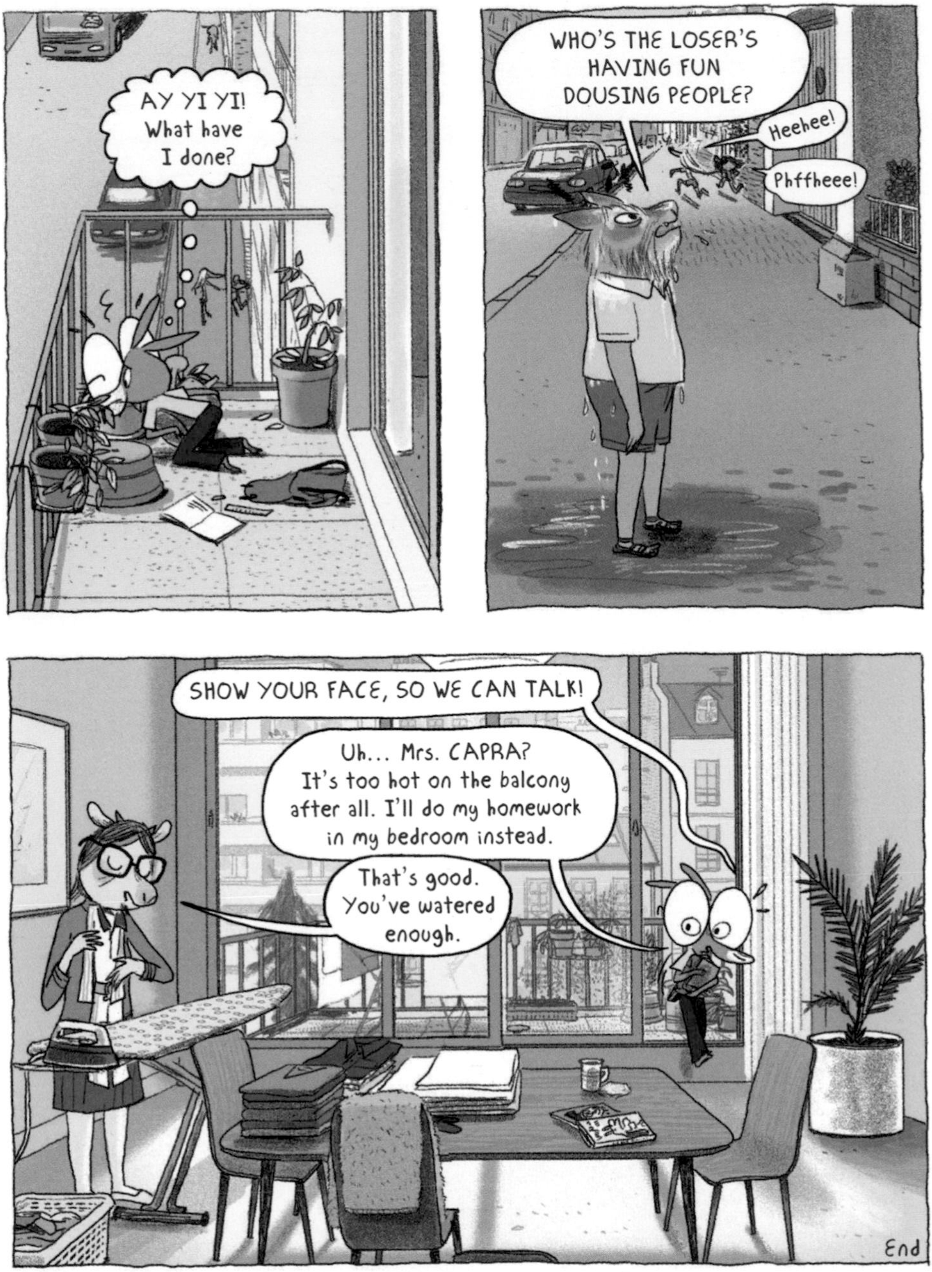
AY YI YI! What have I done?
WHO'S THE LOSER'S HAVING FUN DOUSING PEOPLE?
Heehee!
Phffheee!
SHOW YOUR FACE, SO WE CAN TALK!
Uh... Mrs. CAPRA? It's too hot on the balcony after all. I'll do my homework in my bedroom instead.
That's good. You've watered enough.
End

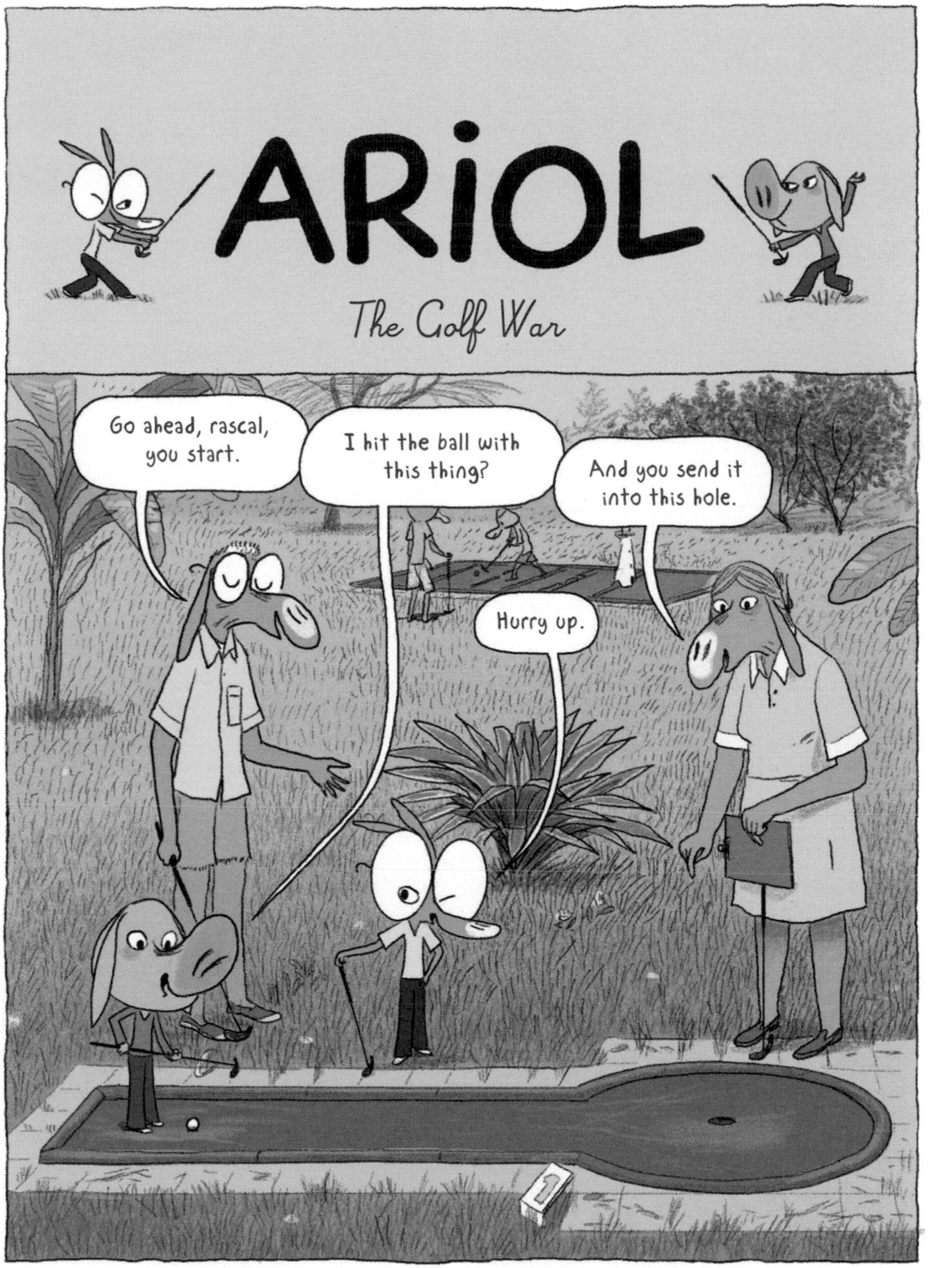
ARiOL
The Golf War
Go ahead, rascal, you start.
I hit the ball with this thing?
And you send it into this hole.
Hurry up.

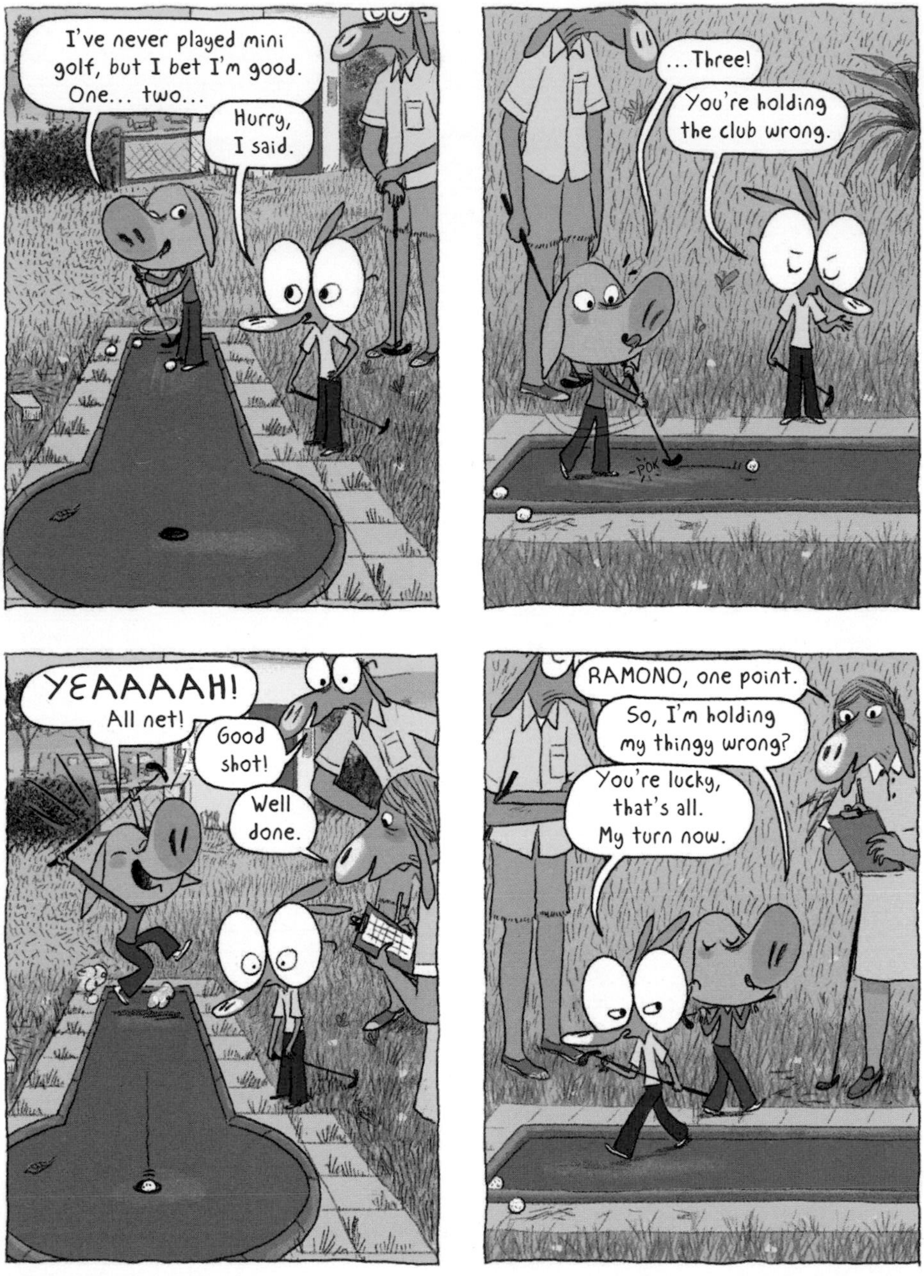
I've never played mini golf, but I bet I'm good. One... two...
Hurry, I said.
...Three!
You're holding the club wrong.
POK
YEAAAAH! All net!
Good shot!
Well done.
RAMONO, one point.
So, I'm holding my thingy wrong?
You're lucky, that's all. My turn now.

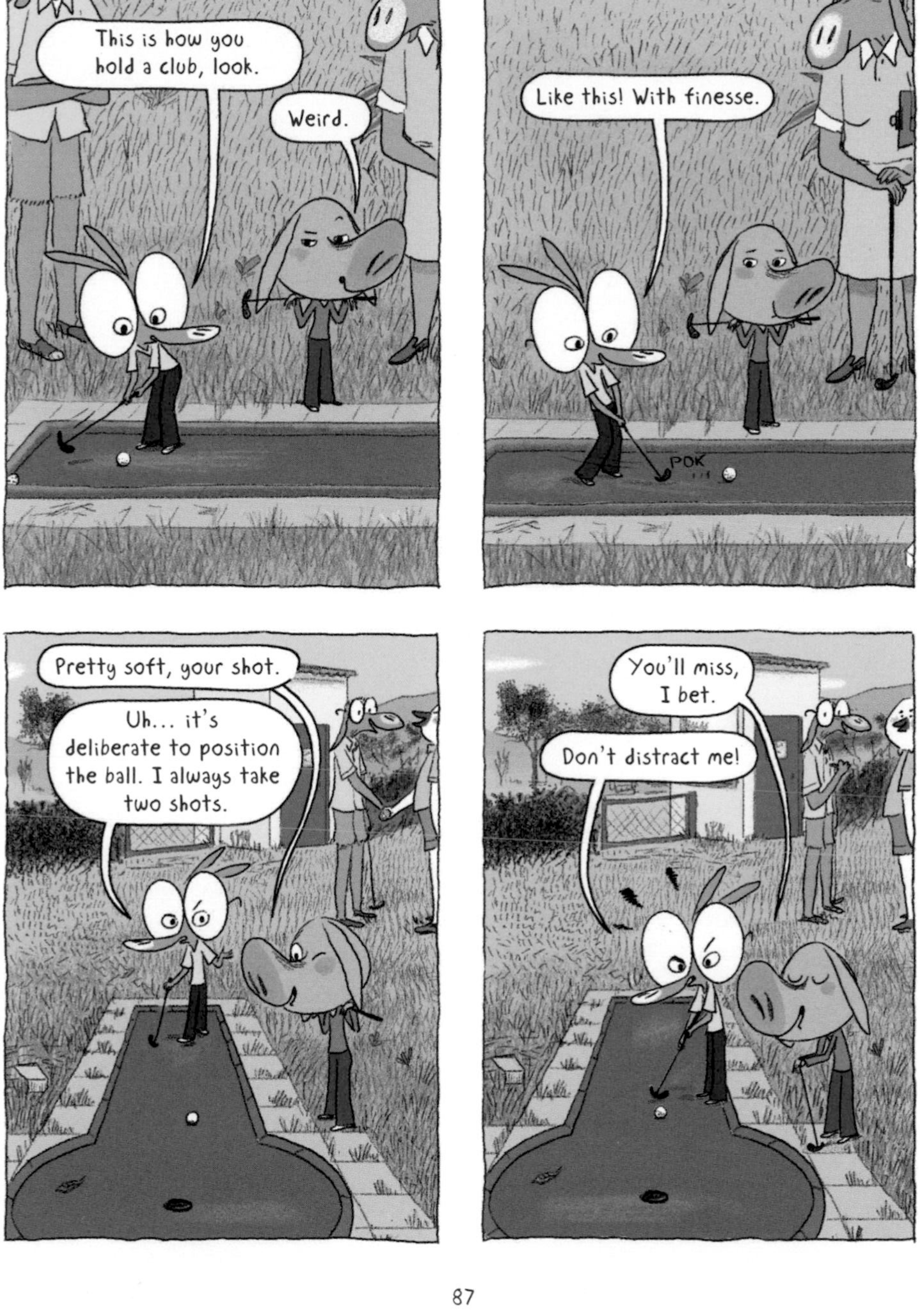
This is how you hold a club, look.
Weird.
Like this! With finesse.
POK
Pretty soft, your shot.
Uh... it's deliberate to position the ball. I always take two shots.
You'll miss, I bet.
Don't distract me!

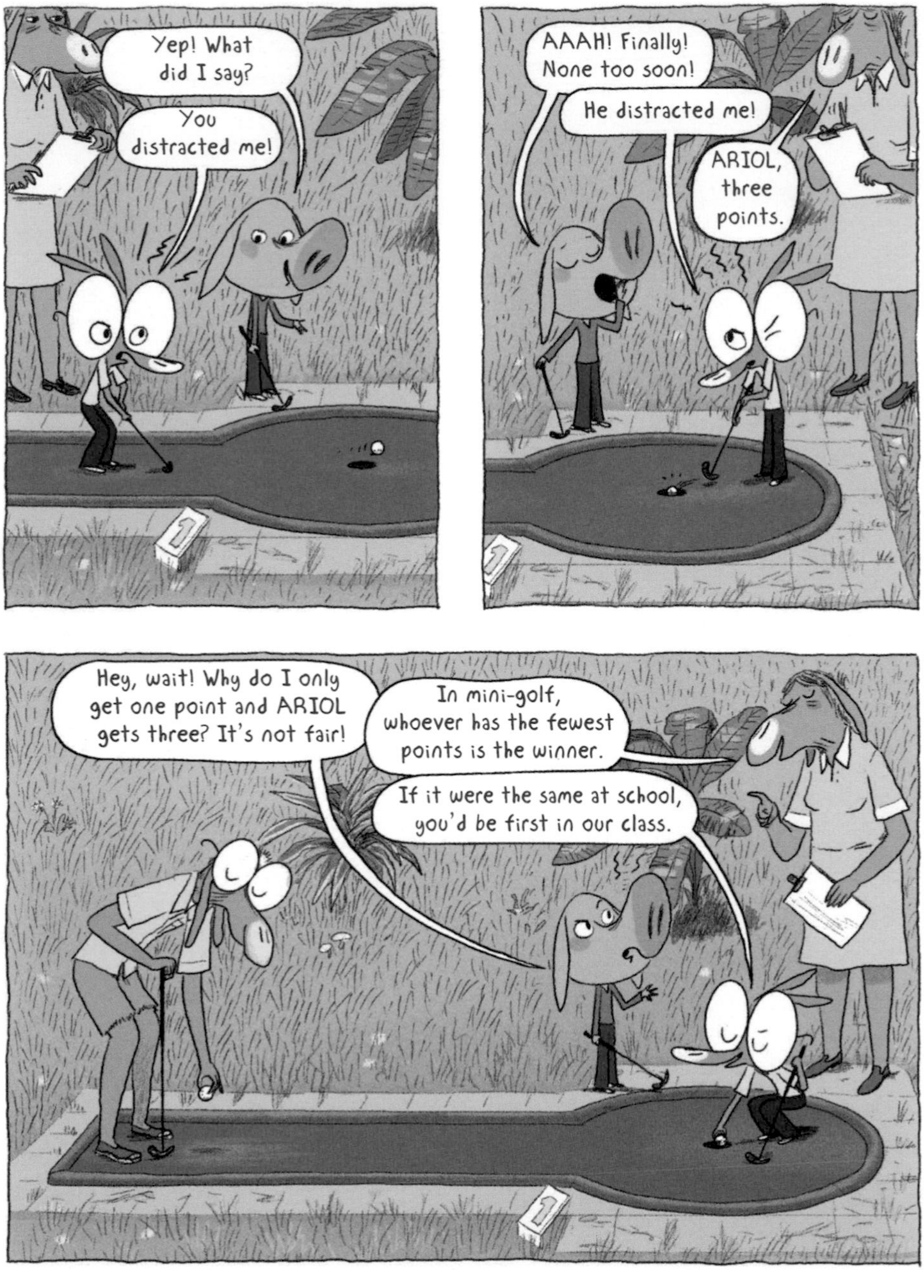
Yep! What did I say?
You distracted me!
AAAH! Finally! None too soon!
He distracted me!
ARIOL, three points.
Hey, wait! Why do I only get one point and ARIOL gets three? It's not fair!
In mini-golf, whoever has the fewest points is the winner.
If it were the same at school, you'd be first in our class.

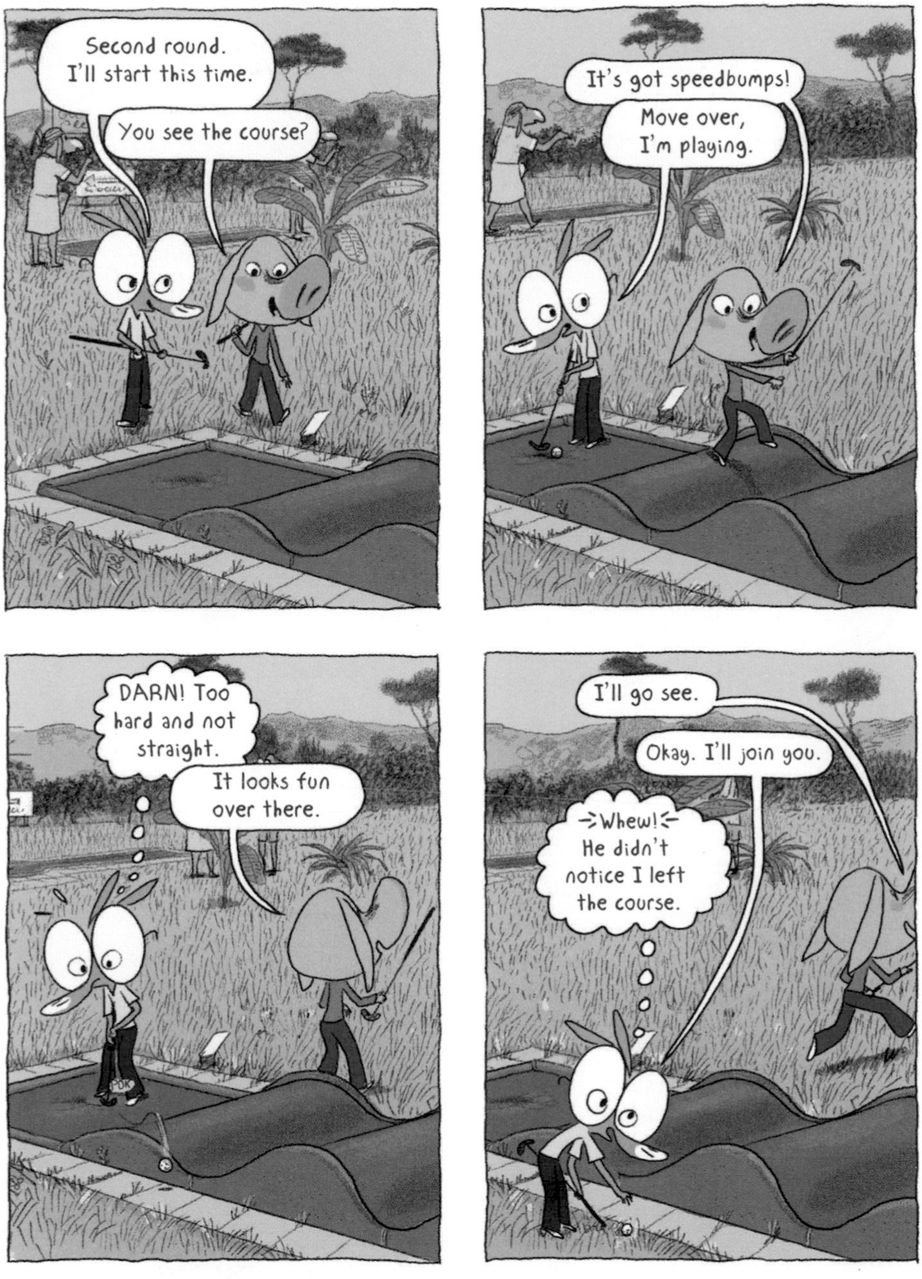
Second round. I'll start this time.
You see the course?
It's got speedbumps!
Move over, I'm playing.
DARN! Too hard and not straight.
It looks fun over there.
POK
I'll go see.
Okay. I'll join you.
Whew! He didn't notice I left the course.

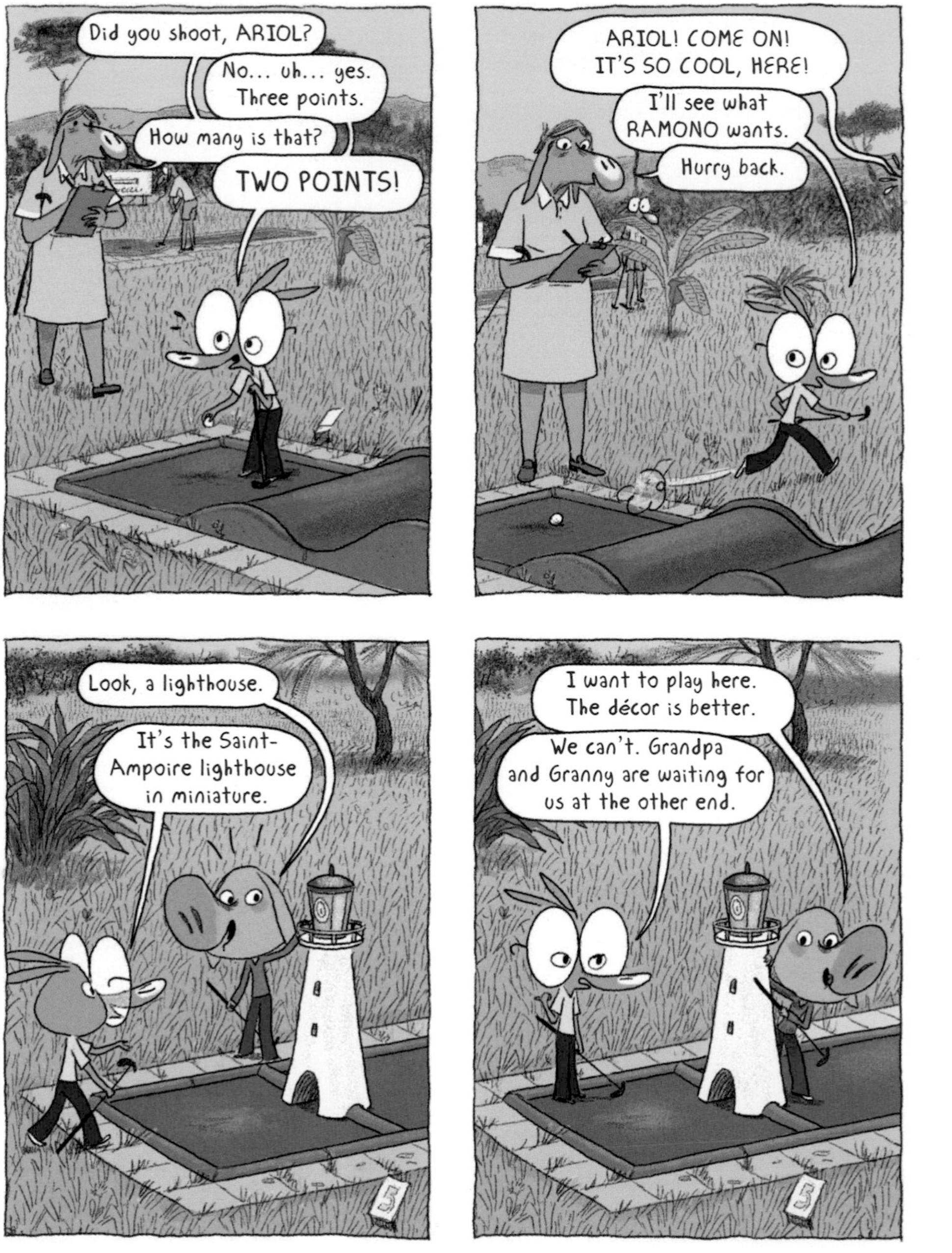
Did you shoot, ARIOL?
No... uh... yes. Three points.
How many is that?
TWO POINTS!
ARIOL! COME ON! IT'S SO COOL, HERE!
I'll see what RAMONO wants.
Hurry back.
Look, a lighthouse.
It's the Saint-Ampoire lighthouse in miniature.
I want to play here. The décor is better.
We can't. Grandpa and Granny are waiting for us at the other end.

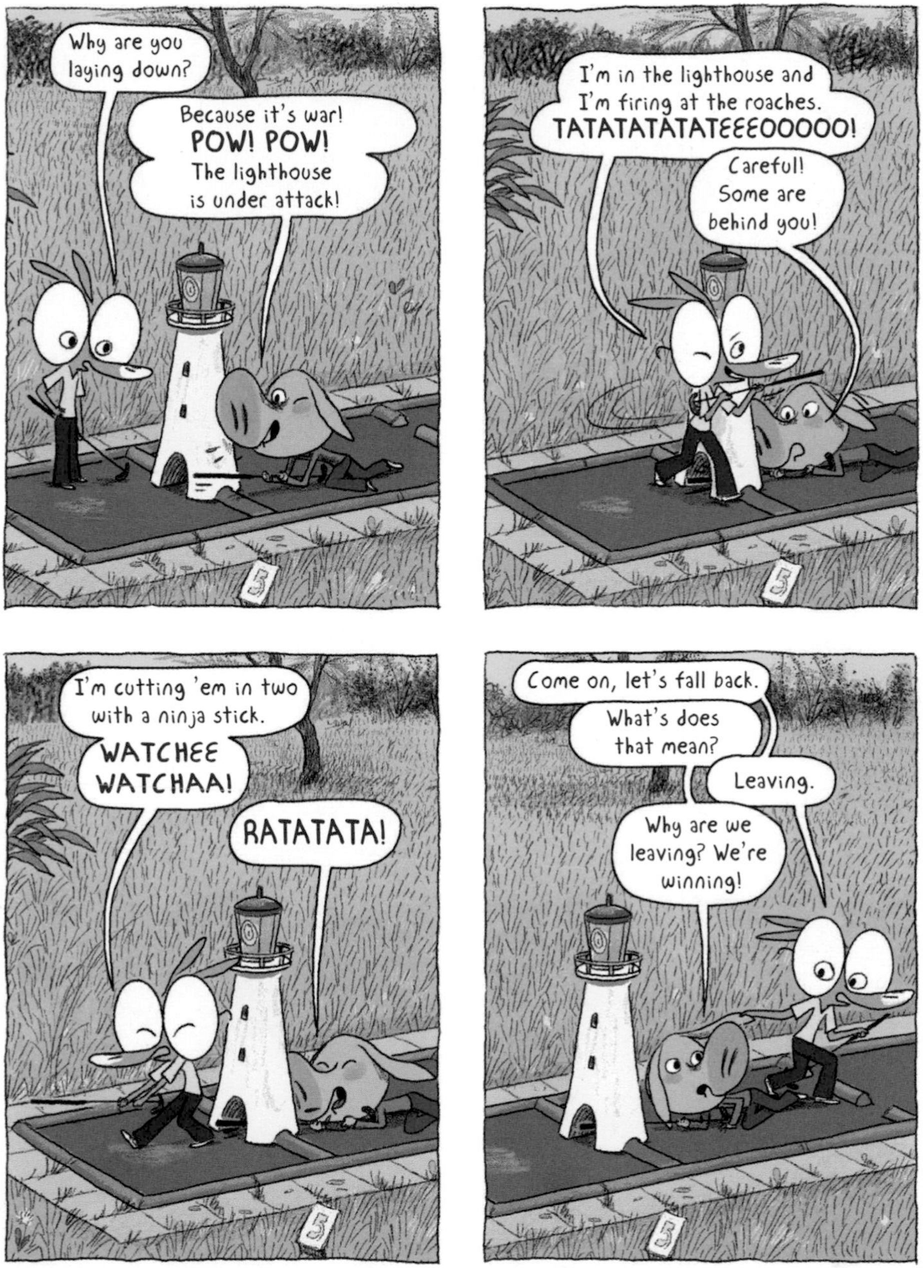
Why are you laying down?
Because it's war! POW! POW! The lighthouse is under attack!
I'm in the lighthouse and I'm firing at the roaches. TATATATATATEEEOOOOO!
Careful! Some are behind you!
I'm cutting 'em in two with a ninja stick.
WATCHEE WATCHAA!
RATATATA!
Come on, let's fall back.
What's does that mean?
Leaving.
Why are we leaving? We're winning!

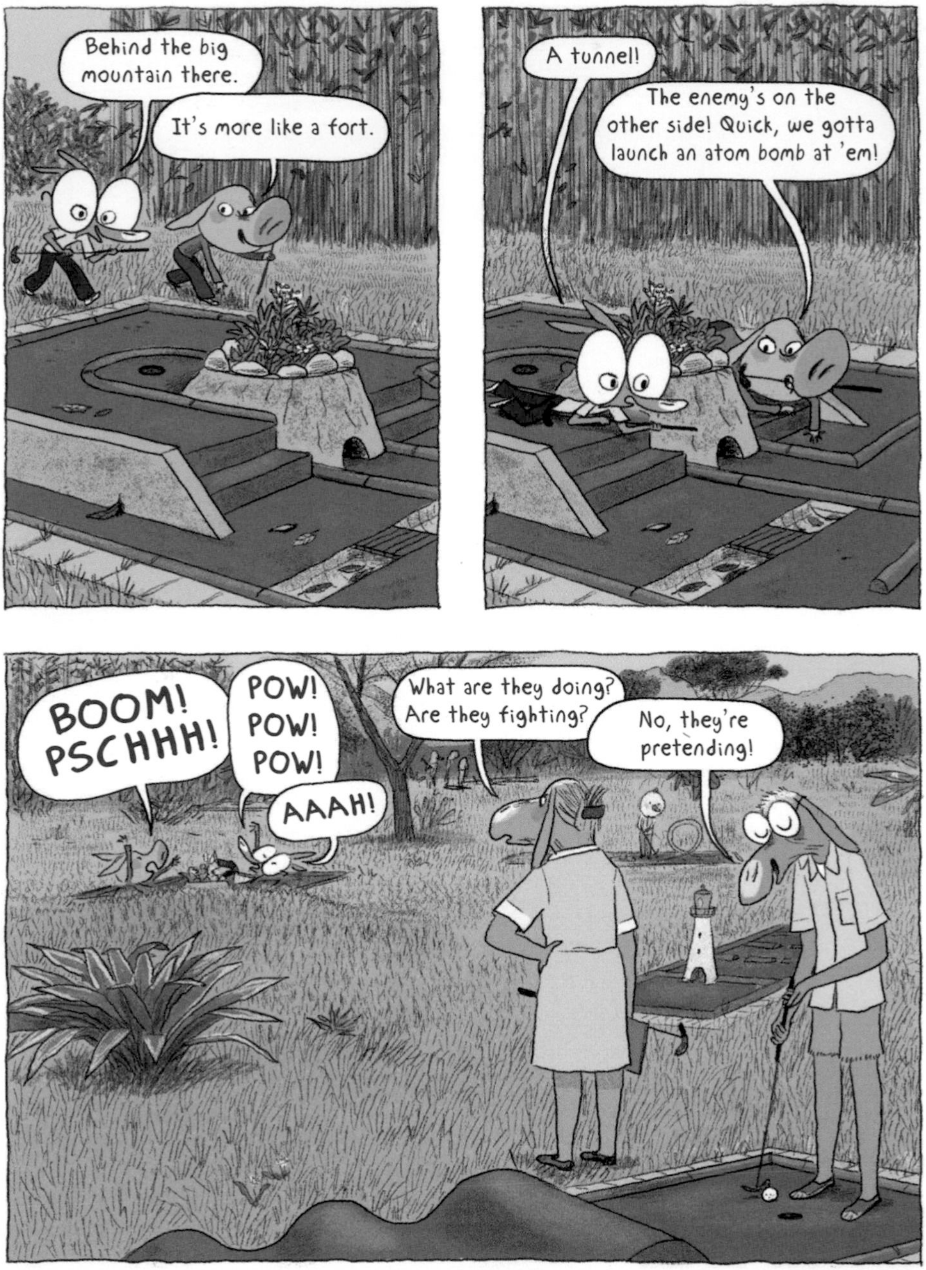
Behind the big mountain there.
It's more like a fort.
A tunnel!
The enemy's on the other side! Quick, we gotta launch an atom bomb at 'em!
BOOM! PSCHHH!
POW! POW! POW!
AAAH!
What are they doing? Are they fighting?
No, they're pretending!

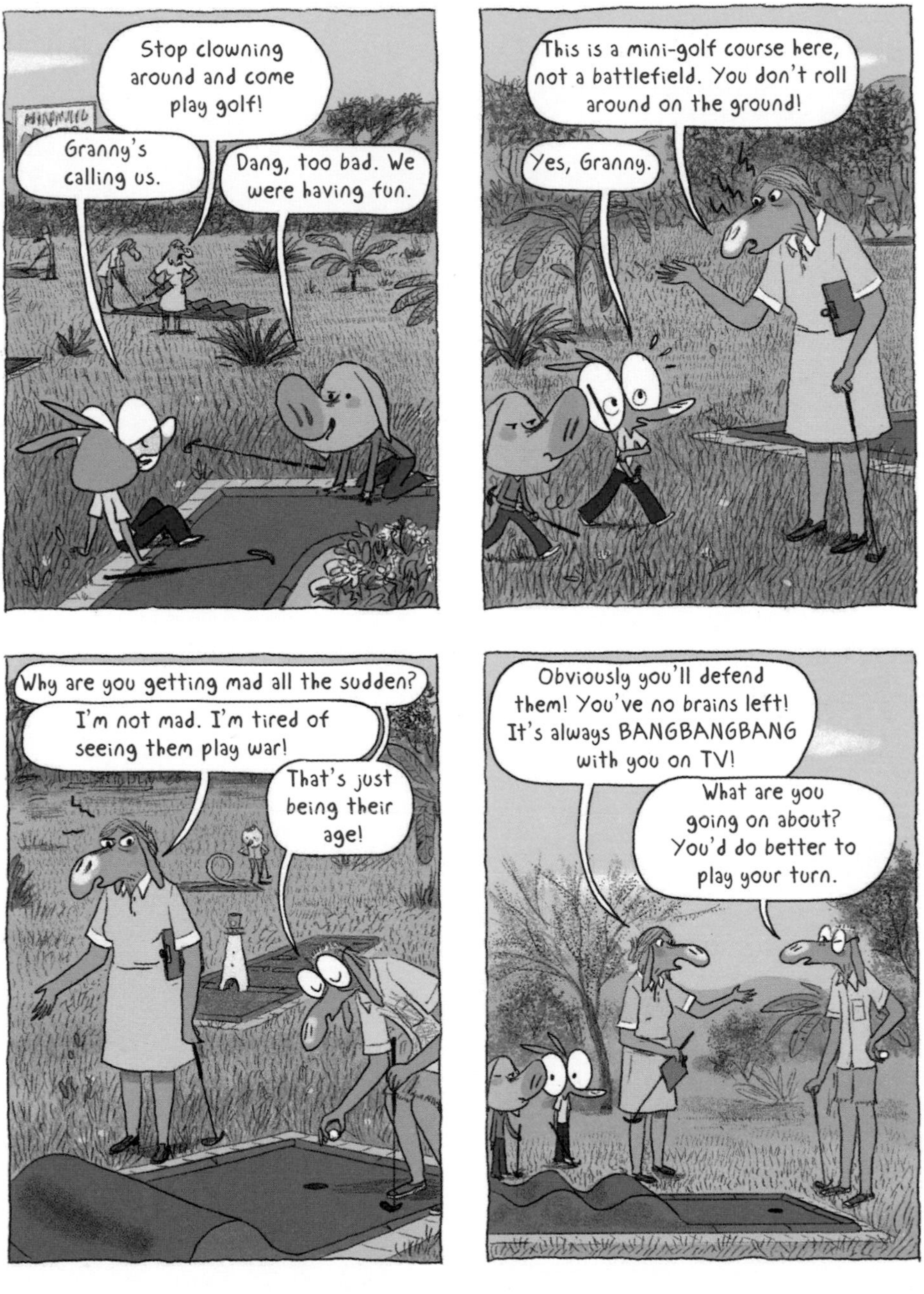
Stop clowning around and come play golf!
Granny's calling us.
Dang, too bad. We were having fun.
This is a mini-golf course here, not a battlefield. You don't roll around on the ground!
Yes, Granny.
Why are you getting mad all the sudden?
I'm not mad. I'm tired of seeing them play war!
That's just being their age!
Obviously you'll defend them! You've no brains left! It's always BANGBANGBANG with you on TV!
What are you going on about? You'd do better to play your turn.

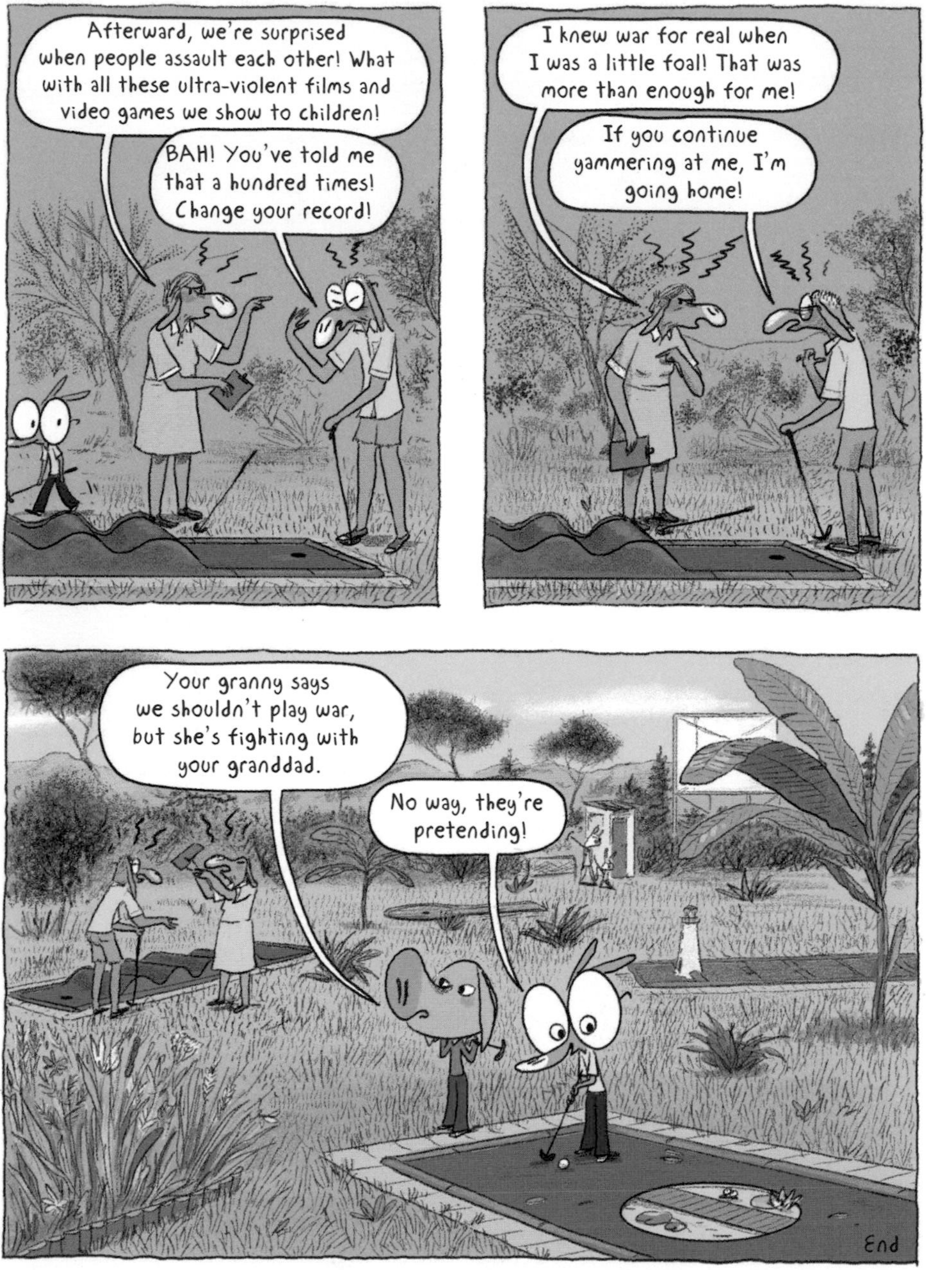
Afterward, we're surprised when people assault each other! What with all these ultra-violent films and video games we show to children!
BAH! You've told me that a hundred times! Change your record!
I knew war for real when I was a little foal! That was more than enough for me!
If you continue yammering at me, I'm going home!
Your granny says we shouldn't play war, but she's fighting with your granddad.
No way, they're pretending!
End

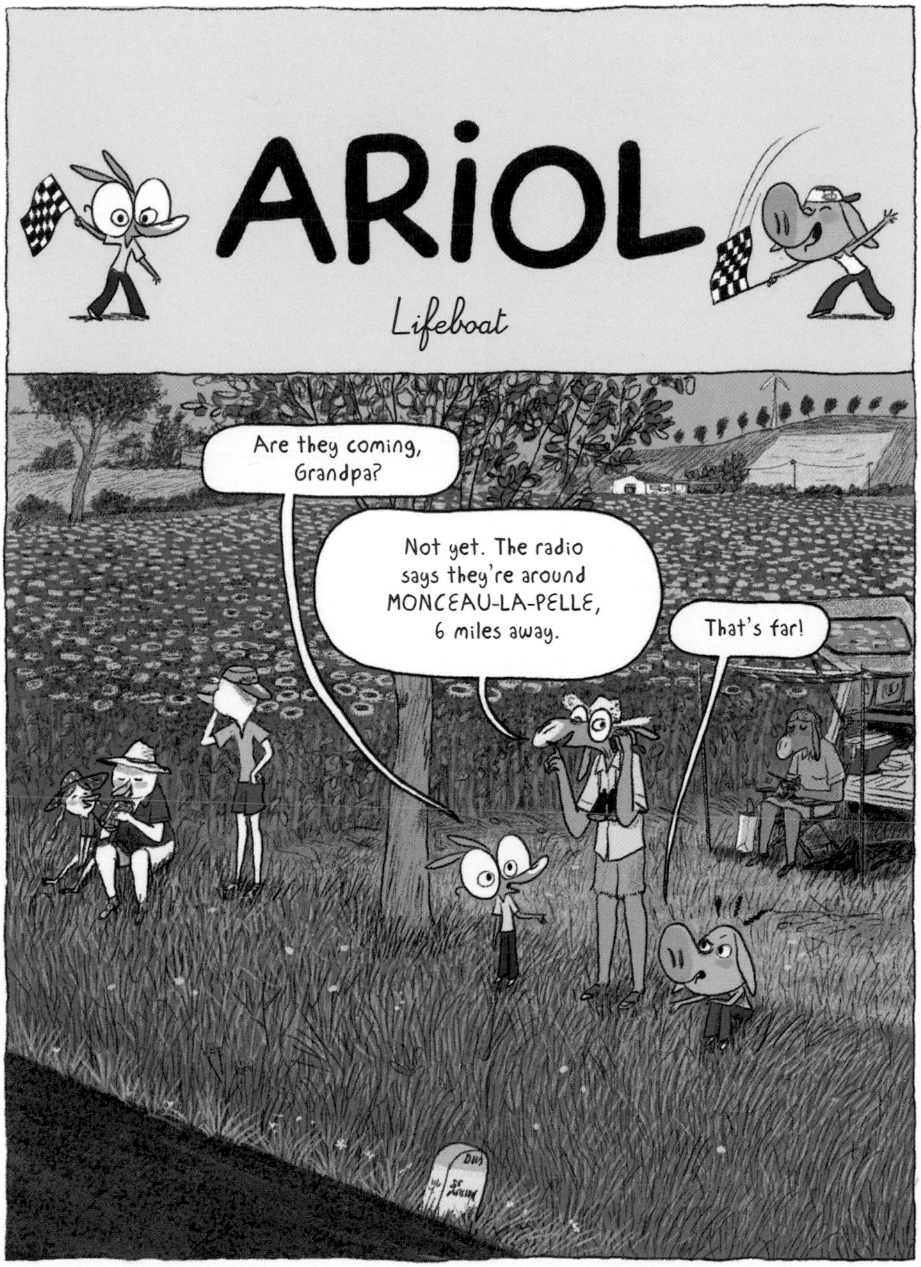
ARiOL
Lifeboat
Are they coming, Grandpa?
Not yet. The radio says they're around MONCEAU-LA-PELLE, 6 miles away.
That's far!

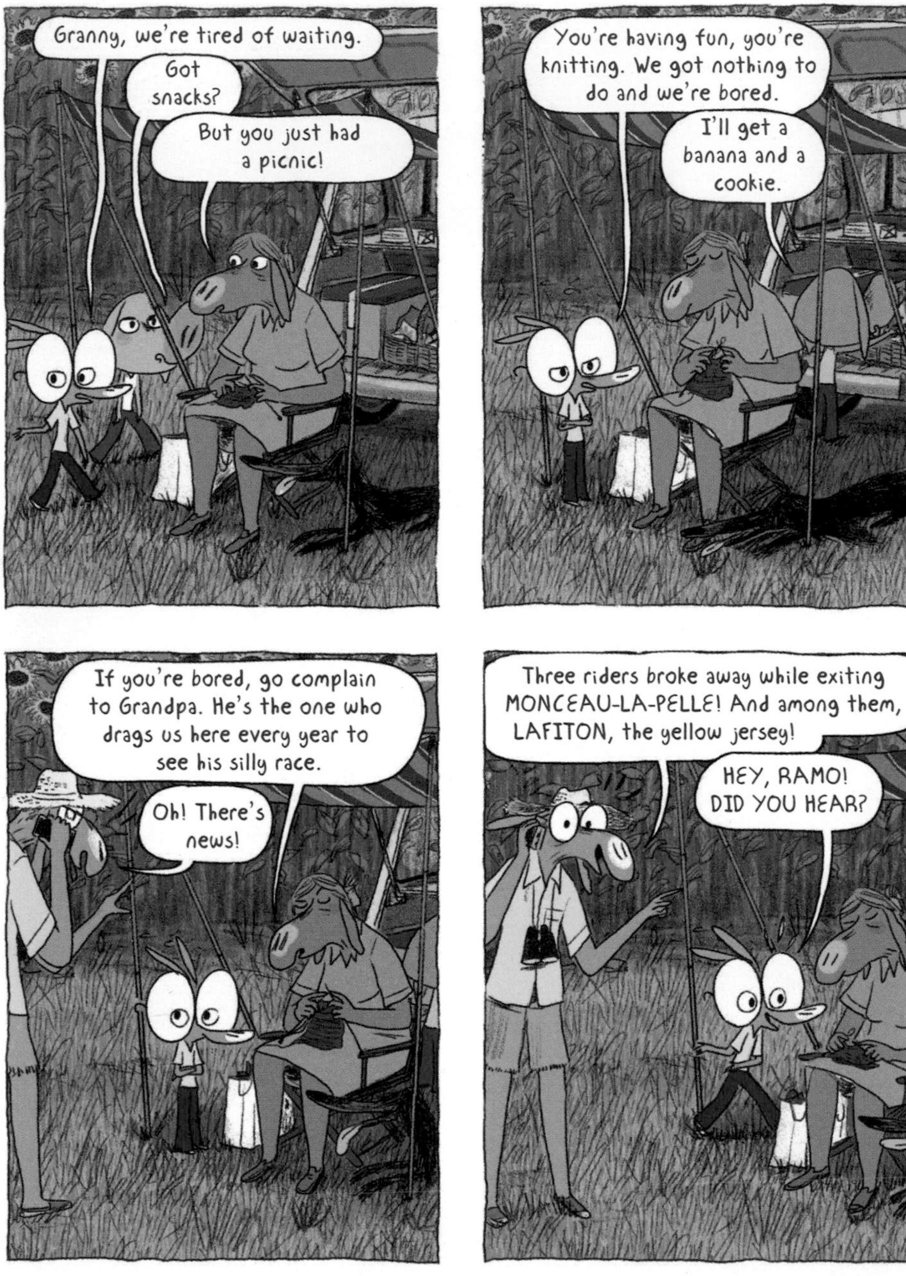
Granny, we're tired of waiting.
Got snacks?
But you just had a picnic!
You're having fun, you're knitting. We got nothing to do and we're bored.
I'll get a banana and a cookie.
If you're bored, go complain to Grandpa. He's the one who drags us here every year to see his silly race.
Oh! There's news!
Three riders broke away while exiting MONCEAU-LA-PELLE! And among them, LAFITON, the yellow jersey!
HEY, RAMO! DID YOU HEAR?

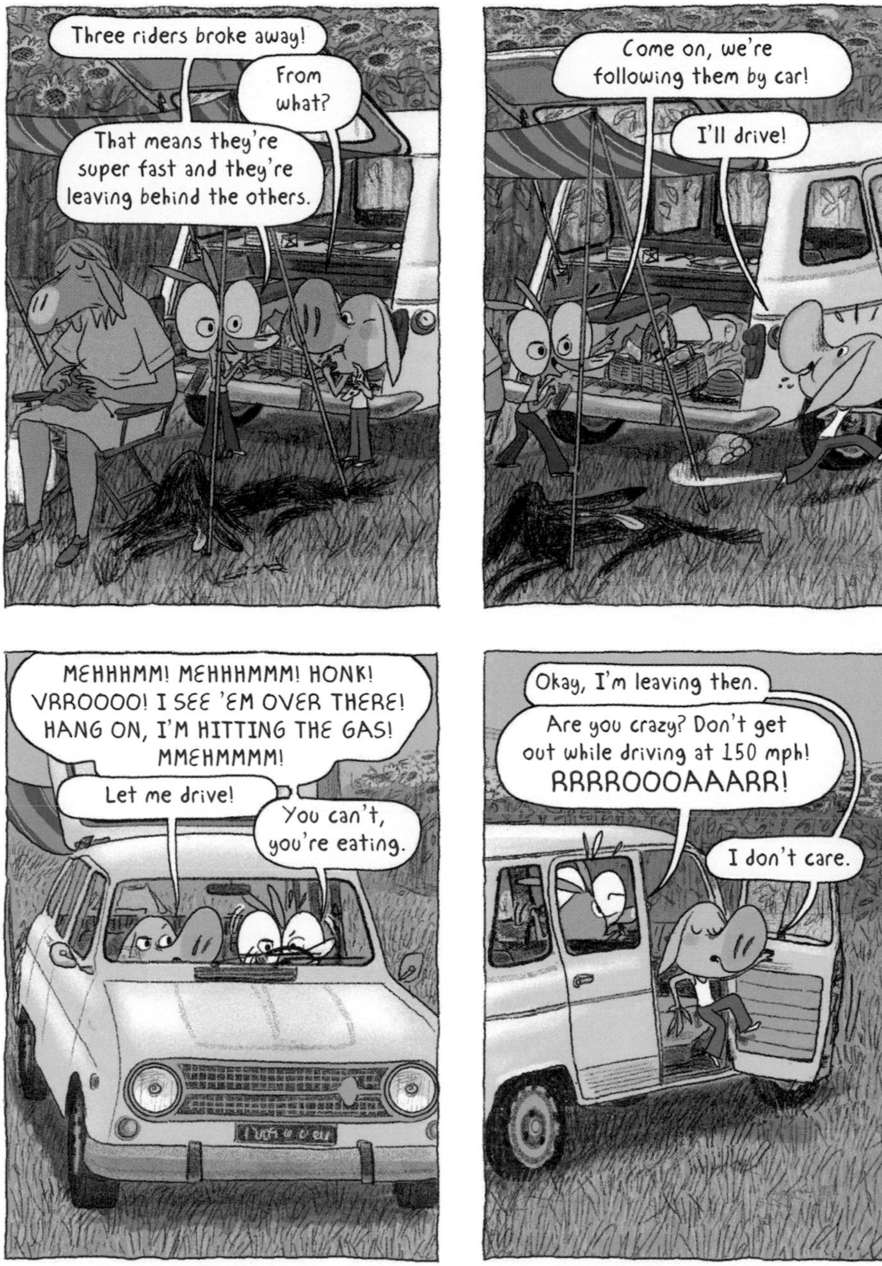
Three riders broke away!
From what?
That means they're super fast and they're leaving behind the others.
Come on, we're following them by car!
I'll drive!
MEHHHMM! MEHHHMMM! HONK! VRROOOO! I SEE 'EM OVER THERE! HANG ON, I'M HITTING THE GAS! MMEHMMMM!
Let me drive!
You can't, you're eating.
Okay, I'm leaving then.
Are you crazy? Don't get out while driving at 150 mph! RRRROOOAAARR!
I don't care.

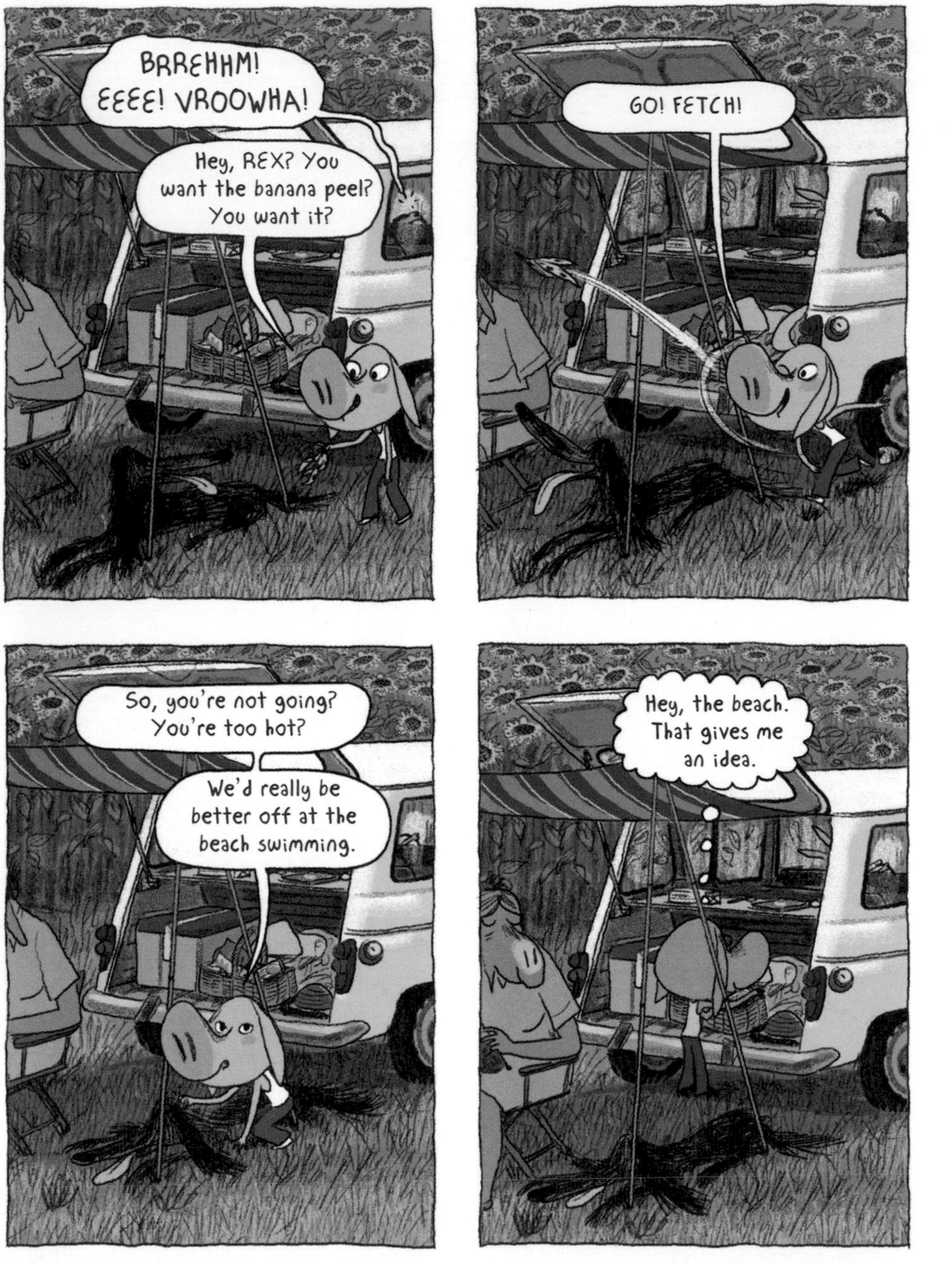
BRRЕHHM! EEEE! VROOWHA!
Hey, REX? You want the banana peel? You want it?
GO! FETCH!
So, you're not going? You're too hot?
We'd really be better off at the beach swimming.
Hey, the beach. That gives me an idea.

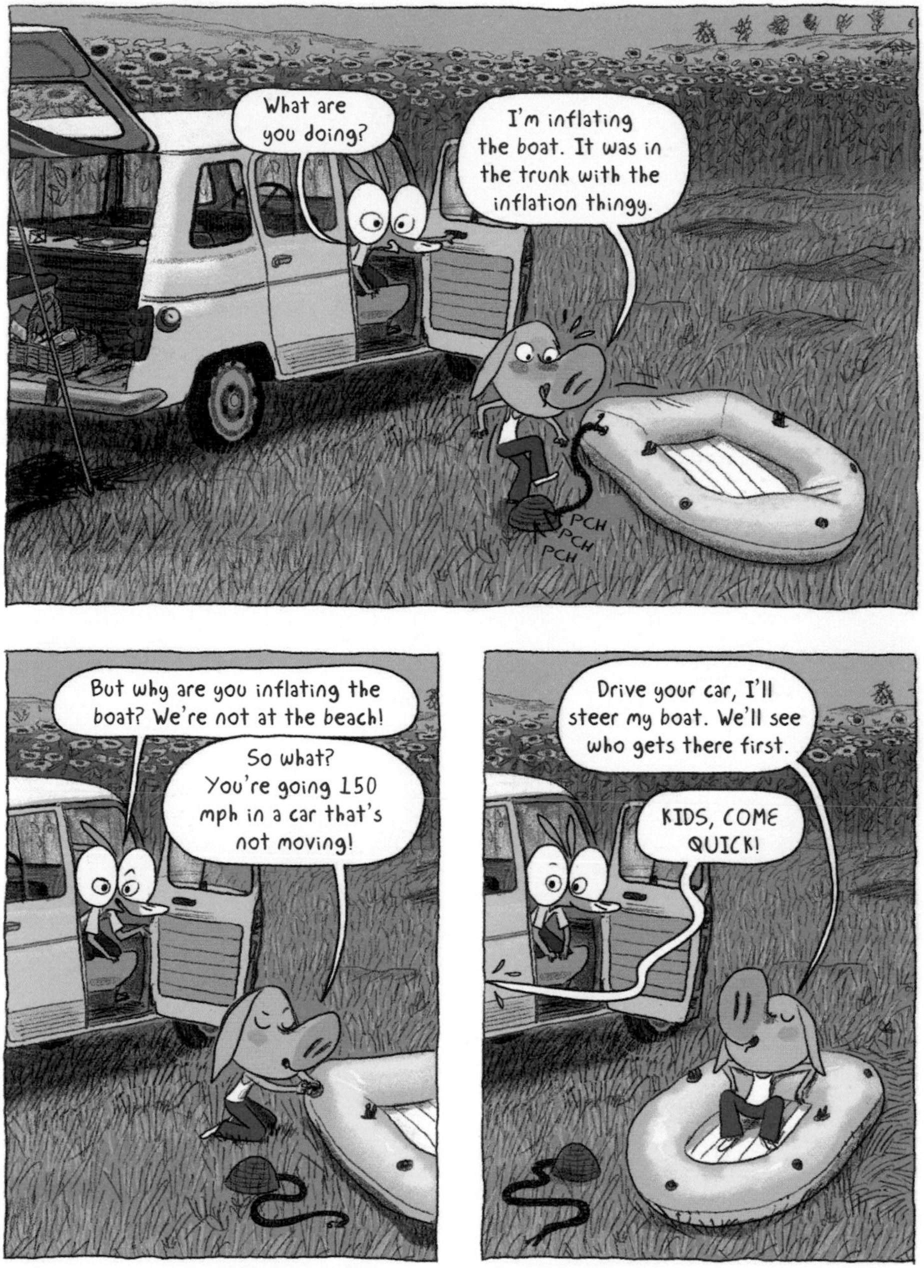
What are you doing?
I'm inflating the boat. It was in the trunk with the inflation thingy.
PCH PCH PCH
But why are you inflating the boat? We're not at the beach!
So what? You're going 150 mph in a car that's not moving!
Drive your car, I'll steer my boat. We'll see who gets there first.
KIDS, COME QUICK!

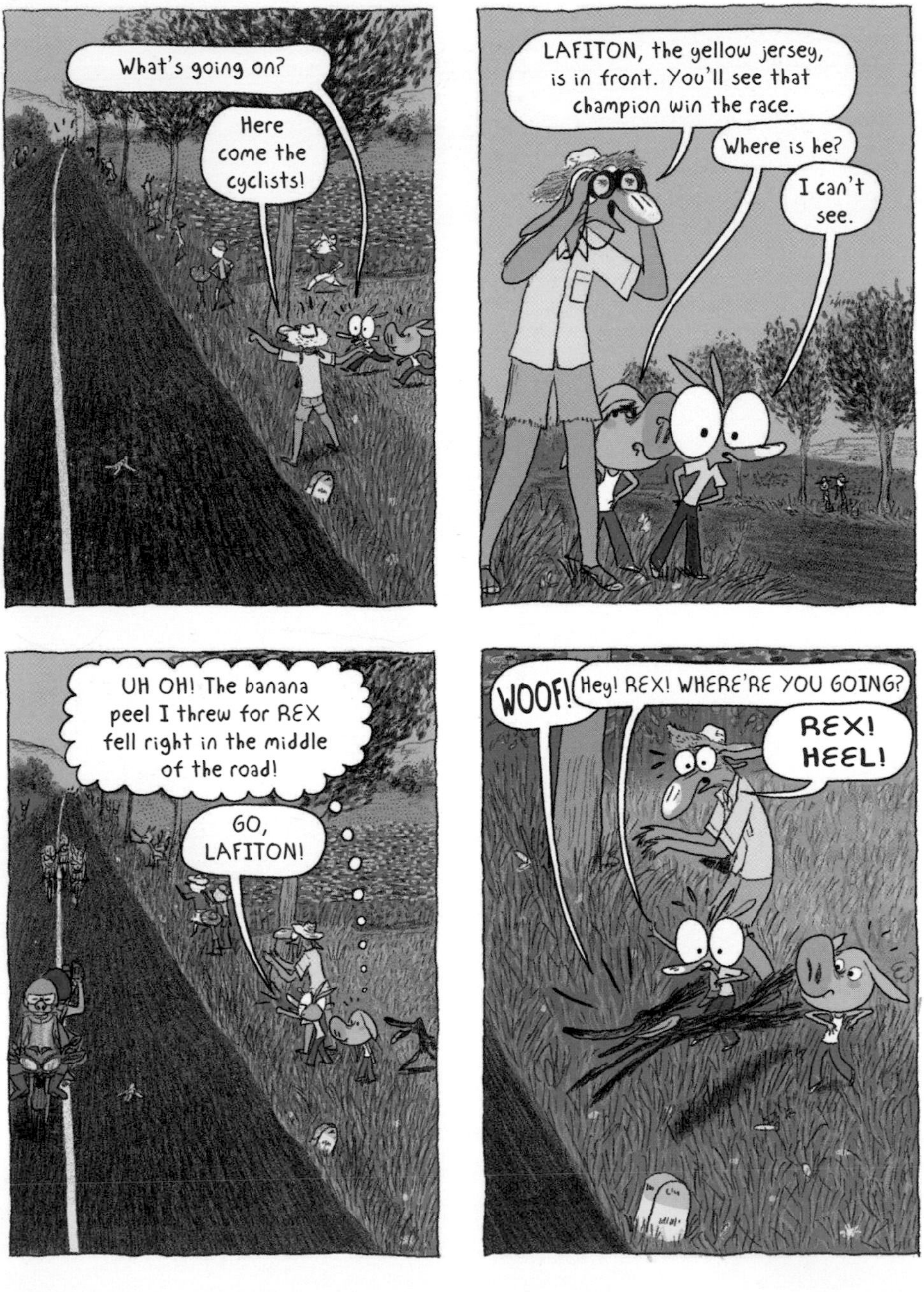
What's going on?
Here come the cyclists!
LAFITON, the yellow jersey, is in front. You'll see that champion win the race.
Where is he?
I can't see.
UH OH! The banana peel I threw for REX fell right in the middle of the road!
GO, LAFITON!
WOOF!
Hey! REX! WHERE'RE YOU GOING?
REX! HEEL!

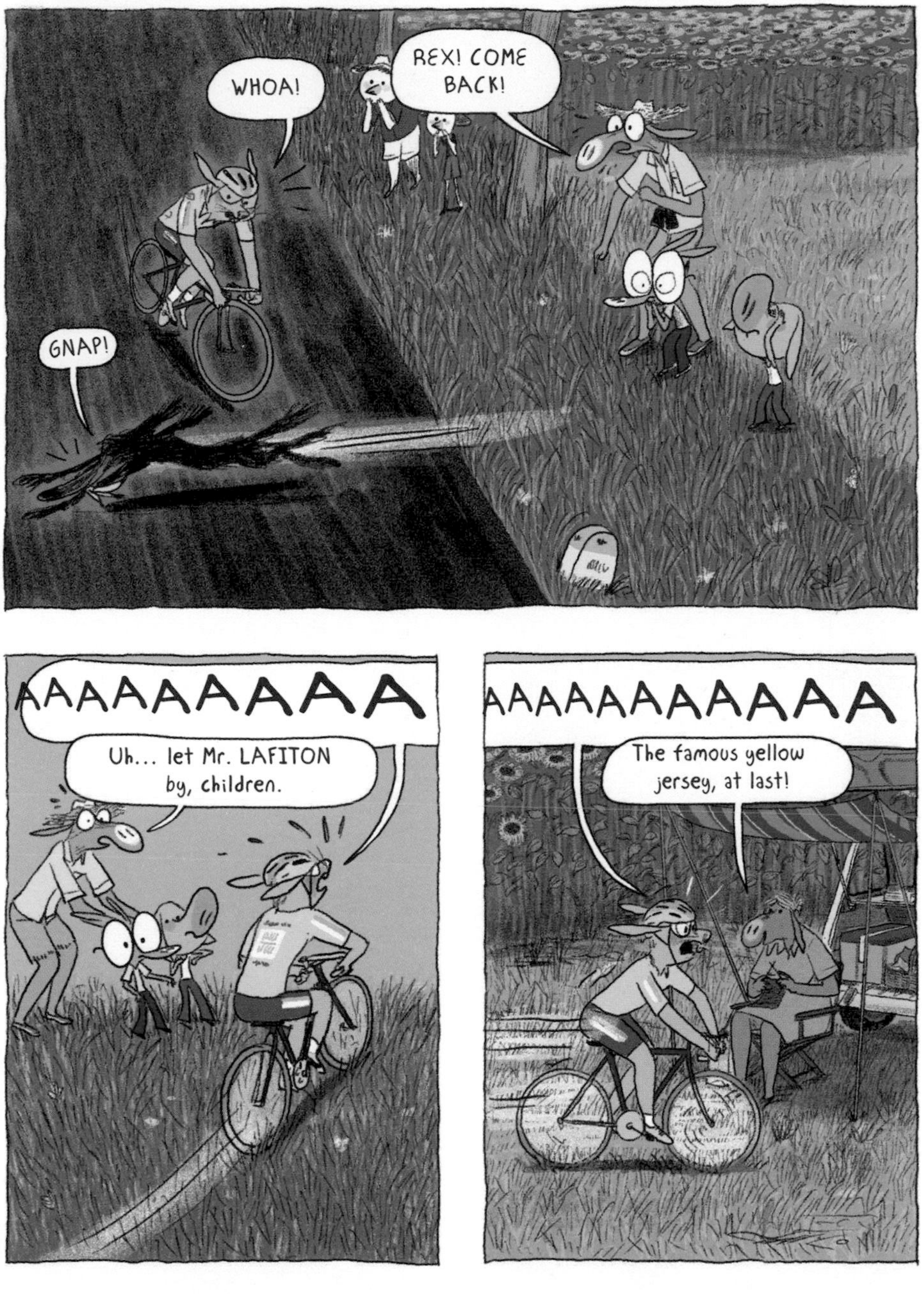
WHOA!
REX! COME BACK!
GNAP!
AAAAAAAAA
Uh... let Mr. LAFITON by, children.
AAAAAAAAAAAA
The famous yellow jersey, at last!

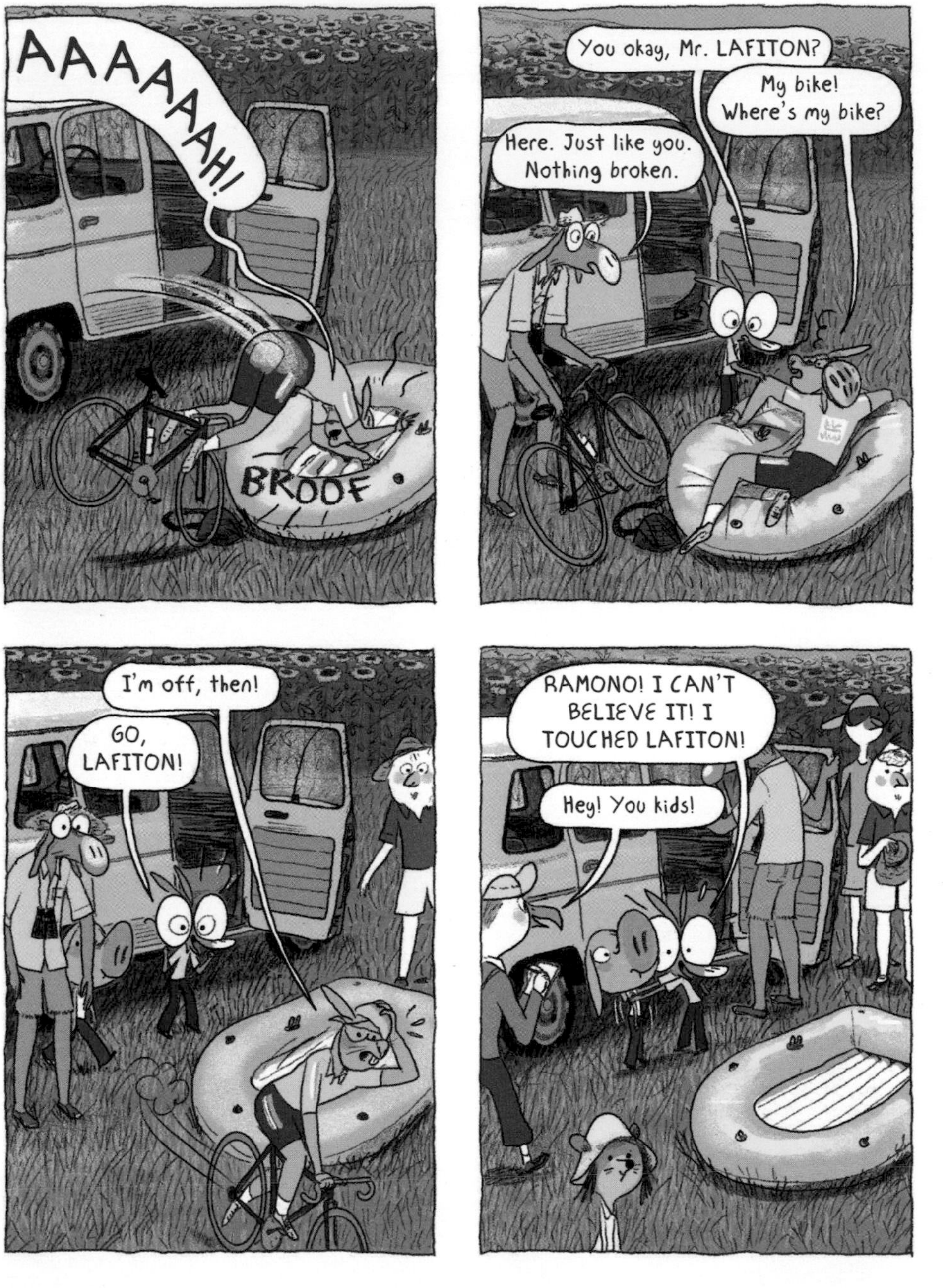
AAAAAAAH!
BROOF
You okay, Mr. LAFITON?
My bike! Where's my bike?
Here. Just like you. Nothing broken.
I'm off, then!
GO, LAFITON!
RAMONO! I CAN'T BELIEVE IT! I TOUCHED LAFITON!
Hey! You kids!

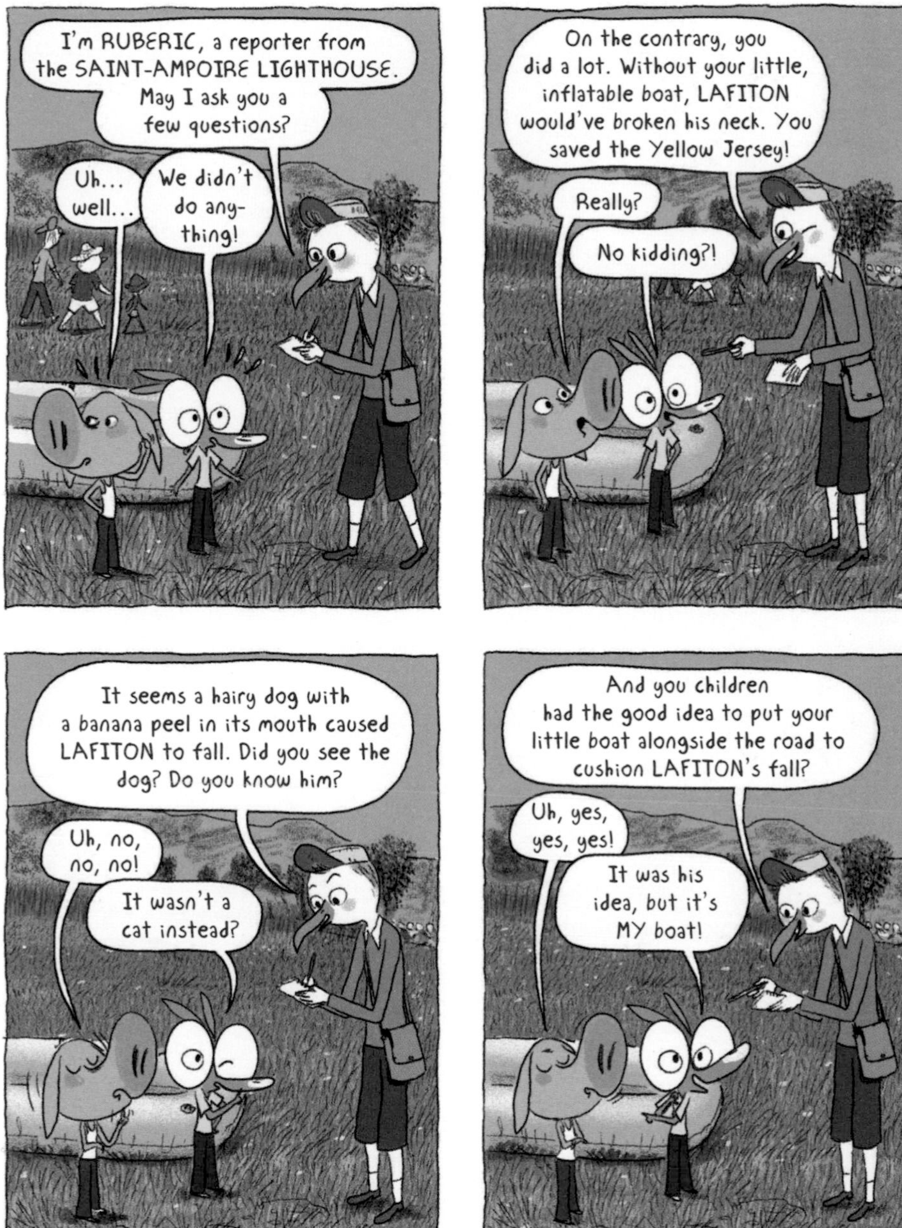
I'm RUBERIC, a reporter from the SAINT-AMPOIRE LIGHTHOUSE. May I ask you a few questions?
Uh... well...
We didn't do any-thing!
On the contrary, you did a lot. Without your little, inflatable boat, LAFITON would've broken his neck. You saved the Yellow Jersey!
Really?
No kidding?!
It seems a hairy dog with a banana peel in its mouth caused LAFITON to fall. Did you see the dog? Do you know him?
Uh, no, no, no!
It wasn't a cat instead?
And you children had the good idea to put your little boat alongside the road to cushion LAFITON's fall?
Uh, yes, yes, yes!
It was his idea, but it's MY boat!

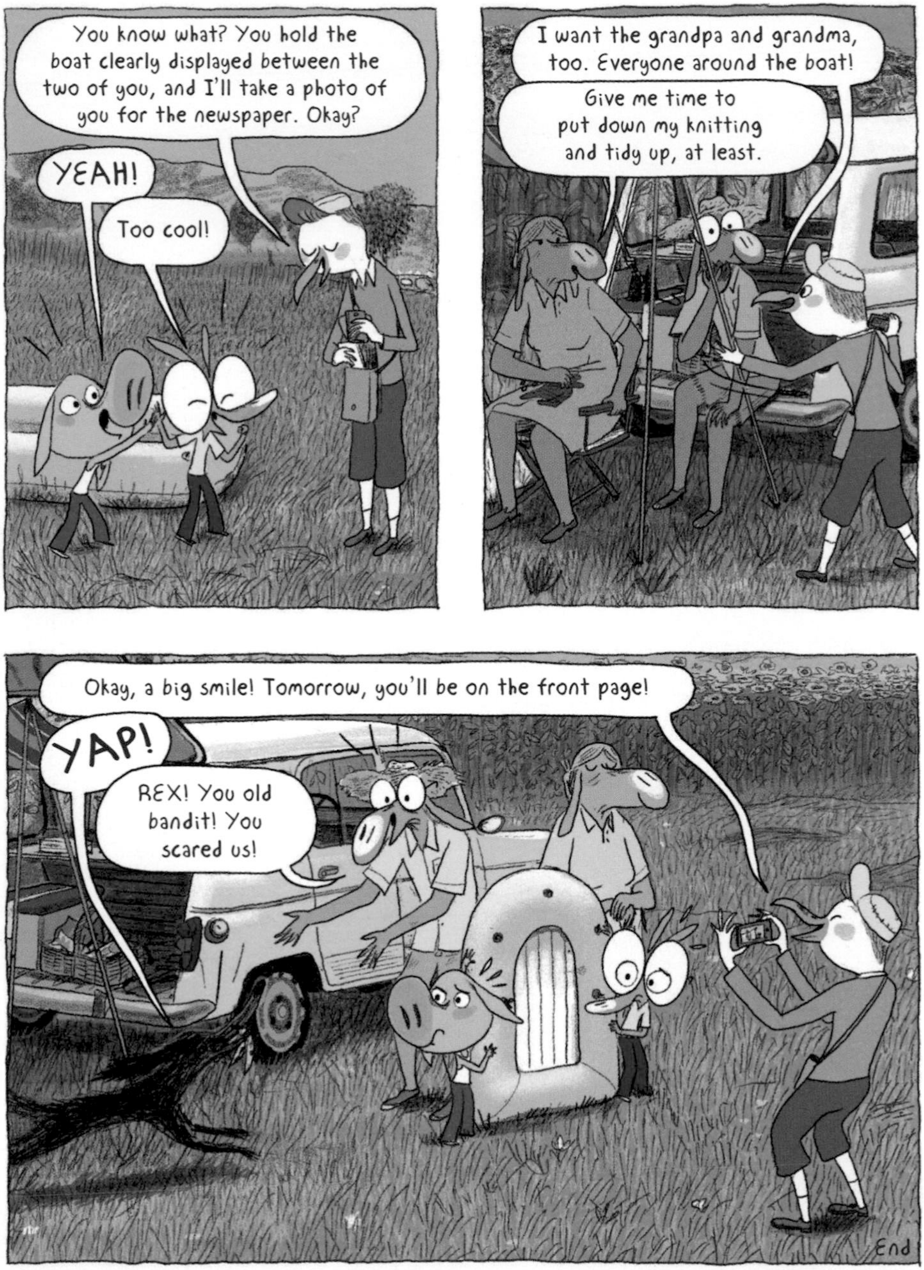
You know what? You hold the boat clearly displayed between the two of you, and I'll take a photo of you for the newspaper. Okay?
YEAH!
Too cool!
I want the grandpa and grandma, too. Everyone around the boat!
Give me time to put down my knitting and tidy up, at least.
Okay, a big smile! Tomorrow, you'll be on the front page!
YAP!
REX! You old bandit! You scared us!
End

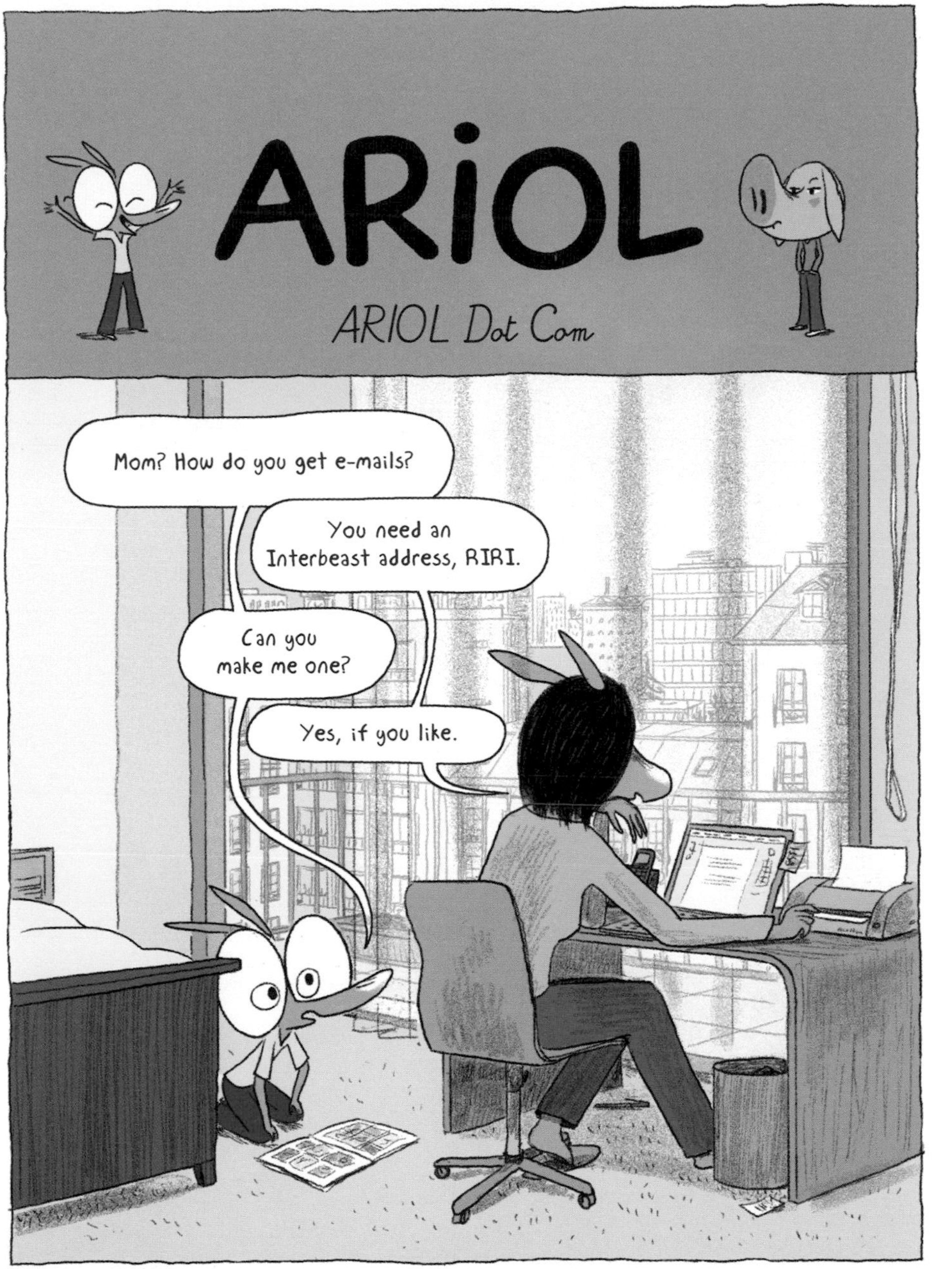
ARiOL
ARIOL Dot Com
Mom? How do you get e-mails?
You need an Interbeast address, RIRI.
Can you make me one?
Yes, if you like.

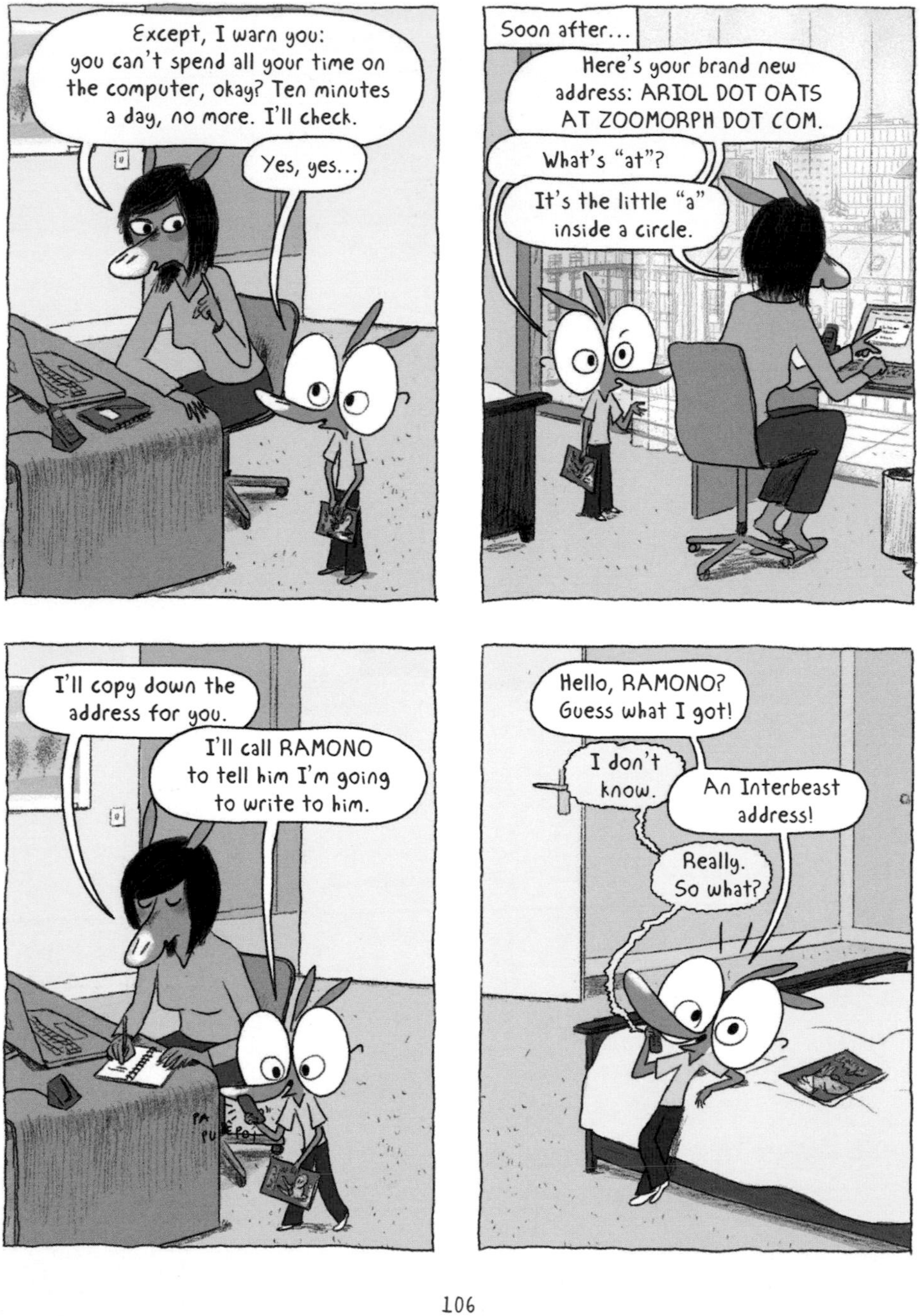
Except, I warn you: you can't spend all your time on the computer, okay? Ten minutes a day, no more. I'll check.
Yes, yes...
Soon after...
Here's your brand new address: ARIOL DOT OATS AT ZOOMORPH DOT COM.
What's "at"?
It's the little "a" inside a circle.
I'll copy down the address for you.
I'll call RAMONO to tell him I'm going to write to him.
Hello, RAMONO? Guess what I got!
I don't know.
An Interbeast address!
Really. So what?

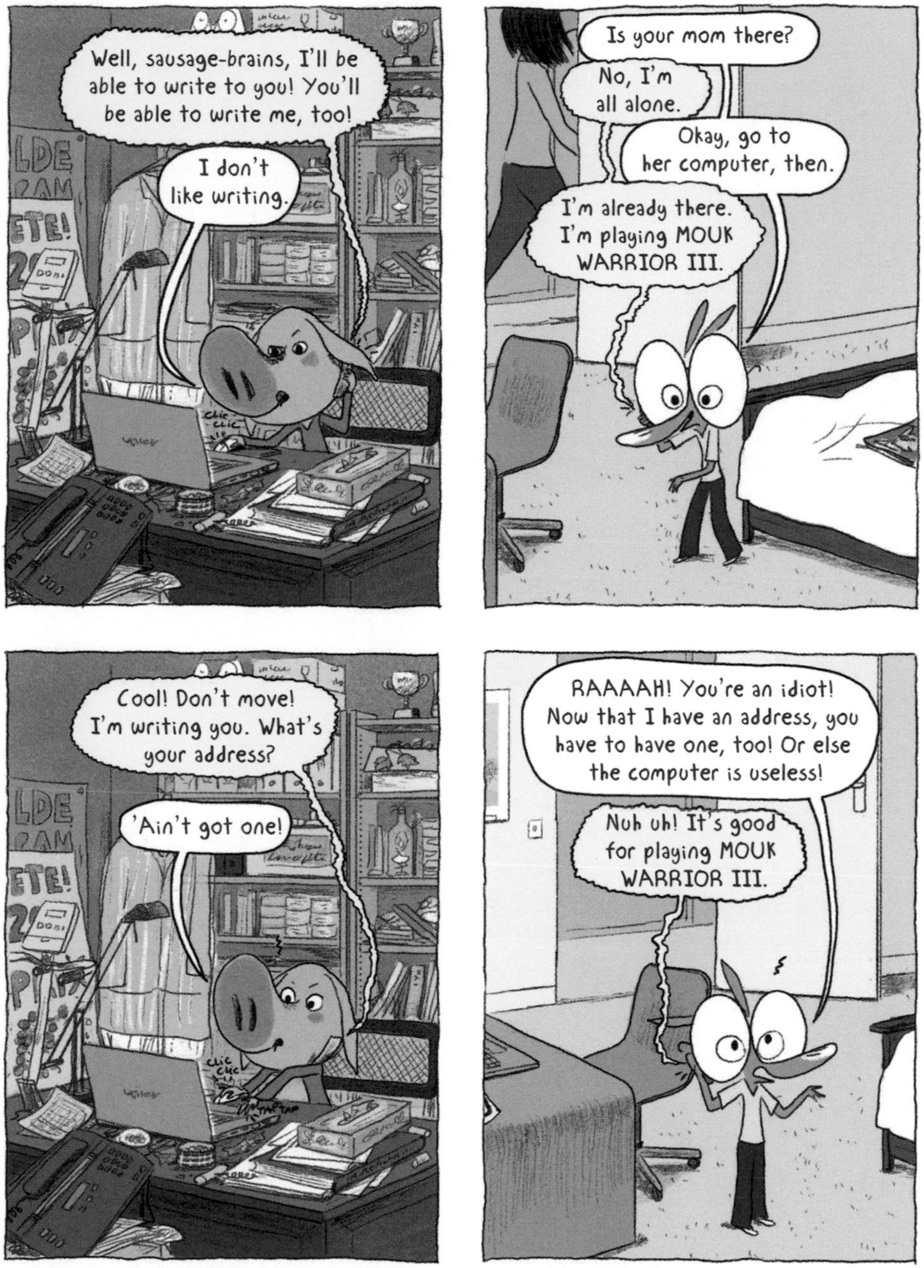
Well, sausage-brains, I'll be able to write to you! You'll be able to write me, too!
I don't like writing.
Is your mom there?
No, I'm all alone.
Okay, go to her computer, then.
I'm already there. I'm playing MOUK WARRIOR III.
Cool! Don't move! I'm writing you. What's your address?
'Ain't got one!
RAAAAH! You're an idiot! Now that I have an address, you have to have one, too! Or else the computer is useless!
Nuh uh! It's good for playing MOUK WARRIOR III.

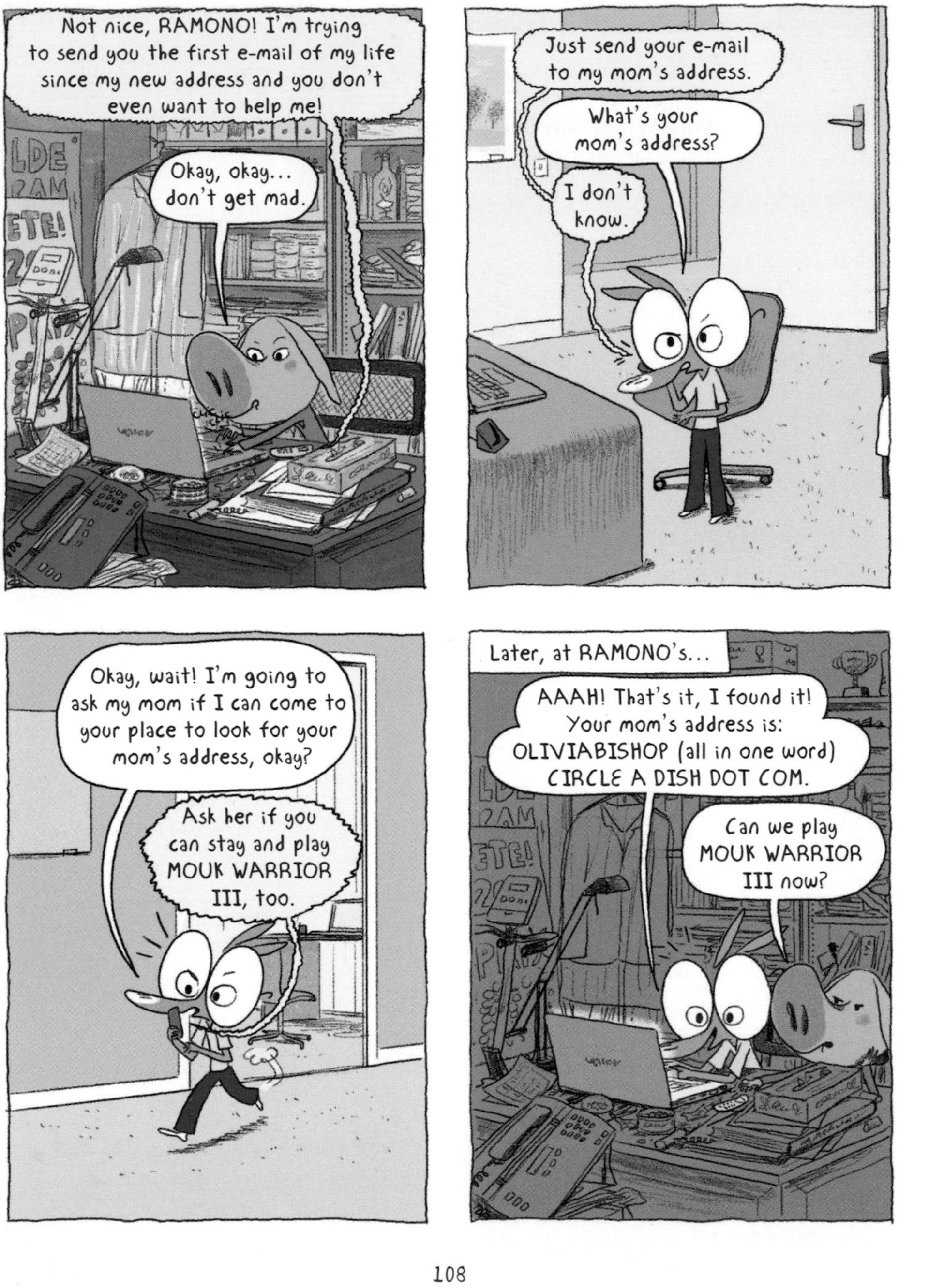
Not nice, RAMONO! I'm trying to send you the first e-mail of my life since my new address and you don't even want to help me!
Okay, okay... don't get mad.
Just send your e-mail to my mom's address.
What's your mom's address?
I don't know.
Okay, wait! I'm going to ask my mom if I can come to your place to look for your mom's address, okay?
Ask her if you can stay and play MOUK WARRIOR III, too.
Later, at RAMONO's...
AAAH! That's it, I found it! Your mom's address is: OLIVIABISHOP (all in one word) CIRCLE A DISH DOT COM.
Can we play MOUK WARRIOR III now?

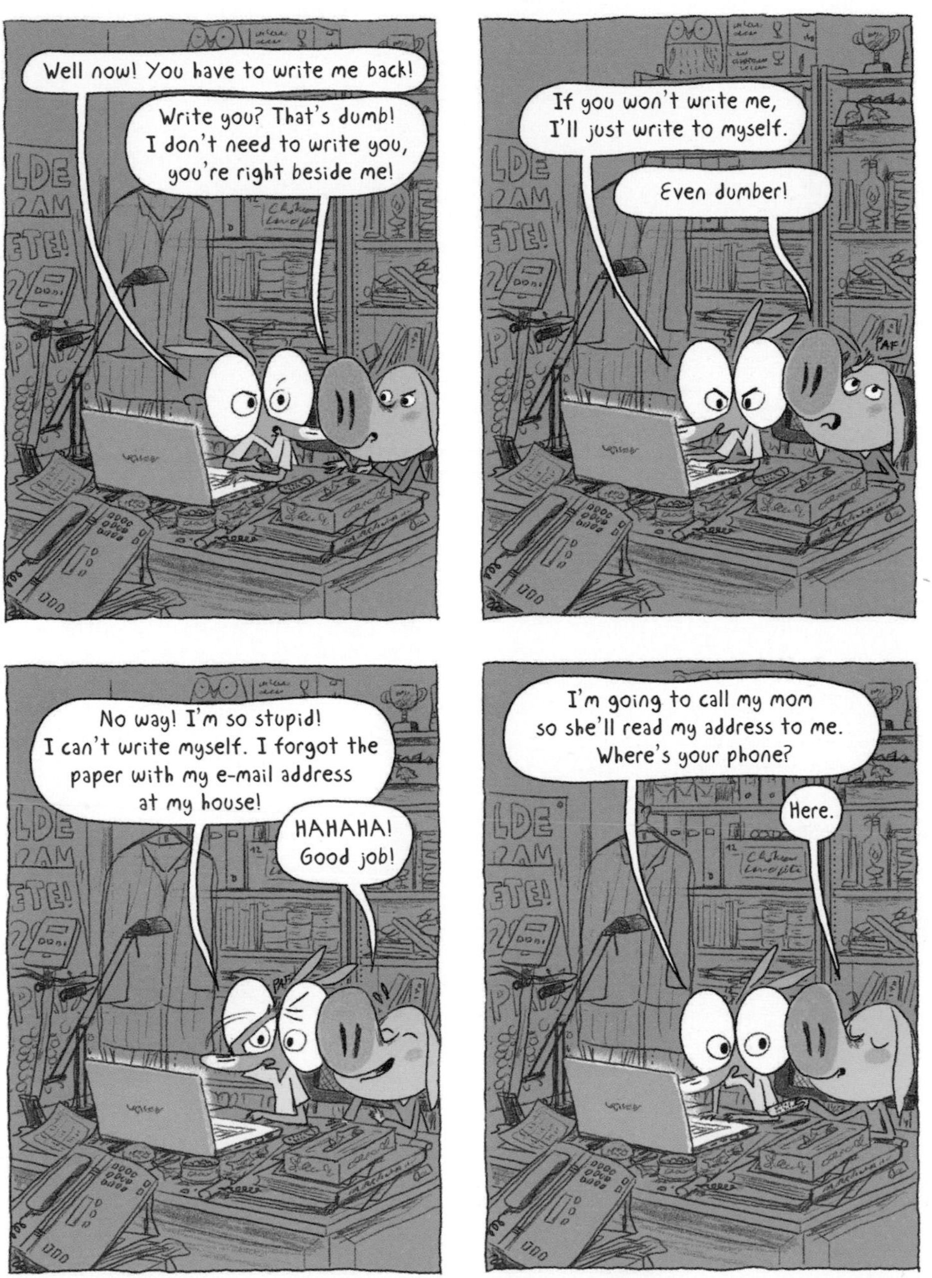
Well now! You have to write me back!
Write you? That's dumb! I don't need to write you, you're right beside me!
If you won't write me, I'll just write to myself.
Even dumber!
PAF!
No way! I'm so stupid! I can't write myself. I forgot the paper with my e-mail address at my house!
HAHAHA! Good job!
I'm going to call my mom so she'll read my address to me. Where's your phone?
Here.

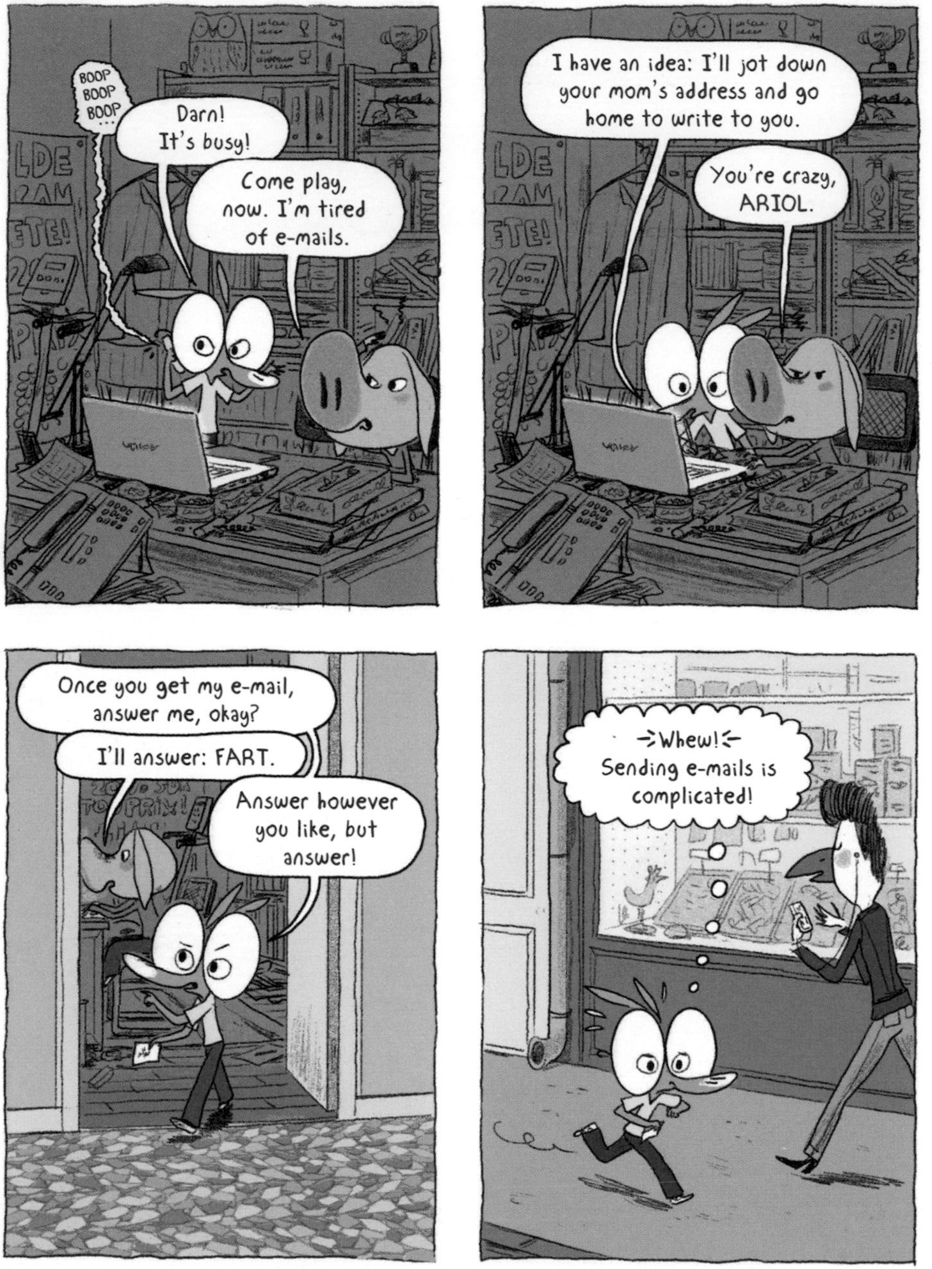
BOOP BOOP BOOP ...
Darn! It's busy!
Come play, now. I'm tired of e-mails.
I have an idea: I'll jot down your mom's address and go home to write to you.
You're crazy, ARIOL.
Once you get my e-mail, answer me, okay?
I'll answer: FART.
Answer however you like, but answer!
Whew! Sending e-mails is complicated!

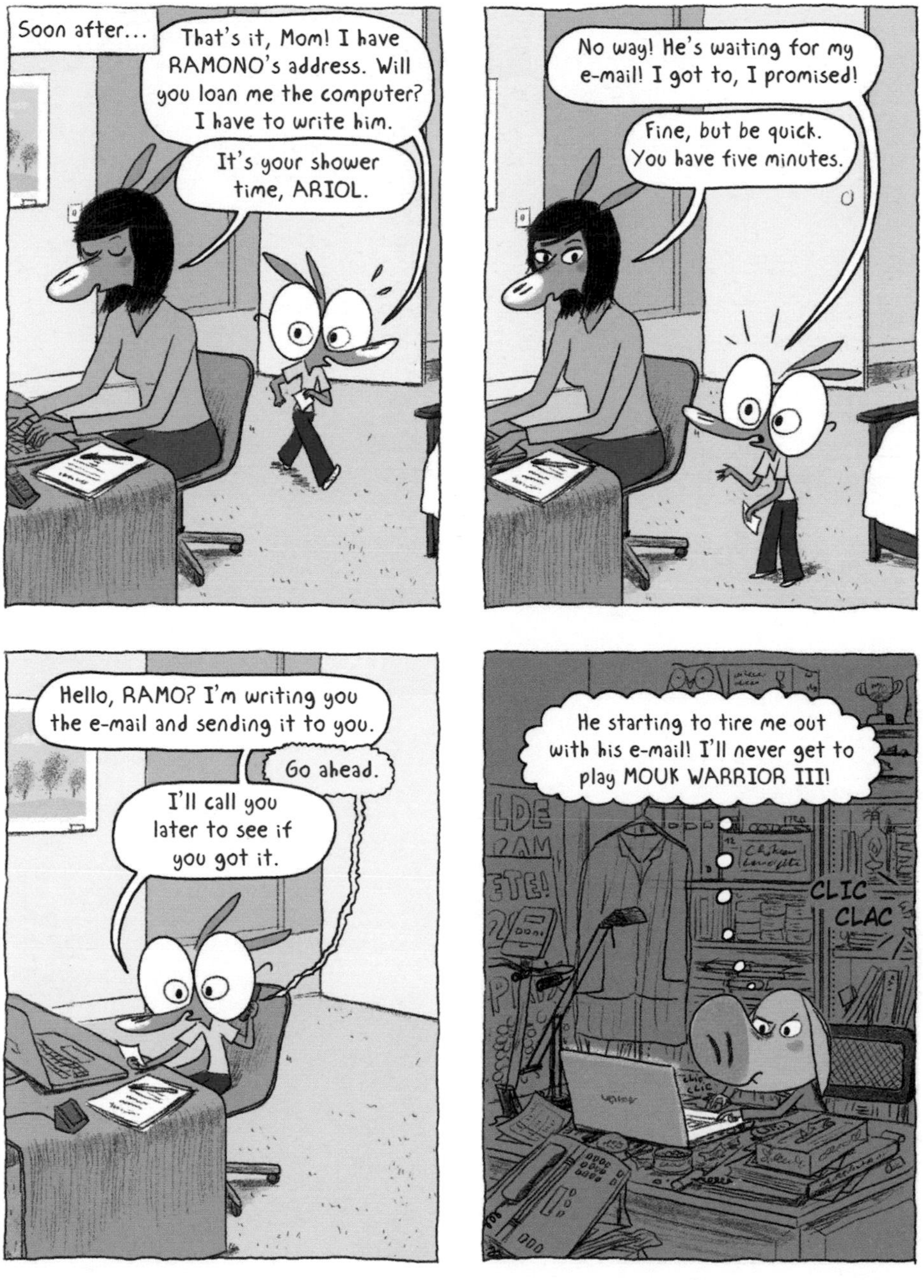
Soon after...
That's it, Mom! I have RAMONO's address. Will you loan me the computer? I have to write him.
It's your shower time, ARIOL.
No way! He's waiting for my e-mail! I got to, I promised!
Fine, but be quick. You have five minutes.
Hello, RAMO? I'm writing you the e-mail and sending it to you.
Go ahead.
I'll call you later to see if you got it.
He starting to tire me out with his e-mail! I'll never get to play MOUK WARRIOR III!
CLIC
CLAC

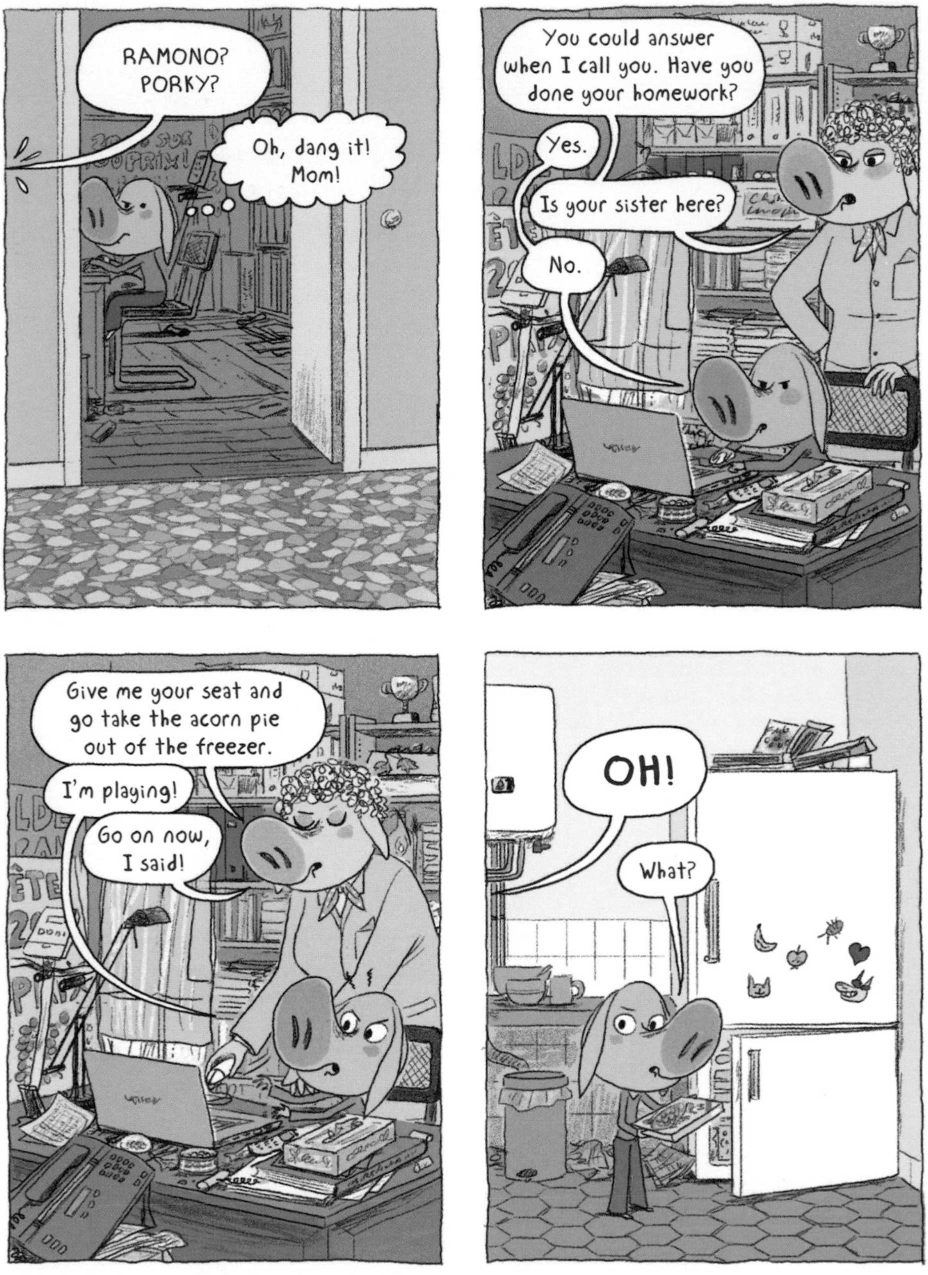
RAMONO? PORKY?
Oh, dang it! Mom!
You could answer when I call you. Have you done your homework?
Yes.
Is your sister here?
No.
Give me your seat and go take the acorn pie out of the freezer.
I'm playing!
Go on now, I said!
OH!
What?

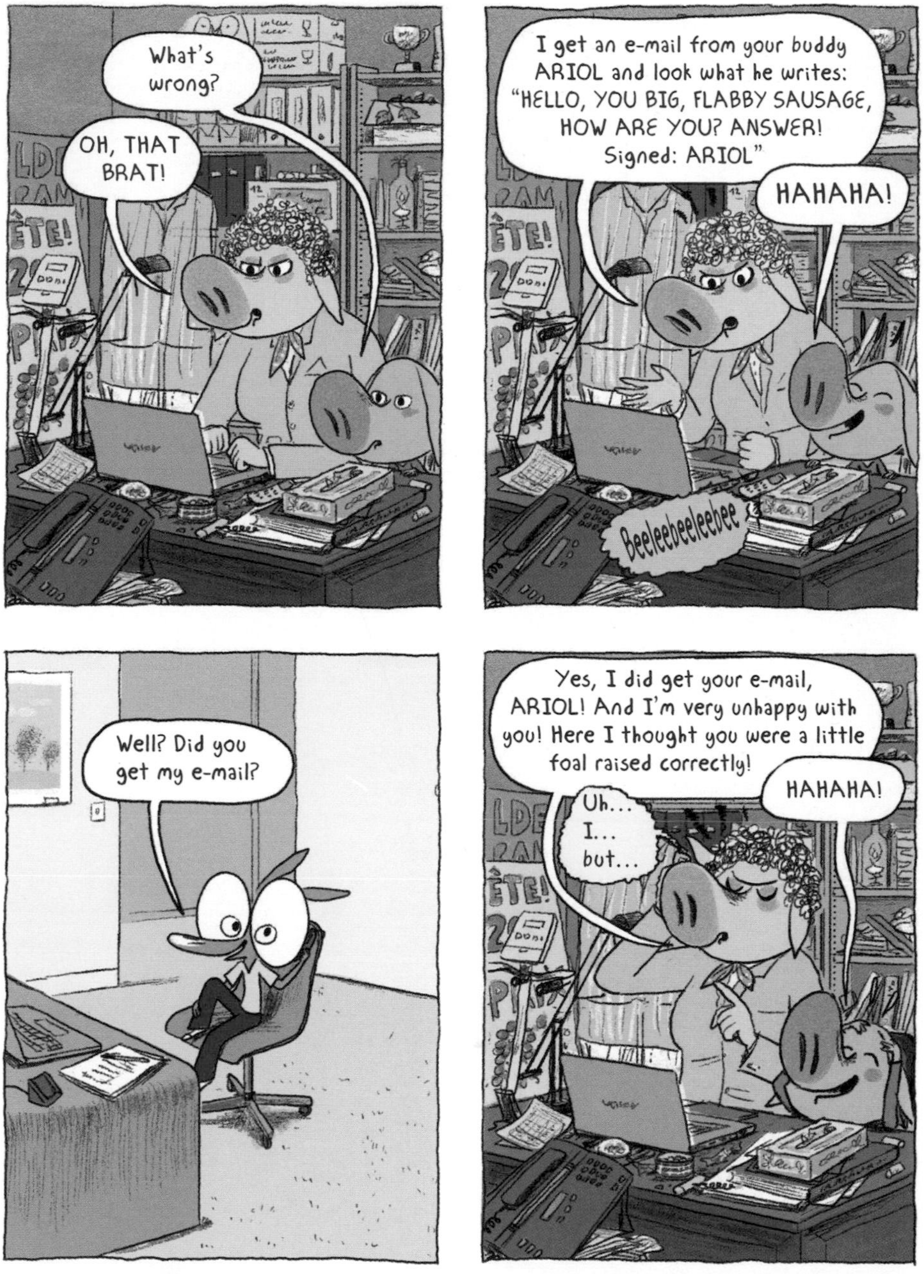
What's wrong?
OH, THAT BRAT!
I get an e-mail from your buddy ARIOL and look what he writes: "HELLO, YOU BIG, FLABBY SAUSAGE, HOW ARE YOU? ANSWER! Signed: ARIOL"
HAHAHA!
Beeleebeeleebee
Well? Did you get my e-mail?
Yes, I did get your e-mail, ARIOL! And I'm very unhappy with you! Here I thought you were a little foal raised correctly!
HAHAHA!
Uh... I... but...

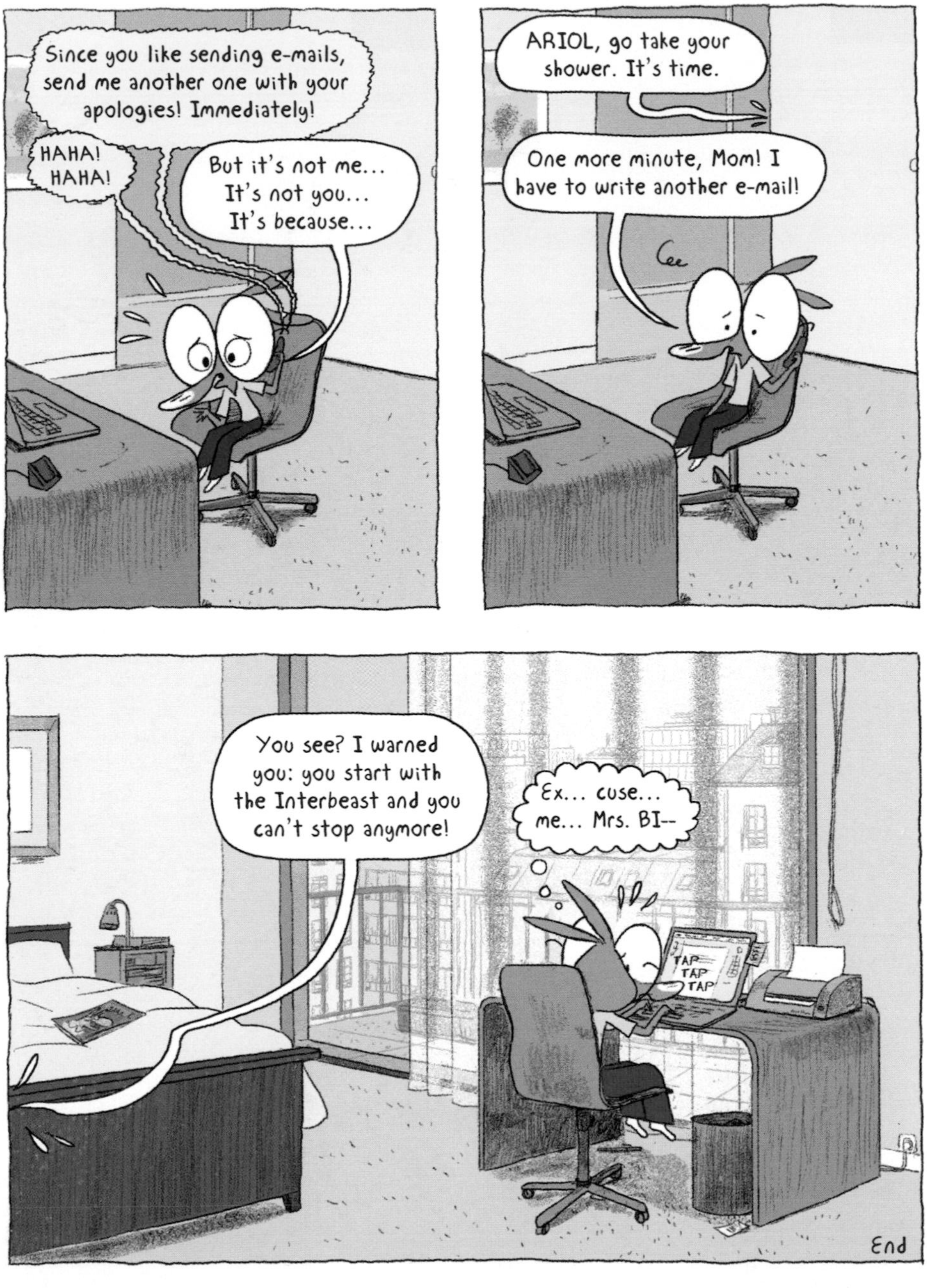

Since you like sending e-mails, send me another one with your apologies! Immediately!
HAHA! HAHA!
But it's not me... It's not you... It's because...
ARIOL, go take your shower. It's time.
One more minute, Mom! I have to write another e-mail!
You see? I warned you: you start with the Interbeast and you can't stop anymore!
Ex... cuse... me... Mrs. BI--
TAP TAP TAP
End

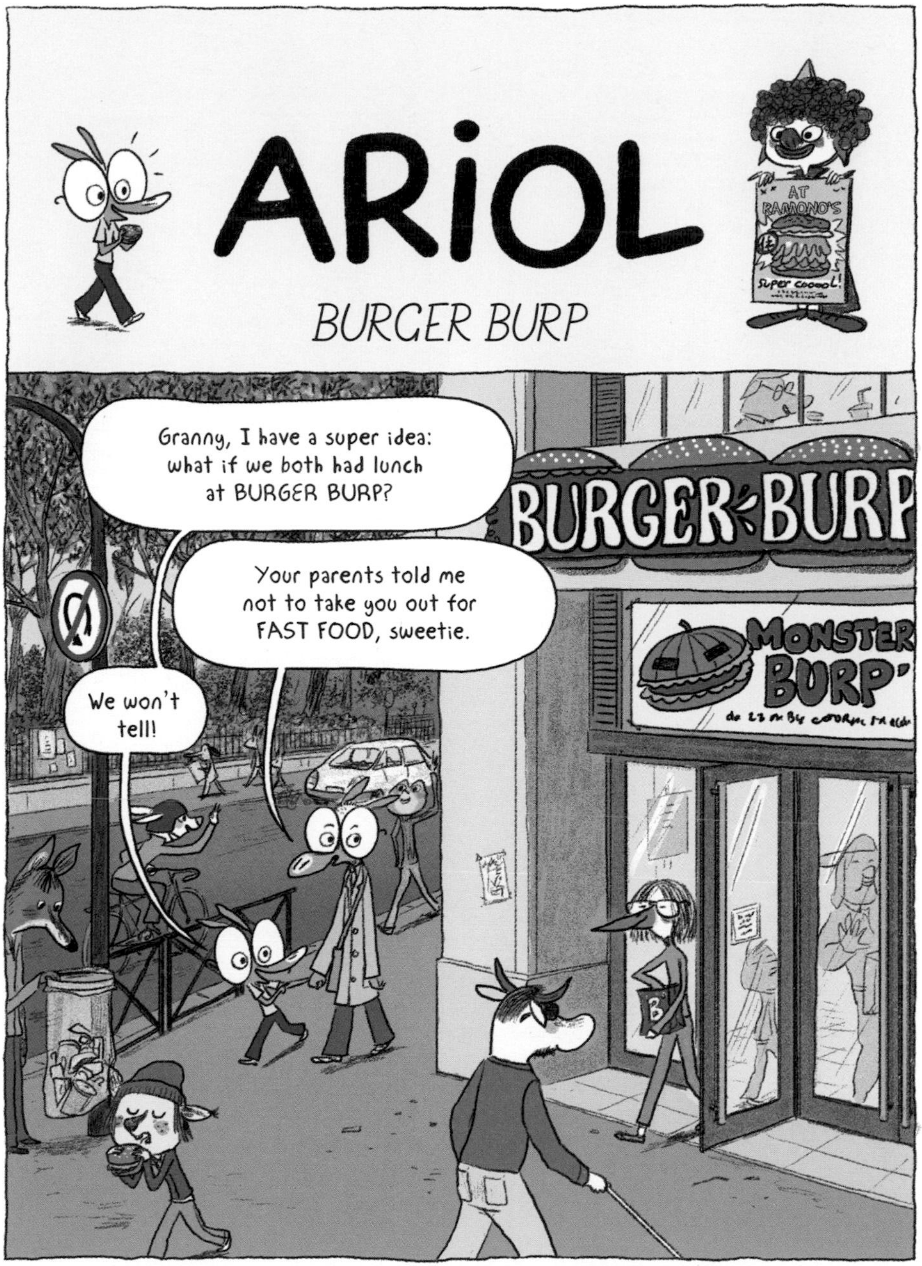
ARiOL
BURGER BURP
AT RAMONO'S
Super coooool!
BURGER BURP
MONSTER BURP
Granny, I have a super idea: what if we both had lunch at BURGER BURP?
Your parents told me not to take you out for FAST FOOD, sweetie.
We won't tell!

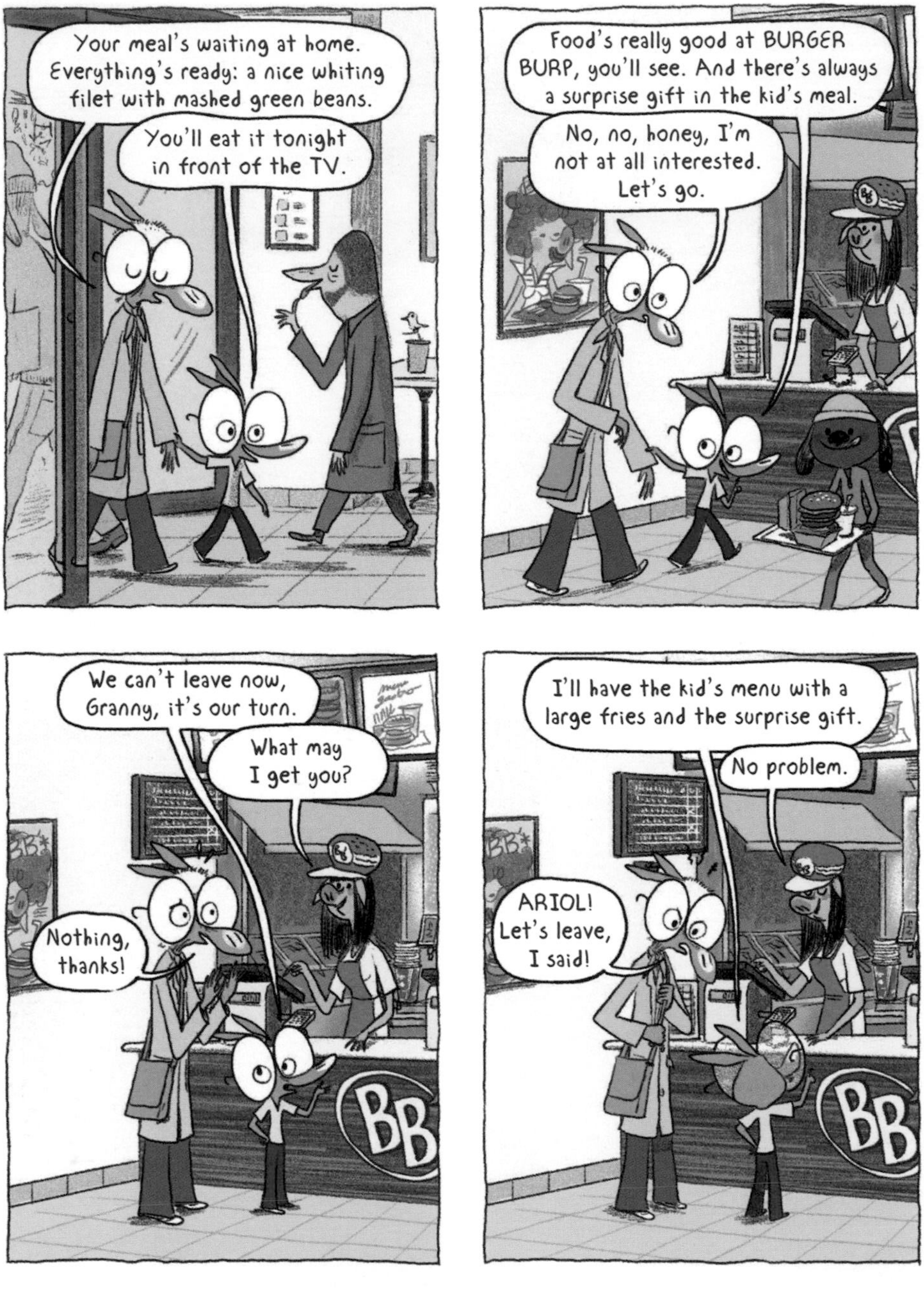
Your meal's waiting at home. Everything's ready: a nice whiting filet with mashed green beans.
You'll eat it tonight in front of the TV.
Food's really good at BURGER BURP, you'll see. And there's always a surprise gift in the kid's meal.
No, no, honey, I'm not at all interested. Let's go.
We can't leave now, Granny, it's our turn.
What may I get you?
Nothing, thanks!
I'll have the kid's menu with a large fries and the surprise gift.
No problem.
ARIOL! Let's leave, I said!
BB
BB

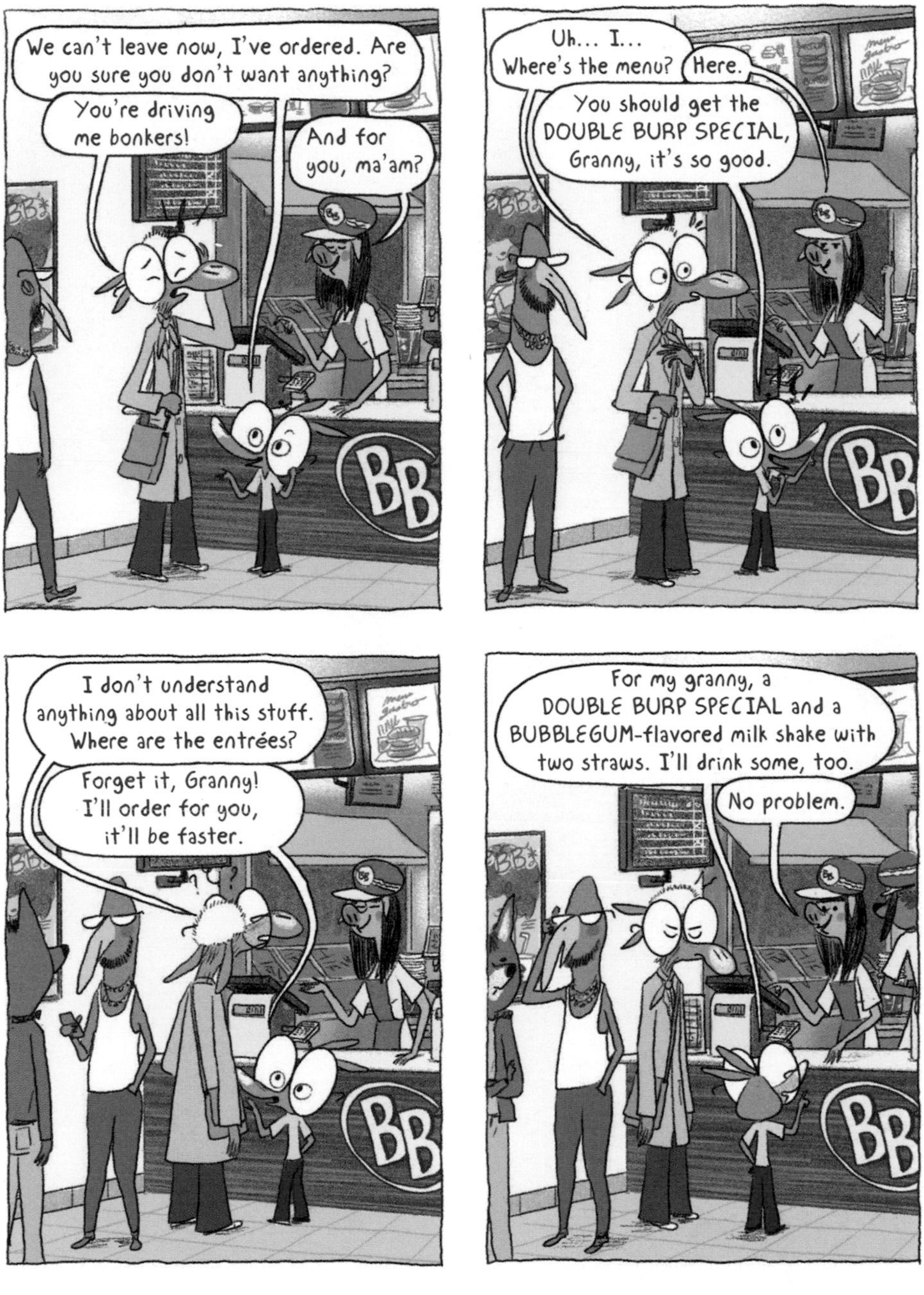
We can't leave now, I've ordered. Are you sure you don't want anything?
You're driving me bonkers!
And for you, ma'am?
Uh... I... Where's the menu?
Here.
You should get the DOUBLE BURP SPECIAL, Granny, it's so good.
I don't understand anything about all this stuff. Where are the entrées?
Forget it, Granny! I'll order for you, it'll be faster.
For my granny, a DOUBLE BURP SPECIAL and a BUBBLEGUM-flavored milk shake with two straws. I'll drink some, too.
No problem.

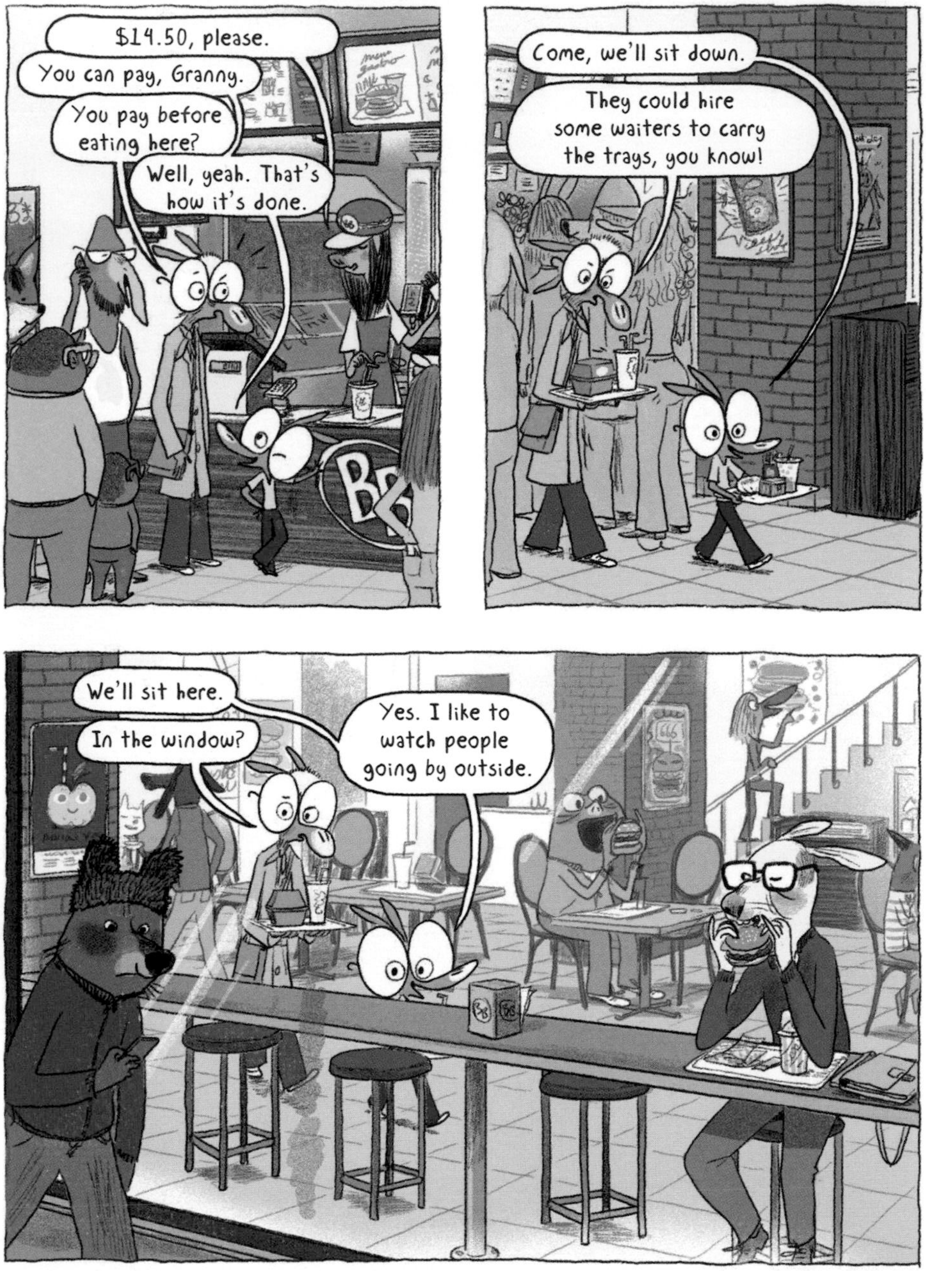
$14.50, please.
You can pay, Granny.
You pay before eating here?
Well, yeah. That's how it's done.
Come, we'll sit down.
They could hire some waiters to carry the trays, you know!
We'll sit here.
In the window?
Yes. I like to watch people going by outside.

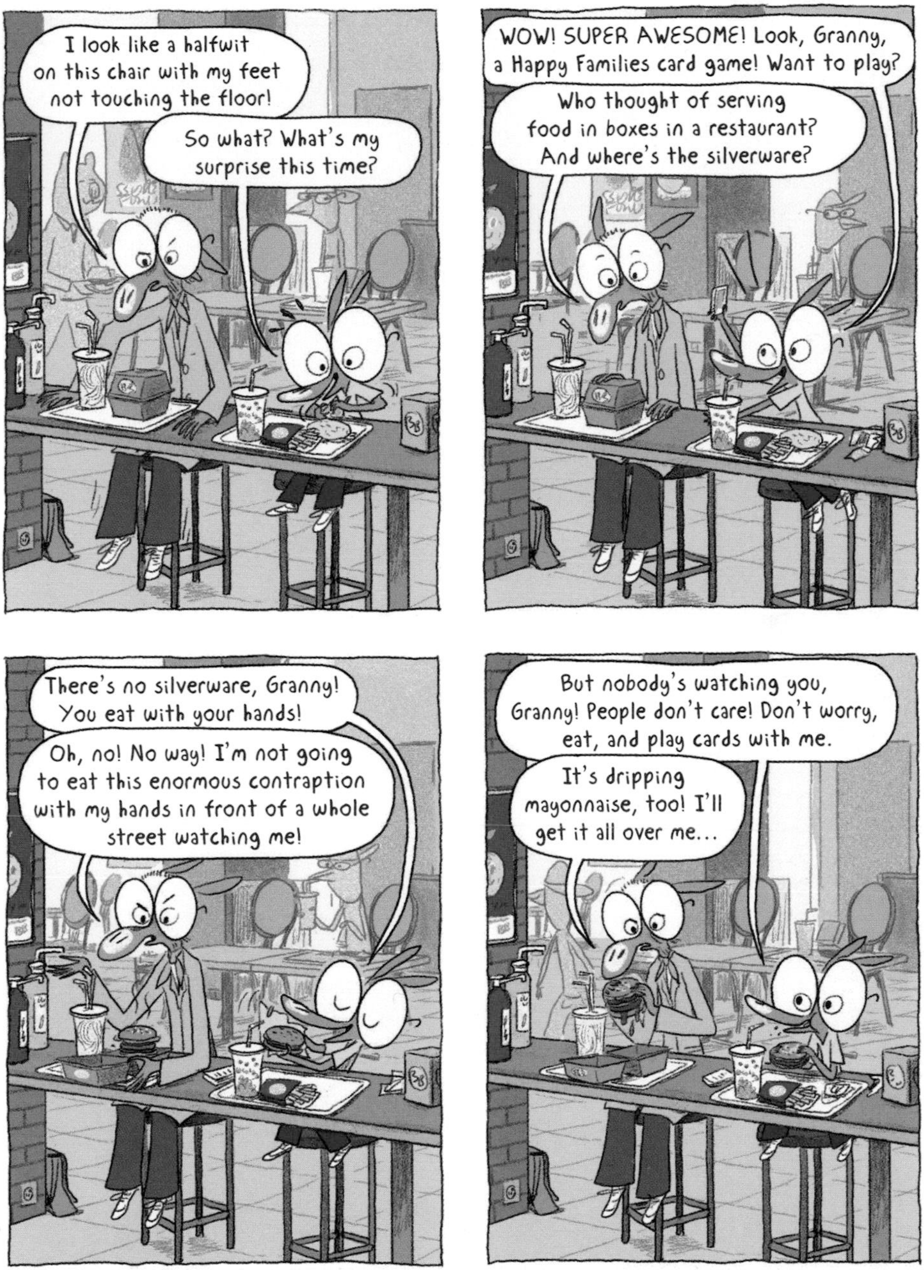
I look like a halfwit on this chair with my feet not touching the floor!
So what? What's my surprise this time?
WOW! SUPER AWESOME! Look, Granny, a Happy Families card game! Want to play?
Who thought of serving food in boxes in a restaurant? And where's the silverware?
There's no silverware, Granny! You eat with your hands!
Oh, no! No way! I'm not going to eat this enormous contraption with my hands in front of a whole street watching me!
But nobody's watching you, Granny! People don't care! Don't worry, eat, and play cards with me.
It's dripping mayonnaise, too! I'll get it all over me...

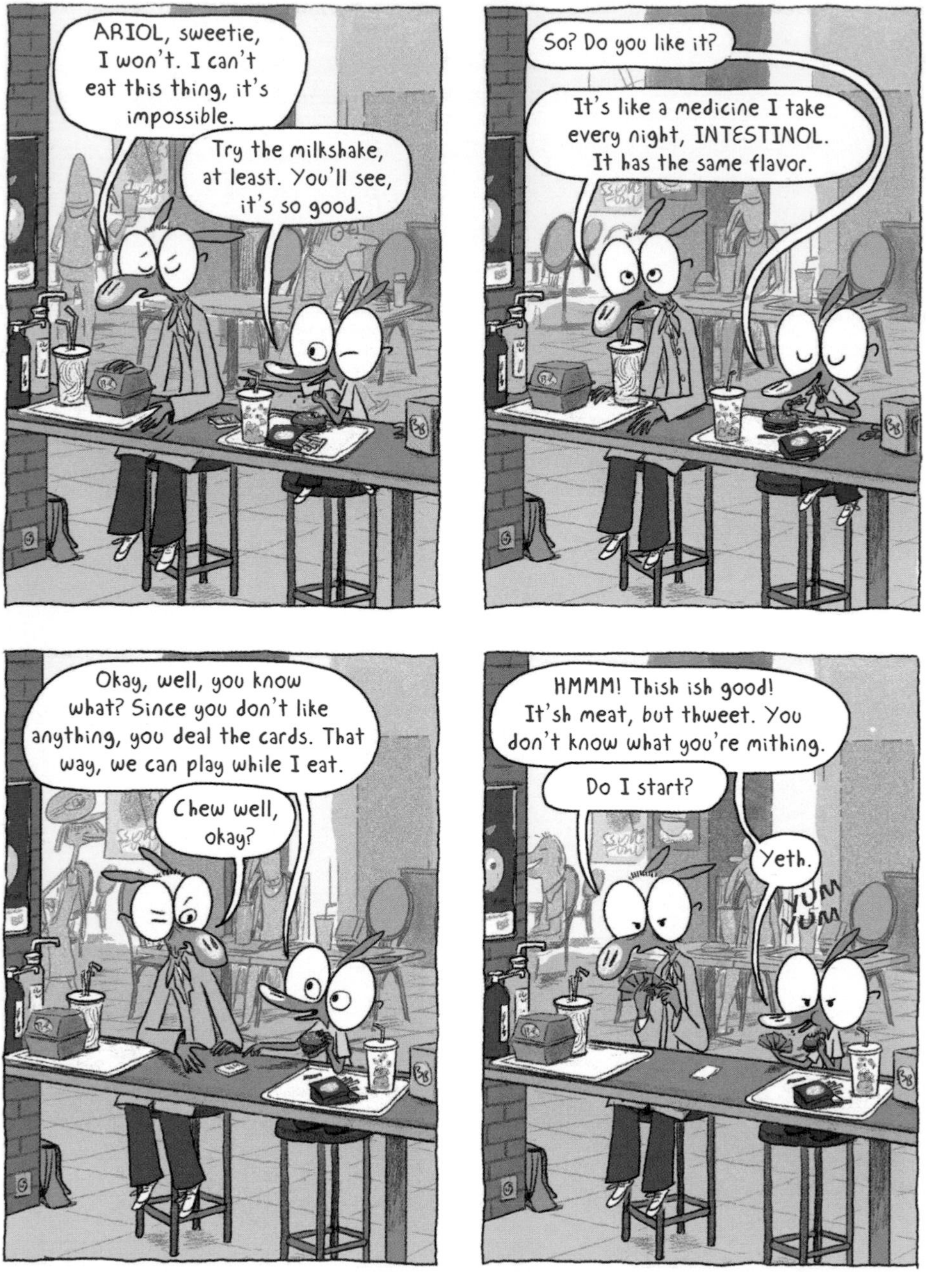
ARIOL, sweetie, I won't. I can't eat this thing, it's impossible.
Try the milkshake, at least. You'll see, it's so good.
So? Do you like it?
It's like a medicine I take every night, INTESTINOL. It has the same flavor.
Okay, well, you know what? Since you don't like anything, you deal the cards. That way, we can play while I eat.
Chew well, okay?
HMMM! Thish ish good! It'sh meat, but thweet. You don't know what you're mithing.
Do I start?
Yeth.
YUM YUM

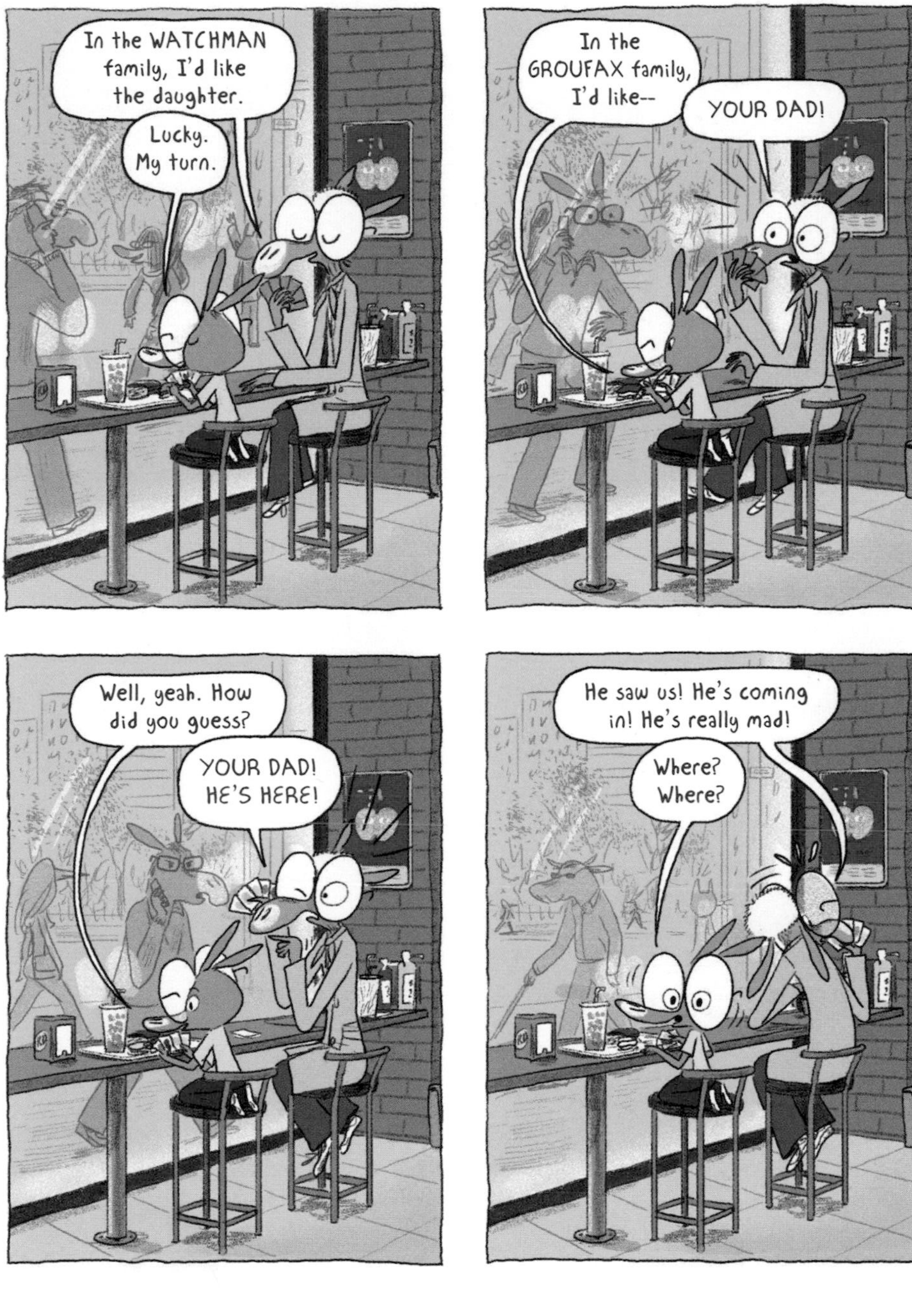
In the WATCHMAN family, I'd like the daughter.
Lucky. My turn.
In the GROUFAX family, I'd like--
YOUR DAD!
Well, yeah. How did you guess?
YOUR DAD! HE'S HERE!
He saw us! He's coming in! He's really mad!
Where? Where?

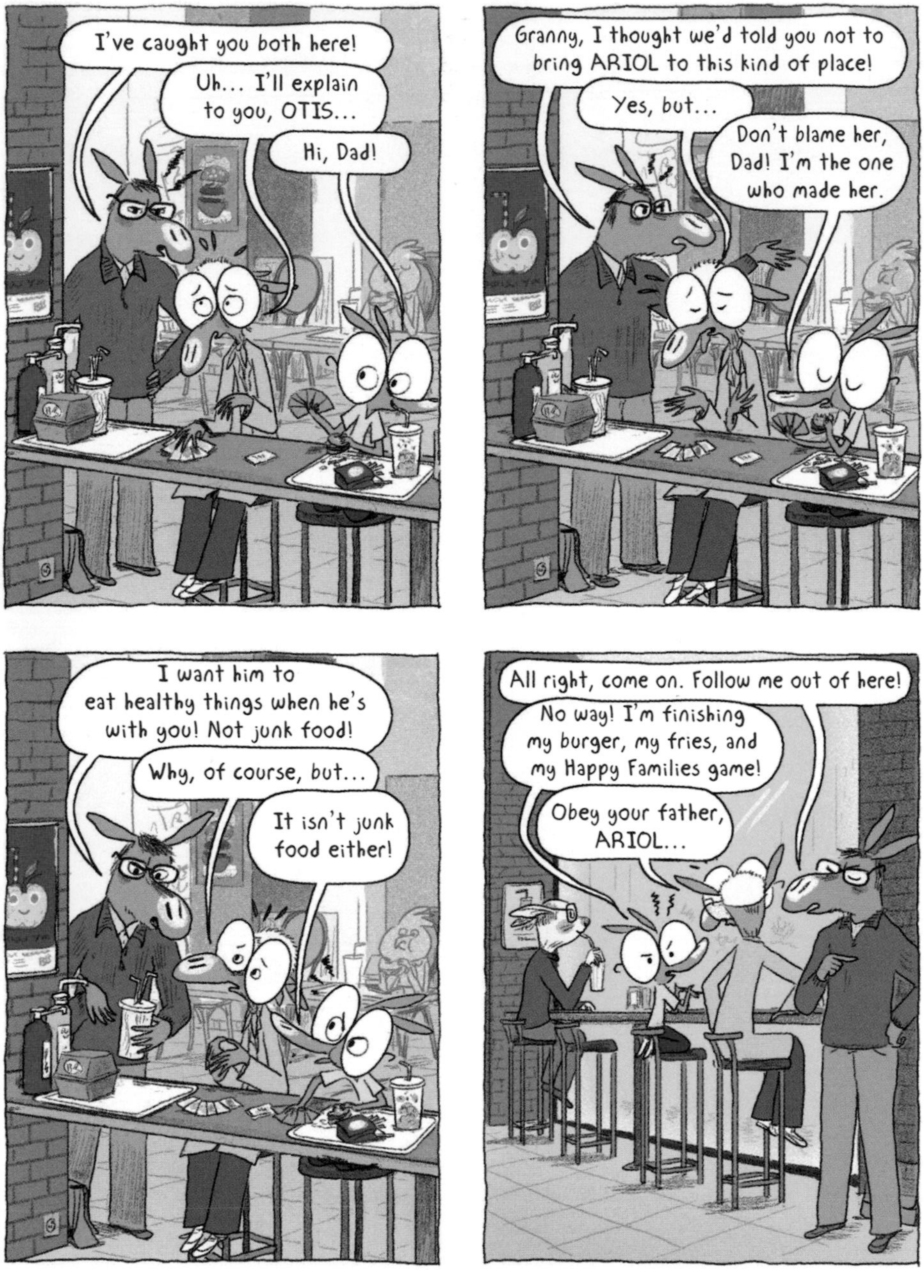
I've caught you both here!
Uh... I'll explain to you, OTIS...
Hi, Dad!
Granny, I thought we'd told you not to bring ARIOL to this kind of place!
Yes, but...
Don't blame her, Dad! I'm the one who made her.
I want him to eat healthy things when he's with you! Not junk food!
Why, of course, but...
It isn't junk food either!
All right, come on. Follow me out of here!
No way! I'm finishing my burger, my fries, and my Happy Families game!
Obey your father, ARIOL...

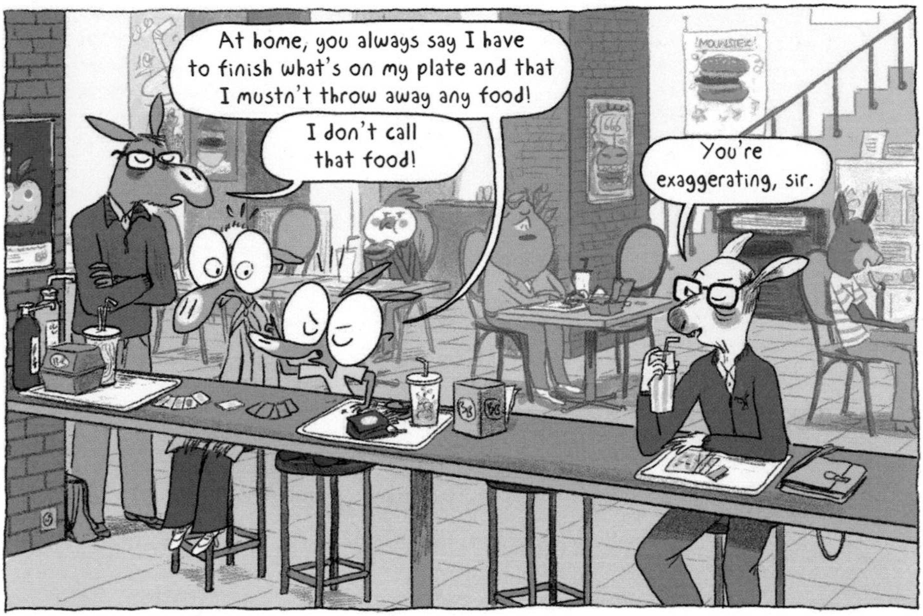
At home, you always say I have to finish what's on my plate and that I mustn't throw away any food!
I don't call that food!
You're exaggerating, sir.

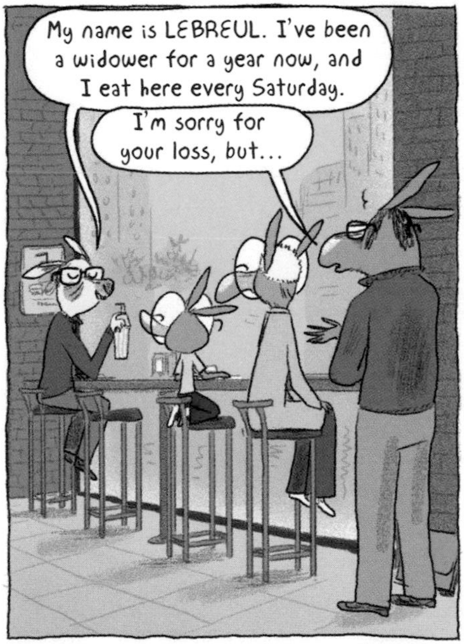
My name is LEBREUL. I've been a widower for a year now, and I eat here every Saturday.
I'm sorry for your loss, but...

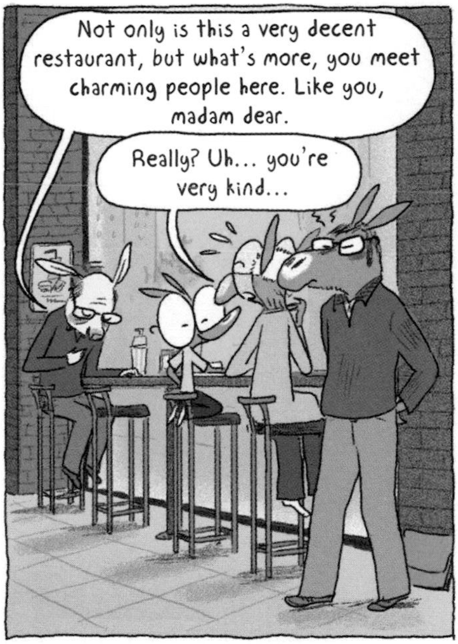
Not only is this a very decent restaurant, but what's more, you meet charming people here. Like you, madam dear.
Really? Uh... you're very kind...

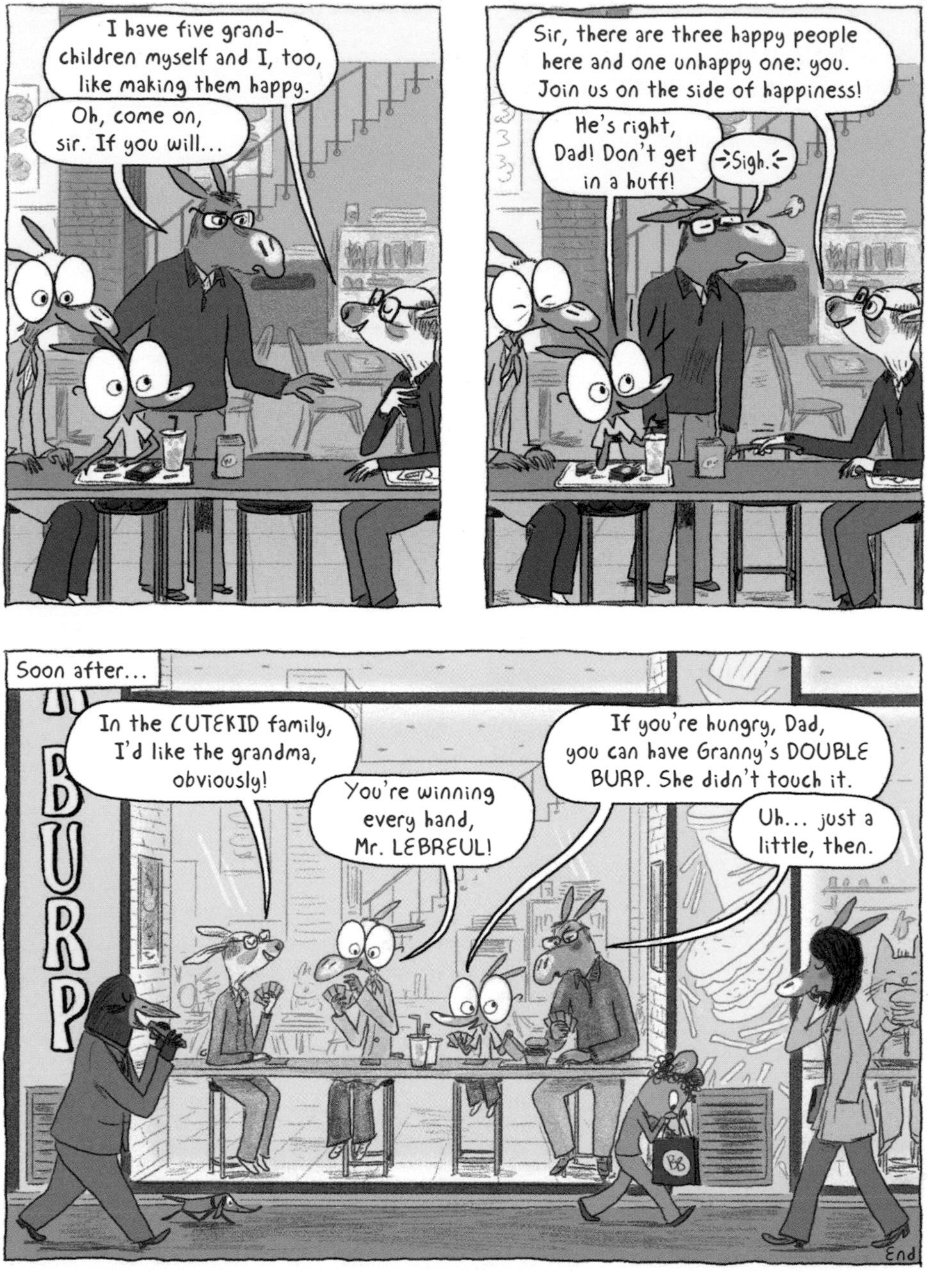
I have five grand-children myself and I, too, like making them happy.
Oh, come on, sir. If you will...
Sir, there are three happy people here and one unhappy one: you. Join us on the side of happiness!
He's right, Dad! Don't get in a huff!
Sigh.
Soon after...
BURP
In the CUTEKID family, I'd like the grandma, obviously!
You're winning every hand, Mr. LEBREUL!
If you're hungry, Dad, you can have Granny's DOUBLE BURP. She didn't touch it.
Uh... just a little, then.
End

# WATCH OUT FOR PAPERCUTZ™

Welcome to the nifty, naturalistic, ninth ARIOL graphic novel, by Emmanuel Guibert and Marc Boutavant, from Papercutz-- those crazy people dedicated to publishing great graphic novels for all ages. I'm Jim Salicrup, Editor-in-Chief and Ariol's substitute teacher. I'm here to let you know that in addition to the wonderful ARIOL graphic novels that we proudly publish, we also publish other graphic novels that you may also enjoy. Now, you could just go to papercutz.com to actually see all those other wonderful graphic novels, but while you're here, there is one in particular that I want to tell you about...

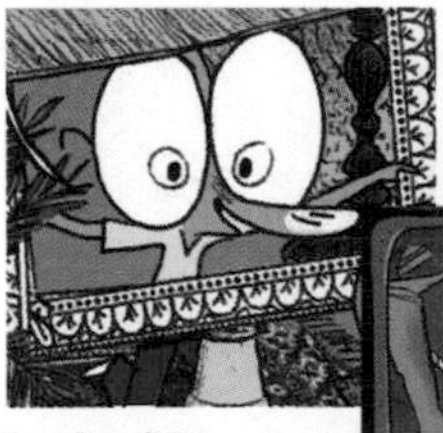

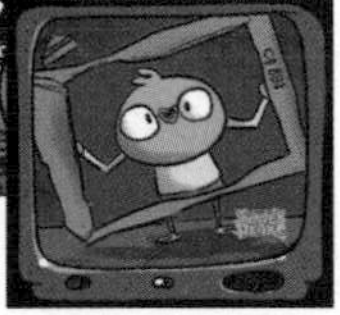

Harvey Beaks © 2016 Viacom International Inc. All Rights reserved.

What made me think of it was when Jeff Whitman, Assistant Managing Editor at Papercutz, was assistant managing editing this volume of ARIOL, he mentioned that Ariol and Ramono were doing what Harvey Beaks, Fee and Foo are doing in NICKELODEON PANDEMONIUM! #1 "Channeling Fun." When the power goes out at Harvey's home, he and his friends decide to make their own TV for Harvey's parents to watch. As Foo says, regarding the challenge of creating original programming, "It's not as if this stuff is hard to write." I loved the shows they dreamed up, especially a game show called "Can You Punch That?"

NICKELODEON PANDEMONIUM! is an all-new Papercutz graphic novel that is brilliantly written, beautifully drawn, and delightfully designed, that features a collection of comics starring such Nick stars as *Sanjay and Craig*, *Pig Goat Banana Cricket*, *Breadwinners*, *the Loud House* and, as we mentioned, *Harvey Beaks*. There's a loose TV theme tying all the stories together, and it's fun to see how there are other similarities to ARIOL running throughout NICKELODEON PANDEMONIUM! For example, we all know that Ariol and Ramono's hero is Thunder Horse-- whose adventures they faithfully watch on TV and collect in comics. Sanjay and Craig are huge fans of erstwhile movie action-hero Remington Tufflips, and that reminds me of one of my heroes when I was a boy, and his connection to a certain TV show...

There once was a show that was all about pranking people (Something *Pig Goat Banana Cricket* could appreciate!) while they were being filmed on hidden cameras. No, I'm not talking about Ashton Kutcher's *Punk'd*, but the show that started it all, Allen Funt's *Candid Camera*. That show was so popular, that on a cover of a comicbook, Mr. Funt had caught Clark Kent in a phone booth changing into Superman, as Mr. Funt exclaimed, "Smile! You're on Candid Camera!"

And while I realize that Ariol didn't mean to douse that poor guy on the street with water, it really was an accident, it would've been fun if Ariol responded to the Soaked Guy's complaints with, "Smile! You're on *Ariol Camera!*" Of course, not too many non-Baby Boomers would've got that joke, but hey! You never know when one day, a total stranger (who looks like a little blue donkey) may turn to YOU and say, "Smile! You're on *Ariol Camera!*"

Thanks,

Jim

**STAY IN TOUCH!**


EMAIL: salicrup@papercutz.com
WEB: papercutz.com
TWITTER: @papercutzgn
FACEBOOK: PAPERCUTZGRAPHICNOVELS
REGULAR MAIL: Papercutz, 160 Broadway, Suite 700, East Wing, New York, NY 10038


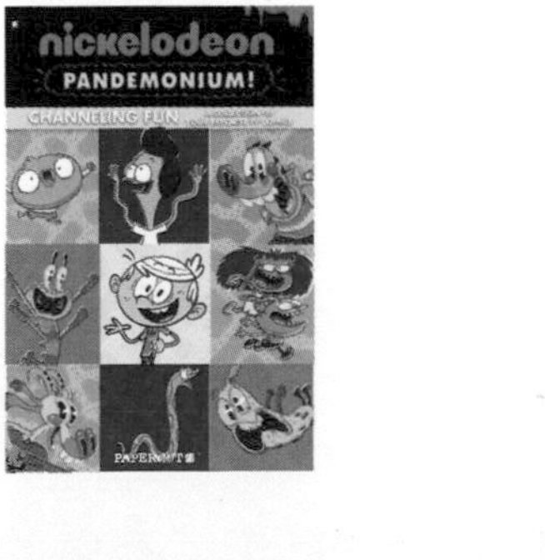

nickelodeon
PANDEMONIUM!
CHANNELING FUN

# Other Great Titles From PAPERCUTZ™

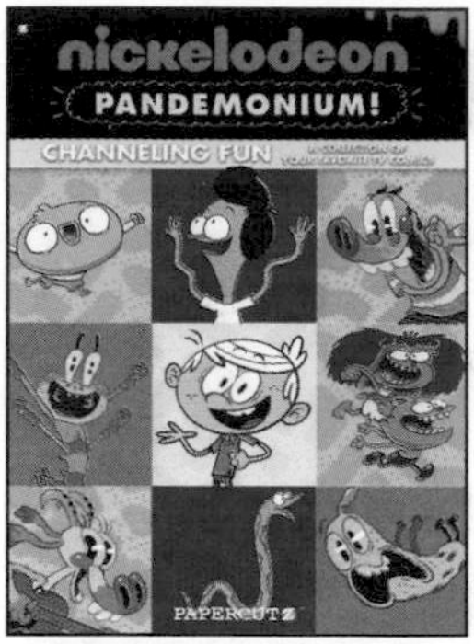
nickelodeon
PANDEMONIUM!
CHANNELING FUN
PAPERCUTZ

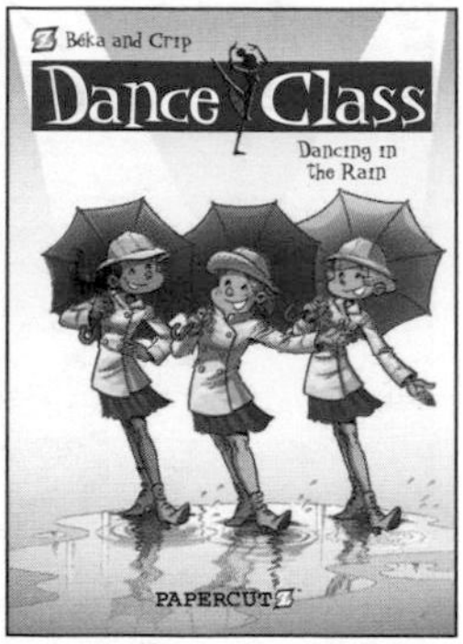
Béka and Crip
Dance Class
Dancing in the Rain
PAPERCUTZ

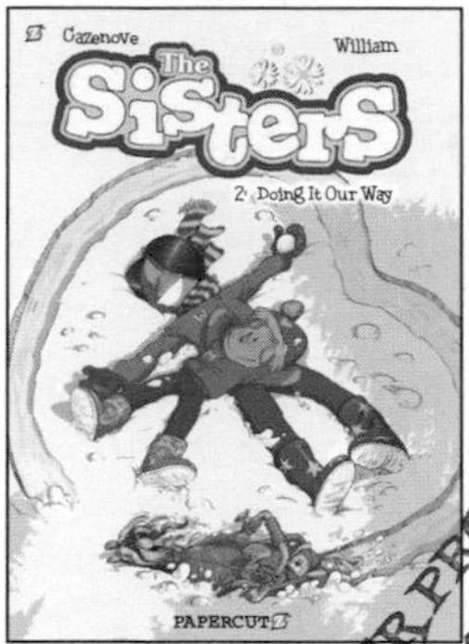
Cazenove
William
The Sisters
2 Doing It Our Way
PAPERCUTZ

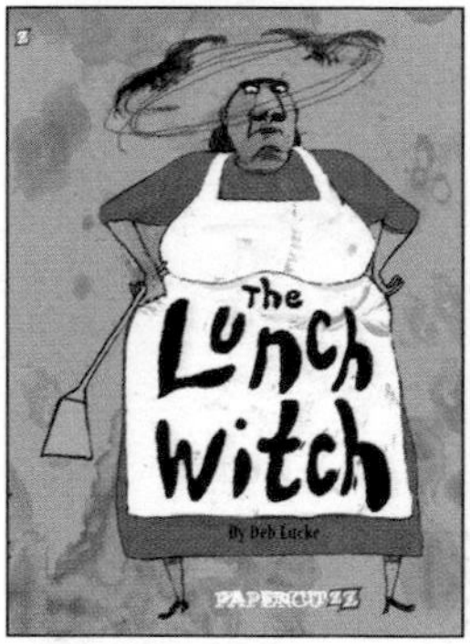
The Lunch Witch
By Deb Lucke
PAPERCUTZ

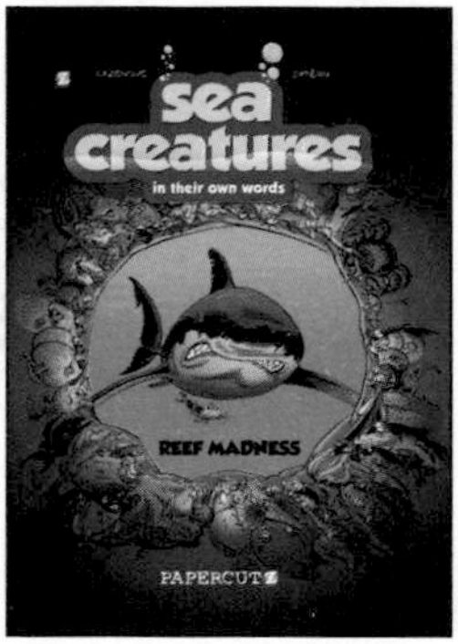
sea creatures
in their own words
REEF MADNESS
PAPERCUTZ

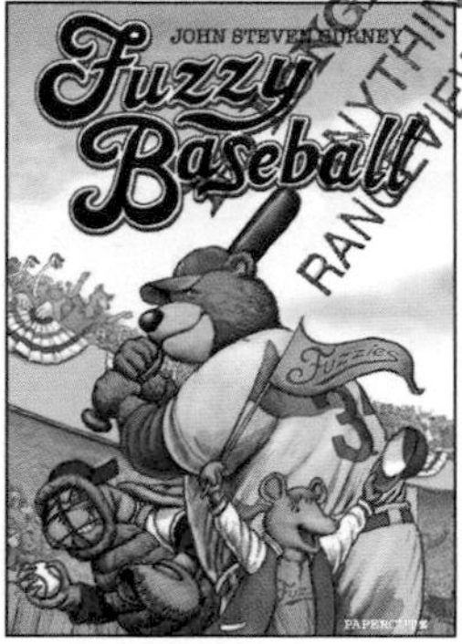
JOHN STEVEN GURNEY
Fuzzy Baseball
PAPERCUTZ





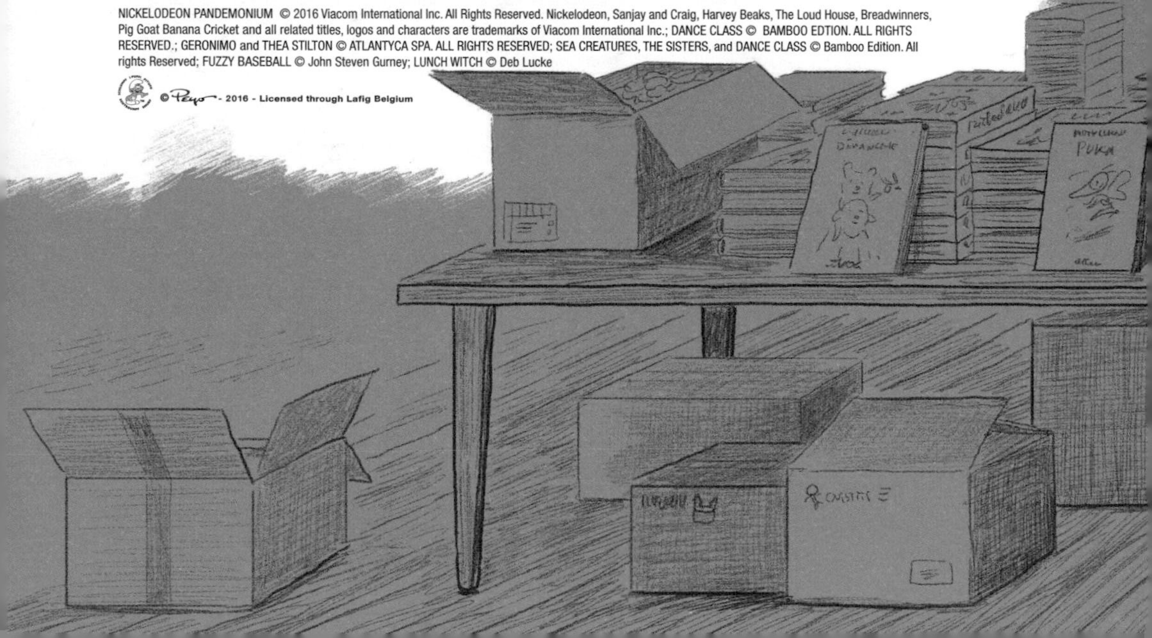

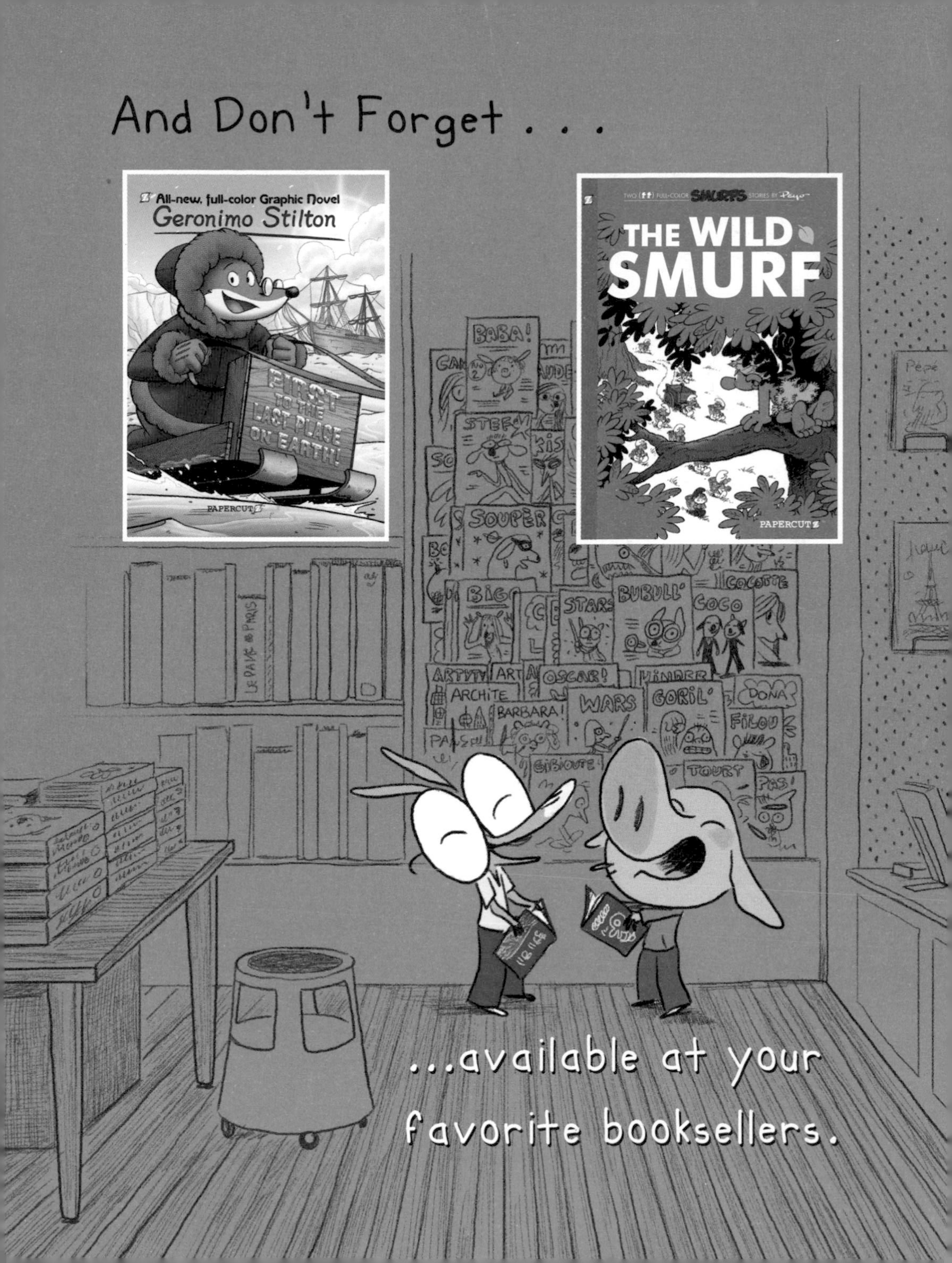
And Don't Forget . . .
All-new, full-color Graphic Novel
Geronimo Stilton
FIRST TO THE LAST PLACE ON EARTH!
PAPERCUTZ
THE WILD SMURF
PAPERCUTZ
...available at your favorite booksellers.